"Each character´s personal journey reflects someho⸺ one case, I found myself mirroring my own wounds.

"From the first few chapters, I found myself stopping to reflect on what was happening and the emotions the characters felt. It was as if I were going through the journey with them." **Amy | Ithaca**

"The Orchid changed my perspective, illustrating that anyone can view life through the eyes of love. It teaches that regardless of past challenges—be it personal struggles, trauma, or guilt—we can choose to forgive and move forward with love and understanding." **Charlotte | Los Angeles**

"A great fiction novel that is easy to read and will make you smile, possibly cry and root for your fellow women friends. You will see some aspects of yourself in the characters and end up loving them. The message is always positive - there is always calm after the storm even if one has to work through some challenges. The reward is worth it." **Claudia | Puerto Rico**

"The Orchid is particularly beneficial for anyone struggling to cope with their current life situation. It's an ideal first step for those not open to or unable to seek professional help. It's also suitable for anyone looking to improve any aspect of their daily life and aspiring to live their best life." **Denise | New York**

"The Orchid is not merely a book to be consumed quickly; it is a rich source of wisdom and insight that demands to be savored, contemplated, and internalized. It's a timeless companion on your quest for self-discovery, offering solace, inspiration, and a roadmap to inner harmony. Allow this book to be a constant source of guidance, a wellspring of empowerment, and a reminder that the journey towards self-love is both infinite and profoundly rewarding." **Fernanda | Mexico**

"This book will give you an amazing and accurate view of what each and every one of us can do to exist with ourselves and each other in the most positive of ways. Even if you're not a believer YET!" **Michelle | Los Angeles**

"…a joy to read. The writing is simple and clear. The detail and imagery is beautifully crafted to transport you to the literal landscape of the heavenly place called The Orchid where the story takes place. The story, the characters and the teachings lead you through an emotional journey of self-discovery always ending in a place of empowerment and love." **Vanessa | Hong Kong**

THE ORCHID

a novel

The Secret Code of Modern Goddesses

Rocio Aquino  **Angel Orengo**

The Orchid: The Secret Code of Modern Goddesses
Copyright © 2023 by Rocio Aquino and Angel Orengo
All rights reserved.
Published and printed in the United States of America
First Edition February 2024

Thank you for purchasing an authorized edition of this book!

We deeply appreciate your respect for copyright laws, refraining from reproducing, scanning, or distributing any part of this work without permission.

Reproduction of this publication in whole or in part, or incorporation into a retrieval system, or transmission in any form or by any means, whether electronic, mechanical, photocopying, recording, or otherwise, is not permitted without the prior written consent of the publisher. The sole exception is brief quotations in critical reviews and certain other non-commercial uses permitted by copyright law.

Enjoy your reading!

THE LIBRARY OF CONGRESS HAS CATALOGED THE HARDCOVER EDITION OF THIS BOOK UNDER THE CONTROL NUMBER: 2024901337

English ISBNs: Paperback/979-8-9894882-1-6 | Hardcover/979-8-9894882-0-9
E-book/979-8-9894882-4-7 | Audiobook/979-8-9894882-6-1

ISBNs en español: Rústica/979-8-9894882-3-0 | Rígida/979-8-9894882-2-3
E-book/979-8-9894882-5-4 | Audiolibro/979-8-9894882-7-8

Collaborators:
Editorial Consultant: Kitt Walsh
Illustrations: Vitana Makovskaya, Muktadir H., Cuauhtemoc Rodríguez S.
Editing: Marisol Robles, Julie Lind
Cover & Book Design: Cuauhtemoc Rodríguez S., Alex Salnikov

All Rights Reserved © 2023 For The Highest Good Press
Comments about this book or its contents can be sent to
info@theorchid.me

This is a work of fiction. Names, characters, businesses, places, events, locales, and incidents are either products of the authors' imaginations or used in a fictitious manner. Any resemblance to actual persons, living or dead, or actual events is purely coincidental.

www.TheOrchidBook.com

DEDICATION

To all who journey through these pages: may you be inspired to rewrite your own narrative and live a life of love, free of limitations, and enriched by the knowledge that you are powerful beyond belief.

Table of Contents

Authors' Message / 8

I. Introduction
Chapter 1: Mary / 13
Chapter 2: The Orchid / 21
Chapter 3: Sofia / 25
Chapter 4: Congratulations / 33

II. Arrival
Chapter 5: Welcome / 37
    Property Map
    Teachers and Healers
    The Guests
    The Rooms
Chapter 6: Olivia / 51
Chapter 7: First Dinner / 57
Chapter 8: Nicole / 67
Chapter 9: Evening Council / 75
    Gazing

III. Awareness
Chapter 10: Morning Prayer / 97
Chapter 11: Meditation / 99
Chapter 12: Writing / 105
Chapter 13: Journaling / 109
Chapter 14: Breakfast / 113
Chapter 15: Stephanie / 117
Chapter 16: I Want to Be Perfect / 125
Chapter 17: Awareness / 129
    The Spectrum of Inner Growth

Chapter 18: Limiting Beliefs / 137
Chapter 19: Dance / 151
Chapter 20: Jennifer / 157
Chapter 21: Watsu / 169
Chapter 22: Breath and Sound / 175

IV. GRATITUDE
Chapter 23: I Give Thanks / 185
Chapter 24: The Energy in Our Body / 197
Chakras

Chapter 25: Letting Go / 205
Chapter 26: Letters of Gratitude / 211
Chapter 27: Activities / 223
Chapter 28: Evening Council / 225
I Am Grateful

Transforming Energy

Chapter 29: Trust Yourself / 237

V. FORGIVENESS
Chapter 30: Morning Reflections / 245
Chapter 31: Asking for Forgiveness / 249
Chapter 32: Silence / 253
Chapter 33: Releasing Heavy Energy / 257
Chapter 34: Silent Meditation / 259
Chapter 35: A New Day / 263
Chapter 36: Labyrinth / 267
Chapter 37: Tarot / 271
Chapter 38: Blue Tape / 289
Chapter 39: I Forgive Myself / 303
Chapter 40: Celebration / 309

VI. Acceptance

Chapter 41: A Place to Love Themselves / 315

Chapter 42: I AM / 319

Chapter 43: Find Your Truth / 327

Chapter 44: Unconditional Love / 333

Chapter 45: The Power of Acceptance / 337

I Love Me

I Accept Me

I Accept Others

Chapter 46: The Power Within / 349

Chapter 47: Prayer / 357

VII. Intention

Chapter 48: Morning Reflections / 363

Chapter 49: Self-Empowerment / 367

Chapter 50: LifeScript / 377

Chapter 51: Activities / 399

Chapter 52: Closing Ceremony / 401

Tunnel of Love

A New Beginning

VIII. Farewell

Chapter 53: Connect with Mother Earth / 415

Chapter 54: Because I Am You and You are Me / 419

IX. Acknowledgements

Authors' Message

In the mosaic that is life, every thread tells a story, each a vibrant testament to love, discovery, and rebirth.

Our story, entwined and colorful, has been a journey of shared dreams, challenges, and wisdom gathered from the myriad of souls we've encountered. It has also been a journey of self-growth and transformation in which we have come to learn that all we have been searching for, awareness, gratitude, forgiveness, acceptance, intention, happiness and love, has always been within us. It is from these personal and collective experiences that *The Orchid: The Secret Code of Modern Goddesses* was born.

We are Rocio and Angel, partners in life and spirit, wanderers who found home in each other's hearts. Our journey together has been filled with many cultures, beliefs, and encounters with both the ordinary and extraordinary. In every corner of the world, from the bustling streets of some of the world's largest metropolises, to ancient cities and the tranquil silence of hidden temples, we have found knowledge, understanding, and the essence of what connects us all.

This book is more than just a fictional story about wonderful and powerful women; it's a reflection of our lives, the lessons we've learned, and the profound truths we've uncovered along the way. It's a tribute to the resilient spirit of all the women in our lives, those we have lived with, and those we've met along the way, whose stories of courage, transformation, and triumph have inspired us profoundly.

The Orchid is not just a place we want to bring to reality, but a symbol of hope and healing, a sanctuary we've envisioned where every human soul, regardless of its journey, can find understanding, solace, strength, wisdom and self-discovery. It's a place where we can remind each individual of the incredible power they already have within.

As you turn these pages, we invite you to walk with us through the lives of five extraordinary women, each at a crossroads, each seeking something more. Their stories, though unique, reflect a universal quest for self-acceptance, and self-love.

In sharing this story, we share pieces of ourselves, our beliefs, and our vision for a world where every woman recognizes the goddess within. May you find in *The Orchid* a mirror, a mentor, and a message that resonates with your own journey.

With love and light,

                            Rocio and Angel

The Orchid

If you want to find the secrets of the universe, think in terms of energy, frequency and vibration. —Nikola Tesla

Part I
Introduction

The Orchid

Chapter 1

Mary

Mary had been raised right. She was the only child of devoted parents who saw that she wanted for nothing. Shopping trips for seasonal wardrobes, travel to Europe in the summer, piano and French lessons with the best tutors, a horse of her own to practice jumps and dressage, ballroom dance and etiquette instruction, and a room fit for a princess with a white canopy bed and a zoo full of stuffed animals.

When she was older, Mary was sent to finishing school, where she would learn how to plan a dinner party for twenty, enough about classical music and opera to hold her own in any conversation, and how to manage a staff of servants.

Mary was expected to make the most of her physical assets, good manners, and breeding to complement her future husband but not to ever challenge or overshadow him. She was to greet him at the door with a chilled martini, listen devotedly to how his day unfolded, cheer him up when he was down, bear him at least two perfect children (one should be male to inherit his father's business empire) and never complain.

It was to be a fairy tale life. To Mary, it seemed like a shiny prison.

Mary was bored to tears by her upbringing and wanted to break free, see the world, have some adventure, and find a man who was dashing, daring, and a little dangerous.

But instead, she found herself studying art history at Smith College, one of the famous Seven Sisters Schools, where women were expected to pass the time until they earned the only degree that truly meant anything—the "MRS," which referred to women who got engaged or married while pursuing higher education. Then they could quietly retire to one of the white clapboard houses in the wealthy residential communities of Westchester, Greenwich, or Boston's Back Bay, learn to play bridge, and wait for their husband to come home from the law firm or bank, where he is now an up-and-coming junior partner, a young man to keep an eye on.

But times were changing. The pill had been introduced in 1960, freeing women to have sex for pleasure, not just procreation. The war in Vietnam had attracted thousands of young people to protest marches and sit-ins. Everyone was smoking pot or trying psychedelics, and to be sitting in a stuffy classroom surrounded by other rich girls seemed to be a colossal waste of time. Mary wanted more. She wanted to live. She wanted experiences and challenges and to make a mark on the world. She was on fire with youthful idealism and ready to buck her upbringing and throw her fate to the wind to see what destiny would bring her.

What it brought her was Michael. She met him at a protest sit-in when he plopped down beside her on the ground. He had wild, uncombed long hair, a scruffy beard, and the bluest eyes she'd ever seen. As the afternoon passed, between chants, they talked for hours. Michael was a graduate student at the University of Massachusetts in Amherst, there on a full scholarship. He was some sort of technical genius. He had ideas, big ideas, and he was working on RSS security messages that at present were only sent from university to university but would soon be the way everyone communicated. The messages were called "e-mails," and Michael believed that they needed to be protected, encrypted like the coded messages sent during WWII, except for private use. Letter writing was on the way out.

Michael was creating encryption keys and planning on opening his own company in his parents' garage in Quincy, near Boston. Then he was going to change the way everyone in the world spoke to everyone else. He would help control the flow of information across the globe.

Mary didn't really understand everything he said, but she was attracted to his passion, romantically and intellectually. Here was the man to whom she could hitch her wagon. He was going to be a star. She just knew it.

Their relationship grew strong in a very short period. Mary spent many late nights listening to Michael talk about how technology was going to bring the whole world together. No more would kids around the world have to starve because they didn't have the same educational opportunities as kids in the States. Now all information could be shared for free and almost instantly.

During his last year in graduate school, Michael talked up his company, MFE Industries (which stood for Michael's Foolproof Encryptions), to everyone and convinced enough students to kick in a few bucks, assuring them that as initial investors they'd make their money back a hundred-fold once he got going. Mary, who by now was convinced that her Michael was going to change the world, chipped in all of her allowance, which her parents kept increasing at her request, not knowing the money wasn't going to beauty salons, shopping, or school supplies.

After Michael's graduation, Mary decided to drop out of school to help him build his company. So, after her sophomore year ended, she told her parents that she wouldn't be coming with them to Europe over the summer, that she was "interning" at an art gallery in Boston and staying with "friends." She loved her parents but lying came easily when her future was unfolding before her eyes.

The couple went to live with Michael's parents, who let Mary stay in the visitor's room across the hall from Michael's (and turned a blind eye toward nocturnal visits between the two). During the day, they rigged used transistors, miles of cable, many extension cords, and more in the garage. While Michael worked on writing code and inventing a reliable encryption method to safeguard information sent and received via the infant computer network, they had to leave the door open and fans blowing to keep the equipment from overheating.

Word of their work got out fast, and when Michael was asked to speak at scientific conferences, Mary helped write his talks. He provided the tech details, and she did her best to make them understandable. She even drew MFE's first logo for the front of brochures she designed to lure investors and for business cards for Michael to hand out at conferences. The fledgling company got its own phone line, and Mary answered all calls as if the company were ensconced in a glass office tower somewhere instead of a dirty, hot garage in suburban Boston.

But it all started to come together and Michael won a large grant to fund his work (Mary wrote the prospectus). Real investors started sending money, and soon MFE Industries was a serious company. In no time, Michael began acting as a consultant for companies who saw the writing on the wall regarding the new high-tech world.

It was all very exciting: working side-by-side all day, squeezing into Michael's childhood twin bed at night to make love until the wee hours, and then talking, over endless cups of coffee, about how to build their dreams in the morning.

Mary's parents, unaware of all that was happening until the school informed them that she had dropped out, were quite upset at Mary's duplicity. They demanded to meet this Michael, and so she brought him to their home for dinner one night.

Her parents grilled him about his upbringing, his family, his bank balance, and his prospects. Her father asked him point-blank what his intentions were towards his daughter, and Mary was quite surprised when he answered, "I love her. We are getting married." But his declaration changed nothing. Mary's parents had already dismissed Michael as a "dirty hippie" and predicted a dire outcome if Mary stayed with him. They also threatened to cut her off and leave her without a dime if she did. But Mary would not be deterred, and so, without her parent's approval, she and Michael married one Saturday at the courthouse with two strangers as witnesses.

The first few years were tough, as the young couple poured every penny they could get their hands on back into the business. They ate a lot of canned tuna and lived with Michael's parents. But then the tide turned and money started pouring in.

They bought a townhouse in Boston and a commercial building in Worcester to house MFE. Their staff grew to hundreds of people, and the government contracts they were awarded funded expansion after expansion. Michael became renowned as an expert in computer encryption, and Mary became the vice president of worldwide marketing.

They were very happy together, and, when baby Julia came along, their little family seemed complete. Mary set up a crib and playpen right in her office, and Julia spent her early years on the hip of either parent as they moved from meeting to meeting. She became the unofficial mascot of the company. Luckily, she was a good-natured child with an even temperament, always smiling, and she grew into a lovely girl who adored both her parents.

For the next twelve years, the company flourished, and Julia and her mother became inseparable. Julia was helpful, naturally polite, somewhat shy, and as steady as a rock. Mary was much more emotional. She was quick to anger (she did not suffer fools gladly), got highly offended when anyone criticized her husband (no matter how mildly), and was so fervently in love with Michael that it was almost hard for people to watch. Working by his side, being his sounding board and confidante, helping him manage the business, and raising their daughter was all she ever wanted in life. Mary's dream for her future had come true.

For his part, Michael left his dirty hippie days behind him. His beard was gone, his hair was now cut by a renowned Italian stylist, and he wore tailored suits. He had even taken up jogging, a new pastime sweeping the nation. It was while running through the park one evening that he met Patty.

She was in her final year at Boston University School of Law and show-stoppingly beautiful. Patty's parents lived in the area, and she was at her parent's home for the weekend. Her long black hair fell over her face as she sat on the ground crying and rubbing her ankle. She had twisted it on a cobblestone, and Michael stopped to help. She stood up with difficulty, threw her arm around his neck, and tried to hobble along. When that proved too painful, he offered to drive her to her parent's house a few blocks away. Patty called him "my hero." When Michael dropped by a few days later to check on her recovery, he had taken off his wedding ring.

It all happened so fast; Mary never saw it coming.

Michael announced one night that he was going to divorce her. He would split the now-considerable company profits and buy out Mary's stock shares. She would be rich, set for life, with plenty of money to take care of their twelve-year-old daughter. He gave her full custody as he "planned to have more kids soon enough."

Mary was more than heartbroken. She felt shattered, and she sobbed, night after night, for months. Julia was frightened watching her parents' marriage fall apart and her mother crumbling as a result. Eventually, being in the same town with Michael became too much for Mary. She couldn't stand seeing photos of him and his new girlfriend at social functions that she and Michael had been too busy to attend. When the engagement announcement appeared in the newspaper, Mary knew she had to get out of town.

She withdrew Julia from school, re-invested all of her wealth in the burgeoning computer industry, and began traveling to all corners of the world, searching for a surcease to her pain. She wasn't sure exactly of what she was looking for, but she tried all sorts of healing methods and practices with the hope that the pain would subside.

During her journey, Mary sought wisdom from diverse spiritual and wellness practices. She immersed herself in the tranquility of meditation and yoga and practiced it in both silence and darkness for weeks at a time. She tapped into the harmony of her body and mind, further accessed by acupuncture and tai chi. Studying the principles of feng shui, she fostered a sense of balance with her surroundings. Her exploration extended to reiki, chanting, and the use of mantras, while she also delved into sound healing, chakra alignment, and the principles of energetic frequencies.

Mary accessed the profound wisdom of Aboriginal dreamtime in the Australian outback and experienced the purifying power of the Hawaiian "*Ho'oponopono*" prayer. Her adventurous spirit led her to swim alongside majestic marine creatures, commune with monkeys while sleeping in treetop huts high up in rainforest canopies, and learn gentleness with strength while feeding tamarind to the massive elephants of northern Thailand.

Ascensions to ancient sacred sites broadened her perspective. Her travels in Egypt were particularly transformative. Along with many meditations inside the pyramids, Mary devoted significant time to visiting archaeological wonders, exploring temples, and immersing herself in the rich tapestry of their culture. This nurtured a profound respect for the wisdom of ancient civilizations. Continuing her journey, living with indigenous tribes further enhanced her understanding of diverse cultures. Sitting with shamans and native healers, she experienced their powerful, time-honored practices firsthand. She discovered the transformative power of medicines found in plants and fungi, deepening her bond with the natural world.

Mary later learned about the cleansing rituals of the *Temazcal* ceremony held in a sweat lodge, the emotional liberation of art therapy, and the tapping system known as the Emotional Freedom Technique (EFT). She dove into the insightful domains of spiritual psychology and navigated through enlightened models of human development and consciousness. Her journey also led her to explore mindfulness and compassionate communication practices, improving her self-awareness and interpersonal relationships.

Mary was drawn to the therapeutic properties of natural elements and experienced the rejuvenating effects of thermal waters, mud and ice baths, holy wells, and hay saunas. Her curiosity about the human mind led her to explore diverse therapies ranging from Freudian and Jungian psychoanalysis to hypnosis and past-life regression.

Consultations with mystics, astrologers, tarot readers, and crystal healers enriched her knowledge of esoteric wisdom. She studied ancient religions and prayed at many historically significant shrines, lighting candles, leaving offerings, and always asking for clarity and for her purpose to be shown to her.

Dietary exploration was also a part of her journey, as she practiced a raw foods diet, breatharianism, veganism, prolonged fasting, and Ayurvedic nutrition.

Mary's journey represented a quest for inner growth, healing, and harmony. In exploring such a myriad of practices, she found a deeper understanding of herself and the world, highlighting the interconnectedness of her mind, body, and spirit. She was searching for relief from her pain and what she found was much greater.

The overwhelming message she received from all of her exploration and experiences was that the universe was *love*, and that awareness, gratefulness, forgiveness, and acceptance were necessary so as not to block that love. She learned that she was enough, a spiritual being who came forth from love to be loved. Like a mother loves her child, so the universe loved Mary, and, at last, she understood. She knew that she needed to help other women find what she had found. They may be unable to discover the knowledge that Mary had found through the teachers and therapies that she sought out while traveling the world, but she could bring the world to them. A profound thought began to take shape in Mary's mind.

One night, ten years later, she sat with her daughter, Julia, who, from an early age as her mother's traveling companion, had absorbed spiritual wisdom far beyond her years. As they talked late into the night, staring into a fire before them, Mary shared her nascent idea with Julia.

"What if we could gather an array of teachers and healers from all over the globe and place them in one single location?" Mary said, haltingly, as though she were listening for the first time herself to the words formed on her tongue. "There they could exchange ideas and co-create the most powerful laboratory of personal healing and transformation the world has ever seen."

She continued, her voice rising with excitement.

"It would be a safe and sacred place where women could come to learn how to achieve a radical shift in consciousness and mindset and, through that shift, experience fuller and more fulfilled lives. They could then take what they learned and share that knowledge with others, creating an ever-widening circle of higher consciousness, where ever more women would understand and experience universal love."

As Julia's eyes grew wider seeing the vision her mother was describing, Mary looked at her daughter and knew that she must build such a place for the woman Julia was becoming and for all the women being born into a world

The Orchid

too often narrow and blind to the glorious truths the universe could reveal. It was her destiny, Mary now knew. She would build this sacred and beautiful place, and she would name it The Orchid.

With the business acumen Mary had built over her years with MFE Industries, her nearly inexhaustible supply of money—which, thanks to the meteoric growth of the computer industry in which she had invested, now exceeded a billion dollars—, and her equally inexhaustible passion for the work, her vision became a reality. Healers, teachers, and practitioners from all around the world were chosen, offered handsome compensation and the freedom to design their own programs, and invited to reside at The Orchid. From all over the globe they came, inspired by Mary's mission of love.

Once The Orchid was receiving visitors, Mary began to see the power of what she had created. All of the women who passed through its loving and supportive environment and became familiar with the many tools and methods taught at this unique educational facility began to experience change. Not everyone responded the same way, but, because there were so many modalities available, everyone always found at least one with which they could connect.

Just as in Mary's own life, the cumulative effect of the knowledge and collaboration of all the teachers and healers was what was needed to create a meaningful impact for every woman who attended. The Orchid has been transforming lives for more than twenty years.

Chapter 2

The Orchid

Towering high above its verdant foothills, the Cascade Range skirts the coasts of Northern California, Oregon, and Washington, stretching its arms into British Columbia. In places, the range is so tall, clouds drape over it like a shawl. Its higher altitudes cradle alpine meadows, tundra (home to big cats, deer, and bear), and ice blue glaciers.

Amidst this dense forest, not far from the mystic silhouette of Mount Shasta, lies the haven of tranquility and transformation known as The Orchid. Spanning over 400 acres of pristine land, this property is a living tableau of nature's beauty, adorned with lakes, creeks, and waterfalls, cradled by rocky ledges and vibrant meadows. It boasts sun-dappled groves, winding earthen trails, and craggy overlooks. Remote yet accessible, it welcomes guests with a collection of unique state-of-the-art facilities and structures, each distinct in its design and purpose.

The atmosphere is serene but not silent, as the property is alive with birdsong, the soundtrack to the scene. Juniper, leaf mold, and pine resin scent the air, and the leaves and tiny branches on the forest floor crunch under the feet of passersby.

There are no uninvited guests at The Orchid, and all who enter its gates are welcome. Part of what they learn will be taught by the topography itself. It might be a leisurely stroll through the invigorating citrus-scented orange groves, a meditative walk through the inviting labyrinth, a quiet moment in the vegetable garden and adjacent plantations, or a peaceful observation period at the edge of the bamboo forest. Perhaps it will be watching the pond for the lightning flash of gold that is the koi surfacing or the soul-soothing tranquility of sitting at the Meditation Center during sunset.

The Orchid

These are some of the lessons in this great schoolroom, and their moments of solitude do much to heal the most tumultuous of spirits, but there are other treasures.

Catering to guests' nutritional needs, the main dining hall presents a carefully curated selection of meals. The buffet tables showcase an array of fresh fruits, a variety of international cheeses, and produce harvested from local organic gardens. Guests can also choose from freshly baked breads, flavorful salsas and dips, and a modest selection of homemade desserts offering guilt-free indulgence for those who have denied themselves such pleasures.

For the body, The Orchid's comprehensive gym caters to a variety of fitness interests and expertise levels. It provides a dynamic range of activities, from the adrenaline rush of high-intensity interval training and strength-building routines to the serene, mind-body synergy of Pilates and yoga. Dance lovers can lose themselves in the rhythm of a large variety of classes, while cycling enthusiasts can challenge themselves in spinning sessions.

The Orchid is home to a splendid spa facility, a sanctuary devoted to relaxation and rejuvenation. Here, guests can avail themselves of a variety of soothing treatments, from tension-relieving massages and skin-nourishing facials to restorative hydrotherapy and purifying saunas. Notably, it incorporates natural, plant-based treatments that align with its holistic approach, thereby offering guests a transformative journey of sensory pleasure and inner peace.

As the day concludes, cozy lounges come alive with the warm glow of fireplaces, while, come morning, large windows allow the natural light to flood in, ensuring the constant circulation of fresh mountain air.

Hiding around the property, the guests' accommodations reflect a strong commitment to originality and creativity. Each dwelling is a unique expression of architectural inspiration drawn from a wide array of global aesthetics. These abodes are seamlessly integrated into the natural landscape, using the existing topography and local materials to provide guests with a singularly distinctive experience.

All of this underscores a deep respect for the natural surroundings and a dedication to innovative design. Each accommodation is an embodiment of this philosophy, fostering an unforgettable connection between guests and the serene beauty of the environment.

Guests come together in shared spaces and learn lessons in various courtyards and venues scattered throughout the site. Each person embarks on a journey of self-transformation, lending and receiving support from others along the way. Guests arrive as strangers but depart as changed, freer individuals, ready to share with the world the gifts they've received during their stay.

Becoming a guest involves three crucial steps: securing a referral from a former attendee, demonstrating a keen interest in the program through a completed application, and showing a sincere commitment to the mission of The Orchid. Each woman's decision to take these steps is influenced by her unique life circumstances and readiness for change.

The Orchid

Chapter 3

Sofia

Sofia could pinpoint the exact moment she started despising her family.

It was when she was thirteen, on the verge of womanhood, and, once again, her father and mother, Raul and Ana, were having a screaming match in the kitchen of their home in Monterrey, Mexico. Her father's face turned bright red and his voice grew ever louder. Her mother retreated into a corner and dissolved into an emotional mess; sobbing and inarticulate, tears streamed from her eyes.

Raul provided plenty of opportunities for tears. He was a womanizer and a gambler, profligate with money and stingy with affection. He did exactly what he wanted to do whenever he wanted to do it. Keeping his marriage vows was not on that list. Ana suspected him of being unfaithful and kept trying to catch him out by hurling accusations at him when he would come home late, hoping for a confession.

"Where were you?" she'd scream. "Which *friends* were you out with this time?"

"I was out playing cards, Ana. You know that. I told you where I was going this morning. The game ran late so we could make back some losses," he lied.

Lying was Raul's superpower. He could make up a story on the spot for every occasion and make people believe him. He sometimes even believed his own lies. But, Ana, having heard almost every variation of tall tale he could come up with, was his toughest audience. Each time, she had to be convinced anew of his innocence.

Ana herself was not a paragon of parenthood. She thrived in an environment of looking good on the outside no matter how rotten the core, often prioritizing social activities over the needs of her family. She distracted herself from her tumultuous marriage with a whirlwind of breakfast gatherings, luncheons, coffee dates, tennis lessons, and charity events. Shopping sprees were her specialty. After every argument or whenever she couldn't immediately account for Raul's whereabouts, Ana would embark on extravagant expeditions across the border to San Antonio, Texas and spend lavishly on the latest in fashion, handbags, and footwear. She'd unflinchingly charge all her purchases to Raul's credit card, viewing it as retribution for his suspected infidelity. "One lie, one purse" became her catchphrase.

But Ana was also very invested in how other people viewed her family. The country club became her stage and the members her audience. There, with her husband and children, she could paint a portrait of familial perfection. Under Ana's laser-like stare, her husband knew better than to cast his wandering eye on another woman, and the children were expected to look good, mouth pleasant answers to the adults' questions about school, and then disappear as quickly as possible, be seen but not heard.

Ana herself would sport the trendiest swimsuits and large designer sunglasses, layers of gold bracelet running halfway up her arm and a frozen margarita in hand. She lorded over a poolside table and managed to look as though she had a perfect family, even though, for the amount of actual attention she gave them, they could have been cardboard cutouts.

This dysfunctional pattern was not new to them. It was merely the continuation of a historical cycle passed from generation to generation. Despite some changes in gender roles and societal norms, daily life and societal structures remained skewed towards men. Such disparity often set couples like Ana and Raul on a collision course.

Raul had been taught, as were most of his male friends, that he could have fun, go to school, earn degrees, and go on to have a successful career. A woman was a crucial part of this life equation. Every man required a "good" woman to become a wife, manage his household, and bear him children. A man, conversely, was expected to earn a good living to provide for his family and keep his wife relatively happy. But that scenario didn't preclude a man from having a little fun on the side.

Ana, like many women of her generation, was conditioned to be an obedient daughter, marry well, be a "good" wife, cater to all her husband's needs, manage an immaculate home, stay impeccably dressed, remain physically attractive, and bear children. She had also been taught that the most important day in her life was the day she married, an occasion that marked the passing of her stewardship from her father to her husband. Any ambition beyond these set boundaries was often discouraged, deemed unnecessary, or flat-out forbidden. The only part of this set-in-stone reality that Ana could control were the social gatherings and shopping sprees. They were her only outlet for satisfaction and fulfillment. It was like being trapped and her rage simmered in such imprisonment.

Ana and Raul did their best, but the societal pressures and their ingrained beliefs always tipped the scales, adding more dysfunction to their relationship. The only time they worked together was in running their family businesses—two grocery stores and three apartment buildings. The revenue from these efforts provided them with financial security, which helped ease some of the tension.

But the arguments continued, and, as the years passed, the frequency and intensity of their fights increased. Sofia and her brother learned to stay out of the way and keep quiet whenever their parents fought, but that didn't mean they didn't listen to everything that was said. As they got older, they saw their father slap their mother around many times, and they couldn't understand why Ana didn't fight back.

After a particularly violent episode, Sofia picked up a kitchen knife to defend her mother herself, and, when she ran forward, knife raised, her father hastily retreated and made for the exit. Sofia felt triumphant and powerful, certain she had finally changed the situation. But though her mother and father slept in separate rooms for a few weeks after that, it wasn't long before Ana and Raul began to act as though nothing had happened and went back to projecting their smoke-screen perfection to the outside world. Just like the many that preceded it, that incident was never mentioned again. Swept under the rug, it joined a legacy of pain, silence, and secrets.

This toxic environment served as a disturbing schoolroom for Sofia and her brother, who started to mirror what they learned, the aggressive behavior they constantly witnessed. Once they were old enough, they began displaying it towards each other. As a result, Sofia frequently found herself fending off her brother's bullying, which once resulted in Sofia getting her jaw dislocated. She would retaliate aggressively whenever she could and often gave better than she got. Her parents, so wrapped up in their own drama, barely noticed what was going on in their children's lives, but even if they had, Sofia was sure that they would not have interfered.

The Orchid

These painful experiences gradually hardened Sofia, causing her to form protective walls around her heart, which eventually turned to stone.

I will not let anyone push me around and take advantage of me, she vowed to herself. *I'd rather be dead. I'll never let anyone treat me like a piece of shit.*

During all of this time, the only solid and peaceful relationship that Sofia had was with her friend, Monica Reyes. She spent much time with Monica and her family, and each time she was with them, she noticed that their interactions with each other were different than those she had with her family. There was respect, trust, joy, love, patience, and peace between them. They handled disagreements rationally and never felt the need to raise their voices. And they were very successful.

It was the exact opposite of Sofia's family experience. The Reyes' home felt safe and like a true oasis from her tumultuous world. Monica's parents were attentive, shared advice, and were supportive of their daughter's interests and dreams.

They extended this treatment to Sofia whenever she was at their house. It was a bit surreal, except that Sofia experienced it so consistently and for so many years that she knew it to be true. Such support made Sofia wish the Reyes were her family. Over the years, Sofia developed a deep respect for Monica and her family, and it served her as an example of how she wanted to live her life one day.

Sofia saw education as a lifeline, a way to transform her life and escape her present reality. She enrolled at a prestigious university in Mexico City, a move that conveniently allowed her to break free from her tumultuous home environment. Immersed in her studies, she rapidly achieved her degree, her intense dedication allowing her to accomplish it in the shortest possible time frame. This swift attainment opened the gates to the corporate world, fast-tracking her professional journey.

Sofia was thirsty for power and recognition and her career benefitted greatly from this. She soon realized that the resilience and ruthlessness she had developed from facing aggression at home had become an unexpected advantage. They enhanced her skills in sales and management, allowing her to have an unusually fast climb in Mexico's real estate industry.

After Sofia was put in charge of managing several properties, she immediately found ways to squeeze money out of them, which prompted strong approval and recognition from her superiors. One of the first things

Sofia did with the properties, a few apartment buildings, was raise all the tenants' rents by 40 percent. Those who couldn't pay would be evicted. No sob story swayed her. It was as if she had a calculator in place of a heart.

With the commissions she earned, she started her own portfolio. She began buying up small apartments around Mexico City, fixer-uppers, which she would turn over to a small crew of laborers that she had assembled. They would make cosmetic improvements *only*. She would then use the same tactics she was using at her job: jack up the rents, evict those who couldn't pay, and fill the apartments with higher paying tenants. She would also sell the properties before anyone noticed that roof leaks had been painted over or that rusty pipes were held together with plumber's tape. She paid off inspectors, took her profits, and did it all over again.

Soon Sofia had enough money to leave her job and cast a wider net. She had her eyes on an old residential hi-rise in an up-and-coming area of the city. The cost, however, was a little out of her league. She'd need a partner, and she knew just the person to ask.

It was then that she reached out to her childhood friend, Monica, who knew her very well. Since Monica was from a wealthy family with an extensive business background, she would be a fantastic partner. She also knew that Monica was learning how to manage her family's ever-growing real estate portfolio. She and Sofia had kept in touch over the years and Sofia thought that Monica might be interested in this new opportunity.

Sofia made a lunch date with Monica and put a proposal before her. The two of them would each contribute 50 percent of the purchase price of the building, with them both listed as co-owners on the mortgage. They would use Monica and her family's name to get in the door, and some of the many tricks Sofia had learned to squeeze money out of the project and eventually flip it for a huge profit.

Monica was glad to see her old friend, but after listening to the proposal, she shook her head with a firm "no." She wouldn't consider it. "I'm going to pass on your offer, my dear friend. Thank you very much."

Sofia, somewhat surprised, asked her, "But why? It's such a great opportunity. Think of the money we could make."

Monica gestured for the check and then calmly explained her thinking to Sofia.

"I'm not interested in doing business that way, Sofia. It's not right and I don't want to be part of that."

"What are you talking about?" Sofia was puzzled.

Monica hesitated before saying what was really on her mind. Looking into Sofia's eyes, Monica asked, "Sofia, can I be totally honest with you?"

"Yes, of course," Sofia said. "We've been friends for a long, long time. I expect you to be."

"You changed a lot from the young girl I grew up knowing. I hear that working with you is not ideal. You've taken advantage of many people, and the word on the street is that you only care about yourself, that you always cheat, and that you are always angry. You are infamous around this city for blowing your stack. I love you very much, but I'm not going into business with someone with such a quick temper. You overreact, you jump to the wrong conclusions, you have a giant chip on your shoulder, and you'd rather burn a house down than ever give the appearance that someone got something over on you."

Monica continued, "I also know that you truly believe that unless you cheat, you won't advance."

Sofia interrupted, "Ok, why don't you tell me how you really feel."

With a wan smile, Monica replied, "To be fair, I asked you before saying anything. "You know my family, Sofia. We don't subscribe to that type of behavior, and I don't either. I've learned to be aggressive but also transparent and fair in all my dealings, and I have been highly rewarded for being that way. Besides, I sleep better at night."

Sofia, who always had a ready answer to everything, was silent and pensive after hearing her friend's words. She found her voice again and said defensively, "Thanks for your comments, Monica, but I don't have the benefit of a wonderful family behind me. I've only done what I had to do to survive. Otherwise, people would take advantage of me."

Monica calmly responded, "I hear you, but the choice is always yours. There are other ways to be successful."

"Well, I don't know any other way," Sofia started to argue, seeing her chance for a profitable partnership with her friend slip out of her grasp.

Monica looked at her with compassion and said, "You know, Sofia, maybe it is time for you to consider another path, another way of doing things. You don't have to carry all the pain, anger, and resentment with you for the rest of your life. Some of the women in my family, me included, have all gone to a place where we have learned a different way of thinking. This opened the doors to dramatic improvements in our lives. I know you've seen that reflected in us all. I would highly encourage you to look into this place. Perhaps it can also work for you.

"It is called The Orchid. I'm happy to recommend you and provide you with the information to apply if you want it. If you decide to go, I'll sit down with you afterwards and talk about whether we might work together."

The Orchid

Chapter 4

Congratulations

Sofia received a lovely letter on stationary made from pressed flowers and botanicals. A subtle scent of rosemary and lavender arose from the letter, which read:

Congratulations, Sofia, on your acceptance into The Orchid.

You've joined a dedicated group of women who, like you, have shown a willingness to work on personal transformation. We're pleased to welcome everyone who shares this dedication, and we're thrilled that you'll be joining us on this journey.

I remind you that the program requires your commitment, and that its results are directly proportional to the effort and dedication you put into it. However, I assure you that by attending and completing the course you will have taken a profound step towards a more powerful existence.

Our entire staff, including an unparalleled team of healers, teachers, and practitioners, are all ready to welcome and support you.

I look forward to seeing you soon.
Until then, wishing you many blessings,

Mary Rose
Founder & Director

A second sheet added necessary details, such as the date chosen for the recipient's arrival, giving Sofia and the other twenty-nine women who would attend on that particular week at least a month's lead-time to arrange their

The Orchid

---

work schedule, child-care, or any affairs that needed to be put on hold. It was expected that the guests would focus only on themselves during their time at The Orchid.

A QR code for downloading a round-trip airline ticket was included, and it was explained that ground transportation to and from the retreat center would be provided.

The women were asked to leave any valuables at home as well as any electronics, as their use was disallowed during their stay. Cell phones would be kept in a lockbox for the duration of their program, but each guest could be reached and had access to a phone at the front desk. The number was provided on the sheet as was a Guest Services number for any further questions the guest may have.

They were asked to bring any medications (but no recreational intoxicants); to designate a contact in case of emergency; and to only bring undergarments, a bathing suit, running shoes, and the clothes needed for travel, as all other garments for their stay would be provided. The women were also asked to provide their clothing and shoe sizes.

They were also informed that all food and meals would be included and asked to advise of any allergies or nutritional requirements. Finally, a separate card was included with the message:

> Your stay at The Orchid is without any financial obligations, a privilege realized through the selfless donations of our founder and numerous prior visitors. They've gained invaluable insight from the wisdom and teachings shared here and, in a spirit of thankfulness, aim to provide similar opportunities for others.
>
> We anticipate that you, too, will feel driven to share the knowledge you gain, recommend our program to those seeking enlightenment, and contribute in your own way to the cycle of giving.
>
> With love from sisters to sisters, from all corners of the world.

Namaste,
The Orchid Team

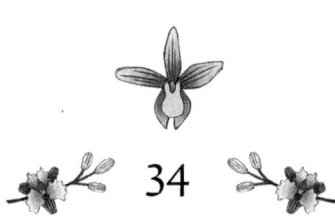

Part II
Arrival

The Orchid

Chapter 5

Welcome

Sofia was driven to The Orchid by an impeccably dressed driver in a beautiful black electric sedan.

The drive was a moving meditation in itself. As the car glided quietly through the forest, the road ran upwards as though headed for the clouds. Every shade of green passed the window and whole meadows of flowers could be seen through breaks in the trees. A carefully curated music list played in the background to help each guest relax and stimulate a shift in consciousness prior to their arrival.

Sofia opened the window of the car to see if the scene outside smelled as good as it looked. It did. Spruce, fir, and balsam mixed with a hint of unidentifiable wildflowers added to the sensory experience. She felt a lessening of tension in her neck and shoulders as she relaxed into the calm rhythm of the journey.

Time seemed to slow down.

"We have arrived," proclaimed the driver. Her voice had an air of formality. Swiftly, she stepped out and navigated her way to the passenger side, gently opening the door for Sofia. She proceeded to unload the luggage and arrange for its transport to Sofia's assigned room. Then, with a slight bow, the driver excused herself.

Two staff members stepped forward, arms open, and introduced themselves. "Welcome to The Orchid, Sofia. We are so grateful that you have chosen to join us. I am Mia," said one. "And I am Ela," said the other.

"Hello, and thank you," said Sofia, observing all her surroundings but still a bit sluggish from her travels.

"We have the honor of welcoming you and helping you set an intention to release and relinquish any heavy energy you may be carrying as you enter,"

The Orchid

Mia explained. "As we circle you and smudge you with sacred sage and burning palo santo wood, close your eyes and ask the universe to take all heaviness from you so that your spirit may ascend like the smoke from the smudging."

Sofia didn't quite believe she was carrying heavy energy but closed her eyes nevertheless to allow for the blessing.

Ela lit the incenses in an abalone shell, and, when it began to smoke, she walked clockwise around Sofia, wafting the smoke up and down her body with a colorful feather. When she had completed the circle, she heard the following words, said by Mia, with a beautiful smile: "These doors are open only to our invited guests and to the divine light of living love. Sofia, you are the vessel of such light, we are grateful for your presence, and we are deeply honored to have you."

With that, Mia and Ela directed Sofia to walk up with them towards the reception area. Along the way, they passed a rock with two bronze plaques embedded in its surface. Both were burnished by thousands of hands that had touched them in passing, as if trying to absorb their messages through their fingertips.

The first read:

> We recognize and honor the Indigenous people of the Shasta Tribe, who are the original stewards of this land. We pay our respects to their elders, both past and present, and acknowledge their spiritual connection to this region. May we always remember and honor the significance of these lands and the people who have called them home.

The other:

> Your task is not to seek for love, but merely to seek and find all the barriers within yourself that you have built against it. —Rumi

**

Everything about The Orchid was akin to the experience of being in a five-star hotel in some exotic location. However, the ambiance didn't just promise sensual pleasure and relaxation; it also hinted that hidden wisdom was about to be unveiled.

The Reception and Guest Services Center was a seamless fusion of indoor and outdoor environments, as if nature itself had crafted it. The room was alive with the sight of countless orchids of every imaginable hue, each one different, each one unique. These wonderful plants not only beautified the place but also served as symbols of the diversity of the women who visited The Orchid.

Instead of confining walls, the room opened up entirely, embracing the surrounding natural splendor. A gentle breeze danced through the space, carrying with it the scents of the blooming flowers, intertwining their fragrances with the earthy perfume of the nearby forest.

A small stream gracefully wound its way around the reception desk. Moss-covered stones lined its edges, and the stream's melody, a symphony of nature's rhythm, invited guests to sit and immerse themselves in the calmness of the flowing water.

The staff ensured that every woman felt seen, heard, and cherished in this new world they had entered. With serene smiles and soothing voices, they guided each of them through the check-in process, guaranteeing their every need was met with grace. It was here that they kindly requested the surrender of phones and other electronics, recognizing their temporary absence as essential for the inward journey. The simplicity of this request spoke volumes about The Orchid's expectations.

In every aspect, it was evident that this was no ordinary place; it was a sanctuary with a clear and serious purpose.

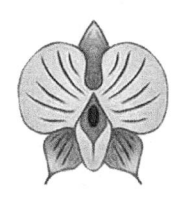

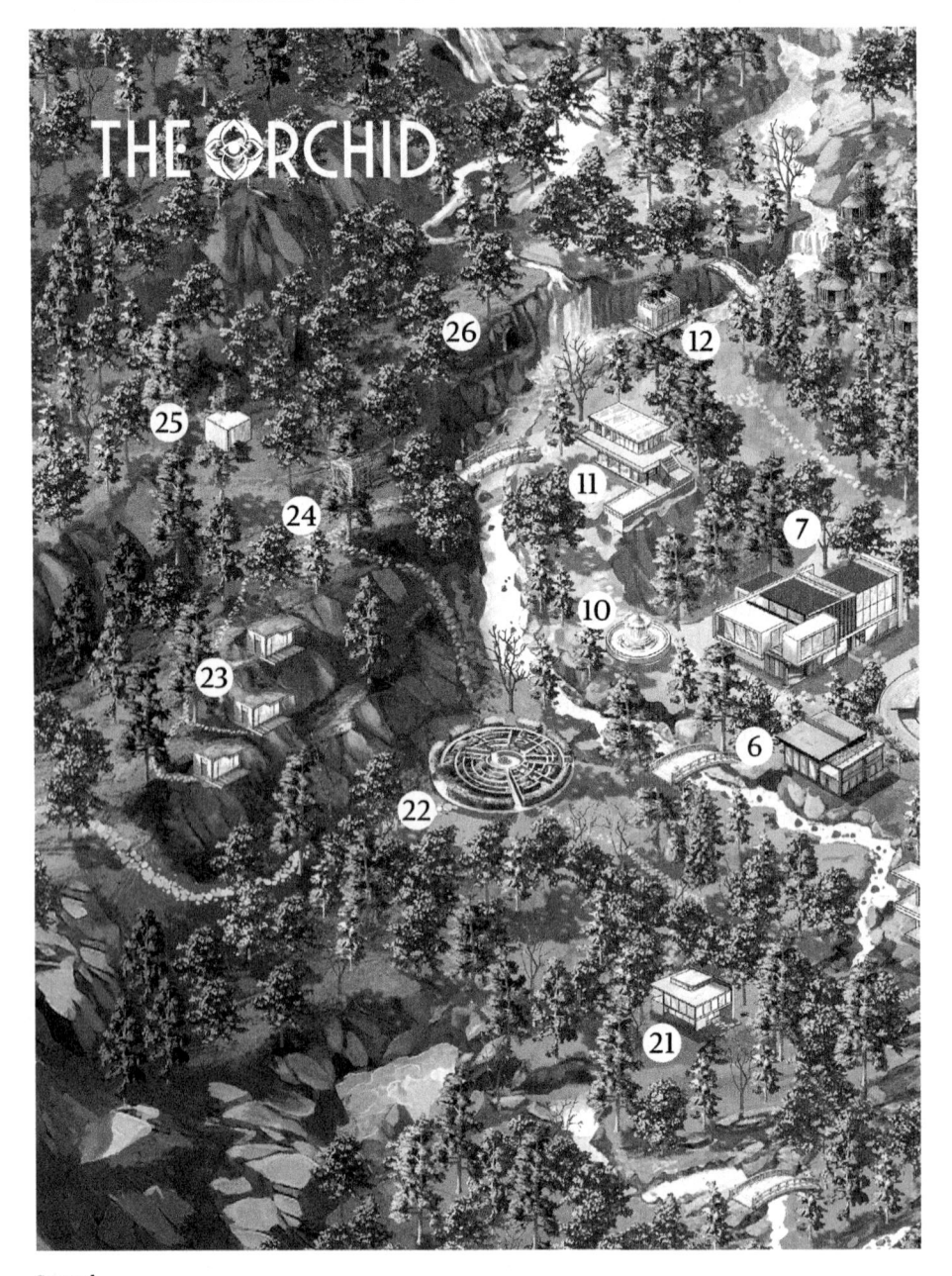

The Orchid

Legend
1) Main Gate/Parking 2) Love and Ancestral Acknowledgement Stone 3) Pond 4) Reception/Guest Services
5) Central Plaza/Fire Pit 6) Main Offices 7) Activity Center 8) Sanctuary 9) Dining Hall 10) Fountain
11) Aquatic Center 12) Canopy Room 13) Tree House Village #1

40

Property Map / Welcome

14) Dance Studio 15) Meditation Center 16) Observatory 17) Bamboo Forrest 18) Vegetable Garden
19) Plantations/Orchards 20) Ceremonial Arch 21) Heaven Spa 22) Labyrinth
23) Cliff Rooms 24) Nest Room 25) Mirror Room 26) Cave Room 27) Tree House Village #2

41

The Orchid

MAGDA
Divination
Ireland

LEYLA
Physician, Seer
Turkey

SISTER D.
Buddhist Monk
Bhutan

RANI
Masseuse
India

ISABELLE
Breath and Sound
France

AISHA
Watsu
Iran

FLAVIA
Dance
Brazil

Teachers and Healers / Welcome

Mary
Founder
United States

Lucia
Head Nutritionist
Italy

Wakinyan
Shaman
United States

Silvia
Shaman
Peru

Samara
Languages & Writing
United Kingdom

Ruby
Social Worker
Rwanda

Teena
Psychologist
New Zealand

Name	Sofia Aguilar	Olivia Munson
Age	28	50
Title / Occupation	Business Owner	Dir. Economic Development
Related Industry	Real Estate	Non-Profit
Parents	Ana Aguilar Raul Aguilar	Loretta Munson Tyrone Munson
Children	None	None
Marital Status	Single	Single
Education	B.S. Business Admin.	Ph.D. in Political Science
Place of Birth	Monterrey, Mexico	New Orleans, Louisiana
City of Residence	Mexico City	Washington D.C.
Areas of Opportunity	Anger, resentment, aggressive behavior, lack of trust in others, hyper vigilance, interpersonal conflicts.	Panic attacks, migraines, insomnia, overbearing behavior, emotional guardedness, anxiety, stress, burnout, strained relationships, and difficulty relinquishing control.
Recommended by	Monica Reyes	Penelope Schriever
Assigned Room	The Cliff 1	The Canopy Room

Nicole Moretti	Stephanie Henry	Jennifer Clairborne
30	35	37
Science Teacher Volunteer EMT	Designer	Finance Manager
Education	Fashion Design	Insurance
Isabel Moretti Gregorio Moretti	Mei Wong Fang Wong	Patricia Clairborne Paul Clairborne
None	2	2
Single	Married	Single
M.A. Physics and Biology		B.S. Business Management
Houston, Texas	Singapore	Lansing, Michigan
Houston, Texas	New York City	Lansing, Michigan
Struggles with self-acceptance. Grappling with feelings of shame and guilt, due to parental pressures and personal beliefs regarding gender. Lack of self-confidence, fear of losing familial support.	Body image issues, extreme weight loss, unhealthy relationship with food, struggles with intimacy, fear of vulnerability, anxiety, low self-esteem, and post-traumatic stress.	Struggles with letting go of past relationship, unresolved emotions, attachment, lingering feelings of loss, lack of self-love, struggle with self-esteem, feelings of unworthiness, depression, sadness, and a general sense of despair.
Malena Rodriguez	Natasha Pawlowska	Rebecca Smith
The Cave	The Mirror	The Nest

The Orchid

The Rooms

As Sofia was guided through the pathways of the luxurious complex, every detail caught her attention. She pondered over the maintenance costs, the materials used, and the decisions behind each construction. Even though she was surrounded by beauty, her analytical mind wouldn't allow her to fully immerse in it.

Upon reaching her room, she was awestruck. A glass balcony offered a panoramic view of a cliff which, while breathtaking, also gave her a sense of vertigo. The room's interior was a perfect blend of luxury and rustic charm. Every element seemed to have been chosen with intent.

As the guide outlined some particulars of her lodging, Sofia was reminded of moments from her childhood, triggered by a small welcoming detail - a plate of churros and a jug of hot chocolate. However, these memories also brought echoes of pain, which Sofia quickly pushed out of her mind.

She tried to engage the guide in a deeper conversation about the design and inspiration behind the room, but the young woman was already at the door, ready to leave. *She probably doesn't know anything anyway,* Sofia thought. *She's just an employee. I'd like to meet the owners and ask my questions directly.*

Approaching the desk, she admired the vintage telephone, the pewter inkwell with a refillable fountain pen, and a small note on the table that read:

> Leap and the net will appear.

Reflecting on the meaning of those words and the experience awaiting her, she thought, *What the hell does that mean?*

**

As she followed her guide down the path, Jennifer was overwhelmed by the grandeur of the place. Often, when she felt nervous, she'd resort to constant chatter as a defense mechanism. However, something about the guide's serene and self-assured presence made her hold back, choosing not to break the silence. Instead of speaking, Jennifer opted to delve into a deep sea of memories and reflections about her life.

At the end of the trail, they encountered lodgings that looked like a massive bird's nest among the trees. The guide announced, "Here we are, at your room," pointing upwards. In awe, Jennifer followed the guide up hidden stairs leading to the nest. Once inside, she found a circular room made of intertwined branches, mud, and leaves, evoking the sensation of being in a natural haven. A clay fireplace in the center radiated cozy warmth, and a hanging bed promised nights of rest beneath the starry sky.

As Jennifer explored, the guide began to share details: "On the desk, you'll find a journal to capture thoughts or moments of beauty. If you need anything, call the reception. At 6:00 p.m., you'll hear the bell announcing dinner. During your stay, we suggest wearing the clothes we've provided, which can be found in the closet by the sauna." Jennifer nodded, thankful for the information.

Little details, like a teapot with chamomile tea and cinnamon cookies, stirred warm memories of her family. Yet, despite the beauty and tranquility of the place, Jennifer grappled with her own insecurities, especially regarding her divorce. She felt alone. She also questioned her abilities as a mother. But as she reflected, a note on the desk caught her eye:

> We may not write all the chapters of our life, but we can decide how to live them.

These words offered her momentary solace, reminding her that despite challenges, there was always hope and a way forward.

**

As Stephanie walked through the lush forest, her guide suddenly stopped and, with an enigmatic smile, pointed upwards. Stephanie followed her finger and discovered a nearly invisible structure, camouflaged by mirrors that reflected the surroundings. The guide led her to a glass elevator that took them straight to this architectural marvel.

Upon entering, Stephanie was amazed by the panoramic view of the forest, thanks to the one-way glass walls. The minimalist design, with cool and elegant tones, contrasted with the warmth and life of the exterior forest. The guide showed her the amenities, highlighting a bathroom with a glass shower that could turn opaque with just the flip of a switch.

This must be for guests who aren't used to showing everyone every part of their body like me, she thought.

"On the desk, you will find a map of the property and your schedule for the week," the guide informed her and excused herself.

However, what truly captured Stephanie's attention were the mirrors. There wasn't one, but two standing mirrors. *Strange*, she thought. *Why do I need two mirrors?*

Stephanie walked to the first and took a quick look at herself, automatically adjusting a bit as she used to. She placed one foot in front of the other to minimize the width of her hips, sucked in her stomach, pushed back her shoulders, and tossed her glossy black hair.

Then, as always, she started an internal critique: Was her waist getting fat? She'd have to check with the measuring tape she always carried. She automatically looked around the room for the toilet and thought: *We'll see each other after dinner, my friend.*

Sighing over her imperfections, she approached the other mirror and, upon looking into it, nearly screamed. Her reflection was completely distorted! It was wavy and made parts of her body look enormous and clumsy, and her head as small as a pin. Moving a bit to the right, the reflection changed. Now she looked as thin as a stick and as tall as the bamboo stalks found everywhere.

It was a funhouse mirror, like the ones found at carnivals! Inscribed on its frame it read: "What is reality?" Stephanie pondered that question.

On the desk, besides the map and schedule, was a teapot with a jasmine flower and a bowl of Tau Huay, a dessert from her childhood. Her mother's words on beauty and weight flooded her mind: "We don't eat that in this house, Stephanie. You must stay thin. No one will want you if you're fat and ugly."

But then Stephanie saw a small card on the desk that read:

> My true power lies in accepting myself as I am.

Reflecting on this idea for a moment, Stephanie took a spoonful, and her eyes closed in ecstasy.

**

As she walked, Nicole felt enveloped by the melody of the birds, which gradually gave way to the distant roar of falling water. Following her guide, the sound intensified until they stood before a majestic waterfall crashing forcefully onto a rock, creating prisms of rainbows in the air.

The guide led Nicole on a path behind the waterfall, revealing a surprise: a door that opened to a cave transformed into a truly unique room. The interior was lit by Moroccan lanterns hanging from the ceiling, adorned with bright-colored cushions and tapestries embellished with mirrors and bells. A luxuriously dressed bed beckoned for rest.

As Nicole looked on in awe, the guide showed her a corner that housed a cedar sauna and a bathroom with colored glass tiles, reflecting the light from infrared lamps. The guide pointed out a bag with essential amenities and informed her about the evening's scheduled activities before bidding her goodbye.

Once alone, Nicole explored further. On the desk, she found a samovar with cardamom tea whose aroma enveloped her. Next to it, a tray with rainbow cookies.

Nibbling on a cookie reminded Nicole of her Nonna and her warm embraces; her bosomy chest always smelled of semolina and sun-warmed tomatoes. She had loved Nicole without reservations.

"That is true love, *amore mio*," she heard Nonna's voice in her head. "Loving your *famiglia* is as natural as breathing."

A clear thought crossed her mind, *Elena is also my family. Perhaps this place can help me proudly announce that to the world.*

She then noticed a small white card beside the cookie tray. It read:

> When a woman loves herself, she's no longer at the mercy of forces greater than her, for she becomes the powerful force herself.

**

Though she had agreed to hand over her phone, Olivia knew she would have a devilish task trying to shut off her brain. She had a brilliant mind and didn't know how to turn it off. It had been operating at full throttle her entire life. But Olivia knew things had to change or she would be of no use to anyone. Burnout was near, or perhaps it was already here.

The Orchid

She arrived at a treehouse, elevated about thirty feet from the ground. She walked up the winding stairs encircling the structure. Upon entering, she was amazed by the spaciousness and brightness of the place and its large windows.

The guide showed her every detail of the room. Olivia felt transported to another world, one filled with luxury and comfort. The bathroom, in particular, caught her attention with its vintage tub featuring whirlpool jets and an array of ointments and oils with scents that reminded her of her mama.

After the guide left, Olivia explored on her own, finding little details that made her smile, like the fluffy towels and pink slippers. However, what truly delighted her was discovering a plate of hot beignets and a cup of chicory coffee on a bistro table, next to a bouquet of fresh flowers. It was a reminder of her home in New Orleans and the simpler, happier moments of her life.

As she reflected on the decisions she had made, she found a note with these words:

> Be still, and know that I am God. —Psalms 46:10

Olivia let that thought sink in a little. *Be still, eh?* With nothing else to occupy her mind, she realized she *was* hungry and took a bite of a beignet. *Oh Lord*, she thought. *Maybe the world can spin without me for just a little while.*

She carried the delicious treats and coffee out to the balcony, found a small table there for her mini-feast, and looked up at the sky and over to the mountaintops while she ate.

"*Yes Olivia, you have climbed high in this life, but you've never climbed this high,*" the voice in her head said.

And then she heard her mother say, "*Don't matter how high you climb. Jez' remember, there is only one God, Livy, and you ain't him.*"

Chapter 6

Olivia

"... ladies and gentlemen, that is the only outcome that we should be aiming for. The time has come to take action, to eschew empty promises and extend our hands, sharing the bounty we all enjoy with those who have nothing, and to do something meaningful for the less fortunate. Time and time again, research has shown that when we support and educate women, communities flourish. If we don't act, we will be handing them a death sentence." The speaker cast her gaze at the assembled United Nations delegates and seemed to meet everyone's eye. After a momentary hush, there was loud applause from most of the audience, except for the delegates of those countries who had a different agenda.

Passion was the speaker's gift. Dr. Olivia Munson was as eloquent as she was intelligent, and when she drew her fleshy frame up to its full height of nearly six feet, she looked formidable indeed, like the queen she might have been in a previous life. Even to her colleagues, she was known as *Madam Olivia*, as though addressing her without some title was unthinkable for someone as naturally regal as her.

Olivia had been born in New Orleans' infamous Ninth Ward, a place of hardship and poverty but where people like Loretta, Olivia's mother, developed a spine of steel and an unbreakable will. You wouldn't make it on those mean streets if you didn't. The Ninth Ward was no place for sissies.

Her Mama, as she called her affectionately, had scrubbed white folks' floors and even brought their laundry home at night to starch and iron before starting early the next morning and doing it all again. She took three buses and then had to walk seven blocks—sometimes through drenching rain—just to get to work, then had to slog all the way back with that heavy laundry bag. She did it all without complaint, but not without comment.

The Orchid

"Sugar, I scrub the devil's own behind if'n it helps you break free from this damn bayou," she said.

Loretta had wanted a better life for her Olivia. She wanted it so badly that she made Olivia want it too.

Olivia worked hard in school, took every extra credit opportunity and advanced placement class offered, and haunted the library until she almost became a fixture there. Everyone in the community thought that she was special.

"That girl, Olivia, is gonna be something," the librarian would say to her assistant. "Her nose is always in some book or another and she eats up learning like it's ice cream."

She was right. To Olivia, learning *was* nourishment, and she'd eat her fill until she was full enough to get out of the Ninth Ward and get her Mama out too.

Olivia had a dad, and unlike many of her classmates' fathers, he actually lived in the household. He just wasn't living there all the time and, when he made an appearance, he was rarely sober. He couldn't, or didn't care to, hold a job and had relied his whole life on the toil of others—first his mother, then his various lady friends, and now his wife.

Tyrone had always been a player. He was a good-looking man still, though his looks were fading from his drinking. Still, Loretta did use to light up when he came home ... until the hitting started. One wrong look or ill-chosen word and *crack*! Olivia's father would reach out and slap Mama square across the face. Sometimes he even bloodied her nose, and, like the color red to a bull, the sight of that blood would enrage him further. The open-handed slap turned into a closed fist, and Mama would be on the ground screaming and covering her face against further blows.

As Olivia got older, she tried to step in when Dad started swinging.

Once she grabbed his shoulders from behind as he drew back his fist, but he shook her off and turned his fury on her. Olivia wore sunglasses for a week or so after that. But she doubled down on her studies, intent on getting an education and taking herself and her mother far away from her father and that shotgun house on Deslonde Street.

When she won a place on the student government and helped her Model UN team win the state competition, Olivia knew she had found her calling. She would become a legislator and craft laws to help erase the terrible, unyielding conditions under which the urban poor, like her mama, labored day and night for a wage that barely covered groceries.

Olivia won a scholarship to Tulane University right there in the Crescent City, and now it was she who took three buses and a trolley to get to campus. She majored in political science and was enthralled with the discussions going on all around her about the conditions of the world and what they, the next generation, could do about them. When she graduated, she went right to work on getting her doctorate. The title of her dissertation was "Emerging Nations and the West's Responsibility." When she earned her doctorate, becoming Dr. Olivia Munson, it was the proudest day of her life.

She just wished Mama had been alive to see it.

Her father hadn't killed her after all. The tumor did. He had not been there when she passed, but he showed up after, drunk and blubbering how Loretta was "the finest damn woman the good Lord ever made" and sobbing to all that would listen: "I jez don't know what I'm gonna be doing without her."

He soon figured out what he was going to do without her and before long drifted away with yet another woman who should have known better. Olivia drifted away from her father too and practically *ran* to her new life as the senior staffer for an NGO in Washington, DC.

Her sights were now set on a larger stage. Rather than just helping the urban poor in the United States, now she was going to use her talents and skills to help women the whole world over.

For three decades, through very hard work, she had succeeded, helping set up collectives so women's handicrafts could be sold through an international distributor to help them feed their children through times of famine. She added her talents to a project for desalinating water to bring relief to drought-stricken areas. She even organized a holiday catalogue where wealthy donors could buy a cow or a flock of sheep for a village—like pet adoption with livestock. Such creative resource-building projects were Olivia's life's work, and she was proud of her contributions.

But now she was engaged in one of the biggest fights of her life. The 2020 pandemic had disrupted all economies around the world, and women suffered particularly, with childcare responsibilities and scant resources at the best of times. A recent UN report had found that millions of women would be thrown into poverty because of the COVID-19 pandemic. In addition, they also experienced an increase in domestic violence, as many of them found themselves unable to leave their homes and abusive relationships.

Lastly, women found it difficult to find jobs, as, naturally, those available would almost always go to men first.

Olivia had to convince the member nations of the UN to authorize the necessary funding. Using every contact she had cultivated over the years, she had wrangled a chance to plead her case in front of the General Assembly, and she vowed to present the problem in such a way that the delegates could not refuse her.

At the end of the day, when the applause had died down, the Council took a vote. Olivia had convinced them, and her initiatives got their funding. She shook a few hands and soon made her way out of the assembly floor to make room for the next speaker.

As she exited, members of her staff came towards her, smiling and congratulating her for the incredible performance. But Olivia would not have any of it. Immediately she went off, complaining about the many things that had gone wrong. "Next time, let's make sure that the speech is complete and written exactly as I dictated it. The point about the research was not underscored correctly and not written up the way I instructed. And what good is it that the speech is well-written if the microphone is not working properly? Whose damn job was it to make sure that it was? And me, well, I better learn how to speak. I sounded like a fool out there mispronouncing the names of several people. Those should have been spelled out phonetically on the teleprompter."

It was one of the biggest wins of her life, and Olivia could not get past the little errors. Her brilliance and accomplishments were being overshadowed by her need for control and perfection. Instantly she was tired and could barely keep her eyes open. She begged off celebrating with her staff and other well-wishers and headed back to her hotel room, her quiet, empty hotel room, feeling a little like a deflated balloon.

It's too soon for congratulations, she thought to herself. *Don't think for a second that this is all there is to it. There are still dozens of hurdles before the money is transferred and available. This outcome was largely just luck. And you are getting sloppy. There were so many mistakes today. If this is how you are going to do it, you will fail.*

She shook her head to shake such thoughts out of her brain. It wasn't like her to be so cynical or discouraged.

"Snap out of it, Olivia. You can do it. Live to fight another day. Find that fire in your belly." She heard her Mama speaking those words.

But within her she only felt dying embers, not the raging blaze she knew she'd need if she were going to continue her work.

All of a sudden, she felt her heartbeat speed up, thumping crazily in her chest. She thought for a second that she was perhaps having a heart attack. She felt extremely anxious and dizzy, and she couldn't breathe. "Oh, keep me safe, dear Lord, I still have so much to do," she whispered.

This had happened before, but this time it lasted a few more minutes than the last. It was enough of a scare for her to find her way to the floor where she remained sitting a long while. She eventually made her way back to her bed and went to sleep. *Sleep will do me good, and all will be better in the morning,* she thought.

When her assistant called to wake her up the next day, Olivia gave one excuse after another for her lateness. She couldn't help but worry that the panic attacks were getting worse each time. Perhaps she should listen to the advice that her friend and former mentor, Penelope, had given her: that she should attend that program at the retreat center.

Penelope and she had worked shoulder-to-shoulder in some of the worst regions of the world. They had weathered the brutalities of war and the loss of human lives and been witnesses to the erosion of dignity in many refugee encampments.

Olivia had always admired Penelope's drive, daring, and unconquerable spirit. At least it appeared unconquerable, until the day Penelope said she was quitting. She mentioned burn-out and said she couldn't go on anymore. The poverty and disease and children with bloated, starving bellies had gotten to her, and she couldn't face another day.

Then Penelope disappeared, off the radar, for more than a year. Olivia tried calling and emailing and the only response she got was a terse, "I'm fine. Don't worry." Then nothing, until a few months ago, when a different email arrived from Penelope.

> Dear Madam O,
>
> I'm sorry I have been distant, but I needed to get away for a while.
>
> When we last saw each other, I barely had the strength to go on, and I didn't know what to do or where to turn. I took some time off to get some perspective. An old friend of mine recommended I go to a place called The Orchid, a retreat center in California. The seven days I spent there literally saved my life.

The Orchid

I know how hard you work and how depleted you must feel. I'm pretty sure this place will help you too.

I can hear you now, even across the miles, so let me answer your first unspoken question. No, it is not a cult, and yes, they do have amazing massages, so what do you have to lose?

By the way, the woman who owns and runs the place is someone who will amaze even you, my dear friend. I hope you take me up on this offer.

With lots of love,

Penelope

A few days after receiving that email, Olivia had already researched the place and even completed the online application. She knew she needed help and was intrigued by both Penelope's endorsement and what she read about it.

Though she didn't have confirmation yet, in her team meeting later that day Olivia asked her staff to begin thinking about the possibility that she would take a vacation. The notion that Madam Olivia would take a vacation was novel, and her staff scampered to arrange things. Getting Madam O off their backs for some time would be a vacation for them, too.

Chapter 7

First Dinner

Nature seemed to quiet itself, as though the world were holding a deep breath, as the sun began to set, lighting the sky above The Orchid in shades of rose, gold, tangerine, and crimson. The stars were eager for the moment when the dome above would turn navy blue so they could rush the sky and throw themselves forth, spilling like diamonds from a jeweler's pouch. All was still as the guests began the trek from their rooms to the dining hall, each woman absorbed in her thoughts.

Just then, the low, melodious tones of a Tibetan bell was heard reverberating through the forest, announcing the coming of the evening and seeming to give permission for the night bird and insect songs to begin. The air was heavy with the night-blooming jasmine's perfume, its tiny flowers shining even whiter in the gathering dusk, and each woman took a cleansing breath without even being aware she was doing so, breathing in beauty and slowly entering into the rhythm of this wonderful place.

The vista finally opened, and each guest saw before them a structure seemingly sprung straight from the ground, like the trees of the forest. The roof was woven twigs and the body twisted bamboo that fashioned into a sinuously curving construction, evoking a woman's own anatomy, a womb for gathering and growth.

The path to the two entrances was flanked by a row of brightly burning torches beckoning each guest inside. The interior was much larger with a ceiling taller than it appeared from the outside, as though a magic trick had been performed to it. Each woman was greeted by the hostess, who possessed a calm, Zen-like attitude and sported a slight smile, as she led the guests to their respective seats at a long wooden table. On other nights, the women could choose where to sit, but, for this first night, they were seated so as to relieve any social pressure. It was important that everyone was made to feel included and equal.

The guests were all dressed, as were the attendants, in all-white organic cotton and linen clothing, only differentiated one from another by personal touches some of the women had chosen. Stephanie had perfectly applied full-face makeup. Jennifer's uncombed hair was gathered in a neon pink scrunchy. Sofia wore a golden chain necklace and Nicole, eye-shielding sunglasses.

All the guests stealthily sized up the other women, making judgements, fair or otherwise, based on body shape, age, physical beauty, and the way in which each guest held herself. Some were slumped, eyes down; others scanned the room, their faces alive with curiosity. Some looked uncomfortable and shy. A few scowled angrily, the tightness in their shoulders visible from across the room. Others looked like natural royalty, all eyes drawn to them as they held their heads high.

Olivia's head was one of those. The last to arrive, she bustled in with a colorful scarf hiding her double chin. "So sorry to be late," she said as she joined the others at the table, not really sorry at all. "I had to finish up a very important call, and having to do so through the front office's switchboard was a pain. I wish I had been able to keep my cell phone."

"I know, right? I don't know how I'm gonna survive all week without mine," said Jennifer, who was sitting right next to Olivia.

Sofia bristled a little internally at Olivia's comments: *Well, if I knew we could just waltz in whenever we wanted, there were a few dozen calls I could have been making,* she thought to herself. *Who does she think she is, a big shot or something?*

After her tepid apology for being late, Olivia introduced herself to the women sitting at her corner of the table. "Hello all. I am Dr. Olivia Munson. Everyone I work with calls me *Madam* Olivia. It is a pleasure to meet you all," and she turned her gaze to Jennifer, who would have liked to skip the formalities but was pinned by Olivia's direct gaze. "Who are you, and what do you do?"

"Um, hi everybody. I'm Jennifer Clairborne, and I am, well, I work at, I mean, I hope I still work at an insurance company." Realizing that what she had said was a little scattered, she tried to regroup. "I'm a ... I'm divorced," she said, her voice trailing off at the end. She recognized she had made being divorced sound like a profession. *Well, perhaps I've made it one,* she thought.

After a bit of an awkward silence, Sofia, who spoke with a bit of an accent, broke the ice.

"I'm Sofia Aguilar." With a smile, she added, "real estate mini-mogul from Mexico City."

Everyone laughed at her description, as she turned to Nicole on her right.

Removing her sunglasses, Nicole announced, "My name is Nicole Moretti, and I'm a high school science teacher from Houston, Texas."

Then, all turned their gazes to Stephanie, whose beauty had them side-eyeing her through everyone else's introductions. "My name is Stephanie Henry. My husband, my two daughters, and I live in New York City and I own a design firm."

Sofia piped up, "You are not a model? With those looks, I would have bet money you were a model."

Stephanie, enjoying the attention, smiled and said, "Well, before my marriage I *was* a professional model, but I retired from that life."

Sofia, still pressing, said, "If I looked like you, I'd keep modeling and piling up the money till they stopped wanting me to pose."

Stephanie, a trifle annoyed that she had to explain her decision to a total stranger, replied a little icily, "Well it is not as easy as it looks, and that way of life comes with its own trials and troubles. Sometimes people get hurt...." Realizing she had said too much, she snapped her lips together and turned her head away from Sofia.

Nicole, hater of conflicts, smoothed the angry tension out of the air by saying, "I'd like to be piling up money, but, as a teacher, that's not likely, though sometimes I think we should at least get extra pay. Teaching teenagers is like trying to get cats to march in a parade."

Everyone in the group laughed, and the tension in the air dissipated some.

As conversations continued, attendants served the women a choice of two tasty and colorful mocktails, a passion fruit martini or a pomegranate mojito. A welcome appetizer was also served, a slice of cucumber topped with an avocado and red pepper hummus, served on a small plate that seemed to belong in a doll's collection rather than in a fancy restaurant. As the servers placed the dishes, they murmured that the main meal would be served soon.

Olivia continued the conversation, "Oh, I know about trials and troubles at work, except I hear about them shouted through headphones in twenty-seven different languages."

Nicole said, "What do you do, Olivia? I mean *Madam* Olivia."

"Oh, don't worry, darling, it's fine," said Olivia out loud, secretly enjoying the correction. She then regaled the group with a short introduction to her work with the NGO, explaining the manner in which it helped people. The other women listened respectfully except Jennifer, who was having trouble focusing. Her sense of inferiority was deafening her.

Jeez, they are all so accomplished! Next to them I feel so small, like I'm back at square one. I might as well be still at my first day of work. Hi, I'm Jennifer, when is lunch? And where's the bathroom? And what exactly am I supposed to do here? I'm close to losing my job, I've got no real career, I'm divorced, my kids….

Her interior litany of doom was interrupted when Olivia leaned over and said, "So, Jennifer, do you have kids?"

"Yeah, I do. Two of them. A ten-year-old boy and an eight-year-old girl."

Olivia continued, "And you are raising them alone?" She didn't wait for an answer but went on. "I was raised by a single mother, and, in my work, I have met thousands of single mothers. You are the strongest and bravest women in the world, and you are all heroes."

Jennifer blushed and started to say that she wasn't doing too good a job at it and surely was undeserving of the compliment but instead said nothing, feeling gratitude towards Olivia well up in her. "Thank you," she finally murmured and smiled back at her.

"Well, I don't have time for kids or husbands or barely even friends," piped up Sofia. "I am the busiest person in the world, juggling my business. I buy, sell, and manage residential and commercial properties." She finished in a rush and looked around as though the others would burst into applause.

"Good for you. If it weren't for landlords, a lot more folks would be sleeping on the street," said Olivia with only a hint of irony.

Conversations were interrupted when a small chime was hit by a wooden knocker held in the hand of a woman who introduced herself as Lucia, the head nutritionist.

When she had everyone's attention, she said, "Good evening and welcome to The Orchid. We hope you found your accommodations comfortable and that you will enjoy the food you will be served throughout your stay with us, beginning with this evening's meal. As head nutritionist, my role is to ensure that all our farm-to-table meals are of the highest quality and nutritional value.

"Our bodies are magnificent machines with all sorts of systems performing the most incredible feats. We have mechanical systems: our blood circulation system is our very own transportation department, and our brain excels at electronic storage and flow. We even have our own regenerative repair system, meaning that we are also able to heal ourselves. Imagine that. You have everything you need in your body to lead a healthy life to avoid and even to combat disease, and it all begins with good nutrition. The Buddha said it best, 'To keep the body in good health is a duty ... otherwise we will not be able to keep our mind strong and clear.'

"All our food is organic, and much of it is provided by our own on-site farm, greenhouse, and orchard. We eat communally, as the sharing of food is a way to learn about each other and celebrate together the bounty this beautiful world supplies.

"In your applications, each of you answered questions providing an outline of the quantity, type, and style of nutrition you are interested in receiving this week. Your meals will continue to be served based on those specifications. If at some point you would like to make any changes, please let me know so that we can accommodate you.

"We go out of our way to ensure that our dishes suit your preferences and dietary needs, as will be explained by our wait staff as your food is served. After dinner, we will gather in the adjacent building, where our official program will begin. Until then, I will be here, so please feel free to reach out if you have any comments or questions. Again, welcome. We are so happy to have you here with us. Enjoy your dinner."

Servers, attentive to the guests' every wish, poured fruit-flavored spring and sparkling waters, freshly squeezed juices, and iced cardamom tea to sip during their meal. Then the dishes began to be presented. All the meals were vegetarian, but a vegan menu could be requested.

The first course was a rich, red tomato soup with fennel from the herb garden. It was served in a large oval bowl with white broad borders that accentuated the deep ruby color of the soup. A trio of perfect basil leaves and roasted cherry tomatoes floated on a skim of coconut yogurt in the bowl's center, and it was accompanied by a slice of whole grain bread, fresh from the oven.

Jennifer simply stared at the bowl. *This is so beautiful*, she thought. *I wish I had my phone to take a picture of it. Who knew a tomato soup could be so spectacular?* She then took a taste of it and was stunned at how the flavors burst on her tongue.

She wasn't alone in her appreciation.

Nicole thought, wryly, *I was impressed with the room, and now there is this gorgeous food. Even if this place doesn't help me figure out how to go on living, at least I'll die well-fed.*

Olivia, who knew her way around a restaurant, said, "I have been to some of the world's finest restaurants and eaten lots of soups in my time, but let me tell you, this one ranks high on the best of the best list."

Then she and the others were quiet for a time as they enjoyed every drop.

"That was great," said Sofia. "I wonder what comes next?"

Stephanie hoped it was a salad. Though organic and no doubt healthy, she wasn't sure that the soup hadn't been made with some high-calorie ingredients, maybe cream or butter to give it its richness? She had eaten it all, though. Its explosion of flavor had seemed to activate her appetite, and, in Stephanie's mind, that wasn't a good thing.

The next course was indeed a salad—a fresh and colorful one. It was a mixture of red peppers, green avocado, broccoli, edamame, yellow baby corn, purple radishes, onions, toasted almonds, and quinoa.

Eating around the corn and almonds, Stephanie found herself truly hungry and gobbled all the rest with a speed Olivia noticed, just as she noticed that Stephanie had skipped some of the ingredients. *Ok, now I know why she is so skinny. That girl has an eating disorder.* She wondered if Stephanie knew that about herself.

The next plate could be smelled even before the servers placed it before each of the women. Bright orange sweet potatoes had been roasted in a curry of ginger, cinnamon, and cumin.

Sofia, who liked spicy foods, smacked her lips at the aroma. "Now we are talking," she said to no one in particular. "The spicier food is, the better I like it."

"Growing up in Texas, I learned to like spicy food from the time I was in diapers," Nicole chimed in. "Elena can't stand spicy food and much prefers when I make my mother's Italian recipes."

"Who is Elena?" Sofia asked.

Nicole turned bright red. "Um, oh, um Elena is my best friend, um a really close friend, she's my roommate, and, well, we eat together a lot and…."

"So, she's your partner, huh?" said Sofia, ever direct.

Nicole felt all the air leave her lungs as she whispered, "Well, I don't know if I would call her that...."

Sofia pressed on. "What do you call her then?"

Nicole felt like a small animal caught in a trap and was mustering an answer when she was saved from replying by the next course served. Sautéed tofu supplied the meal's main protein, served alongside black and red beans swimming with peppers and sautéed onions.

In the center of the table were heads of baked cauliflower, which none of the women reached for until Olivia led the way. "Where I grew up, in New Orleans, you didn't waste food," she said. "This is delicious and y'all ought to try it."

Stephanie, fixated on the purity of the food, checked the cauliflower for any trace of butter or sauce. Once sure it contained neither, she placed a tiny bit in her mouth and continued to chew it persistently long after the flavor had vanished.

Olivia struggled a bit with how to ask this diplomatically, "Honey," Olivia said, watching Stephanie, "do you always eat so little? You can't be on a diet. You are barely big enough not to blow over in a stiff breeze."

Stephanie, a bit bothered by the question, blushed a bit but muttered, "Oh, I eat plenty. But as my mother used to say, if I don't keep an eye on my figure, nobody else will either."

"Well, a person would have to be blind not to think you are beautiful," Olivia replied. "Maybe you are too hard on yourself. I'm sure your husband thinks you are perfect."

"But I'm not," Stephanie snapped back. "I'm not perfect, but I should be."

"Who told you that, child? My mother always said all the perfect people are in Heaven," Olivia reported. "The rest of us gotta do the best we can."

"With me, there is a lot of room for improvement," murmured Stephanie and turned her head to end the conversation.

Olivia turned back to her meal, a festival of freshness and flavor that might turn any person into a vegetarian. The portions were moderate but filling. Seeing the lovely, light fare, Olivia knew she was going to miss that special one-time-only welcome treat of beignets back in her room but was pleased with the choices being presented.

Girl, you know you could stand to lose a few pounds, her inner self said. *I know, I know. I'll be good*, she replied, smiling as she realized she was talking only to herself.

Jennifer still hadn't gotten over the soup and was astonished at how one course after the other was both beautiful and delicious. *Maybe the kids and I should grow a vegetable garden at home*, she thought. *I'd probably kill all the plants, but it might be a good project for us to try.*

Dessert was a selection of fruits from The Orchid's own farm. It included raspberries, apples, figs, pomegranates, apricots, cherries, plums, peaches, and nectarines. A beautiful, tasty apple pie was also served, with a collection of herbal teas, nestled in a teakwood box, from which the women could choose their favorites.

Stephanie was pleased at the fact that all dishes were nutritious and vegetarian but still held back from consuming the full amounts of the portions that were served.

This is too much food, she thought, aghast when the servers brought out yet another course. *I really should only eat one of these meals a day. I wonder if they are watching me to see how much I eat? I am not going near those sweet potatoes, that is for sure, and fruit has such a high sugar content*, Stephanie thought, sipping her sparkling water. *Perhaps I can just put some of the food in my mouth and spit it out after the meal?* She began plotting her latest battle in her war on food.

The chatter grew louder in the dining hall as the guests continued to comment on the lovely surroundings and the fabulous dinner.

"Well, if we are going to eat this well, it's a good thing there are plenty of perfect hiking trails throughout this property," Sofia chimed in. "I stay thin because I basically run everywhere. You're pretty thin, Nicole. How do you stay in shape?"

"Sometimes I think I just worry away any extra weight," Nicole blurted out.

"What are you worried about?" pressed Sofia, who wasn't the best at observing social cues.

"Well, I ... it's some of the things I'm here to learn to talk about," Nicole said and diverted the conversation over to Jennifer, who wasn't saying much.

"Why are you here, Jennifer?"

Jennifer had no guile and didn't hesitate in her answer.

"I have been making stupid mistakes, and I'm having trouble focusing on my job and my family life," she admitted. "My bosses have known me since I was a kid, and they recommended I come to this place. I got a sort of ultimatum to get my act together or I'd get canned. I'm hoping I'll save my job and maybe I'll learn a thing or two while here."

Jennifer's courage, honesty, and vulnerability set a tone for some of the others to do the same.

"Maybe you will, darling," said Olivia in her deep, rich voice. "Maybe we all will. I've been having panic attacks, and a friend recommended I come here in search of answers."

"I'm told I've got a little of an attitude problem, and that I don't really trust anyone," admitted Sofia, "though I don't see how that is a problem."

"That's because some people just can't be trusted, and they can wound you so deeply you might never stop bleeding," murmured a small voice.

Everyone turned towards Stephanie, who hadn't said another word (nor eaten another bite) for a while. Her voice was so low it was as though she were speaking to only herself. Her downcast eyes never left the tabletop.

Before anyone could react to her words, Lucia rang the chime again.

She addressed all the women in the room: "Dinner is now concluded. We hope you all enjoyed it. Good food nourishes more than the body, it also feeds the soul. We hope you are sated and getting more comfortable with each other.

"Please take a moment to look around the room at all of the women here with you tonight."

She allowed a few seconds for every woman to see the others present.

"Believe me when I tell you that by the end of this week, some of these wonderful people, all with their own beauty, strengths, and imperfections, will become powerful allies in your journey towards a more free and bountiful existence. And now, if you will all please gather at the front of the room and follow me, we will transition to the Sanctuary, where our Evening Council will be held."

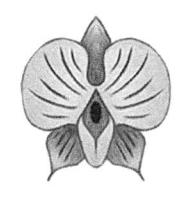

The Orchid

Chapter 8

Nicole

By the time Nicole went to Catholic school, most of the legendary torture stories of such an education were in the past; kids no longer had to kneel on pencils for misbehaving, no one's forehead was slammed into the blackboard for a wrong answer, and the bishop didn't slap anyone's face to make them a "soldier for Christ" during the sacrament of confirmation.

She had heard all these stories from her Nonna, her beloved grandmother who lived with Nicole and her parents. Nonna had gone to St. Vincent's Catholic School in the 1940s, a time when everyone stood whenever a priest entered the room, when Mass was still said in Latin, and when nuns, the bane of generations of children, were the schoolteachers.

At home, at Nonna's insistence, the family still said grace before every meal and knelt in the living room to say the rosary every night. No one dared miss Sunday Mass unless they were practically on their deathbed. Nonna, who still wore widow's black for her husband, who had died forty years earlier, was the de facto ruler of the roost at home, and Nicole's very pious parents adhered happily to her rules. Nicole also followed the rules, because it never occurred to her that she had any choice in the matter.

One of those rules was that Nicole would attend St. Vincent's just like her parents had and her Nonna before them.

Things had changed with the school since Nonna's time. The parish, built by Italian immigrants who came to establish truck farms in Post Oak at the turn of the century, was now home to many different ethnicities (even the parish priest was Polish) and Masses were now all said in English from an altar that faced the congregants. The nuns had largely all left, turning to social activism or nursing during the AIDS epidemic, and the faculty was now comprised of all lay people, with the exception of Sister Consuelo Fernandez, who now ran the school.

Sister Consuelo was a brilliant administrator and kept the building updated and the curriculum top-notch, but, in a time when dwindling enrollment meant higher expenses, one of the cost-saving measures was that Sister Consuelo herself oversaw the school's science department.

Nicole, a quiet and studious girl, loved science *and* Sister Consuelo. She hung to her every word in class and lingered in the lab to talk with her afterwards whenever possible. Sister Consuelo knew a kindred spirit when she saw one and took Nicole under her wing, discussing with her articles in *Scientific American* and the latest scientific advancements. The nun knew that Nicole, painfully shy, wasn't finding adolescence easy.

The other girls spent much of their time talking about the opposite sex, tossing their hair, and giggling when one of the "cool" boys was nearby. Notes were passed about who liked whom, and homework was forgotten in favor of hours spent looking through teen magazines, gossiping about why a couple broke up or got together or making elaborately-hatched plans on how to get Daniel, Robert, or Joey to like Amy, Natalie, or Sarah. Sister Consuelo knew all about these conversations, of course (she'd been a teacher a *long* time), but aside from confiscating the magazines that made untimely appearances in her classroom, she largely ignored the goings-on … but she *did* notice.

One of the things that caught her attention was how, when the girls gathered in groups at recess or lunch, Nicole either sat alone or hovered at the outskirts of any group, always a bit apart. Sister Consuelo had been a bright, shy girl once, knew Nicole would benefit from a little extra adult attention, and was glad she could help Nicole, even in a small way. What Sister Consuelo didn't understand was how very important that attention was to Nicole.

It wasn't just that Nicole's home life didn't allow for her to speak to her conservative parents or dictatorial grandmother or that she was too painfully shy to claim her place in the rough-and-tumble social hierarchy of adolescence; it was because Sister Consuelo was the only one who let Nicole be Nicole.

She didn't have to pretend interest in things she didn't care about (or else risk being mocked as a nerd), join in on the nasty bullying of other girls, or suffer from embarrassment when she wasn't invited to a party or sleepover. With the nun, Nicole could just be who she was, no pretense required.

Smart as a whip with a mind eager for knowledge, Nicole saw Sister Consuelo as a role model, someone she would like to emulate when she grew up. Nicole wanted to be a teacher and had even prayed, fervently, to God to send her a vocation, an irrefutable calling; she felt a longing to join a religious order and become a nun. But her prayer went unanswered, and no vocation came, and soon she learned the reason why.

Nicole had a secret. Passion had, in fact, grown in her but not for religious life.

Nicole discovered she was gay.

A new girl had joined the class mid-year, and with the arrival of Carol Rossini, Nicole's life would never be the same. A fire was lit within her. It was all she could do to pay attention to what was happening in class rather than just stare at the waterfall of Carol's dark hair.

Various times, Nicole found herself outside the wrong classroom after following Carol as she walked down the hall, or she couldn't eat her lunch as Carol, instantly popular with the other girls, always held court at a nearby table. At night, the appearance of Carol's face in her mind kept her from sleeping. Nicole didn't know what to do with the strange feelings and physical sensations Carol awoke in her, but she knew she couldn't speak of how she felt to anyone.

Yet Sister Consuelo knew something was bothering Nicole and asked her about it after class one day. To her shame and surprise, Nicole burst into tears and fell into the nun's open arms. She could do nothing more than sob, and though she couldn't speak of the reason for her anguish, she'd never forget Sister Consuelo's whispered counsel: "Give all your problems to God, Nicole. He will send you comfort and help. All you need do is ask in prayer," she said. "And Nicole, I will always be here for you, to listen and remind you that you never have to go through anything alone."

Those words sustained Nicole for years, and she did pray, even when she wasn't sure anyone was listening.

Years passed, and Nicole graduated with honors from St. Vincent's without ever confessing her love for Carol or the other "Carols" that followed, and she never told anyone, particularly her family, about her sexuality.

She deflected all talk of why she had no boyfriend by telling everyone she was too busy with her studies. Nicole was determined to make her dream of becoming a science teacher a reality and applied herself to that goal with a single-minded ferocity. She won a scholarship to Rice University and continued living at home. She thus avoided dorm life and explanations of why she never went out with a boy and was always there to help her mother, who, after Nonna died, took over cooking dinners every Sunday with exactly the same menu Nonna used to make. Nicole allowed no time out for a social life, therefore excelling at school even if loneliness threatened to consume her. She tried to push all romantic and sexual longings to the very back of her brain, hoping they would just go away, starved by inattention.

But love found her anyway in the only place it could: the book stacks of the campus library. That's where she first met Elena, as they were both reaching for the same book. Elena was a materials engineering major, studying the medical uses of polymer, and after laughing and agreeing to share the textbook, the two shared a reader's table and a quiet conversation about some recent developments in the field. That conversation led to another, and another, until they were meeting for coffee, and then a movie, and, at last, a thrilling kiss behind the student union. After months of discussion, the couple decided to share an apartment off-campus. Nicole told her parents she was getting a teaching fellow stipend from the science department to offset costs (true), and that the apartment was only so she could make those early-morning lectures and late-night lab work possible (untrue). She would, she assured her parents, still always be home for Sunday dinner.

Elena was as free and happy a spirit as Nicole was constrained and full of self-loathing. Ever the good girl, Nicole was awash in Catholic guilt and what her family had taught her about sin. Thinking love and marriage was only sanctioned in God's eyes between a man and a woman, Nicole knew she was sinning. Despite the logical brain that made her such a star in science, Nicole's illogical emotions still convinced her she was headed to Hell for what she was—a bad girl, a deviant, a sinner. Her family would disown her if they knew how she and Elena were living.

So, she never told them.

She pretended that Elena was her friend and roommate and was sure to arrange visits with them when Elena wasn't around. This worked for quite a while. Sometimes, on special occasions, she would bring Elena along as any girl would bring her best friend home for dinner. But such dinners were awkward for two reasons: Elena didn't appreciate having to hide her sexuality and their relationship, and the talk around the table always turned to the "nice young men" Nicole's mother had dug up for the two of them to meet. Mother was sure Nicole and Elena would make some "lucky men" great wives. Of course, she was also not shy about stating that she expected Nicole to produce grandchildren. Nicole ignored and dismissed her mother's behavior as harmless and tried to convince Elena that it would eventually stop.

Elena took this in stride, understanding that Nicole, at some point, had to come to the realization that she had to stand up to her family (and overcome her conservative upbringing) to claim her life as her own and her relationship with Elena proudly and without shame. She knew Nicole loved her, but after many years of this pattern, her patience was wearing thin.

Nicole distracted herself by giving back to the community as a volunteer emergency medical technician, instructing people in the use of cardiac paddles, how to perform CPR (Cardio-Pulmonary Resuscitation), and the proper way to administer Narcan to overdose victims. At work, she was an excellent and well-regarded science teacher, one of the top in the state, making sure to look out for the shy kids like Sister Consuelo had done for her. Nicole still kept in touch with the nun, now long retired, and visited her once a month at the Mother House of her order. They both treasured this time together and often took walks during which they caught up on each other's lives and other issues. A bit stooped with age, Sister Consuelo still could manage a brisk walk and a strong hug, and, as ever, she had a willing ear.

Little did Nicole know that she would find herself in dire need of Sister Consuelo's loving support now more than ever.

It was supposed to be one of those typical dinners like the many Nicole and Elena had attended before. They would simply show up, enjoy delicious home cooking, put up with Nicole's mom's comments, and go home as they always had. This time, though, it was different. Upon entering her parent's home, Nicole's mother greeted them at the door with an unusually devious smile on her face. Then she immediately dragged them both to the living room, where there were two handsome "Christian" young men waiting to meet them, Nicole's mother proudly announced. There wasn't enough time to think about an exit strategy, and it all went downhill from there.

Nicole and Elena put up a façade that allowed them to get through the dinner and, at the end, dismiss the two young men without any major harm. The same was not true for Nicole and Elena's relationship. The incident was the proverbial last straw for Elena, and she let Nicole know that she had reached it.

Nicole was given an ultimatum. "I love you with all my heart, but I can't do this anymore. Either you come clean to your family about our relationship or it's over," Elena said. Such was the clarity in Elena's mind that the comments and demands were made without major drama or a raised voice. She then made other arrangements to stay with some friends, packed a bag, and left their apartment.

By the time it was Nicole's scheduled monthly visit with Sister Consuelo, Elena had been gone for a week. Weighed down by absolute despair and growing panic, Nicole went to visit her friend. When Nicole arrived, the nun, now in her eighties, immediately began to speak with the excitement of someone who had few people to talk to. Their shared love of science always made conversation between them lively and easy. Sister Consuelo wasted no time bringing up the recent accomplishments of the Webb telescope, the most powerful telescope that had been launched into space to date, and mentioning all the new photos of the universe it was capturing.

It took Sister Consuelo a minute to realize that Nicole wasn't listening.

"Is everything ok, dear? Sister Consuelo asked. "You know you can always talk to me about anything." She delivered those words with great warmth. Her loving arms embraced Nicole as they had many times before, and Nicole, who could no longer hold the weight of her situation, simply erupted into tears. Such was her relief that Nicole summoned the strength to tell Sister Consuelo what had happened with Elena and said out loud for the first time that she was gay.

Nicole was silent, waiting for some sort of reaction from her mentor and wise friend.

Without acting a bit surprised and handing Nicole a tissue from her sleeve like she always did when Nicole was a young girl, Sister Consuelo softly said, "I know, child. I've always known. Hush now," and she wrapped Nicole in her arms as she sobbed. "Love can be painful at times, I understand, but it is very rarely fatal. You'll live through this and God will be there for you to help. Remember we are all his children."

The two held each other in silence for some time. Enough for Nicole to unload some of the heaviness and pain she was carrying, even if the relief was only temporary.

As Nicole's sobbing abated, Sister Consuelo broke the silence with some profound words.

"Nicole, I've known you for a long time. I've always treasured our relationship and my love for you is beyond words. I've always supported you, and I've always been honest with you. So please, listen to me as I say this: Nicole, you are a grown woman, capable of making your own decisions. At some point, perhaps now, you need to stand up for what Nicole wants, even if that goes against the wishes of some of the people around you, even your parents. God will love you right through it all."

Nicole continued to cry. Sister Consuelo paused and said a quiet prayer for her to be shown the right thing to do or say to help Nicole and was answered with a sudden thought. She spoke it aloud.

"Perhaps you need some time away from your family and your situation to clear your mind and understand how to move forward with your life. I may know a place where you can do just that."

"You want me to join the convent?" Nicole asked, laughing and crying simultaneously.

"No darling, I know you well enough to know that is not your calling. A woman I know never took her final vows as a nun and left the convent, but she never stopped seeking spiritual truth. Her path differed from mine in the end, but it seems she found peace and a new connection with God. She wrote about it in a letter to me just the other day, saying she had been confused and lost about what path she should take in her life, and a visit to this retreat center helped her set the right course. I cannot remember the name of the place, but I remember that it was something familiar. Let me try to find that letter."

Sister Consuelo went to her room and rummaged through her nightstand drawer.

As she returned, she announced, "The Orchid, that's what it was called. Come on, look for it on your phone. Let's learn more about this wonderful place together," she said.

"It says here it offers a seven-day course of study, reflection, and healing *free* for anyone that applies and is accepted," Nicole read out loud, "but you need to be recommended by someone who already attended."

"If I ask her, my friend will recommend you, I'm sure. I will contact her tonight. I think you should apply, my dear. We nuns know a thing or two about the healing power of retreats. I even attended some where we all observed the Great Silence, cloistered away from people and communing only with God. I always came back refreshed in my vocation and my purpose. You may find the same thing from spending time at this place. I think it's worth investigating."

"You may be right, Sister, and thank you so much. What would I do without you?" Nicole said as she hugged her friend, tears still rolling down her cheeks and the weight of the world only slightly lessened on her shoulders. But she did feel a vague new sensation. She felt a slight pulse of what felt like hope.

Chapter 9

Evening Council

As they walked towards the building, a drum could be heard beating quietly and rhythmically, like a human heartbeat. From the outside, the Sanctuary stood as a testament to the age and wisdom contained within. It was a large, imposing circular structure, hewn from the earth itself, with walls of rough, unpolished stone that stood resolute against the elements. The top expanded towards the sky, its height exaggerated by the ever-present silhouettes of flickering candlelight seeping through the windows or slits in the walls.

At the apex, there was an unassuming opening, a small portal to the heavens and the rhythm of its celestial bodies. Cultural symbols and motifs, carved meticulously into the stonework, suggested an air of reverence and purpose. Despite its rugged and imposing demeanor, the Sanctuary was inviting, promising a warm sense of community within.

Stars shone through the opening, but their lights paled because of the hundreds of lit candles adorning niches and shelves throughout the chamber, casting shadows on the rough-hewn walls. The reflection from the flames danced along the floor and illuminated the colorful cushions and rugs that covered it, arranged in a semicircle around a large fire pit. The fire itself, shooting sparks of gold, silver, and blue, seemed alive with a spirit greater than any human presence. Its smoke, fragrant with sage and pine, wafted heavenwards, giving the impression that the structure itself was breathing.

As the women entered, they grew hesitant in their steps, and their conversation wound down into hushed whispers. Looking up, they saw long shadows dancing on the walls, ending in a dark pool near the arched roof. The stars shining down to meet the flames from the fire created a nearly unbroken column of light. The walls were rough, as though the prayers and intentions of all those who had come before them had etched the surface as they winged their way upwards.

Every sound in the space had the clarity of a bell, and the herbs, thrown by handfuls into the sacred flames, completed the feeling that they had ventured into a cathedral.

The hundreds of candles filling the room with a thousand points of light added soft illumination to the faces of all who entered, erasing marks of care and worry that were worn on so many faces like medals bestowed after a battle. Dressed all in white, the women looked like angels, and they smiled at all the beauty around them, never realizing that they were adding to that collection of loveliness themselves.

The atmosphere was magical and magnificent. An enchanting energy pulsed throughout the room and all its occupants, as though they were plugged into a cosmic current. All fatigue and apprehension left them. They all felt as if they had come home.

The spell was broken when Sofia whispered loudly to Jennifer, "Jesus, it looks like a church in here."

"Not like any church I've ever been in," Jennifer whispered back.

Nicole tried to hush them, "Keep your voices down," as though she were speaking to her students. "Can't you feel that we are in the presence of…of…."

"Of what?" Sofia shot back.

"I don't know. Something holy," Nicole finished her sentence.

"Spoken like a true Catholic school girl," Sofia said and started to chuckle.

Nicole blushed a little.

"Okay, you got me pegged," she said. "It just seems to me we should be more respectful."

"I confess, respectful isn't in the top ten of my character traits," Sofia boldly stated.

"Sometimes respect is just what is called for," Olivia interjected, and the three other women stopped talking.

Olivia led the group and held back a moment to assess the situation before choosing a seat near the fire. Jennifer, Nicole, Sofia and Stephanie followed her. All sat together, having already formed a bond over dinner, and waited to see what would happen next. Though they were curious and some, like Stephanie, slightly nervous, staring into the flames was calming and set a mood for reflection for even the most distracted among them.

A few minutes passed and expectations began to build. Soon after, a woman entered from a hidden doorway on the far side of the fire. She was tall and lithe, and her long silver hair barely moved as she stepped gracefully towards the audience. Dressed in a caftan of the finest white silk, Nicole had a fleeting image of wings on her back, before she shook her head and the vision cleared.

The other women also had similar, intense reactions to seeing Mary for the first time.

Olivia was reminded of Athena, the goddess of wisdom, who had sprung fully formed from the head of Zeus. To Olivia's eyes, Mary looked like she was slightly otherworldly, wise, and semi-divine. *How odd*, Olivia thought. *I am usually not so easily impressed by someone at first glance*, and she quickly remembered her friend's email. *I wonder if she's the owner?*

Stephanie saw otherworldly beauty in Mary. *How does she project that loveliness?* she thought, always feeling unlovely herself. *It is as though she is translucent and absorbing the light itself. She is glowing.*

Jennifer, who always felt "less than," was intimidated beyond words and thought, *Omigod, if she's the teacher, I'm gonna flunk this class.*

Even Sofia was impressed. *Now, there is a woman with power*, she thought, expecting Mary's eyes to be cold and calculating, taking the measure of all the women before her, but was instead very surprised to see only a warm light of kindness in Mary's gaze. Momentarily confused, Sofia regained her clarity and thought, *she really knows how to work a crowd.*

For her part, Mary stood quietly and calmly, allowing each woman to form and absorb their first impression of her. She knew the reaction her appearance would cause. She had seen this many times and had claimed her power long before and had never lost it since.

The drumming stopped as Mary began to speak.

"Good evening," she said, her voice low and throaty but easily heard throughout the room.

"My name is Mary, and I am the founder of this wonderful place. With all my love," she said, placing her right hand on her heart, "I welcome you."

She stopped as if to let the words sink into the minds of all sitting there.

"This is our Council Fire and we are very glad to have you all here."

Her chestnut brown eyes, set in a nest of wrinkles caused by years of smiling, met those of every woman in the room.

Indeed, she is the owner, and what an interesting accent, thought Olivia, though she couldn't quite place it. *Strange*, she continued, *I've heard most of the world's languages in my work. Her accent sounds like a mix of several. She must be well-traveled. I'll ask her when I speak with her. We can compare notes on globe-trotting.*

Stephanie, ever mindful of appearances, judged Mary to be between fifty-five and sixty, though there was an air of timelessness about her that confounded Stephanie's calculations. *She's not young, but she's not old*, Stephanie thought. *But her skin is so lovely; I wonder if she has had work done?*

For her part, Jennifer was dumbstruck. *Gosh, she's just beautiful*, she thought. *I bet she never had kids.*

Nicole was also noticing Mary's beauty but was concentrating more on her inner beauty. *Wow! She is just shining, like she is lit from within. If I could feel even a fraction of the calmness showing on her face, I'll do whatever this place asks of me during my time here.*

Sofia, distracted again, was barely listening, thinking of her business back in Mexico and wondering how she was going to make a few phone calls, when she felt Mary's eyes upon her, immediately bringing her attention back to the room. She felt how Mary's power commanded that all eyes be on her despite the fact Mary hadn't really said anything about that or even raised her voice. Mary just smiled warmly, gathering all the woman in. Sofia squirmed a bit on the carpet she was sitting on and thought, *Hmmm, no table pounding or yelling to get attention. What a powerful presence. I may be able to learn a thing or two from this woman.*

Looking around the room, Mary continued to speak, "I hope you found your accommodations to your liking."

The group excitedly affirmed that they had, and Mary continued, "And that your first meal was delicious and satisfying?"

Again, the woman nodded and murmurs of "delicious" and "fantastic food" were heard.

Olivia, used to commanding attention herself, a trait learned when engaging with the monumental egos of some of the world leaders, raised her hand,

and, when acknowledged, she said, "I hope I speak for everybody when I say that the room, the food, and really every single detail has been exceptional. Thank you very much."

Mary gave Olivia and the group a dazzling smile and said, "Good, I am so glad. We want you to feel special and be comfortable and relaxed. It is our hope that when you leave here, you will feel love in your heart for yourself—all of yourself—your past, with all your experiences, and your present, with all its imperfections, so that you can accept all of who you are and go forth into a joyful and limitless future."

Mary paused.

"I know many of you hear my words and think, 'She doesn't know who I am, what I have done, or what's happened to me. It's not that simple to change my whole life.' But I say back to you, there is nothing you have done that I or one of our healers and teachers haven't done. No grief, pain, or anger we haven't experienced. We'll use our knowledge to create a space and lovingly make available the tools we found useful in our journeys. We offer the same tools for you to use in your journey here this week to discover who you truly are.

"After your work here, you will be able to wipe off the mirror of your perception and see yourself more clearly—as the powerful being that you really are.

"During this week, we will help set your feet on the path toward that knowledge, but it is *you* who must walk the road. The work we'll ask you to do will be rigorous. It is no small feat to pry open an oyster to find the pearl inside.

"We will ask you to dive deep within yourselves, but know that what you find and must confront may be challenging. Pushing outside your own comfort zone is often difficult, but we ask that you be brave and persevere. You will first discover awareness. Then we will introduce you to gratitude, forgiveness, and acceptance, and lastly you will be empowered to act with intention.

"The reward for your hard work will be worth it. Understanding will lead to freedom, and you will be able to put down the mental and emotional shackles that have kept you bound as immoveable as any prisoner ever chained to a wall. The difference is you would have found the key within you to unlock those chains.

"We will help you find it.

"We ask only that you commit to the process 100 percent. It is very simple: if you do not do the work, you will not get the results. But if you do, your life will change for the better and the obstacles that have held you back until now will melt away like ice in a river when spring arrives.

"These claims are well founded. Our team has been conducting these retreats for more than twenty years and thousands of women have discovered their way out, up, and through their difficulties and disappointments.

"I was first among them. I traveled the world, studied cultures and religions and rituals, sat at the feet of some of the great spiritual leaders of our time, and met many others from the past through prayer and meditation. I brought those tools and lessons with me and assembled a most transformative team of experts to help me share them with you, in the hopes you, too, can change your life and share what you learn with others. In this way, we can expand our spiritual sisterhood and change the world.

"So, again, welcome. I am so very happy you are here."

After a few moments to allow her words to sink in, Mary spoke again.

"And now, it's my pleasure and honor to introduce you to one of my dear sisters, who will continue with this evening's very special ceremony, which is known as The Council."

Emerging from a door inset in the wall behind the fire stepped a character straight from a history book dressed in traditional ceremonial clothing: a soft deerskin tunic and boots adorned with intricate beadwork. Around her neck and wrists were layers of silver and turquoise jewelry. Her glossy hair, black as ink, was plaited with feathers, stones, and copper rings, and her face was painted with one eye outlined in blue and black marks painted between her lips and chin. She wore a white buffalo cowhide blanket and clutched a bunch of twigs capped with eagle plumes, sacred symbols of her tribe.

Mary folded her hands together, brought them to her heart, bowed to the assembled guests, and turned to bow to the figure in front of her before hugging her as she exited the stage and walked to the back of the room.

The majestic woman took her place in front of the fire, and the flames rising behind almost paled in significance to the power emanating from her.

Her gaze was clear and direct as it passed over the assembled women. Her very being commanded respect, and her audience gave it. They sat in awe for a few seconds, taking in the natural nobility of her presence, and then all unconsciously leaned forward when she began to speak.

Her voice was deep and resonant.

"Welcome to you all. I am Wakinyan, 'Sacred Thunder Wings' in your language, the twelfth in the line of *wakȟáŋ*, shamans, from my family, members of the Lakota tribe, also known as the Teton Sioux. I come to you from our tribal land in North Dakota. I am also a member of the White Buffalo Cow Society, the most respected women's society of my people, now dedicated to the protection of women and children from domestic violence and rape."

At the mention of the word "rape," Stephanie visibly shivered, a movement Olivia, whose shoulder was touching Stephanie's, felt run down her own arm. *What caused that reaction?* Olivia thought. *That little girl is in lots of pain. Perhaps I'll talk to her and offer what counsel I can, or maybe a hug is all the situation really needs.* Olivia then turned her attention back to the speaker.

"It is my pleasure to guide you tonight in a Ceremonial Council.

"Our Council derives its meaning from the fire rituals that many native people around the world have used to bring their tribes together and discuss issues of importance. It is a way for us to remain connected and to emphasize our belonging to the group and to each other, to come together as one. It is a safe space that creates an opportunity to be with, see, and listen to each other with transparency, openness, vulnerability, and without judgement.

"Today, I will pose a thought, and we will go around so that each of you can share as your heart and soul desires."

Wakinyan put down the sacred twigs and took up a ceremonial stick, a tree branch decorated with amulets, beads, and bright paint. She held it tightly in her hand.

"We will use this ceremonial stick and whoever holds it is the one to share. Before we start, let's call on our higher spirits and set an intention for our sharing."

She then raised her arms as though to amplify the strength of the words she then spoke.

> "Oh, Great Spirit, we are all relatives, united by you and all that we share in this world. We know we dwell in the presence of sacred love.

We gather to remember that we are whole and boundless, as you have shown us since the beginning. But our minds, our thoughts, and our experiences have created illusions and we've forgotten our true nature. We have started to believe that we are fragmented. We have started to believe that we are not sufficient. We have started to believe that we are not a reflection of your sacred love. Guide us in shedding these burdens that restrain our spirits and the veils which blind us from recognizing the sacred within each of us. Enlighten our vision and awaken our hearts."

She paused now, holding the stick in the air with both hands.

"We are all related. We are one," she concluded.

Sweeping her eyes across the group, Wakinyan said, "Thank you all for staying connected to the love and the universal energy. And now, recognizing the power and sacredness of this circle, let's begin.

"Our sharing today is about what weighs on your soul right now. I remind you all that the greater the depth of your sharing, the greater the level of healing that you will experience. So do your best to go deep. I will begin, and whoever wants to can follow.

"What is weighing on me right now is my fear of being restrained by my ego. I am concerned that it may lead me to not try hard enough, to give up too soon, to turn a deaf ear to my intuition and the messages from my higher soul. I fear that I may lose sight of the fact that I am here to serve *you*, and that I am one with all of you."

Wakinyan's words came across as heartfelt and strong, but there was also a softness to them.

Then she placed the ceremonial stick on a cushion that had been placed in front of the fire and invited whoever was ready to begin the sharing to come and claim it.

Taking a deep breath, Nicole got up. She picked up the ceremonial stick and sat down again. After a brief silence, during which she was admiring the stick's beautiful amulets, she began to speak.

"I am Nicole and I am being torn in two by a choice I must make. I must reveal myself to those I love and I'm afraid they won't love me anymore when they hear who I really am."

A tear started down her cheek, and she dropped her head and said no more.

"I thank you for your courage to speak first, Nicole," said Wakinyan, then asked her to decide whether to send the stick to her right or her left. She chose left, and it was Sofia's turn.

"I'm afraid that I may have left a lit candle in my room," she said, laughing, "I hope it doesn't burn down the place while we are here."

This aside was well received, and the rest of the women also let out small, nervous giggles. It served as a reminder that as serious as the search for inner peace was, all of them must also enjoy the journey and not take it or themselves too seriously.

"Okay," she said, starting again. "I am Sofia, and I'm trying to start a business partnership with an old friend, but she doesn't like the way I do business. She says that I am too cynical, untrusting, and harsh with people, so any partnership we formed would fail. I'd like to make this happen, but she is right that I am cynical and trust nobody. I learned those lessons very early, while growing up with a very dysfunctional family."

Olivia heard a gasp at Sofia's last words and realized the sound had come from her.

Sofia passed the stick to Olivia, who began speaking.

"I'm Madam Olivia. Well, really just Olivia. I also had a very dysfunctional family. My father was unreliable and abusive," she said, inclining her head towards Sofia. Then she went on, "Because he couldn't be relied on, and my poor mother damn near killed herself trying to be both mother and father to me, I learned to be overly responsible to make up for him. That trait is ingrained in me. It helped make me the success I am, but now I see it as a stumbling block. It is getting in the way of my health, my peace of mind, and my growth. I'm becoming someone I don't want to be and am hoping my time here can help fix that."

She handed the stick to Stephanie.

"Hello, I'm Stephanie, and, well, I can relate to not being able to trust men. When I was a model, I was young and very naïve. I had grown up protected and knew very little about the world. In my first big job, my boss … didn't treat me well. It was really my fault for being so young and dumb, and now I'm having trouble trusting even my husband, who is a really good man." Stephanie stopped and took a deep breath. "I'm not really ready to talk about this yet…." With that she started trembling, tears began sliding down her cheeks, and she covered her face in her hands.

Wakinyan, radiating warmth with her kind smile, said to her, "Take a deep breath, Stephanie, and be kind to yourself."

Jennifer, who was sitting to her left, patted her back, her motherly instincts clearly taking over. Stephanie then passed the stick to her. "Oh, my turn?" Her eyes grew wide, and bringing both her hands to the front and holding the stick tightly, she spoke.

"Jennifer is my name, and I'm a divorced mother with two beautiful young kids. I love them and do my best to take care of them, but I'm not doing the greatest job of it right now. I'm even screwing up at work because I just feel overwhelmed all the time. My loser ex-husband left us, and he helps very little with the kids. I've felt lost, miserable, and alone ever since he left, and some days I can barely breathe. I'm about to lose my job, and my bosses, well-meaning as they may be, gave me an ultimatum about coming here and making some changes."

Jennifer quickly passed the stick to the woman on her left.

"I am April, and what weighs on me? I'm afraid of continuing to feel that I'm not enough." Enunciating each word very, very slowly and with tears running down her cheeks, she continued,

"Every … single … day … I wake up, and all I feel is that I'm not enough: that I'm not smart enough, not pretty enough, not happy enough, not rich enough. I'm tired of feeling this way, but I don't know how to get out of it. It's been with me all my life, as far back as I can remember, I can't stand it anymore, and I'm sick and tired of it."

As though the stick represented her self-hatred, she thrust it into the hands of the woman next to her, who took it and simply held it in silence. After the few women who had already spoken, a certain momentum had begun, but this woman didn't speak. The silence caused a few of the women to feel uncomfortable. A few looked around the circle trying not to stare at the woman. Most dropped their eyes.

It was all Olivia could do not to speak to the woman directly, urging her to speak with some well-meaning advice, but she bit her tongue. *Maybe*, Olivia thought, *like Stephanie, she wasn't ready to speak … yet.* That thought surprised her.

Usually, Olivia was surrounded by people so eager to speak, they almost talked over each other. *This woman is sitting here physically,* Olivia's thought continued, *but her spirit isn't.* She was sitting like a dejected doll, shoulders forward and hair covering her face as her head dipped down. Olivia felt a rush of compassion for her, and, instead of interfering by speaking, she offered up a quiet prayer for her. Eventually, the woman passed the stick without having said a word.

The next woman was also silent for a while, unable to articulate anything. Her emotions were intense, and they paralyzed her.

When she was finally able to speak, she said, "I'm Susan, and for as long as I can remember, I have been afraid." She continued, raising her voice slightly. "I've been afraid of pretty much everything. Of the past. Of the future. Of doing something different with my life. Of failing. I've tried everything, or lots of things, and nothing seems to work. Or nothing seems to work long enough for it to be significant enough to make anything change."

The stick went around the room, and the stories continued. Many issues were shared. Some women were angry. Others felt lost, as if they didn't know who they were and didn't even know where to start to find out.

Some had lived through traumatic experiences and had never spoken about them, let alone been able to overcome them. All were hurting from limiting beliefs, paralyzing thoughts, and physical or emotional abuse that had either happened long ago or was happening currently. It was an emotionally charged sharing experience for everyone present.

After no one else had anything more to share, Wakinyan spoke again. "Thank you all for taking a leap into the uncomfortable, for being vulnerable, for being honest, and for honoring the sacredness of this Council. You are all incredibly courageous for finding the strength to come forward and speak from your heart. I know that much of what was said resonated with me, and I suspect with many of you also, whether you could bring yourself to speak yet or not."

"One of the most important lessons from tonight's sharing," Wakinyan continued, "is that you are not alone with the burdens you carry. Every one of us is working on figuring out this journey we call life. And we have each other. When we speak from our heart, when we are no longer superficial, when we allow ourselves to be vulnerable, we begin to see each other in a different light. A burden shared weighs less heavily on your spirit. It is then we start to see each other as the amazing women that we are. We put aside the judgement, the criticism—of others and of ourselves—and we begin to see—really see—each other as sisters."

Understanding began to appear on some faces around the circle, and everyone raised their heads as Wakinyan put down the ceremonial stick and turned again to the assembled group.

"Our next exercise will build on the energy that is present now. If I may ask you all to please stand and find a partner."

The women rearranged themselves according to Wakinyan's direction.

"Now, without speaking, touching, or dropping your eyes, I want you to stand directly in front of your partner, about two feet apart. Our goal is to gaze into each other's eyes. Try to see past the color or shape of your partner's eyes, instead looking into what lies behind them, her very soul. This might seem uncomfortable to you, staring into the eyes of a stranger, but you will soon see, there really are no strangers here. We are all the same, vessels for the Great Spirit.

"We will look into each person's eyes for approximately thirty seconds. I will then ask you to switch and find another partner to repeat the exercise. All here will be seen, some of you for the first time."

Olivia moved to face Jennifer. The look in the younger woman's eyes reminded Olivia of a scared rabbit in the headlights of an oncoming car. Jennifer's eyes darted back and forth, slightly intimidated by the depth and wisdom she found in Olivia's eyes. Then something happened that Olivia was not expecting.

All of a sudden, Jennifer's eyes started to well with tears. It was as though a door swung open behind her eyes, and Olivia was able to peer in. Olivia was overwhelmed with affection for Jennifer. *Poor girl*, Olivia thought, *look at the pain she is carrying.*

Not much different than your own that other voice in her head whispered.

Nicole was paired with Stephanie, and the two stared at each other as though they were engaged in a competition.

Both women seemed determined to reveal nothing to the other, but soon even Stephanie, absorbed in her own anguish, could see the pain in Nicole's eyes. It echoed her own. In that moment, both shared a deep connection during which Stephanie's heart began palpitating strongly, and she, too, started to tear up. *I'm just a mess,* Stephanie thought, *a soggy mess. Why am I crying so much?*

Sofia was facing April, who earlier shared about not being enough. *This is stupid*, thought Sofia, feeling highly uncomfortable. Facing the unyielding stare of her partner, who at the time felt more like an opponent, Sofia wanted to push back or even walk away, but she wouldn't give up. She stayed there, standing, and did all she could to continue staring at April's eyes, though sometimes she avoided her gaze altogether by simply focusing on her forehead or nose.

The exercise continued in complete silence for about twenty minutes. Each woman had the opportunity to gaze at the eyes of all the others present, with mixed reactions and experiences. After the exercise was over, Wakinyan asked everyone to sit down once again and form a circle around the fire.

"Would anybody like to share what you've experienced?" she asked.

Sofia was the first to raise her hand. "The first time, I found it very difficult and wanted to avoid it at any cost." She turned to April and said, "Nothing personal. But then, something *did* happen. I started to see my partners differently. I was ... moved. It then got a little easier and I got more relaxed."

Jennifer was next to speak. "I, too, was moved. I was looking at one of my partners, and I saw her strength in her eyes, and I simply started to cry. It was such an unexpected, strong connection for me. You know, it was nice to be seen by someone who was not judging me. Or at least I don't think she was," she said jokingly.

A few other women also shared. They mentioned how uncomfortable it was at first, while others spoke of how peaceful and serene their experience had been.

All of them, one way or another, acknowledged that the encounter, while uncomfortable, had led to a deep connection, one they either rarely experienced or had never experienced at all.

After all were quiet, Wakinyan stood up and spoke.

"Often, one of our biggest issues is that we feel disconnected from others: from our family, our friends, the rest of the world and, most tragically, from ourselves. However, I can assure you that we are not disconnected. Our thoughts, work, children, partners, and other unending distractions make us feel so. Our goal, by the end of the week, is to help you see that all that disconnection you feel is nothing more than a mirage. You have surrendered your reality and adopted thoughts that would have you believe you are alone. Such misbelief has come to control you. We will help you help yourself. We will assist you in becoming aware and ultimately releasing those damaging beliefs and fears that are holding you back from understanding the amazing person you already are.

The Orchid

"I know that tonight's exercise was a stretch for some of you. I ask that you give yourself a chance. Go at all these exercises at your own pace, but stretch yourself to the point of being uncomfortable. That is where growth and transformation truly happen, and that is why you are here.

"And now, I would like to conclude tonight's Council."

She signaled a drummer in the corner of the room to begin playing and she started chanting in the Lakota language as she circled the fire, knees lifting from and returning to the ground in a rhythmic pattern while she shook the sacred twigs with eagle plumes she had reclaimed. It sounded like an atonal song at first, and then Nicole realized that what she was hearing was a prayer ... a prayer for the women gathered ... and she bowed her head.

Wakinyan stopped dancing and stepped before each woman, shaking the sacred twigs over them in a type of benediction.

At last, she said, "Sisters, I have asked the Great Spirit to watch over you and lead you through the untamed lands of your souls. I have asked you be given protection and the strength you need to fight the ghosts of fear and despair like the warriors you are. As the Lakota's most famous warrior, Crazy Horse, said, 'I salute the light within your eyes, where the whole universe dwells. For when you are at that center within you, and I am at that place within me, we shall be one.'

"Following tonight's exercise, I recommend a warm bath or shower and lots of sleep. It may not be obvious to you, but we just moved a lot of energy and it is important to give the body and mind some time to integrate all of it. So, I suggest honoring yourself with love, kindness, and lots of rest."

Wakinyan finished speaking, and then looked to Mary, standing in the back of the room, signaling for her to take over. Mary walked to the fire and began to speak.

"Thank you for all the hard work today. It has been a long day of travel, meeting new people, and sharing lots about yourselves," she said, smiling. "I know it is a lot, but we are trying to accomplish many things this week."

Mary paused and was quiet for a moment, while continuing to make eye contact with all.

"Before we end for the evening, I wanted to provide you all with an opportunity to ask any questions you may have."

Sofia's hand shot up immediately. "Will we have to do this staring thing again every day?"

Mary smiled slightly at her description of "this staring thing" before answering. "Maybe. There will be many exercises throughout the week, which will help you dust off your mirror. Some will be easier for you and some may be harder, but all are designed to help you take a few more steps along your path."

Nicole asked the next question, "I'm a schoolteacher and I guess I am accustomed to having a lesson plan. Could you maybe sum up what we are expected to learn this week?"

Mary replied, "It is different for everybody. But, generally speaking, you will learn who you are, and that you have the power to become anyone you want to become. You have all the tools within you to effect that transformation already. You are actually in control of your lives, though it might feel more like experiences are happening *to* you rather than that you are creating them, but that is only a matter of perception. What you seek, you already have. We are all here to help you realize that."

Nicole frowned, not much more enlightened than when she had asked the question.

Sofia raised her hand again. "Um … I'm not comfortable with praying. I haven't been for a long, long time," she said as she lowered her hand. "But it appears to be an important part of what you do, umm, what we do, here. I'm not sure how I feel about it."

"Thank you," said Mary, with an unmistakable note of kindness and love infusing her words.

"First, let me say that I see you, and I respect you and your position." She paused, and then continued to speak. "I guess I would ask, when you need help, when you need the type of guidance that is beyond you, from where do you get it?"

Sofia quickly answered, "From within. From myself," she said.

Mary walked towards her and said, "Then I encourage you to continue doing just that. But because we have many voices within, my advice is to ensure that you are uttering those words to the incredible wise power that you already have inside. Here we call that power our 'Higher Self.'"

Mary thanked her for the brave and honest question and began to scan the room for whomever would ask the next.

"Is one week enough for the type of transformation that you are suggesting can happen to us?" asked Stephanie, who was carefully wiping the tears in her eyes.

"Yes and no," Mary responded, feeling Stephanie's strong emotions. "You see, there are no rules for growth and transformation. Every moment, every fragment of every second, every amount of energy dedicated to observing and truly loving yourself, transforms you. And that transformation continues and builds on the previous layer. My suggestion to you is to use your time here to the fullest."

More hands were now raised, as the women became more comfortable asking questions in front of each other.

One of the women said, "I'm uncomfortable with the idea of being in the water, and I noticed you have an aquatic center on the property, and I want to know if I have to participate in any water exercises myself."

Mary answered, "Thank you. As you will learn, there are a number of different tools and practices that we use to help you go within. Exercises in the water is one of them. Not all the tools are for everybody, but we have many experiences here. That diversity allows us, and you, to find what will best suit you in your journey."

Mary turned slightly and away from the woman who had asked the question, as if the thought were complete … then she deliberately turned to face her again.

"However, because we are here to grow, we only ask that, when you encounter these uncomfortable feelings, that you ask yourself, why are they present in the first place? The fact that you are uncomfortable with it could mean something. What might that be? A lesson to learn? A heavy energy to get rid of? I encourage you to be curious and to explore that someday, perhaps this week. You may find that the answer to that question may be an important step in your transformation. But to answer again your specific question … the choice to use any particular tool or method is ultimately always yours."

"How will I know how deep to go?" asked another.

Mary looked at her, smiled with great appreciation, and asked, "How much do you want to heal?"

The woman accepted that answer and sat quietly again.

Mary continued, "At any time, the depth of your experience will depend on the depth of your effort. If you want to become an expert swimmer, then you need to stop training in shallow waters and dive courageously, with proper training, support, and guidance, of course, into the depths of the ocean. Then your skills will strengthen and your growth will be exponential. Like anything else, the benefit you'll get will depend on the effort you put into it. My advice to you … go as deep as you can so that you can have the greatest growth."

"Is it going to be painful?" Jennifer asked.

"Yes, no, perhaps," said Mary, enigmatically.

"It is different for everyone. For some the pain is excruciating. For others, it may take no more than a slight realization, a click that magically connects two points with the simplicity of two drops of water joining as one. However, and this is the part that you need to consider, though it may be or seem painful to talk, share, acknowledge, and relive the pain, consider the amount of energy you have expended holding onto that pain. You have filled your mind and heart with ideas and stories, about yourself and others, that just aren't true. You have held them close to you and made decisions, sacrifices and life choices based on those perceptions. Are you going to continue to hold tightly to that pain? I'd rather walk through fire for a few minutes to lighten my load than continue carrying issues that weigh my spirit down for the rest of my life. You can choose to continue to live under such a weight, but my choice will be always to let go. You need to decide on your own choice."

Another woman asked, "How do I start? If there are so many tools and so many options, where and how do I start?"

"Thank you," said Mary. "We have five simple steps here: we become aware, we learn to be grateful, to forgive, to accept, and ultimately, to discover how to be intentional in our actions. It helps that we set an intention for this week and speak it aloud. I, Mary, would like to work on this particular aspect of my life. I want to be free of judgment or I want to do away with these misguided beliefs of my own unworthiness and embrace my absolute self-worth. Or I want to live free of guilt, courageously and without fear. Or I want to forgive my parents, husband, lover, children or whomever, for whatever they did to me."

Mary looked around the room and then continued: "Those are some examples, but only you know what is best for you. The clearer you are about your intention, the clearer you'll be about the tools you can use and the actions you must take to help you get where you need to go.

"As you've heard us say a few times now, we believe that every one of you have all the knowledge needed to address your own issues. So, I'm confident that you'll find the answer that best suits you. Remember, we will be right by your side, supporting you as you make those choices. We won't make the choices for you. They are yours and yours alone to make, but we will support you. We've got you."

Mary continued to address all questions with the patience and love of a woman who had all the time in the world and who lived for no other moment but *now*. She was present and engaged and attentive to every word and question that was asked. Her answers were clear, direct, and completely loving. Every woman there felt it. They felt a connection that they had not experienced in a long time. For some, it was honesty. Others felt unjudged for the first time ever. A few even felt an energy inside of them that was moving throughout their entire body.

Once there were no more questions, Mary thanked them once again for their courage and for their energy.

"Please, don't hesitate to come to me, or any of our team members, with any other comments or questions. We are here to listen and we want you to have all the answers your mind, heart, and soul require.

"Now, I invite all of you to close your eyes and take a few deep breaths. Think about this moment. Forget all that has happened before now, and stop thinking about the future. Just think of here and now. Bring into your mind any image that inspires and fills you with love and hold onto that image. Begin to feel the love course through you. As you do, breathe in … one, two, three, four," she said softly, "and out … one, two, three, four and in…." She continued to ground them until the serenity and love in the room were palpable.

"Now, think of what you hope to accomplish here this week. The areas you aim to work on. The areas that you want to change. Pick one, perhaps two. Hold those thoughts in your heart." Mary paused.

After a few seconds, she continued. "What would change look like? If you managed to lovingly address those areas you identified, what would change feel like? Those thoughts of change, imagined and envisioned, can be real. In fact, by merely thinking about them, you have begun to materialize them.

You've taken another step in your transformation."

She waited a few moments and invited them to open their eyes.

And with that, Mary placed her palms in front of her heart, making eye contact with all again.

"Thank you all for a wonderful and magical evening full of love, strength, and growth. Have a good night's rest.

"Until we see each other again, Namaste, which means 'The Divine in me, recognizes the Divine in you.'

"Tomorrow, we begin bright and early. The topic of our day will be 'awareness.'"

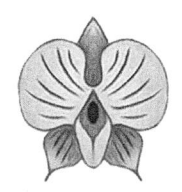

Part III
Awareness

The Orchid

Chapter 10

Morning Prayer

Anyone might have expected this to be a soundless place near dawn, but it wasn't. It was a world alive with the melodious symphony of feathered creatures. Night birds stood watch and then made way for the arrival of other avian performers who greeted the dawn. Amidst the harmonious chorus of these delightful creatures, the Tibetan bell reverberated with a deep and sonorous tone that rippled through the tranquil atmosphere. Both were a reminder that this was a place for uncovering the glories of the soul and that such a search was marked only by divine rhythms.

Olivia began her day as she did every day, kneeling by her bed in prayer. She was a Christian who had been saved by Jesus and professed her faith by being baptized as a young girl at the New Hope Baptist Church in her New Orleans neighborhood. It was to that same church where her mama and grandma walked her every Sunday morning when she was growing up, all three of them dressed in their finest, her grandmother always sporting a hat with feathers and ribbons. They would nod, smile, and give a genial, "Good morning, y'all" to the other families they saw walking along the way.

Some families had their father walking with them to church but not Olivia's. Her dad never went to church, and as a little girl, she never understood why.

"No-good, do-nothing fool," her grandmother would mutter to Olivia's mother, Loretta, as they walked. "Can't find a way outta some whore's bed or some gin mill to see to his family and honor the Lord's Day."

Loretta always defended her husband, though as Olivia grew, she realized he deserved no defense.

They would continue in tight-lipped silence until they got to the church, where they were greeted with hugs and kisses from the congregation, who were so close they seemed like family themselves. After everyone had pushed together to fit more into a row of pews, the singing would start. There was a choir behind the altar, dressed in scarlet robes with gold collars, and when the organist hit the first few notes of "I Won't Be Back," that choir would sing to shake the very rafters.

When the reverend took the podium, he would read the Gospel and then give a thunderous sermon, accompanied by loud calls of "Amen" and "Speak it, brother" shouted out by the congregation.

Olivia did remember one sermon, though, where the reverend read the story of the Prodigal Son, a young man who scorned his father and went out into the world to do some terrible things. But when he came back home, his father forgave him, took him in, and held a party for him where something called "a fatted calf" was served. Olivia was pretty sure that was their version of Sunday dinner. She remembered the sermon because of the big fight her mama and grandma had about it on the walk home.

Loretta said to her mother, "You see, even the Bible talks about a Prodigal Son coming home, and that no matter what he's done, like the father in the story, we should forgive him, Mama."

Her mother spat back, "Tyrone ain't no Prodigal Son and this ain't a Bible story. Open your eyes, Loretta. That man of yours ain't no good and never will amount to anything".

Mama *did* forgive Papa, over and over again, Olivia remembered. No matter how Dad cheated on her or stole her money or beat her body, she forgave him … right up till the time she died of overwork and worry caused by him. Olivia was the one who couldn't forgive him. She wasn't sure she ever could, but she took to her knees to pray anyway.

> Dear Lord, thank you for the gift of life. Thank you for allowing me one more day of life. I ask, Lord, that you strengthen my faith, that you help me become a better person, and that you take away my sins and my pain. Thank you for bringing me here. Show me what you want me to do, Lord. Help me use all of me—my talents and troubles, my skills and shortcomings—to serve you, Lord. In Jesus name I pray. Amen.

Creaking a bit at the knees, Olivia rose up from her bedside and dressed for the morning group meditation.

Chapter 11

Meditation

As the dawn cast a warm glow over The Orchid, the early risers moved gracefully towards their first meditation. Their soft footfalls barely disturbed the serenity of the awakening day. The world around them stirred lazily into life—only the sounds of nature broke the stillness with dew-kissed leaves rustling under the caress of the morning breeze. Scattered along the paths they trod, signs bore inspiring words and quotes, like breadcrumbs of wisdom for their journey. Each sign they encountered seemed to resonate with a timely message, stirring their spirits.

> Knowing yourself is the beginning of all wisdom. —Aristotle
>
> Today is the first day of the rest of your life. —Charles Dederich
>
> Awareness is the greatest agent for change. —Eckhart Tolle
>
> What is the greatest lesson a woman should learn? That since day one, she's already had everything she needs within herself. It's the world that convinced her she did not. —Rupi Kaur

Each women's face lit up, mirroring the dawn's soft radiance as they read, internalized the messages, and were moved by these inscriptions.

On the top of one of the highest summits stood the Meditation Center, a circular building with a stone foundation and an upper half composed entirely of glass. Designed to capture the views of both the sunrise and sunset, as well as the lush green forest canopy below, it was a place dedicated solely to meditative introspection, a place to shed one's earthly woes, silently appreciate the majesty of nature, and connect with the oneness of the universe, both externally and inside of one's soul.

The Orchid

Mary was already waiting at the doorway, speaking to another of The Orchid's healers, Silvia, as the guests made their way up from the campus below.

Silvia's ancestral ties could be traced back to the Andes, the mountainous region home to Machu Picchu, known to many as a vortex of great energy and spiritual power. Her thick, long, straight black hair was perfectly held in a single braid that reached her waist. She and Mary smiled and laughed as they engaged in light conversation with each other and with a few others.

As the women entered, they sat facing East to experience the magnificence of the rising sun against the beautiful landscape. They found their seats on cushioned mats and chairs.

After some minutes, Mary formally greeted everyone. "Good morning! How did everyone sleep?"

"I had not slept this well in ages. Considering I sleep practically in a nest, I now understand how birds must feel," Jennifer replied, laughing lightly.

"I slept soundly too. The sound of the waterfall beside my room was incredibly soothing. I completely lost track of time. If it weren't for the wake-up call, I would still be asleep," added Nicole.

"I'm so glad. I hope everyone is enjoying the accommodations," said Mary as she looked around the room.

"Today's theme is awareness, and the first stop in that journey is meditation. As we assume not everyone here is familiar with it, I invited Silvia to guide us through its fundamentals."

"Hello everyone, and thank you Mary," Silvia said as she took center stage.

"Meditation is a key tool to understanding and changing yourself. By learning to calm your thoughts and to listen to your inner voice, you will become more aware of everything around you. This increased awareness gives you greater understanding over your life and everything you do, because you learn to know yourself better.

"It's a journey of continual self-improvement, with the outcome being that you are constantly becoming the best version of yourself you can be. That is why we recommend that you meditate every day."

Silvia paused for a moment and then continued.

"Get comfortable in your current position. It doesn't matter whether you are sitting cross-legged on the floor or on a chair with your feet flat. Just remain relaxed and alert.

"The first thing to focus on is your breath. Feel the air entering your nostrils, filling your lungs, and then leaving your body. Your breath is a natural anchor, drawing you away from distractions and towards inner stillness.

"At first, your mind will likely be full of thoughts, like a busy highway. Instead of trying to clear them, simply notice these thoughts without judgement, then calmly return your attention to your breath. Each time you do this, you're strengthening your ability to focus and bringing yourself back to the present moment.

"In the beginning, you might only be able to maintain this focus for a few seconds. But with practice, your ability to sustain it will gradually increase. Remember that there's no right or wrong way to do it; the key is consistency."

Silvia paused yet again.

"And so, we will begin. Please close your eyes." Silvia reached in her pocket and pulled out a small chime, which she tapped, producing one clear note.

"Take a deep breath," she said as she counted, "one, two, three, and four.

"Now exhale, one, two, three, four," she said.

"Inhale again, and exhale. Do that several more times. Concentrate on your breathing and go inward. I will now allow you to continue on your own."

Silvia went quiet, allowing each woman to follow her own experience in trying to reach past her conscious thoughts to that pool of divine energy within. She watched as some seemed to instantly relax, a look of peace coming over their features. Others furrowed their brows or had trouble keeping their eyes closed, as though they'd miss something if they weren't ever watchful.

Once they experience it, they will feel lighter and freer, they just need some practice, Silvia thought, and she reminded herself that each of them would find their way in their own time.

Sofia, whose brain ran 10,000 miles per hour, had a hard time settling down to "slow her mind," but she was competitive by nature and determined to be able to successfully master meditation.

Silvia smiled, seeing Sofia's determination in her clenched jaw.

Olivia kept veering into talking to Jesus in her mind, rattling off things that were bothering her and even making some pretty strong suggestions about what He could do about those things.

The Orchid

She stopped herself. *Quit giving orders, Olivia,* she thought. *Try taking them for a change.*

Nicole seemed to have the easiest time. Her face took on a glowing calm that showed she was tapping into the energy.

Jennifer couldn't keep her eyes closed, but when she caught Silvia glancing at her, she slammed them shut like a kid caught doing something naughty.

Jennifer immediately gravitated to the one thought that had consumed her for the past five years—her divorce from Brian.

She felt guilty about the idea of letting go. It was as if she was not ready. Nevertheless, she understood that it was weighing her down and keeping her from living. She worried about what it was doing to her and the kids. She had begun writing the night before in her journal. *Brian, I wish you could read what I wrote,* she thought, *maybe then you'd understand how much you hurt us.*

Stephanie sat upright and perfectly still, a statue of loveliness, with a single diamond tear escaping her eye.

A palpable air of tranquility had enveloped the room. At the end of thirty minutes, which for some seemed like an eternity, Silvia tapped the chime again.

"Come back from your travels, my dears," she said softly, and she waited some time for all to return from their experience.

Then she gently broke silence. "How did that feel for everyone?" she asked as she surveyed the room.

A few women opened their eyes, blinking as if emerging from a dream.

Jennifer began to speak in a soft voice, "I've never felt such peace. I thought I wouldn't be able to quiet my mind, but it just ... happened."

Sofia shared next. "I was very skeptical, but I could actually feel myself drifting away from my everyday thoughts. It was like I was in a different world."

For Stephanie, it was more emotional. "I felt a deep connection with myself. It's like I reunited with a part of me long forgotten," she shared.

Each woman had her own unique experience, but the thread of newfound awareness and serenity was common in all their narratives.

As the conversation continued, a few others confessed that they nearly fell asleep. "It was so relaxing, I felt like I was floating on a cloud," one said with a twinkle of humor in her tone.

Another had a different perspective. "I didn't feel a significant change. I tried to concentrate on my breath as you instructed," she said to Silvia, "but my mind kept wandering," she admitted, sounding a tad disappointed.

When all who wanted to had shared, Silvia smiled understandingly at her students and said, "Remember, the journey into meditation is as diverse and personal as each one of you. No two meditations are alike, so be kind to yourself and remain open to trying again. With time, the process will become simpler. However, each time you meditate, approach it with a beginner's mind, as if it's your first experience. This openness will be key to deepening your practice." Her words carried a sense of gentle wisdom that reassured the group, wrapping up the session with a note of encouragement.

Before departing, Silvia took a moment to introduce the next session.

"We've found that following introspective activities such as meditation, it can be beneficial to engage in some form of writing," she explained. "Writing allows you to process and articulate the energy stirred up during these activities. To illuminate further the importance of written words, I'd like to invite Samara, another of our esteemed teachers, to join us."

The Orchid

Chapter 12

Writing

A small older woman, hair elegantly covered with a hijab in adherence to her Islamic faith and wearing an all-white tunic that shined against her nut-brown, weathered skin, rose to her full five feet in height and padded softly to the front of the room. Her tiny stature belied the fact that she had a powerful presence, and as her amber eyes swept the room, she interrupted the brief silence.

"Good morning," she said with a hint of a British accent. "I am Samara." Her voice was vibrant and her diction so precise that it was obvious that language was her passion.

"What a wonderful experience we just shared. That tremendous meditation lifted the energy of the room, all of us sitting herein." Some of the women nodded their heads as she continued speaking.

"Thank you, Silvia, for leading us," and Samara gave her a short bow as Silvia exited the room, relinquishing the space.

"Congratulations for allowing yourselves the opportunity to explore the depths of your spirit through meditation. You have just completed a profound journey within, a journey I hope brought you some moments of serenity and self-discovery. But the journey does not need to end here. The exploration of our inner selves is a continual process, and it's one that is beautifully complemented by the power of written words.

"Like everything else in the universe, words carry energy impacting us on a deeper level. Not only do they influence emotions in others, but they also affect us and our surroundings.

"This morning, I'm here to introduce you to the transformative power of journaling and free-style writing. These two practices provide a mirror of your soul, an echo of your thoughts, and a blueprint of your spiritual progress. They create a sacred space for you to witness your own evolution, to unravel the many layers of your being, and to make sense of your thoughts and emotions. Let's begin. Have you all received your journals?"

Many of the women nodded in response.

Jennifer, having already poured her heart out in her journal the previous night about her ongoing inability to let go of her divorce, felt a twinge of satisfaction. She felt like a teacher's pet, already ahead with her homework.

"I invite you to see journaling as a quiet dialogue with your true self," Samara continued, "a conversation that happens beneath the surface of daily routines and distractions. Journaling can be a potent tool of self-reflection and clarity. As you pour your thoughts, ideas, emotions, and experiences into written words, you'll find that you begin to understand yourself better. The simple act of expressing your thoughts on paper can make your inner world more manageable. Over time, you'll notice patterns, growth, and an incredible narrative of resilience and transformation. As the poet Rumi said, 'The quieter you become, the more you are able to hear.'

"Then there's free-style writing. If journaling is a gentle conversation with the self, free-style writing is an unfiltered stream of consciousness, a direct pipeline to your deepest feelings and thoughts. Those words should flow unrestrained, just as they come to you, without concern for punctuation, grammar, or sense. You're not writing for an audience; you're writing for you and you alone. This practice can unearth buried emotions and memories and release pent-up energies, revealing your authentic self in its raw, unadulterated form.

"We recommend you perform your free-style writing in the form of a ceremony. First, find a quiet place where you will be undisturbed. Then light a candle, get your paper and pen, and, when ready, take a deep breath and begin to write. You may feel resistance, fear, and hesitation. These feelings are natural. Remember, you're not seeking perfection. You're seeking release, understanding, and freedom.

"Write as long as you need to, and once you're done, do not read what you have written. Instead, sit next to your chimney, or simply use the flame of the candle to burn that which you have written. The act is symbolic. It's a ritualistic release of the energies you've unveiled and a clearing of space for new beginnings. One last thing, accompany the act by always saying, 'I am releasing all this heavy energy for my highest good and the highest good of all concerned.' We end with that phrase as a powerful affirmation that we are seeking well-being and healing for ourselves and those around us."

At the request of someone in the audience, she repeated the sentence. "I am releasing all this heavy energy for my highest good and the highest good of all concerned."

She waited for those who were taking notes to complete their scribbling. Once all eyes were back on her, she continued.

"Words are the wings of your inner journey, providing you with the freedom to soar to heights unseen and dive into depths unexplored. They can heal, inspire, liberate, and transform. I encourage you to embrace this practice with an open heart and a curious mind. Observe how it changes your relationship with your inner self, your spirit. Every word you write is a step closer to understanding and loving yourself. Remember, the power of words lies in their truth, and you are their author. Write. Unearth. Release. Grow."

She then paused in her speaking, providing them a moment to reflect on what she had shared.

"And now," she said, addressing them as a teacher would a classroom full of students, "I am releasing you back to your rooms so that you may do your writing exercise now, before breakfast, and to get ready for the rest of your day. Know that you go with all my love and best wishes for a fruitful writing session."

Chapter 13

Journaling

The journal each woman had received was bound in white leather and embossed with an open heart containing the engraved name of its new owner. Inside, blank, unlined pages were ready to capture the owner's most intimate revelations. Inside each book was a note reminding the woman that she could write anything she wanted to write, but in case she felt a bit stuck, there was a writing prompt which read, "I am...."

Olivia lit a candle and chose to continue with her early-morning reverie related to her father and her childhood. The fact that this period of her life wasn't something she thought often about made her focus on it even more. *Why did Mama put up with so much? No, that isn't the right path to take in this exercise. I must write about myself,* she thought, *the only person I can do anything about anyway.*

Jennifer gravitated to what she had written in the journal the night before and immediately had an instinct about burning all those pages. She felt guilty about the idea of letting go. It was as if she was not ready. Nevertheless, she understood that it was weighing her down and keeping her from living. She also worried about what it was doing to the kids. Then, she realized, *Here I go again with my obsessive thinking.* Determined, she willed herself to focus on the task at hand. Without further thought, she sat by the chimney, tore the few pages from the journal, threw them into the fire, and watched them burn.

For Nicole, the obvious subject was to write about her parents and not being able to disappoint them. *Why is it so difficult for me to tell them the truth?* she asked herself. She began writing immediately, determined to find an answer.

Sofia's thoughts were about being taken advantage of. She carried with her the weight of so many occasions on which she felt betrayed by different

The Orchid

people in her life: her parents, her brother, even herself. Most recently, there was an incident with a friend to whom she had made a large loan. She should have known that she was never going to see that money again. She might as well have thrown the cash in the garbage. *Selfish, that's what people are.* That was the first word she wrote on the page facing her. *Selfish.*

Stephanie was the only one who began writing from the prompt. "I am … stupid," she wrote and put down the pen.

As the exercise ended, a few didn't follow the instructions and began reading what they had written. Others corrected their spelling, scratched out phrases, rewrote sentences—all were just self-imposed diversions from the important work they had begun—revealing themselves to themselves. They had hidden for most of their lives. It was time to not hide any longer. But it had to be their choice.

Most women finished the exercise and saw to the burning of the pages they had ripped out. All over The Orchid, white smoke rose from chimneys, dissipating heaviness on the currents of hope, light, and love borne on the wind. Fears began evaporating, hate started to dissolve, painful memories became less sharp-edged. Gradually but steadily, the transformation of the women's lives unfolded as they continued their journey towards unveiling the love that lay inside all of them.

Journaling

I am...

The Orchid

I am...

Chapter 14

Breakfast

The sun was now higher in the sky and shone down on the treetop canopy, filtering through to the flower gardens and vegetable plots, as the women made their way to breakfast. The mood of the guests in the dining hall seemed a bit subdued, as though many were still writing, adding to their journals in their minds. But soon, as the plates of jeweled fruits and fragrant grains were passed, the women found their voices again.

"How are you all feeling this morning?" Olivia spoke first to the group at her table.

"Pretty good, thank you," Nicole answered. "And you?"

"Fantastic, honey, thank you," Olivia replied. "I've never been better."

This last may not have been literally true, but Olivia believed in setting goals every day and her announcement was raising the bar for herself. She *was* going to feel better. She was determined. Abraham Lincoln had said, "Most people are as happy as they make their mind up to be." She was choosing to believe that statement and put it to work in her own life.

Jennifer, after having selected foods from the buffet table, asked everyone, "How did you all sleep?" Not really waiting for an answer, she continued, "I know I said this already, but I love my room. I slept so well, it's like I had had a few glasses of wine. Except I didn't."

"My room has the most amazing view and a wrap-around balcony from which to relish it," Olivia offered. "Sitting on the balcony seems to demand I slow down and relax. It is perfect for daydreaming, something I don't do enough of."

"I agree, mine is pretty incredible too," Sofia said, chiming in. "It stands against a cliff overlooking a valley. The balcony floor is clear, which is very cool, but I've got to gather my courage up to go on it. Really, it takes a little faith."

Stephanie, feeling encouraged, said, "From the outside, my room isn't visible; it's covered in mirrors, so that it blends with the surroundings, as though it is camouflaged," she explained. "But once inside, I can see everything outside—the trees, the animals, even the stars at night. It's like being part of the forest but hidden at the same time."

"I think my room, which is a literal cave, with its entrance behind a waterfall, may be the most special of all," Nicole added. "It's like being inside the Earth itself."

"All the rooms sound so absolutely unique. I have never heard of a place like this anywhere in the world," Olivia said.

"We should do a tour so that we can see each other's rooms," Sofia proposed, and all the women nodded with excitement.

Jennifer steered the conversation and asked, "Did you all enjoy the evening yesterday?"

As the others all agreed the program thus far met and exceeded all their expectations, Jennifer answered her own question, "I especially liked the Council. I thought it was great to be able to just speak and have people listen with respect. Sometimes I find it kind of hard to say what I mean, but it feels safe here somehow and I know it's good to get it out of me."

Sofia smiled gently and looked at Jennifer. "I'm really sorry for the breakup of your marriage. I can see how it still hurts. You must have loved him terribly."

"Yes, I did," Jennifer added, her voice cracking. "I thought we were a team and that we would be together for the rest of our lives. And yes, it hurt a lot. It still does." Pausing, she drank from a glass of water, slightly overcome by emotion.

Nicole, a master at changing the subject, reflexively asked everyone where they were from, and small talk began about their respective hometowns, places they had traveled, and themselves.

Everyone joined in except for Stephanie. She was meticulously measuring out half teaspoonfuls of her oatmeal and moving the majority to the other side of her bowl.

Olivia, noticing this, leaned over and said, "Would you like some honey with that oatmeal? It must taste like wallpaper paste otherwise."

Stephanie looked up, startled to have been spoken to. "What? Oh no, no, thank you, I don't use honey or sugar."

"Are you sure, darling?" Olivia pressed. "Life can get pretty bland and tasteless without a bit of sweetness."

"I said no," Stephanie snapped, more harshly than she had meant to. "Oh, I'm sorry," she instantly apologized, "I didn't mean to be so rude, I just had trouble sleeping and am a little snappish," she lied.

"No need to apologize, we are all feeling a little raw after having to dig down into ourselves for the writing exercise," said Olivia. "I, for one, have a little trouble writing or saying personal things about myself. Give me a huge crowd, and I can speak for hours, but personal stories I find tougher. My mama used to say we shouldn't burden others with our troubles. Folks got enough of their own."

Nicole chimed in, "I think that's exactly why we are here, though. We are supposed to be learning how to open up with ourselves and each other, don't you think?"

"Yes, it always helps to have someone else to call you on your bullshit," said Sofia with a hearty laugh. "I did get some stuff out in my journal already though. I'm like a volcano that seems to be erupting, but it seems there is a lot more lava to flow out. I wrote until I ran out of time."

Turning to her, Sofia asked Stephanie, "How about you, Stephanie? Did you write a lot?"

Stephanie answered, "I only wrote one word and it's the way I feel all the time." And she got up from the table and left the Dining Hall.

The Orchid

Chapter 15

Stephanie

"Darling, you know the sweet buns are only for your father," Stephanie's mother, Mei, scolded her daughter, abruptly taking the bun out of her hand and changing her tone. "We don't eat this. The bookers for the big runway shows in Paris and Milan want skinny girls," her mother continued. "You have to look perfect."

As a child, Stephanie was anything but fat. In fact, she was so slender that some extra-small garments needed to be taken in to fit her. Despite this, her mother remained obsessively critical, focusing not only on Stephanie's weight but also on her skin, hair, walk, friends, boys, and anything else that might distract her from becoming a top model.

Mei did not consider her behavior abusive. She just wanted Stephanie to succeed at any cost. It wasn't even about the money, as the family was well-off. Stephanie's father owned a textile mill that kept him busy and absorbed, so he rarely spent time with her. What Mei wanted was to continue rising in Singapore's social hierarchy. She wanted to be one of the beautiful people, invited to all the best parties, rubbing elbows with those in the highest echelon, and she saw her daughter as her ticket into that glittering world. When Stephanie became a top international model, those golden doors would open even further.

Mei had also been a model and reached a certain level of success herself. She had graced some runways and been featured in a few regional magazines, but, after several years of struggling in the business, she faced the reality that she would never become a top model. She considered herself fortunate to have met Stephanie's handsome father, quickly married him, retired from the business, and soon thereafter turned all her attention towards grooming her daughter to pick up where she had left off.

Mei constantly reminded Stephanie, "Your face and figure are your currency."

Chinese on her father's side and Singaporean on her mother's, Stephanie had inherited the best qualities of both: a tall, slender physique, honey-butter skin, waist-length black hair, and olive-green eyes. Upon seeing her, people were often rendered breathless, confirming that her appearance was indeed her fortune. It didn't take long for agencies to take notice, and, in short order, Stephanie was soon scheduling modeling gigs.

The experiences weren't always ideal, but Mei had every single part of Stephanie's career all planned out in her head and would not be deterred. There would be things her daughter would have to put up with until she made the big leap to the world of European modeling. These privations were just stepping-stones to that great world. She'd just have to endure long enough to get there. When she was old enough, Stephanie and her mother were on a flight to Paris, armed with a packed schedule, including meetings with some of the most important agencies in the modeling world.

**

While waiting in the front office of one such agency, surrounded by the highest concentration of the most beautiful young girls they had ever seen, Stephanie and her mother were, for the first time, a little intimidated. It was also nerve-wracking to see how some of the models stormed out of the office crying and heading straight for the elevator.

Stephanie was ushered into a private office to find a few executives and a photographer reviewing different portfolios. The room was full of smoke from a few lit cigarettes dangling from lips or set on the edge of the overflowing ashtrays. There were cocktails on the table, the ice in them melting in the heat of the room, and a bottle of champagne, with fluted glasses chilling, in a nearby ice bucket. It was clear who was the boss, because all eyes were on one man, he of the perfectly tanned skin and midnight black hair edged with silver. Hunched over the table with a magnifying glass, he examined the models' photos. Everyone else in the room appeared to be waiting for him to move or speak.

No one looked up to acknowledge Stephanie's presence when she walked in. She stood there for a few minutes, as they spoke in French in hushed tones between themselves. Finally, a woman asked in impatient English while holding out her hand, her scarlet, red-pointed nails like daggers, "*Vite!* Where is your portfolio?" Eventually, the man in charge, Francois Bellacroix, glanced up and looked Stephanie over. He started with her breasts, flicked his gaze to her long legs, and, at last, went to her face. His look revealed nothing, and yet Stephanie had never felt more naked.

"Turn around," he ordered, without any other greeting. Stephanie spun in place.

"Hmmmm," he said. "How old are you?"

"I ... I'm 16," stammered Stephanie.

An exchange of rapid-fire French between Bellacroix and an assistant took place, before Bellacroix resumed his study of the photos in front of him.

"*Oui*, good," the assistant said. "That's all for now. Come back tomorrow. You will need to sign some documents and be prepared so we can send you out on some of our backlogged shoots. Now *vite*! Get out."

Stephanie scurried to the door and nearly ran to her mother, who was waiting impatiently in the lobby, to relate just what had happened. Mei shrieked in excitement, hugging Stephanie tightly while raising her eyes to heaven. *At last*, she thought. *At last, my plan is falling seamlessly into place.*

**

Stephanie was starting to feel more secure in her modeling. It had been nearly a year, and she had received lots of training and was already getting high quality gigs, working regularly, and making good money. Soon, she received a telephone call advising her that Bellacroix wanted to have a meeting with her. The meeting would be at his house, and a car would pick her up.

It was not a typical business meeting. In fact, it was not a business meeting at all. From the moment Stephanie stepped from the private elevator into his lavish penthouse overlooking the Seine, it was apparent that Bellacroix only had one thing in mind. Her small and thin frame was no match for his large, muscular body, just as her innocence was no match for his cold and calculated prowess. Bellacroix raped her. No one heard her screams of "No, no, please" or her sobs when her pleas went unheeded.

**

As time went by, Stephanie spoke to no one about the incident, not even her mother.

The agency continued to give her jobs, and eventually she landed some covers in the most sought-after magazines. But no amount of success eased her pain. She internalized all the anger and resentment, blaming herself for what had happened.

Surely, I must have sent some unknown signal or egged him on without knowing it, was the thought she eventually internalized.

Not long after, Stephanie began to develop an unhealthy relationship with food, as though she could starve the badness out of her. She learned to deny herself food and to stick her finger down her throat when she was forced to eat. It became her go-to diet plan, a dangerous one, but at least she was thin, which was important for a model. The practice also gave her some control in a world where terrifying things might happen, unexpectedly, at any moment. Maybe she could eat so little she could disappear. She would just be a pretty face and a very thin body—a mere prop—not a bad girl who deserved bad things like what had happened to her. She fought down the memories of the rape, but the guilt and shame began to eat away at her self-esteem. She vowed she would never tell anyone of the incident.

**

But the harm that *had* been done continued bubbling beneath the surface of Stephanie's increasingly famous face. She felt disconnected from many emotions. She felt undeserving of her success and lacked confidence. She was sure people only cared for how she looked, not for who she was.

Stephanie still had nightmares about the incident. She would wake up with vivid memories of dreams wherein she saw live butterflies pinned to lab display cases, or where she endured photo shoots where the photographer instructed her to adopt a different facial expression only to realize she had no face at all.

She pushed the terrifying memories deeper and buried herself in her work. Despite growing into a successful model in a world where men revered models, she had no love affairs, because she had no love for herself and therefore none to give.

After many years, Stephanie moved to New York City, quit modeling, started a design business, and married James, a wonderful man she had met through friends. He was successful, handsome, and well-bred, the scion of a well-to-do family and very much in love with Stephanie. She wished she could return his passion, but it was as if something inside of her was frozen—a core of ice. But she did want a husband and a family of her own, and James seemed a good choice. She reasoned that maybe his love for her would be enough for them both.

The couple soon had twin daughters. The girls were wonderful and brought a lot of joy to Stephanie's life. She adored them. James was a caring and attentive husband, but her past lived with her like a shadow on an x-ray. She was always afraid he would find out her secrets and reject her. But she couldn't bring herself to tell him, and this eventually affected her ability to be intimate with him. She assumed if he found out what she was, he'd leave her. In her eyes, he loved her only because she was beautiful, even if he didn't say it. Why else would anyone love her? That was all there was to her—a palette for face paint, a mannequin for the latest fashions.

She continued to vomit after nearly every meal and learned how to do so quietly, so James and the girls wouldn't hear. Stephanie panicked if she gained an ounce of weight and constantly checked the mirror for any change in her looks. When she took her children for ice cream, she didn't even dare lick the cream melting down the kids' cones. As if that wasn't enough, Stephanie felt numb at James's touch, so she started to pretend she was satisfied in bed. She had to be perfect so James would stay, and she could keep her family together.

**

One day, Natasha, a model friend from her early days, came to town and reached out. She asked Stephanie to lunch. At first Stephanie refused, because she recoiled at the idea of speaking with anyone who had been close to that traumatic event. Stephanie hadn't spoken to her since leaving Paris, but she did follow her on social media. She knew that Natasha had retired from modeling, that she looked fantastic and very healthy, and that she had opened a string of highly successful yoga studios in France.

Stephanie accepted the invitation but swore she would steer the conversation away from anything to do with the incident. Natasha, though, had other ideas. While Stephanie toyed with her salad, Natasha laid it on the line. "Stephanie, I've been friends with you for a long time, and I know, well I suspect, you *too* are a survivor of Bellacroix's predatory behavior."

The Orchid

Stephanie, stunned by her use of the word "too," gazed at Natasha in profound disbelief. A sharp, piercing pain gripped her chest, and tears welled up uncontrollably. As their eyes locked, Natasha's too were brimming with tears. Silently, the two women clasped hands, finding solace in their shared embrace.

"I've never told anyone before," said Stephanie, taking a deep breath. "But I don't understand, if you were too, how is it that you are doing so well, contented and glowing like nothing bad ever happened to you?"

"I wasn't doing well for a long time, but I am now, and you can be, too," Natasha said. "It's clear that you still suffer from the effects of what was done to you, and I want to help. Part of my recovery came when someone I trusted recommended I spend a week at a place called The Orchid. It is a women-only retreat center where in one week you can rediscover your internal power and, with it, your voice. There you will learn that what happens to you does not define you."

"Thank you," Stephanie offered, somewhat embarrassed.

"But I also want to ask your help in return," Natasha added.

"My help?" Stephanie replied, thinking someone like herself, who was barely hanging on, was in no position to help anyone else. "My help with what?"

"There is great power in women speaking up and telling their stories because it helps other women stand in their truth. I want to expose the modeling industry or any others perpetuating such behavior and exploitation," Natasha explained. "Would you consider helping by sharing your own experience?"

"Me?" Stephanie all-but-shrieked. "But what happened to me was *my* fault."

"It was *not*!" Natasha said adamantly. "We were sexually abused, Stephanie. You and I were *not* responsible for what happened, and I am certain other women will benefit greatly from hearing us tell our stories."

"I couldn't possibly...," Stephanie began.

"Look, I think I understand how you feel, and that you are frightened and think yourself powerless," continued Natasha. "I was, too, and I felt worthless for a long time. But I found my power again and with it I discovered my voice."

"You seem so confident," Stephanie began haltingly. "I don't know … the girls, my husband…. What is the name of that place again?"

"The Orchid," Natasha said. "It is free, and all it takes is a short application and a recommendation from a previous attendee. I will recommend you. Please think about it, and when you've found your voice, we need you."

The Orchid

Chapter 16

I Want to Be Perfect

After having left the breakfast so abruptly, Stephanie veered from the main path that led to the building where the activity was to be held and found her way to a clump of high bushes. Secreting herself behind them, she held back her hair with one hand, bent over, and, with years of practice, stuck her finger down her throat and vomited up the little she had eaten for breakfast.

Yesssss, she yelled triumphantly in her mind. *You probably got it out in time so it didn't settle on your hips, you fat pig. Next time don't eat so damn much.*

As she stepped out of the bushes, shaky and a bit lightheaded, Stephanie straightened up only to find Mary standing in front of her.

"Oh! I umm … I dropped an earring and I…," Stephanie began, the lie forming instantly on her lips.

"Hush now," Mary said softly and wrapped her arms around Stephanie as tenderly as she would a child, holding her for a long moment. She led her to a nearby bench and sat closely next to her, holding both her hands.

"I know what you were doing, Stephanie, and I'd like to speak with you about it, please," Mary said, her voice as calm as the surface of a glassy lake on a windless day. "My dear, I know you believe you are hiding what is going on with you well. You believe this is something you can handle alone, and that you have no need of anyone else. You even feel as though at least you are controlling *something* in your life that seems all too often out of control.

"But you are suffering from a disease of the mind, one that causes you to have a warped perception of yourself. When you look in a mirror, you see a fat woman, when, in reality, you are unhealthily thin. You think you are ugly, when you are beautiful enough that people spent millions of dollars just to have your photo on their magazine cover. You think you aren't enough, that you don't deserve what you have, and that your life is a waste, when in fact you have the love of a husband, two wonderful children, your parents, and now us, your new extended family. What is it that you want to be that you are not?"

Stephanie, embarrassed and ashamed at having been caught making herself vomit, found herself vulnerable but strangely relieved. She surprised herself by answering Mary's question.

"I want to be ... perfect," she heard herself say.

"Ah, well, then you can stop worrying, because the truth is you *are* perfect already," Mary said. "Somewhere along the way, you became convinced you were damaged, that you are less than, that you don't deserve happiness and good things for yourself. You allowed other people's opinions, often just based on what they needed and their insecurities, opinions often not about you at all, but actually about themselves—you allowed these opinions to shape who you think you are and how you live your life. You have chosen instead to internalize strangers' opinions and cause yourself harm in order to fit into their definition of what you *should* be. That was an error, but one that you can correct.

"The vomiting will tear your stomach lining up and cause holes in your esophagus from the stomach acid being raked across it. You will develop osteoporosis, thinning of the bones, from a loss of calcium, your hair will fall out, and your skin grow dull, you can even invite irreparable cardiac harm and possibly suffer an early death—all to fit into an image that is as unreal as any doll. Your mother could lose her daughter, your children their mother, your husband his wife, and the world a wonderful woman. All because you have bought into the lie that you must be outwardly perfect—when in fact you are already inwardly so.

"My question to you is this, Stephanie: Do you love your family?"

Mary waited quietly for an answer as Stephanie, feeling as though cataracts had fallen from her eyes, suddenly saw how selfish the choices she was making were.

"I do love my family," she said softly.

"Do you love them, even though they aren't perfect?" Mary pressed.

"Yes, of course I love them, even though they aren't perfect," Stephanie whispered.

"Do you love them enough to fight to stay alive for them?" Mary asked.

"Yes," Stephanie said more loudly. "I love them enough to fight for them."

"That is wonderful news. If you agree, I want you to meet with our nutritionist, Lucia, and our dietary social worker, Ruby, who suffered from the same eating disorder from which you are suffering. They can help you, so you can begin your reeducation about food. You need a new relationship to it. But you also need a new relationship with yourself and your vision of yourself. The experts here on staff can also make referrals to some medical and holistic practitioners once you go back home to help you continue your journey towards better health. There is no quick fix, but you must be willing to begin the work and see it through. Will you make a start and accept our help, Stephanie?"

"I will," Stephanie said, suddenly flashing on a mental vision of the constant worry in her husband's eyes while he watched her dress. "You are becoming skin and bones, Stephanie," he recently said. She recalled how proud she'd been at his words. She then remembered one of her twins practically begging her, "Mommy, you have to eat something. You never eat anything. Are you going to die?" She'd laughed off her words, saying, "You silly goose, of course Mommy won't die."

But mommies *did* die.

Stephanie remembered her seventh birthday, a fabulous party arranged by her own mother. After the party, Stephanie's mother had asked her to put her new toys away and get ready for bed. But Stephanie didn't want to stop playing and ignored her mother. Much later, Stephanie ran to find her mother asleep on the floor. Stephanie remembered feeling slightly guilty that her party had so worn her mother out that she'd fallen asleep before she'd even gotten to the bed.

"Mommy," Stephanie had said. "Wake up, Mommy," and when she got no answer, Stephanie knelt to shake her mother, but there was still no response.

Stephanie remembered how a chill had run down her spine then, and that she had started screaming, "Mommy! Mommy! Wake up! Please don't die!"

She had been scared nearly to death, and the minutes until one of the helpers rushed in, took in the scene, and called the paramedics felt like hours to Stephanie. Her Mommy might die and it was all her fault.

The heart attack was, of course, not the little girl's fault, but no one ever thought to reassure her of that. Stephanie took in the mistaken lesson: if she had been a better girl or if she had listened to her Mommy, that horrifying incident would never have happened.

Stephanie would have to be better.

Stephanie would never disappoint her mother again.

Stephanie would have to be perfect.

Thinking of the fear in her own children's eyes that she, their mommy, might die, Stephanie felt sick to her stomach. No child should know such fear. She was hurting her own family. Stephanie knew it was time to do something about the way she was living.

"Yes, I will accept your help, Mary. Thank you," she said through the tears.

Mary nodded. "You are a child of the universe, Stephanie. You deserve to take up space. We are going to help you claim it," and she wrapped Stephanie in her arms once more.

Chapter 17

Awareness

The next exercise was located in the Activity Center. The building's exterior was a blend of modern architectural elements with clean lines and large windows, inviting the ample natural light. Its sleek and polished appearance seamlessly integrated with the natural surroundings. Inside, the spacious central area accommodated both classroom and open configurations, creating a dynamic and versatile environment for diverse uses.

At the door a sign read, "Lessons on Awareness."

Awareness of what? Sofia thought to herself as they all waited for whomever was leading the lessons to arrive. *Just today I have become aware, after visiting the buffet, that I really don't like pomegranates. Last night, from journaling, I learned I might be a little pissed off. What more do I really need to be aware of?*

Sofia's train of thought was interrupted when the door opened and Mary and a second woman, who was in a wheelchair, entered the room.

"Hello everyone, great to see you all again," said Mary with a big warm smile, and she found a place in the rear of the room.

The other woman stayed in the front and waited. She always allowed for a long moment before speaking, aware that, with few exceptions, all attendees always had to adjust their attitude about meeting someone with a disability. It didn't matter to her any longer, for she knew they would soon forget she was in a wheelchair, but everyone's first reaction was to be taken aback by her physical condition. When the moment passed, she began addressing the group.

"G'day," she said in a heavy New Zealand accent. "It is so great to meet you all. I've heard so many wonderful things about each of you. It is a blessing to have you here with us. My name is Teena, and I am here to coach you on the power of awareness.

"'Aware of what?' some of you may ask."

Sofia opened her eyes wide, a look of surprise on her face as she asked herself if Teena had the power to read minds.

"Well, all of us carry around a set of beliefs that dictate who we are, how we see things, and how we interpret them. These beliefs dictate how we ultimately live our life."

Teena paused for effect.

"I'm in a wheelchair, for example. Many people look at me and think, 'poor thing' and immediately assume that because of my physical state, I am less than and unable to live life to the fullest. Those people look at me, and they see my condition. They don't see me for who I am, they see their beliefs and their idea of what it means to be in a wheelchair.

"Moreover, awareness is not just about how we see, observe, and eventually judge other people; it is also seeing how we live and judge our own lives. Awareness is the ability to observe ourselves, to witness ourselves, to be an engaged and present audience of our own theatrical performance.

"Awareness is also important in determining our state of being. That takes us to another topic we will touch on today—energy and vibration.

"We are all creatures comprised of energy. All energy creates vibrations in the universe and what frequency we are vibrating on creates our reality."

At some of the puzzled looks, Teena paused and began again. She knew these concepts were new to most of her audience and would have to be explained more fully.

"Humans are like radio stations. One radio station is different from another, based on the frequency on which they transmit, but both are still radio stations. We humans vibrate with energy at different frequencies, but all of us remain human.

"Interesting fact: Do you know who Hellen Keller was?" Some of the women nodded. "If you don't, I invite you to read about her. She was an American writer, activist, and advocate for people with disabilities. She herself became deaf and blind at about two years old. There is so much about her life that is inspiring, but I mention it because some people believed that Helen developed an acute ability to recognize people's vibrational signature.

So much so that once she knew you, she could recognize if you were in the room by merely sensing your presence. Imagine that! Your vibrational frequency may be as unique and specific as your fingerprint."

Teena was now speaking more loudly, her wheelchair darting energetically from one side of the room to the other.

"Our energy or vibrational frequency creates our emotional state and that emotional state guides all that we are. It is the compass of our being."

Teena motioned for a graphic to be projected on to the screen.

"This is The Spectrum of Inner Growth, a concept born from years of shared experiences and observations here at The Orchid. This scale," she explained, "has guided the journey of the countless women that have taken this program during the last two decades, and now yours too."

The Spectrum featured an ascending process of five stages—Surviving, Exploring, Learning, Becoming, and Being—each with an associated range of levels, emotions, and behaviors.

"The initial stage, Surviving," Teena explained, "is about meeting our basic human needs. As its accompanying level, 'unconsciousness,' suggests, in this stage we are steered more by instinct than by conscious thought. Our actions are driven by reactivity and survival rather than by values, intention, purpose, or goals. Emotions associated with this stage encompass fear, anxiety, shame, restlessness, detachment, and loneliness. This is the point at which we find ourselves before realizing that life is about so much more.

"In the second stage, Exploring," Teena continued, "'curiosity' awakens and the quest for answers leads to the cultivation of 'awareness.' This stage carries a blend of wonder, excitement, and self-consciousness. It is here that we finally confirm that there is, indeed, more to life than mere survival. During this period, we may also oscillate between emotional highs and lows more intensely, as we question our motivations, beliefs, and actions.

"Learning follows," she continued. "This stage exposes us to the transformational energies of 'gratitude,' 'forgiveness,' and 'acceptance.' Within these levels we begin to appreciate, let go, understand, and perceive the perfection of the world around us.

"The next stage, Becoming," she stated, "consists of two levels: 'intention' and 'transformation.' It is here that we begin to consciously shape our lives in alignment with our chosen values and aspirations. We establish meaningful goals and discern or clarify our purpose. Substantial personal growth and

The Spectrum of Inner Growth

STAGE	FOCUS	LEVEL
Being	Deep understanding and connection with themselves and the world.	Love
Becoming	Begin to intentionally shape their own development and use their understanding and learning to transform themselves.	Transformation
Becoming		Intention
Learning	Begin to understand the power of positive emotions and attitudes (gratitude, forgiveness and acceptance), and how they influence their experiences and relationships.	Acceptance
Learning		Forgiveness
Learning		Gratitude
Exploring	Exploring environment and their own consciousness. Start to ask questions and seek answers.	Awareness
Exploring		Curiosity
Surviving	Meeting essential needs (food, water, shelter, safety, sustenance).	Unconsciousness

EMOTION	BEHAVIOR
Selflessness, compassion, harmony, joy, serenity, ecstasy, peace, wholeness, fulfillment, love.	Inherent kindness, empathy, and a nonjudgmental attitude to self, others and the world.
Renewal, excitement, anticipation, hope, confidence.	Undertaking major changes in their lives (career, significant relationships).
Determination, ambition, focus, courage, optimism, resilience.	Focused and proactive approach to life, actions align with their stated values and goals.
Understanding, tolerance, patience, calmness, comfort.	Less complaints and resistance dealing with situations; greater ease and peace of mind.
Release, relief, sadness, vulnerability, compassion, empathy, peace.	Less anger or bitterness; more peaceful, serene demeanor.
Appreciation, acknowledgment, contentment, serenity, joy.	Positiveness and appreciative attitude, even in the face of challenges.
Self-consciousness, frustration, realization, understanding, introspection, courage.	Interest in feedback and self-development (books, workshops).
Confusion, uncertainty, anger, lack of clarity, anticipation, wonder, anxiety, excitement.	Inquisitiveness; potential periods of confusion or uncertainty.
Fear, anxiety, apathy, shame, anger, confusion, restlessness, detachment, isolation, loneliness.	Self-absorption; lack of real interest, motivation, or heartfelt engagement.

change occur here, as past experiences are integrated and a higher level of consciousness gradually emerges.

"And then there is Being. In this culminating stage, we experience a profound connection with all that exists. It is when we comprehend, truly comprehend, love." She said this with a slight smile, as though she were privy to knowledge others had yet to discover.

"I suspect that by the time you arrived here you all had already embarked on the Exploring stage, delving into the level of curiosity, perhaps even touching on awareness. You understood why you wanted, or perhaps needed, to be here and were either curious enough or sufficiently encouraged to take action."

Being here wasn't my choice, that's for sure, thought Jennifer, though she was indeed glad that she was there.

Sofia had a similar thought to Jennifer's but had not yet made up her mind about whether or not coming here had been worth her time.

Stephanie found herself haunted by the first stage—Surviving—and squirmed a little in her seat when she read the words "shame" and "detachment" as two of the accompanying emotions. Ever since *that* happened to her in Paris, she had been ashamed and felt detached. Just then she had a flash of insight. She had just thought of the rape as "something that happened to her", not as something she brought upon herself. That was a subtle but startling thought. *This awareness thing might be working on me already,* she thought, before she dragged her attention back to Teena and her instruction.

"I'm going to give you all a few minutes to look at The Spectrum of Inner Growth a bit longer and see if you recognize, or should we say, 'can become aware of,' the level you might find yourself in right now. I would add that the levels are not static or all-encompassing. In fact, you are likely to be vacillating between them. However, what we have often seen is that there is one level in particular in which you may be spending a large portion of your time."

Teena sensed some of the same hesitation and apprehension that had characterized this session in past programs and felt compelled to say,

"If any of you is having some difficulty with the chart and the stage you find yourself in, please don't worry, these feelings are perfectly normal."

She looked again at the graphic now on the screen.

"Think of this as a guide to help us steer towards a destination instead of just drifting through life, like a log on a river, often hitting the banks, sometimes spinning in the current, and eventually just bumping up somewhere not of your choosing. Awareness is a tool we can use to help us steer our log down the river of life."

Nicole disregarded Teena's last words. Her mind was fixated on the word "acceptance." She knew she hadn't reached that point yet and yearned for the courage to share her love for Elena to her parents without worrying about what their reaction, or anyone's reaction, would be. She harbored a hopeful desire to progress up the chart and drew comfort from identifying aspects of herself in the awareness level. Yet, she couldn't help but wonder, *Do I even have it in me to advance from there?*

Olivia, frequently battling feelings of anxiety, anger, and loneliness, identified herself at the lower stage. She recognized that she was often scornful of others who weren't as educated, capable, or well-informed as she. This attitude made her demanding and put a barrier between her and others. In her mind, she heard her Mama say, *Sometimes, Olivia, you've got to go along to get along.* Getting along with others would certainly be a relief and a lot less lonely, she knew. She did find some reassurance in the idea that she regularly took the time to express gratitude, especially during prayer, and that nudged her toward the next stage of her development.

Sofia checked the chart for "clever," "capable," or "intelligent." She was all those things and didn't understand why they were missing. *Useless chart,* she thought. But she resonated with "determination" and "ambition," both emotions of the Intention level. *Intention,* she thought, *that's my category,* though she felt a niggling doubt as to whether she was actually correct about where she stood. *Hmmm,* the thought occurred to her, *maybe that is not where I am after all.*

Jennifer thought that the category in which she found herself was easy to see. *Obviously, I'm stuck in unconsciousness, confused and lonely.* She looked around at the others perusing the chart and then tentatively raised her hand.

"Yes," Teena said, "Jennifer, right? Do you have a question?"

"I do. I want to know: How fast we can climb up the levels and stages? I see myself at the lowest, and, honestly, it's disheartening."

"I understand, Jennifer," responded Teena empathetically. "In one way or another, we all share your struggle. We all have areas that require improvement. And, fundamentally, that is why you are in the program.

But allow me to caution you about attaching importance to the pace of your progress. Everyone is different and unique, so, ultimately, it truly just depends on you.

"To change our lives meaningfully, we must understand who we are and how we live. This self-awareness is the key to personal growth. By cultivating awareness, we can make informed choices, embrace new perspectives, and embark on a journey of self-improvement and evolution.

"And now, let's take a look at how our belief system sometimes gets in the way of that progress."

Chapter 18

Limiting Beliefs

Teena had another list put up on the screen.

"We all have beliefs about ourselves, our loved ones, our enemies, people in general, even groups of people we've never met, the world, politics, religion, gender, the right and wrong way to live, and so on. These beliefs come from many places and imprint on us like chalk on a chalkboard."

Teena continued, this time pointing to the chart being projected.

"We learn or acquire our beliefs from:

- Our age, race, and gender.
- Where we were born and raised.
- Our families (not only our immediate family of origin but our extended family and those we choose to make our families—groups of friends and other loved ones).
- Our socio-economic status.
- Our culture and its customs.
- Our religion.
- Our level of education.
- Our jobs or employment.
- Our experiences.

"So, obviously, a white woman born in the rural southern United States with a culture that taught her of the glories of the Confederacy has a different belief system than a Black sharecropper's wife born into poverty in modern-day Mississippi.

"A fervent Catholic has a different view of abortion than an atheistic feminist.

"A gay child born into a liberal family with two moms would learn a different set of beliefs than a gay child born to a conservative family."

At this point Nicole couldn't help but think, *I would have preferred to have been born to that liberal family instead of mine.*

"Being poor colors your worldview differently than being rich does, and someone unhoused sees society differently than someone who goes home every night to a fully staffed mansion.

"A brain surgeon, for example, may think herself better than a fast-food worker.

"These are some of the beliefs which are imposed on us during our lifetime. What we hold as our beliefs and our truths are ideas and stories that we have heard, received, and accepted from others or have experienced directly. They become thoughts and generate pressures and demands, depending on the degree to which we think they are real. All of our actions start out as our thoughts and those actions are predicated on what we 'believe' and hold to be true."

Teena was now moving all around the room. She was making eye contact with all of the women there and allowing the information to sink in, which, from the look of the faces, it clearly was. It was obvious that she enjoyed speaking on this subject, and she was very good at it. By now, any notion that she had a disability had disappeared, and the women only saw love, eloquence, and intelligence. Power emanated from this incredible being as she shared such life-changing lessons.

"Some of our beliefs can empower us, for example, 'You can do anything you set your mind to do.' Other beliefs can restrict us, such as, 'The only role of women is to bear children.'

"Awareness allows us to be more conscious about what and why we do and believe certain things or act in certain ways. With awareness, we can also come to decide if our beliefs are serving us well, and, the part that is most important, we can come to understand that those beliefs *can be changed*.

"But, first, we need to familiarize ourselves with them. Let's look at some examples of limiting beliefs."

Teena asked for some information to be projected on to the screen again.

"About women:

- Are too emotional.
- Their job is to make babies.
- Are selfish if they don't want children.
- Need to be attractive and pretty.
- Are not supposed to age.
- Need a man by their side.
- Belong in the home.
- Are highly sensitive during their period.
- Cannot get along with/trust each other.
- Are difficult when they disagree or are angry.
- It's better to be a man in this world.

"About my body:

- Is too big for fashionable clothes.
- Needs to be slim to be attractive.
- Is defined by my age.
- Must remain young-looking forever.
- Should not have any visible imperfections.
- Isn't feminine enough.
- Is not fit enough.
- Can't compete with younger ones.
- Should look good for others.
- Needs to conform to beauty standards.

"About men:

- Are in charge.
- Know best.
- Only want sex.
- Don't listen.
- Are not in touch with their emotions.
- Don't cry.
- Don't understand women.
- Are not as mature as women their age.
- Cannot be trusted.
- Are responsible for bringing money home.
- Cannot take care of children.

"About relationships:

- Good love is hard to find.
- There is only one true love for each person.
- I need to fix my partner's problems.
- Even though I don't want to, I need to stay for the sake of the children.
- If my relationship fails, I've failed.
- I can't ask for what I want in bed.
- I need to change myself to be attractive to others.
- I need to put other people's feelings first.
- I must please others to be liked.
- Relationships are supposed to be hard.

"I don't deserve:

- Love.
- To be happy.
- A better life.
- To pursue my dreams.
- Money.
- To be treated with respect.
- To be heard.
- To take time off.
- A successful career.
- A promotion.
- To be here.

"I am too:

- Busy to start a new project.
- Afraid of failing.
- Young to understand.
- Old to try new things.
- Stuck in my habits.
- Afraid to ask for help.
- Worried to enjoy the moment.
- Self-conscious to express my real feelings.
- Afraid that people will laugh at me.
- Cynical to believe in change.

"I need to:

- Have their approval.
- Be in control.
- Do it even if I don't want to.
- Stay quiet even if I don't agree.
- Keep others happy.
- Make sure they are ok first.
- Have a partner to feel complete.
- Always look beautiful.
- Be perfect.
- Be a good _____.

"I cannot:

- Disappoint others.
- Express my feelings.
- Stand up for myself.
- Start over.
- Overcome my fears.
- Break my bad habits.
- Understand complex topics.
- Let go of my past.
- Forgive.
- Achieve success.

"I don't/I didn't/I wasn't:

- Belong in this class/job/position. It's only a matter of time before they realize it.
- Feel qualified for this task. Everyone else is much better equipped than I am.
- Deserving of this promotion/award/grade. There must have been a mistake.
- Competent enough to voice my opinion.
- Contribute anything meaningful to the team.
- Fit into this community. They all have a much better grasp of _____.
- Go to the right school/get the right education.
- Born into the right (country/social class/family, etc.).
- Know how to make the right decisions.
- Know how/Want to ask for help.

"My family/others/they:

- Come first.
- Are not fair.
- Made me feel ____.
- Have a favorite and it's not me.
- Don't understand me.
- Don't appreciate me.
- Don't care what I think.
- Would be disappointed if I ____.
- Know what is best for me.
- Don't listen to my opinion.
- If only they knew that ____.

"My problems are because of my ___.

- Parents.
- Sibling.
- Significant other.
- Children.
- Boss/Job.
- School/Education.
- Country.
- Culture.
- Nationality.
- Skin color.

"About money:

- I am too poor.
- I will always live paycheck-to-paycheck.
- I'm always paying bills.
- I am not rich enough.
- I will never have enough.
- I have to work hard to earn it.
- Doesn't grow on trees.
- I cannot earn it doing what I love.
- Is the root of all evil.
- The rich get richer, and the poor get poorer.

"The world/life is:

- Full of dangers.
- Out to get me.
- Getting worse.
- Only for the rich and powerful.
- Too complicated to understand.
- Gone to hell.
- Cruel and without compassion.
- Totally unfair and unjust.
- Not worth fighting for.
- Filled with deceit and betrayal.

"I'm not _____ enough.

- Smart
- Educated
- Attractive
- Rich
- Worthy
- Confident
- Experienced
- Sexy
- Funny
- Young

"These are just a few of the many limiting beliefs we live our lives by and ultimately allow to control us.

"I'm going to give you a moment to review the list. I invite you to see which resonate with you. Perhaps you have others. If you can and are open to it, go even deeper to determine which may be playing a part in your life. You may even consider writing about it in your journals."

The group was given some time to go through the exercise. After that passed, Teena continued. "Let's explore if your beliefs are serving you well. Let's go around the room, and, if you will, please share one thing you've been told or were raised to understand about yourself, and then tell us if that is still true of you or not. Who wants to begin?" Jennifer, who looked less flustered than she had on day one, raised her hand.

The Orchid

"My mom always insisted that all there was for me was to get married and have kids. 'That was the purpose of a woman's life,' she would say. I fought it for a long time, thinking that I could have it all if I focused on my career first and then the family. But when I gave in to the idea of having a family first, my hus … ex-husband abandoned us. Don't get me wrong. I love my kids like crazy, but I can't help but feel that I screwed up by thinking that I could have it all. Maybe I should have pursued a job in a big city and stayed single." She said this with a hint of sadness.

Olivia followed.

"I grew up in poverty, and no one in my neighborhood believed that there was any way out of that condition. It took a lot of work and determination on my part to see that education was the way out for me and to not give up through that process. I kicked that door down so as not to end up like my poor mama." As she said that, Olivia realized that her whole life had been aimed not at what she could become but rather at what she was trying to avoid becoming. Seeing her life like that was a bit of a shock to her.

Nicole was next.

"I was taught that there were things to avoid doing—sins, many sins, that could actually doom me to hell after death," she said. "I believed that right up till the time that I realized that I was living one of those sins every day, the sin of loving the wrong person. I'm still struggling with how my love can be a sin."

A woman cleared her throat and raised her hand.

"I've always thought that to feel complete, I needed a partner. Lately, I've been feeling down because I didn't have a boyfriend. I've spent my time feeling sad and crying over how lonely I felt. But looking at everyone here, I see that I don't need a partner to feel good. There are many other options."

Her comments inspired another woman with silver braids wound around her head to speak up.

"I'm Lisa, and you got me at the living paycheck-to-paycheck thing. I've done it so long and said it out loud so many times that, if those people who talk about manifesting thoughts are right, I've created a tornado of poverty heading straight for me. I need to change this way of thinking and do something about it."

Lisa was sitting beside Stephanie, and all heads turned her way when she raised her hand.

Stephanie was brief, and it sounded like the words were being pulled from her.

"I was taught to believe that I needed to be perfect. I'm just now beginning to understand that there is no such thing as perfection."

Lastly, everyone turned towards Sofia.

"I grew up watching people who were supposed to be authority figures actually being mean, abusive, and, frankly, useless. I learned that I had to take care of myself, because no one else was going to. This is my belief, and it is a true one. I've had to do what I had to do to get where I am, and I'm not apologizing for that." Sofia set her jaw with those last words and glared rebelliously at Teena.

"There is no need to apologize for our beliefs," Teena said gently. "Only to recognize them, acknowledge they exist, and then examine whether they are beliefs we wish to keep or not. Are they holding us back, or are they pushing us forward? Have we outgrown them, or do they need to be altered in any way?

"Once we are able to observe our thoughts and beliefs dispassionately, as though they are someone else's, we are in a better position to determine if they are serving us well or not. Explore and challenge the truth of the things you have believed all your life. Just because those things have been said to you for as long back as you remember, it doesn't mean they are true. Or they may be someone else's truth—your mother's, your teacher's, an old friend's or enemy's, a past lover's, a culture's, or even the echoes of a colonial past, subtly influencing how you see yourself and the world and potentially holding you back from fully embracing your own truths.

"Determine what is *your* truth."

Teena said this again for effect, "Determine what is *your* truth and whether it serves you well.

"Access your inner wisdom for help with this. We all have inner wisdom, which we can access through meditation. Sometimes it is called 'intuition' or 'Higher Self.' We can use it to search for answers. Continue to meditate on this topic to gain awareness, and then write about it in your journal. As you do, choose some beliefs of yours, examine them, and decide if they are serving you or should be discarded or altered.

"Once you identify ideas and/or stories that are holding you back, then the next step is to free yourself from their control. You can choose to discard or change your limiting beliefs. Meditate on and write in your journal about what beliefs you would like to keep or change. This is an important first step to make changes in your life.

"Remember, all is energy. *Everything is energy.* Discoveries in quantum physics are giving us the understanding that the ocean, the Earth, the planets, water, air, plants, animals, objects, and of course, we humans, including our thoughts and emotions—are energy, all vibrating at different frequencies.

"Surely, you've felt the energy of someone whose enthusiasm is so tangible it seems contagious. Everyone says, 'She always lights up any room.' Or, conversely, we also tend to distance ourselves from that person who constantly exudes pessimism. We say, 'She gives off bad vibes.' These are clear examples of how we perceive and react to others' energy, which clearly is present and real enough to be discernible by us.

"We vibrate depending on our state of being, thoughts, and emotions. It is even speculated that we carry energy over from past generations, and even previous lifetimes, but, at the very least, we certainly lug energy through our lives, and that is the equivalent of dragging an old suitcase behind us wherever we go.

"Recognizing your energetic state is a vital step toward deeper empowerment and freedom. My dears, I say to you, it is time to drop that burden, examine at what frequency we are vibrating, and begin to make decisions about how to steer our life.

"I am passing out copies of the Spectrum of Inner Growth and of the limiting beliefs we reviewed here today to aid in your meditation, and journaling.

"You have all the answers you seek within you. Take the time and create the space to discover them.

"I love you all. Thank you for your attention and for taking this journey with me today."

Limiting Beliefs

The Orchid

Limiting Beliefs

The Orchid

Chapter 19

Dance

Next on the schedule was a dance activity designed to assist the guests in shifting their energy following moments of deep introspection. As the women arrived, they were greeted by the lively tunes emanating from inside the Dance Studio.

The space felt vast, allowing glimpses of the stunning surroundings through its open windows. Illuminated by an abundance of sunlight, the studio exuded a warm ambiance, the polished wooden floors reflecting a gentle glow. The combination of the upbeat music and the inviting atmosphere promised an enjoyable and invigorating session.

Waiting for them was a tall, muscular, dark-skinned woman standing in the middle of the floor, hands on her slim hips. Her smile was large and luminous, and every single woman found herself grinning in return. Even Stephanie managed a smile.

"Hello, my darlings, and welcome! *Welcome!*" the teacher said in a booming and energetic voice. "Come in, gather round." She spread her arms wide as though encompassing them all.

"My name is Flavia," she said in a heavily accented voice, "and I hail from the Bahia region in wonderful Brazil, where we love to enjoy life and dance!"

She shook her hips at these words and winked at Sofia, who seemed a bit taken aback by the motion.

"I am so happy you are here and hope that you enjoy the next hour. You don't have to do much, only allow the music to take control of your body, let Flavia teach you a few moves, and dance! To move is to connect to the energy of the cosmos and come alive. When we move and have fun, we are saluting the universe and our place in it, because, surely, we were all created for joy."

Flavia certainly walked her talk. Her very being radiated joy. She wore a shirt of dozens of different colors, wide orange palazzo pants, and impossibly high platform shoes accented with glitter. There were shells woven into her braided hair, and she wore huge, beaded hoop earrings that flashed in the light from the room's windows. There was no overlooking Flavia. She staked out her spot in the world and fully occupied it.

With her smile and mischievous eyes, she was inviting all the women to join the party. She had an aura about her that was incandescent, and it was obvious to all that she was full of love and energy.

In the background, the music now shifted to a mix of drums and percussion instruments. A song honoring her country's Afro-Brazilian influences made them feel as though they were in the festive streets of Rio de Janeiro during the famous Carnival. Olivia, a veteran of Mardi Gras, found herself laughing out loud. She wouldn't have been a bit surprised if people dressed in feathers and little else, came through the door. The music made her long for her hometown, and she found her feet tapping while Flavia was still speaking.

"Today, my lovelies, we will dance the samba. Once the dance of slaves and even the criminalized, the samba has lived through many incarnations and now is the musical signature of my part of the world. The samba represents freedom—freedom to sway, to tap, to stomp, to twirl, to let loose, and to let your spirit soar. Come and join me!"

Flavia turned the volume higher and spun to face the room. "Begin like this," she said and started moving her athletic body. Her feet went back and then forwards, while at the same time she moved her hips side-to-side. Her long brown arms were bent at the elbows and her hands made circles at the level of her chest. As the music's tempo sped up, so did her movements. Her white teeth flashed, and her long dark lashes swept her cheekbones as her eyes closed and her head fell slightly backwards. Watching her was entrancing. She was sensual and hypnotic.

She seemed to be transported, riding the music like a leaf rides the wind. The women were captivated and soon filled with the same energy. They began to move their feet. As the music wound down, Flavia ceased her movements and opened her eyes.

"It is a spectacular dance, is it not?" she asked the group, her bosom heaving a bit with the intensity of the dance. The faint sheen of sweat on her skin made her appear even more glowing.

Without waiting for an answer, Flavia said to them, "Now, my darlings, we all dance!" and she turned the music to top volume, making the very walls shake with a samba rhythm. "Follow me. There is no wrong way to start, but you must begin to release your soul like the free bird that it is," she yelled above the music, and she nudged the women in two lines and then stood beside them so they could follow her steps.

The time that followed was a celebration of human movement. Flavia demonstrated the proper rotation of hips, which they practiced for several minutes. Then, she focused on the steps.

"First, one foot to the back, then the other foot moves forward slightly," Flavia added. "Then the other to the back again, and the sequence repeats."

She had them practice again and again, explaining that the rhythm and movement of the feet was the most crucial aspect of samba.

Nicole couldn't help but think how *free* and uninhibited Flavia was. "Oh my, she is so amazing. I think she has an extra hinge in her hips that I'm missing," she whispered to Sofia.

"It's in there somewhere," giggled Sofia. "Let's hope we don't break something trying to find it." And she let loose a loud "woo-hoo, woo-hoo!" that had all the women laughing.

Next Flavia explained how to move the arms.

"Let's move our arms sideways in a large motion," she said. "We can, as they say, let it rip."

Olivia held her own, her hips catching the rhythm and making the dance her own.

Stephanie didn't seem to be having as much fun and only slightly swayed to the music, and everyone respected her silent and somewhat somber mood.

But it was Jennifer who proved to be the best pupil of the class. She was dancing samba as though she were born to it.

"Aha!" Flavia said, "A star is born!" and threw back her head and laughed.

"Now, let's add a little spice," she said, opening a large trunk behind her and distributing maracas, tambourines, whistles, and feather boas to all. Soon the entire room, while certainly not moving as one, was energized and dancing together. The percussion beats moved independently of the music, giving rise to a vibrant, rhythmic chaos with feathers flying in every direction. Screams of laughter were heard throughout the room, as everyone was having a grandiose time. Even Stephanie managed a smile as she got bumped sideways by Olivia's hip.

When the class time was up, Flavia lowered the music volume and applauded all the women, thanking them for their love, their energy, and their participation. "You were all spectacular today, dears. *Parabéns*—congratulations!"

She continued speaking while catching her breath some, "Our body is our temple. It is where the spirit resides. Our ability to connect with it, as we just did, and form a singular, energetic experience of body, mind, and soul, is therapeutic, and it brings us to the present moment. The *Now*—the only moment that matters, and where awareness happens.

"I love you all. *Muito Obrigado*," she said. "That's 'thank you' in Portuguese," and she placed her hands together in front of her forehead.

The energy was crackling, and each woman felt as though her spirits were lighter. All were smiling, giggling, almost jumping with excitement. Any sense of fatigue, problems, or concerns seemed to matter less than when they had begun the class. It was a great illustration of how their bodies and spirits were intertwined.

As they were all exiting the room, Flavia crossed and moved towards Jennifer.

"You are Jennifer, right?"

"Yeah," Jennifer answered with a big smile.

"You were awesome! You got the moves, girl. Are you a dancer?"

"No. I mean, I was. I danced competitively in high school, but I haven't really danced since … well, since I got divorced."

Jennifer paused awkwardly, as if something she said had surprised her.

Flavia, noticing that Jennifer's voice cracked with emotion, asked quietly, "Are you ok?"

"Yeah," Jennifer said, coming back to herself. "Thank you. I just realized that this was the first time that I have said those words—'since I got divorced'—without feeling a stabbing pain. It's weird."

"Well congratulations, it sounds like you are becoming aware, and some healing is taking place. Perhaps it is because you are beginning to understand it is up to you to create happiness in your life, or perhaps it's the samba? What do you think?" Flavia asked, winking her eye.

Jennifer laughed out loud, "I think it is both. It's the samba, and I need more happiness in my life," she said.

"Then, my darling, dance! Dance alone in your room, dance while you are cooking, dance while you cry. Movement seems to be one of the keys to freeing your spirit, which has been too long repressed and is ready to take flight. Dance for your life, Jennifer. Invite joy in and give it a permanent seat at your table."

The Orchid

Chapter 20

Jennifer

It was 5:00 a.m., and Jennifer was about to begin her daily routine. Wake up, hop in the shower, cook breakfast, wake the kids, pack their lunches while they eat, pester them to get dressed—*Will they still need reminding to brush their teeth when they are in college?* she wondered—, drop them off at school, and race off to work, always just one traffic slowdown from being late … again.

Her manager gave her the side-eye as she dashed in just a few minutes late and sat at her desk. She shoved her purse in the drawer, realizing she forgot her lunch, which she had left on the dining table.

Damn, I think I forgot my wallet too, she thought. *Oh well, I'll call it intermittent fasting. My hips could benefit from skipping a few meals. Hideous cow!*

Such internal dialogue was pretty much the only adult conversation Jennifer had these days. She was too scattered to form any real attachments with anyone, not even with her colleagues. She was never available for drinks after office hours, as her daycare center charged her five dollars for every five minutes she was late picking up the kids. Once she had gotten them home, it was overseeing homework, making dinner, bathing them, reading them a couple of stories, and finally tucking them in.

By the time she had cleaned the kitchen, if she actually got around to it, thrown in a load of laundry, and double-checked to make sure she had *not* been volunteered by either child to make cupcakes for any school activity, it was 10:00 p.m., and even then, it was not over, since she always had some office work left to do.

She was so tired all the time. Sometimes she thought she might just die of sheer exhaustion.

Time flies when you are having fun, she thought sardonically.

Fun, hell, she felt as though she hadn't smiled in a long time. It was nearly five years ago that her husband, Brian, had walked out on her, had walked out on *them.* Thinking about it made tears well up in her eyes even after all this time. *How could he have done that?* That question was on a constant loop in her mind. She felt the familiar wave of self-pity begin to crash over her. It always happened when she was so tired. The problem was she was always so tired. The tears came more frequently now despite how much time had passed.

To distract herself, Jennifer forced her thoughts to times gone by, when she and Brian had been happy together. She had, like every other girl with a pulse, noticed Brian Coughlin in high school. He had been hard to miss—tall and broad-shouldered with a curl of dark hair falling across his forehead and penetrating eyes. She even noticed them across the room, which was as close as Jennifer got to Brian during the four years they went to East Lansing High. He was captain of the football team and always had his pick of the most popular girls.

For her part, Jennifer was no wallflower. She was a pretty blonde with a nice figure that she kept a strict eye on, as she was a member of the dance squad and had to keep fit. She dated several boys over her school career, but none of the boys set her pulse racing. That phenomenon was reserved for Brian, on whom she had a crush since she first laid eyes on him freshman year. She never acted on her crush. She didn't want to fight her way through the sea of cheerleaders and gorgeous mean girls always surrounding him, and anyway, she had bigger plans.

Jennifer was going to go to a good college, get her degree in business, and use the skills and strategies she learned to open her own company someday. She wasn't quite sure in what field yet, but she envisioned herself swinging down the street of some big city in a fashionable suit, carrying an Italian leather briefcase as she headed for her office, the one with her name on the door.

Her mother, from a different generation, was baffled by this idea, convinced that a woman's first choice should be marriage and children, as was hers. She and Jennifer's dad had been high school sweethearts, marrying just after graduation with Jennifer making an appearance soon after—"like it should be," her mother always added. That scenario never appealed to Jennifer, who was raring to take advantage of the opportunities finally available to women in her generation. She had nothing against marriage and children and saw both of those things in her future, but first she wanted to finish her education, move to a city bigger than her native Lansing, and establish herself in business. She'd find the right man to be her life partner someday, she was sure, but that dream could be deferred until later.

The summer after graduation, she worked at her parents' dry-cleaning stores. They owned two, and her dad made no bones about wanting Jennifer to return after college to work at, and eventually take over, the business. But his not-so-subtle suggestions to that effect fell on deaf ears with Jennifer. In September, off she went to Ball State Indiana on a scholarship she had earned with her excellent grades.

College was hard work, but she did well and was only a few credits from her degree her senior year, when she began looking for a job in the Midwest's biggest cities: Chicago, Columbus, Cincinnati, Cleveland, even as far afield as St. Louis and Minneapolis. But the market was tough, and there were too many graduates looking for too few jobs; finding she was priced out of her longed-for city life, this revealed to Jennifer that she might have to forgo her dreams for a while.

She reluctantly returned to Lansing after she got her diploma but made it very clear to her parents that she was not interested in working with them. The truth was that deep inside, she felt superior or too qualified for the family business. Accepting defeat, her dad helped her get a job at an insurance agency owned by family friends. Jennifer reminded herself that she was just starting out and would at least gain experience for when an opportunity to pursue her bigger dreams came along.

But life had other plans and Jennifer's changed in an instant—the instant she ran into her high school crush again. Not long after her return, Jennifer went out with some girlfriends. She was at the bar ordering a pitcher of beer for the table when a deep voice over her shoulder said to the bartender, "Put that pitcher on my tab." Jennifer turned to see who had spoken and found herself looking into those eyes from her high school daydreams. There stood Brian, even better looking than she remembered him, and Jennifer felt that familiar trip-hammer beating of her heart.

"Hey beautiful, I'm Brian Coughlin. I don't know if you remember me from school," he said, entirely sure that of course she *did* remember him. Everyone *always* remembered him. Truthfully, he barely remembered her but had been admiring her round butt in her tight jeans as she stood at the bar. He asked one of the guys he was with who she was before he made his approach.

Her voice cracked embarrassingly when she answered him, but soon Jennifer and Brian were sitting together at a table for two, her friends forgotten. They talked all night and met again the next and the one after that. Brian enjoyed that Jennifer had a brain (unlike most of the other girls he had gone out with over the years,) and ambition. She had no plans to stick around Lansing for long, and even though she looked at him with definite stars in her eyes, she was sticking to her guns that she had no time for a serious relationship—even with him. She was going places. To Brian, who had always had girls fall into his lap, that sounded like a challenge. The chase was on.

Brian bombarded Jennifer with attention. He took her to the movies, the bowling alley, the amusement park, candlelit dinners, and even brunch dates with her parents (who, like everyone who met him, fell for Brian's charm). The two shared picnics and swam at the lake, met friends for pizza (where Brian kept everyone laughing), and spent romantic evenings alone, where he showed up at the door with huge bouquets of flowers.

Jennifer wouldn't sleep with him, much to his astonishment, since some of their late-night dates turned hot and steamy in the back of his car, but it wasn't a ploy on her part. Jennifer was clinging to her dreams of getting to the big city and starting her own life and was trying to preserve her independence. But, as summer waned, her resistance was being worn down. The more she resisted, the more intense Brian's attempts to persuade her became, and their romance heated up. At the end of the year, Brian proposed, and Jennifer revised her dreams. Now they included a husband, children, *and* her career. She accepted Brian's proposal. Their parents and all their friends were thrilled, and, catching their excitement, eventually Jennifer was, too.

After the big wedding her mother had helped plan, Jennifer and Brian enjoyed a honeymoon—a week in Hawaii financed by his parents—where they finally consummated their love and Brian claimed his trophy. He had won the elusive girl and felt like a conquering hero. Jennifer shelved the last of her dreams of independence, and the couple set out on their married life together, both satisfied with the bargain they had made.

They bought a small starter home—a fixer-upper. It was all they could afford on her salary from the insurance agency and Brian's from his work as a junior sales rep at the local TV network affiliate. It wasn't much, but it was home, and they threw themselves into painting, plastering, and installing laminate floors, working side-by-side. Jennifer was happy she and Brian were a team, laboring to build their lives together.

Soon enough the children came, first Tommy and then, two years later, Michelle. She and Brian had agreed that two children were all they would have to make their family complete. In truth, two children were all Jennifer could handle, because it was Jennifer who was doing all the handling.

Jennifer did all the diaper changing, laundry washing, toy pickup, baby feeding, toilet training, and the thousand other tasks that come with childrearing. Brian was too busy to help much. He was climbing the corporate ladder at the station, first promoted to senior sales rep and then district manager, which necessitated lots of late nights and even trips out of town with clients. Jennifer had to keep her job too. They needed the money, as every penny not absorbed by raising the kids went into fixing the house. There were no more shoulder-to-shoulder home repairs with Brian.

Jennifer was exhausted and overwhelmed, and she looked it. Her glossy blond hair had lost its luster and become straw-like. Drugstore dyes and conditioners had to do, as expensive salon visits weren't in their budget. The dance team figure she had maintained all through high school and college began to give way under a mountain of casseroles and junk food. Jennifer didn't feel like cooking most nights. Brian wasn't there and the kids didn't care. She hated admitting how many times dinner meant frozen waffles. When her "fat pant" jeans wouldn't zip, Jennifer stopped looking in the mirror.

On the increasingly rare times Brian was home, he spent his time watching football and the only real interaction they had was when Brian yelled at her to keep the kids quiet, because he was watching TV. Worst of all, he barely ever reached for Jennifer in the dark anymore. He was too tired, he said, or he had a big presentation coming up at work. Couldn't she please leave him alone and let him sleep?

Jennifer racked her brain about how to change things between them.

She arranged date nights at the local theater for the latest action movie he loved (and she hated). She set up card games with their friends, but the talk between the men always turned to sports, with allegiances divided between competing teams, and that always left Brian argumentative and snapping at her when the evening ended. Jennifer bought bottles of screw-top wine and even sexy black lingerie, but when she went to the bathroom to change into her new purchases, she came out to find Brian already asleep. Aside from the kids, they had nothing much to talk about to each other anymore, and Jennifer felt the panic rise. It was like Brian was slipping away from her.

The Orchid

Something snapped on the night of their ninth wedding anniversary. Jennifer had come home from work early, pawned the kids off on her parents, and spent the afternoon making Brian's favorite dinner: three-cheese lasagna, homemade garlic bread, and Caesar salad. She even made a double-chocolate cake in a heart-shaped pan. She set the table with the china they had gotten as a wedding gift. Against the candlesticks in the center of the table, she propped the card in which she had written, "To Brian, you are still my handsome prince. Happy anniversary. I love you so much. Forever yours, Jennifer." She wore her best dress, though she grimaced a little at how tight it had become lately, put on her makeup, did her hair, and, at 7:00 p.m., she lit the candles to await Brian's coming home from work.

But Brian never came.

At 8:00 p.m., she started calling his cell. It went straight to voicemail. She called again at 8:30 and then every fifteen minutes thereafter. Visions of a car wreck began at 10:00 p.m., and she called every hospital, his parents' house, and, finally, his boss.

At 3:00 a.m., she heard Brian's key in the lock, and she launched at him like a missile.

"Where the hell have you been? I thought you were dead!" Her voice rose higher and her words ran together. "Youforgotouranniversary!" and she burst into sobs.

"Oh shit," Brian said, looking at the still-laid table. "My phone died, so I didn't get your phone calls or messages. Besides, you should have reminded me. I've got a lot on my mind. If you ever took your eyes off the kids for a minute and paid attention to me, you'd know that," Brian shot back. "I'm sure I told you I had a big client meeting tonight. You should have checked my schedule before wasting your time making this dinner to celebrate your anniversary."

Through her tears, Jennifer heard the words, "*your* anniversary," and felt her heart sink.

Brian went on, just to put an end to the drama she was building up to, "We'll do something together this weekend, maybe we'll get a pizza or something. Now I'm beat and I'm going to bed," and he went up the stairs, leaving Jennifer alone.

**

After that night, Jennifer began checking Brian's cell phone. She found some texts from a woman named Ashley. Some were messages like, "I had a great time last night," intermixed with ones that read things like, "Way to close the deal, Brian." The messages weren't definitive proof something was going on between them, but they provided enough fodder for Jennifer to loudly confront Brian with her jealous suspicions.

One day, following many such claims, Brian yelled back at her, "Ashley is a producer at the station, for Christ sakes! We work together. And what in the hell are you doing going through my phone, you crazy bitch?" Jennifer recoiled at the name-calling and tried desperately to believe Brian's denial. She wasn't surprised when he changed the password to his phone to lock her out. He was already locking her out in every other way.

Still, when the other shoe dropped, she was totally blindsided.

One night Brian came home late and told Jennifer they had to talk.

"Jennifer," he began, while she sat on the couch looking up at him, her crossed arms held so tightly across her chest her ribs hurt.

"Jen, I don't really know how to say this any other way but straight out. I don't want to be married to you anymore. I need a divorce...." His voice tapered off.

Jennifer's eyes widened.

"What did you say?" she whispered.

"I don't want to be married anymore. I don't want to be with *you* anymore. I want a divorce."

Jennifer's mouth hung open as though she were a fish gasping for air. She felt her stomach tighten, gut-punched, and the figure of Brian wavered in front of her eyes. She was going to pass out.

She took a deep, ragged breath.

"It's that woman, isn't it?" she accused him.

"It's not about that," Brian yelled back defensively, but Jennifer cut him off.

"You are a liar, Brian. You are a goddamn liar! Yes, it *is* about that woman. Ashley, the one on your phone, isn't it?" Jennifer's voice rose higher. "That bitch is taking you away from me. She's breaking up our family. That fucking whore is…"

When Jennifer called him a liar and his new love a whore, Brian lost his temper and the guard on his tongue.

"She's not breaking up anything. I want to leave. I'm sick of this house, always dirty and noisy and the kids grabbing at me with their sticky hands and you letting yourself go like you have. You got fat, Jennifer, and I'm not interested in sex with you anymore, looking the way you look. Ashley is more mature and more ... I don't know ... sophisticated. She always dresses well and has no kids, and we can sit over cocktails and actually talk over things that interest me. She is interested in *me*, and she knows how to take care of me, unlike you."

Brian continued, protesting, "I'm moving up in the world, and I need somebody who can keep up with me, a woman I can be proud of being with—not a boring and dull girl like you. I deserve better than you."

That last sentence took the air out of Jennifer's lungs. She visibly sagged and went silent.

Seeing her slump, Brian backpedaled a little, "Look, I'm sorry, okay? I didn't mean to say all that stuff. And you don't have to worry. I'll pay child support, and we can set up whatever visitation schedule works for me to see the kids."

Eager to get out of that room, Brian said, "I'm just going to get some of my stuff upstairs, and I'll get the rest later when you are at work."

The only words out of Jennifer's mouth were, "And what will I tell the kids?"

"I don't care. Tell them I'm on a business trip or something," he spat in response.

As he turned towards the stairs, Jennifer's building misery cracked wide open, and she pleaded, "Brian, we can work it out. I can be a better wife. I'll lose the weight and keep the kids from bothering you. We can go to couples' therapy. Whatever it takes. We can fix it. Give us a chance. For God's sake, don't do this."

"No, it's over," Brian said with finality. "I don't want to fix anything, Jennifer. There's nothing worth fixing."

Then, with a blood-curdling scream, Jennifer let it all out. "Get out then! Get out! GET OUT!" And she crumpled to the floor.

**

Even though it'd been years, Jennifer had not been able to accept the loss, and when she slowed down long enough to notice, her life felt empty. She really only had enough energy to keep the household afloat. She managed to keep the kids fed and their clothes clean, but the house, the fixer-upper Brian and she never got to fix up, was falling apart. The ceiling's suspicious rust stain seemed to spread after every rainstorm, and the backdoor was held closed with a sawed-off broomstick. It's not that she was broke, Brian sent child support, though sometimes late and sometimes less than agreed upon, but rather that she just didn't have the capacity to deal with the house or anything really. She was doing the best she could.

Are you? That ever-critical voice in her head said. *If that's so, why is everything such a freaking big mess around here?*

Being a single mother to her kids was sometimes just beyond her, but she tried to shut up that critical voice and pat herself on the back for even getting out of bed some days.

Her mother helped whenever she could, though she was very busy too, taking care of Jennifer's dad, who had had a stroke. He lived and wasn't entirely paralyzed, but he needed extra looking after, so Jennifer tried not to bother her mom with many childcare requests.

Jennifer knew things were getting out of hand. She found herself carrying around a pint glass full of wine as she picked up the clothes and toys strewn everywhere after she put the kids to bed. Sometimes she found herself reaching for a second glass after that just to unwind enough to sleep. It was the only thing that helped her to numb the pain and forget.

Get ahold of yourself, Jen, she admonished herself. *If you keep drinking like this, you'll be in trouble, and what would your kids do if they lost their mom? Then Ashley might take your place!*

That thought usually was enough to make her put down the glass but not always.

Her work was suffering from her inattention, too. When she was at work, she was obsessively thinking about what she should be doing at home, and when she was home, she kept thinking about things at work. People who had been at the company for a shorter amount of time were getting promoted above her, which caused another cavalcade of worry.

What if you lose your job? That voice again. *Someday that child support and alimony will run out, and then where will you be without a job?*

Jennifer had been preparing for a big presentation for a few days. Among her responsibilities were reviewing a report and presenting innovative ideas for a very important client. Unfortunately, she always ended up tackling the pending work at home late into the night, as other tasks took precedence—dinner prep, cleanup, bath-time, the bedtime ritual, and the ever-present pile of laundry, which never seemed to shrink. She wished she had one of those photographic memories that required that she only scan a page and would remember everything on it. But no, there were forty-five pages of the damn report to read and make notes and recommendations on.

Why is everything so difficult? The voice in her head spoke again.

Unfortunately, the presentation she gave was a disaster. She lost her place, got the figures wrong, and forgot to print handouts of the particularly complex charts. Her performance nearly cost the company their account with a very valuable client.

The owners of the company, Rebecca and John, were family friends and had known Jennifer since she was a toddler. They saw Jennifer grow up, go to college, and eventually find love and marry Brian. They didn't think twice when they got the call from Jennifer's dad asking for a job on her behalf.

Their hearts were broken for her when Brian left and the couple divorced and when her father suffered the stroke. Over time, they saw her productivity and her self-esteem deteriorate, and each time she underperformed, they hoped it was just temporary while she grieved. But that day the grieving ended never came. Jennifer seemed angrier, less focused, more guarded, and unkempt every day. She didn't seem to really care anymore about how she looked or acted.

There had been a few issues at work before, but somehow, she had managed to correct her mistakes and contain the damage. But this time it was seriously impacting the business and other staff members were complaining about her not pulling her weight.

As Jennifer settled at her desk, Victoria, the head of human resources, walked towards her. Jennifer reacted quickly, and before Victoria could speak, Jennifer offered an apology for being late.

Victoria acknowledged Jennifer's apology but still asked her if she could come with her for a quick chat.

When Jennifer arrived at the conference room, Rebecca and John were already sitting there having a conversation. Jennifer, of course, was taken by surprise and knew immediately that this was not just about her lateness.

All of a sudden, she heard *I told you so* from that inner voice.

Victoria closed the door and asked her to please sit down.

John was first to speak. "Jennifer, thank you for coming today. We want to talk about what happened at yesterday's presentation."

Jennifer, sensing the imminent danger, interrupted. "John, Rebecca, I know that the presentation was not my best work. I'm very sorry and I can assure you it won't happen again." She lowered her head, not making eye contact anymore, and played with a pencil on the table. "Lately, there's just been lots on my plate. Things at home have been difficult. Dad is not well. Tommy was sick and Michelle, well, Michelle is becoming more demanding and challenging as she grows. I'm just a little distracted, and I'm really sorry. But please know that I am still very committed to my job and to this company. I really appreciate how much you have supported me over the years. I have tremendous respect for the two of you," she said, looking now at Rebecca and John directly.

"Jennifer, thank you for your kind words," John said. "We feel the same way about you. That is why this is tough for us. This is not the first time you didn't perform, and it is happening more and more. Yesterday's incident was too close for comfort. We almost lost an important client, and I think it is best that we part ways."

Rebecca, who until now had been quietly observing Jennifer, began to speak. "Jennifer, this is not easy for us. We've known you for such a long time, dear, during your highs and lows, and it is very painful to see how the light inside that amazing young woman I met so long ago is dimming and dimming."

Those words hit Jennifer hard. She choked and started crying.

Rebecca offered a box of tissues, and John got up and got her a glass of water. There was silence in the room.

Finally, John spoke again, "Like I said, we know this is difficult. We'll make sure to work with you to make your exit as fair as possible. We will give you some extra time, and this will help you while you find another job."

Jennifer continued to cry quietly. She could no longer control herself, the tears just kept flowing and flowing. As she cried, she was feeling a tightening of her chest, and breathing was difficult. For a brief moment she had seen herself in her mental mirror and despised the image in front of her. She felt lost, lonely, and without options. She felt the weight of her own disappointment and betrayal. The voice inside of her once again reminded her of how low she had sunk and how she had failed herself and her kids.

Rebecca, seeing that Jennifer was speechless and that tears were still flowing down her cheek, attempted to comfort her. "Jennifer, darling, take a deep breath and tell me what is going through your mind?"

Jennifer did just that and began to speak.

"That I know you are right." Jennifer was silent again. "The worst part is that I knew this would happen, and I still let it. It is just so difficult. I can see it, and I'm trying, but I don't know how to get out of it. I'm drowning, and I can't swim, and it is all happening in slow motion. I see it, and I can't do a damn thing about it."

Rebecca and John looked at each other as people who are connected often do, communicating a thousand words without saying one out loud. John then looked back at Jennifer and Victoria and said, "Can you please give us a minute?" and he and Rebecca left the room together. A few minutes later, they returned.

When they sat down, Rebecca spoke. "We have some thoughts, and we want to support you, but really the most important thing we need to ask is what do you want?"

Jennifer replied, "I don't know. I don't want to have to do everything all alone anymore. I want my pain to go away. Everything is so difficult. I want to wake up from this never-ending nightmare I'm in." She vomited the words so rapidly out of her mouth that they were almost indiscernible.

Very calmly, Rebecca replied, "I hear you. I can only imagine how difficult all this has been for you and the kids. I know that you are acutely aware of this, but these situations take time to unravel, and the most important thing is for you to take care of yourself first. It doesn't seem like you have been doing that. So really the only question is what are you going to do *now*?"

Still crying, but acknowledging Rebecca's honest concern, Jennifer answered, "I really don't know. I think I need help."

Rebecca turned to John briefly again before extending her hand and touching Jennifer's. "John and I have a proposition for you, but only you can decide if it is something you want to do."

Jennifer, feeling broken, sad, and without options, said, "Thank you. I'll try anything."

Chapter 21

Watsu

Stephanie didn't know what to expect when she found out that Mary had scheduled her for an individual session with a healer at the Aquatic Center that same day.

When she arrived at the large modern structure with its hundreds of panes of glass reflecting the sunlight like the facets of a giant's ring, Stephanie was met at the door by a broad-shouldered woman with hair cropped on one side to better show a row of earrings, all of them divine symbols. There was a crescent moon, the Greek evil eye, a golden sun, Thor's lightning bolt, a small Christian cross, a Celtic triskele spiral, and, at the very top, in the curve of her ear, a tiny golden serpent.

"Welcome," she said in a friendly and melodious voice. "I'm Aisha, and I will be guiding you on your session."

"It's … it's nice to meet you," Stephanie replied, some apprehension in her voice. "Can I just say that I love your earrings?"

"Ahh, thank you," Aisha said.

"I do have some questions before we begin if you don't mind," Stephanie continued.

"I'm happy to answer them all, but let's do so at the pool's edge. Please follow me." And Aisha opened a nearby door.

Inside, light from the many windows reflected off the water of a large pool in the center of the building.

"Is this where I am having my treatment?" Stephanie asked.

"Oh no, this area is mostly used for recreational activities and exercises. Your treatment will take place in a more private area a few stories below from where we are standing right now." As she said this, Aisha motioned for Stephanie to follow her again down a hidden staircase to one side of the building.

They descended, and as they did, the staircase became a dark tunnel lit only by candles carefully placed in alcoves throughout the corridor. The wall became rougher and Stephanie saw they had changed into carved stone. With a sense of unease, she continued to take in her surroundings, feeling nervous and unsure of what awaited her.

Once they arrived at the end of the tunnel, Stephanie found herself in a most spectacular cave. Candles and torches illuminated the space, and a strong scent of roses was present. In the center of the cavern, there was a natural hot spring from which steam was emanating. The water was crystal clear, and the floor illuminated so that the bottom was visible. It was beautiful and inviting, a testament to the fact that nature was the most talented architect of all.

Stephanie was stunned. "Wow. What a special place," she breathed.

"It is, isn't it? Each time I'm here, I experience its wonder like it was my first time," said Aisha. "Besides its aesthetic beauty, there is also the fact that the waters are thermal and carry a rich mix of nutrients and minerals with healing powers. It is as if we were descending deeper into the womb of Mother Earth."

"That's so beautiful," said Stephanie, "I can feel that." Stephanie and Aisha were the only two people there, and the space was peaceful, only the sound of running water in the background.

As she sat on the pool's edge with Aisha, Stephanie asked her first question.

"So, can you tell me about the session: What is it and what does it entail, besides being in this magical place?"

"Of course," Aisha replied. "We are about to have a Watsu session."

"I don't know what Watsu is," Stephanie confessed.

"Watsu is a form of aquatic bodywork. It combines elements of shiatsu, joint mobilization, muscle stretching, massage, and dance to help the body physically. It can lower blood pressure, release tension, help muscles to heal, and increase flexibility, but it is not only the body that Watsu can heal. It can heal your spirit as well.

"So, it's like doing yoga in the water?" Stephanie asked.

"You will be doing nothing but floating." Aisha answered. "Watsu is a passive program where I will be moving your body for you. The pool is only chest deep and the temperature is ninety-four degrees, so your skin doesn't react to it being too warm or too cold.

"You and I will spend some time before we enter the water looking into each other's eyes so that we may connect more deeply, and I may know, intuitively, what movements will help you in your journey.

"I will support your body the whole time, floating you, stretching your muscles, massaging you, and whatever other movements I intuit are necessary. I will match my breathing to yours and listen as your body speaks to me of its needs. I will not drop you nor will I make any sudden movements or submerge your face. You and I are the only people here, and no one will interrupt us. Our session will last ninety minutes and will be largely silent. Nothing is required of you but to lay back and surrender in my arms."

At the term "surrender," Stephanie flinched just a little, but Aisha noticed the small movement and answered the unspoken question.

"There is nothing sexual about Watsu, though it is intimate. I will touch no parts of your body that are considered "private"—such as your genitals or breasts. Try to relax and trust me and the process. I've done this thousands of times, and while every experience is different, everyone leaves having been transformed in some fashion," Aisha said.

"I recommend you have an intention going into the session. Do you have one?" Aisha asked.

"I don't, actually. Can you suggest something?" answered Stephanie.

"Of course," Aisha replied. "How about 'I let the water, fire, air and Earth—the four elements—which surround me, join with my spirit to cleanse me, removing or transforming any energy that is limiting me.'"

Stephanie said, "I like that. It sounds beautiful and powerful. Thank you."

"You are welcome. Have you any other questions before we begin?"

Stephanie shook her head "no," so Aisha spoke again.

"We begin by looking into each other's eyes, so please turn towards me," Aisha instructed. "As you do, repeat your intention in silence a few times."

Stephanie did so. *I let the water, fire, air, and Earth—the four elements—which surround me, join with my spirit to cleanse me, removing or transforming any energy that is not serving me well.*

The Orchid

As the two women gazed into each other's eyes, Stephanie felt a strong connection between them. Aisha's eyes radiated warmth and wisdom, inviting Stephanie into her innermost being. It was a place of peace, and at that moment, Stephanie somehow knew, Aisha *could* be trusted. She felt sure of it.

Odd, she thought, *that letting down my guard a little is a physical feeling, not just an emotional one.*

For her part, Aisha saw caution and fear in Stephanie's eyes and offered up a prayer to the Great Mother to use her talent as a tool to help her heal.

"Now let's take some deep breaths to relax. Breathe in deeply through your nose, hold it at the top of your breath to the count of four, then blow the air out through your mouth, forcefully enough to make your belly rise." Stephanie did so for several breaths and relaxed a bit.

"I will now put floating rings on your calves. They will keep your legs from going under and throwing off the balance of your body," Aisha added. "Now let's begin," she said once done.

The water, the same temperature as her skin, felt like oil to Stephanie. There was no adjustment needed. Strangely, Stephanie immediately felt as though the water was an old familiar place where she had been before and felt totally at home. She'd never been here, but the sense of déjà vu was strong. *Why is that?* She wondered.

Aisha slowly turned Stephanie so she had Stephanie's back facing her and then pushed her gently down by her now softening shoulders. Then she took Stephanie by the forehead and pulled her softly back, until her head was resting on Aisha's right shoulder. Stephanie's legs stayed on the top of the water out in front of her, buoyed by the floats.

Aisha whispered ever so softly in her ear. "Now close your eyes and let me take control of your body's movements. You just breathe deeply and go wherever the spirit takes you."

At that moment, the two became one with the water and began a harmonious and synchronized dance filled with graceful movements and a profound connection that transcended words.

Aisha's intuitive hands detected the slightest cues, responding with empathy and skill. She moved along the spine, pressing various points and creating a loving energy field from Stephanie's head to the tip of her toes. Through specific touchpoints, gentle stretches, and fluid arcs, Stephanie surrendered to the weightlessness, unwinding with each touch, motion, and embrace. Her body effortlessly glided through the water with the fluidity of a fish's tail, shifting in a gentle back-and-forth motion.

It felt wonderful, unlike anything Stephanie had felt before, and she began to drift away from conscious thought as Aisha continued the rhythm. In this dance of trust and compassion, Stephanie's worries began to dissolve, replaced by a profound sense of peace and healing.

As she surrendered her body and soul to the Watsu process, she began to sense the loosening of the energy trapped in her body. As she went deeper, with each breath matched to Aisha's, Stephanie suddenly realized why the warm pool seemed so familiar. *I am inside my mother's womb*, she thought.

Stephanie had become one with the womb or the Earth or the womb of the Earth. It was too hard to think clearly when every feeling was so exquisite.

At that moment she felt unconditionally loved. It felt as though something was opening within her, a space that hadn't been there before; it was not a space hollowed by starvation or obscured by vomit but a radiant space, the light of which was shining out like a little sun. She knew in an instant that she was still a wanted child, a child of the Creator, made in that energy's image and therefore radiant in her own right. Nothing was missing from her. What had happened to her was behind her now and caused no permanent damage to her soul. Her soul remained spotless and shining and … perfect.

Stephanie was unaware that tears were rolling down her cheeks from behind her closed eyelids, but Aisha was aware and maneuvered Stephanie through a move called "The Rolling Accordion," where she drew both Stephanie's knees towards and away from her chest in coordination with her breath. Next, Aisha added a spiral rotation, allowing Stephanie's head to roll side-to-side.

Stephanie felt like a mermaid's baby, and she began to cry in earnest.

Sensing that it was the appropriate moment to do so, Aisha whispered in Stephanie's ear, asking her to repeat what Aisha said. "I let the pain flow out of me. I let it go and with it all the shame and hurt and guilt I have been harboring. I let it all flow out into the water and out of the sea of my consciousness." Stephanie repeated it word by word, and as she did, she felt that energy leaving the center of her body, like a black-winged crow taking flight.

Stephanie's mind was showing her scenes, as though she were watching a movie about her life—her mother's demands, her father's passive love when she needed his protection as her childhood was taken from her, her mother's insistence on Stephanie becoming a model, Stephanie's own belief she wasn't good enough to love if she wasn't perfect, days spent in front of the mirror hating her own body, many terrible times clutching the toilet after she had pretended to eat, the bitter shame she felt when the bathroom scale had ticked up even an ounce, her time in Paris and the brief feeling that at last she was safe and could step out from her mother's shadow and live a life she chose, the painful and terrifying rape, and her efforts to hide her smoldering secret. Stephanie also saw the tender look in her husband's eyes become one of concern when he asked what the matter was whenever he saw she'd been crying.

She also saw how that look changed when he tried to hide his disappointment that she had gotten no pleasure from making love with him. And then she saw and heard and felt her children's love as they wrapped her up in hugs and told her "Mommy, I love you."

Those last happy memories seemed no match for the unrelenting carousel of dark feelings that Stephanie had carried with her for her whole life. But now, being spiritually washed and enveloped in the total love of the Earth's womb, that carousel began to slow down and finally stopped. The dark images began to waver and become more transparent, dissolving like watercolors in the rain. Just like that. Stephanie probed her mind to find those familiar traumas again, but realized they didn't carry the same weight anymore.

She felt clean, free, and lighter for the first time in a long, long time.

She slowly became aware that Aisha was speaking. She focused on the words.

"Here, there is no past," Aisha said. "Here, in this womb, Stephanie, you are reborn."

And so, she was.

Chapter 22

Breath and Sound

Mary greeted everyone at the door with her palms pressed together at her chest, accompanied by a slight bow. She was excited to hear about the day's results from the women themselves, even though she could intuit much from their facial expressions and the change in energy they were exhibiting. The transformation had begun. The program was having its intended effect on these wonderful women and opening new doorways in their experience.

Even after all these years, Mary was still astonished by the changes the attendees experienced in such a short span of time. *How grateful I am that The Orchid exists,* Mary thought. *All that is needed is a safe space, focused attention anchored in pure love, and the help of committed and capable hands.*

Placed on the floor of the Sanctuary, throughout the room were yoga mats spread out like the petals of a flower. When everyone was inside and seated on the mats, Mary walked to the front of the room to speak. She looked over the women; their candlelit faces were upturned in expectation. A cushion, a leather-wrapped mallet, and seven crystal bowls, arranged in a line, were placed in the center of the platform on which she stood. Peace and love permeated the room.

Mary took a deep, cleansing breath and began speaking, "Welcome, my dears. It's so wonderful to be here with you again tonight." She smiled, making eye contact with each of the women gathered, and each felt as though they had been warmly embraced.

"I trust this day has provided you with a deeper insight into what awareness truly is and the power it holds. It's essential to identify those elements—thoughts, emotions, limitations, fears, and beliefs—that weigh us down and distance us from our genuine loving nature.

"The most important thing in your life right now is to become aware of and release yourself from those heavy and limiting energies. When you do, you will be able to find and see the love and limitless potentiality that lies within you.

"Throughout the day, I'm sure there were many opportunities for each of you to have this introspective look at yourselves. Sometimes those inward looks can be painful. We try to encourage you to look backwards, but don't stare, because your life isn't behind you, it is here, now, in front of you at this very moment.

"It's normal to have moments where you become aware of things you could have done differently, but you should not blame yourself for this or think that you could have made better choices. You didn't know what you didn't know, and you always did the best you could at that time. Therefore, it's important to be compassionate, kind, and loving towards yourself and to forgive yourself. Treat yourself as you would treat a cherished friend in a similar situation."

Mary moved across the room and then began to speak again.

"We are extremely lucky because tonight we will be led in a special breathwork and sound bath meditation. If you haven't experienced one yet, you are in for a treat. The benefits of this type of healing session and technique cannot be overemphasized. It is a most powerful and, dare I say, magical, meditative, and healing experience."

The majority of the women in the group had never done a sound bath meditation but by now realized that each activity they had engaged in had been mostly enjoyable. Even those that made them feel slightly uncomfortable had been eye-opening, so they greeted the activity with open minds.

A ripple of excitement flooded the room, and there was some nervous twittering that died down when Mary introduced Isabelle, a middle-aged woman whose vibrant red hair stood out against her long, snow-white dress. Isabelle wore a large golden chain at the end of which hung the Star of David, which sparkled and cast reflections in the candlelight. Her eyes shone brightly as well, adding to the impression that she was glowing with a special energy.

"Welcome to all of you," Isabelle said in a voice that was sweet but forceful enough to be heard throughout the room. "I am a breathwork healer, which is just what it sounds like. I will teach you techniques to help you heal yourself using your own breath. We will practice the technique and then you will begin to feel yourself vibrate. Yes, *vibrate*. Don't be alarmed when it happens. It is a good thing." Isabelle smiled at the somewhat apprehensive look on some of the women's faces.

"Once your body is in a vibratory mode, I will incorporate the most melodious of sounds from these bowls. The sounds will help you experience one of the most liberating energetic sensations you have ever experienced.

"We are going to start breathing together in a synchronized fashion. We'll do two inhalations, the first with the stomach and the second with the chest. Then, we'll exhale. Stomach, chest, and exhale. Stomach, chest, and exhale," she repeated.

"Like this: Uff, uff, ahhh. Uff, uff, ahhh. Uff, uff, ahhh."

The women copied Isabelle as she repeated the rhythm again and again. Little by little, as each woman caught on, the group began doing it in a synchronized fashion.

"Good, you are all doing so well. Now, during this first part of the session, I will be playing inspirational music. After about twenty minutes, you will feel your body beginning to vibrate. When that happens, you'll be well into your journey. At that time, you will return to normal breathing, and I will accompany you by playing the bowls, which will guide and accentuate your vibration even further."

Isabelle knew how the women were soon to feel, having experienced the magnificent journey so many times that she had lost count herself and, more importantly, having witnessed the powerful force as it manifested itself differently for each individual.

"Are there any questions?" Isabelle asked, and since there were none, she continued with simple preparatory instructions. Each woman present had been provided a blanket, a pillow, a cushion for use under her knees or legs, and soft eye masks. Isabelle invited the women to lie down and make themselves comfortable with the provided accessories. Then, she spoke again.

"Relax, enjoy, and think loving thoughts," she said, smiling. "And now we shall begin.

"Stomach, chest, and exhale. Stomach, chest, and exhale," she repeated.

"Uff, uff, ahhh. Uff, uff, ahhh. Uff, uff, ahhh. All through the mouth. I will advise you when it is time to go back to normal breathing.

"Uff, uff, ahhh. Uff, uff, ahhh. Uff, uff, ahhh."

Soon, the pattern of rhythmic breathing was being followed.

"Remember, only focus on your breathing," Isabelle urged. "It may feel a little awkward now, but that feeling will fade very soon. As you breathe, begin to let go of your body and your thoughts."

Isabelle repeated softly, "Uff, uff, ahhh. Uff, uff, ahhh. Uff, uff, ahhh."

All across the room, the women assumed the rhythm. *It is easier now*, thought Nicole, who realized her breathing had strayed a little from the pattern. Isabelle guided her back to the group's rhythm with gentle words.

"Now your breathing pattern will continue by itself, so place your focus on the music. Hear it, feel it, become one with it, and let go of your thoughts."

Leonard Cohen's "Hallelujah" was followed by John Lennon's "Imagine," which gave way to Louis Armstrong's "What a Wonderful World." Beautiful melodies and stirring lyrics filled the room and the spirits of the women there. One song was a chant, repeating the words "I am" over and over. Another invited the listener's soul to awaken and set itself free. Stephanie, whose own spirit seemed cleansed and fresh from its liberation that very day, was transported by the music and lyrics to a wonderful place and felt as though she were floating.

As the music played, the women's breath became one.

"Uff, uff, ahhh. Uff, uff, ahhh. Uff, uff, ahhh.""

As the women entered the last few minutes of the breathing exercise, something amazing happened. Just as Isabelle had predicted, each of them felt their body begin to vibrate. Some, like Stephanie, felt like they were floating, others as if they were birds flying freely through the sky. A few felt as if they had entered a different realm in which the energy of their body was released and it became one with the music, the room, and everything and everyone in it. They became aware of their oneness with the universe.

Isabelle knew the moment had come and she urged them on enthusiastically, "Let yourself go, and let yourself vibrate, and become the essence of energy that you truly are. Your bodies are merely a vessel transporting the energy that you are feeling inside of you now. It is the energy of your soul."

"Now, allow yourself to go back to your normal breathing and relax," Isabelle summoned them as she began lightly striking the crystal bowls with the leather mallet. Methodically, she continued with a circular motion around the bowls' rims, creating a sustained and soothing sound. The vibrating bodies were now in complete unison with the vibratory waves of the bowls themselves. Their spirits rose even further through space.

For some, visions began appearing behind their closed eyelids. Jennifer was one of those.

She first saw her children. They were sitting with her at the dinner table, laughing as they shared what was happening in their lives now. They were older and living on their own. They seemed happy, confident, and accomplished and were now talking over each other as siblings do. Jennifer paid attention to them both, asking questions about their stories. But, vaguely at first, and then more clearly, Jennifer realized they were not alone. She looked at the normally empty fourth seat at the table and there sat Brian.

He looked as he had looked when they married—happy and with love in his eyes. For *her*. Not like he had looked later, uninterested and bothered. She liked this vision of Brian better.

As she watched, Brian turned back to the children to listen to the story their daughter was telling.

Jennifer spoke to get his attention.

"Brian...." She realized her voice was only a croak, so she cleared her throat and tried again.

"Brian, I am so mad at you. What you did was unforgiveable. You were careless with me and with the kids. You were so selfish. I trusted you, and you let me down. I trusted you, and you broke me. Sometimes it is too much to bear." She choked the words out, tears clogging her throat.

Even in the vision, Jennifer felt a pang of guilt at admitting that she was broken and that the thought of just packing it all in, laying down, and dying had crossed her mind. Then she would feel the wave of guilt that she had thought about leaving her kids. What kind of mother am I?

Brian seemed to read her thoughts.

"You are a great mother, Jen. You've always been. Look at our kids. They are strong, funny and loving, thanks to you. You did such a great job with them. Thank you for standing by them through their lives, for taking on the job of being a great mother, and sometimes even a father, to them. But, most important of all, please forgive me. I was so wrong to do what I did."

The Orchid

At those words, Jennifer felt a pang in her heart that felt like it might cleave in two. Hearing those words from Brian meant the world to her.

She cried and cried, letting out a torrent of emotions that seemed to have no end. But even through her tears, she felt another emotion emerging strongly from within. It was anger, a pure and unadulterated rage that shook her from the depths.

Without opening her eyes, Jennifer suddenly sat up, gasping, as if desperately seeking a respite from the avalanche of feelings.

Immediately, a staff member appeared by her side. As Jennifer removed the eye mask, soaked with tears, the assistant sprayed a eucalyptus-scented mist near her, offered her some tissues, and helped her lie down again.

Isabelle, with her fine-tuned intuition, sensed Jennifer's internal storm. She decided to switch instruments and, with great care, picked up a small harp, making its strings dance in an attempt to reconnect with her. Approaching, she placed the delicate instrument on Jennifer's stomach.

At that moment, the harp's vibrations felt like gentle caresses, like waves coming and going, bringing with them a balm of calm. Jennifer felt how those vibrations wove a comforting cloak around her being, embracing and soothing her emotional turmoil. It was as if the harp, with its resonance, was conversing with her soul, offering her a serene refuge in the midst of the storm.

After some time, Isabelle allowed the last notes to resonate, letting them fade into the air. The room was immersed in an atmosphere of introspection and emotion, marking the end of an event that had touched the depths of the soul.

Subtly, she guided the women: "Breathe calmly and naturally. Awaken your limbs, starting by moving your toes. Then, flex your hands and stretch your body gently. Allow your movements to return gradually, and give your body time to wake up. There's no rush; when you feel ready, slowly transition to a sitting position."

All of them were still recovering, somewhat dazed and still in the thrall of the trance. After about five minutes, they emerged from the deep and profound journey, and all the women sat up. They were quiet and deeply moved by the experience they just had.

Isabelle waited patiently and lovingly until everyone was fully present. She then asked if anyone wanted to share anything about their experience.

Jennifer wasn't sure she had the words to describe what had happened to her so she decided not to share. *That emotion came from a vision, which is a kind of a dream, isn't it? But Brian never sat at the kitchen table asking for forgiveness. It hadn't been real. But it certainly felt that way.* She was so confused. Her thoughts tumbled over one another in her turbulent mind. *What the hell am I supposed to do with that rage? And what am I so mad about? And who am I mad at?*

Stephanie spoke up, surprising her new friends, who knew how closed off she had been and how infrequently she shared anything. "I loved it so much. It was very special. My entire body was really vibrating. I know you had said that was exactly what was going to happen, but since I had never experienced such a thing, I simply couldn't wrap my head around it ... until it happened. And then ... oh my gosh. I was weightless, like a balloon." Stephanie's smile was wide when she finished.

Another woman picked up where Stephanie had left off. "I felt some tears start and I began crying, which I guess was the type of release I needed. All of a sudden, the answer to a question I've been mulling over for quite a while, about if I should end a long-time business partnership, came to me clear as day. Suddenly, I just knew what I needed to do. I'm certain of it and feel released from the weight I've been carrying around about that topic."

A few more women shared their experiences. One said that she had not had any major insights, but that she felt incredibly relaxed. Others said they felt lighter, filled with a kind of inexplicable joy.

When the sharing hit a lull, Isabelle continued to speak. "As with many of the sessions that take place here, a lot of energy has moved here tonight. Of course, every one of you is quite different, so the experience, and therefore the movement of energy, is different for each of you also. It is important that you give yourself the time and the space to allow that energy to channel itself properly through you.

"Our recommendation is that, following the closing of tonight's meditation, you abstain from discussing your experience with anyone else right away. There will be plenty of time to do that once you have been able to digest it. So, please go to your rooms; remain in silence; engage in journaling or free-style writing; take a warm shower or a bath; prepare yourself a nice, relaxing tea; and simply go to sleep. Rest.

"One more thing: please note that tomorrow our theme is 'gratitude.' We all have so much to be thankful for and one of the things for which I am particularly grateful is all of you. Thank you all for being so present today, for your hard work, for your commitment to yourself and to your healing," Isabelle said with a loving smile.

She closed the evening with a beautiful prayer of gratitude:

> Dear Universe,
>
> I am filled with immense gratitude for the wisdom and power that surrounds us. Thank you for our bodies, for music, and for the vibratory energy that we experienced here today. Thank you for the endless opportunities for growth and learning, and for the power of meditation and awareness. And, of course, thank you for the company of these amazing souls. I ask that blessings of love, happiness, strength, abundance, clarity of intention, and ease of issue resolution be with us now and for the times ahead.
>
> So be it.

Part IV
Gratitude

The Orchid

Chapter 23

I Give Thanks

As the first hint of dawn began to tint the sky, the sounds of the Tibetan bell rolled across the lush landscape, announcing the onset of the third day. The bell's call, already a familiar part of the morning, echoed amidst the equally familiar melody spun by the avian chorus serenading the air. The guests, having spent two days attuning themselves to this serene place, felt the soothing invitation to wake and entertain the promises of a new day of discovery and enlightenment.

In each room, the women began their morning rituals. Some had experienced a restful sleep but were still feeling exhausted. This was normal, for though they had not performed any strenuous physical activities, they had been taking in, consciously and subconsciously, lots of information and had performed exercises that had begun to shift the energy within them. Becoming aware, it seemed, was a physically, mentally, and spiritually demanding task.

Despite that, their experiences in the program had gotten easier and seemed more natural as the days passed. The fact that they were clearer on what to expect, and what was expected of them, helped tremendously. The staff, teachers, and healers were exceptional people who inspired trust. All the guests knew they were in good hands. Even mistrustful Sofia felt the sincerity of everyone she'd met since her arrival. No one seemed to have any agenda but to help people with open hearts and loving hands. *They must be well paid to give such service*, Sofia thought, used to contractors and employees who did as little as they could get away with on any job. *I wonder how I can get my people to work like that?* Making a mental note to pay special attention to Mary and her staff, Sofia finished splashing water on her face and headed for the door.

Stephanie practically ran out the door, for once barely running a brush through her hair first. *It doesn't matter what I look like,* she thought. *No perfection is required of me to get love from these people.* She felt a chuckle bubbling up in her.

Nicole took longer to get out of bed. She wanted to continue to hide under the covers and sleep. Usually, she slept like the dead, rarely troubled by the doubt that haunted her waking hours. Nicole could feel things shifting inside of her, something coming to a head like an infected blemish that needed lancing. She would need to make a decision about Elena and soon. She knew that, but for just one more day, she could still hide from that decision. She pulled the covers up closer under her chin and listened to the waterfall splashing outside of her room. *I'll get up in a few minutes, just a few minutes more.*

Olivia had already completed her morning prayers and began to get ready for the day. *Gratitude is the theme, eh?* she thought to herself. Olivia wouldn't have much problem with that topic. She knew her life held many reasons to be grateful. Her real challenge was slowing down long enough to count her blessings.

Jennifer was still confused when she woke up. A residual bitter taste was in her mouth from that rage she felt in her vision yesterday. It was like she had been swallowing ashes all night. She scrubbed her teeth and tongue even more thoroughly than usual and wondered why she still felt that wild anger, simmering now but definitely still on the stove of her soul. Looking in the mirror, she said out loud, "What is happening to you, girl? Pull yourself together." But, as she turned from the sink, she still felt unbalanced, off-center, a little unsteady. *Weird,* she thought, *maybe I am coming down with something.*

She hoped the feeling would fade during the day. She didn't like it. *Maybe a good breakfast would help,* she thought, and headed out the door.

There was a slight chill in the air, courtesy of the disappearing night, coupled with a faint early morning mist and a touch of drizzle that gently moistened the path. Despite this, the awakening sun, rising over the horizon, promised a mild day. Lining the trail up to the now-familiar circular building at the summit, were signs inscribed with affirmations and uplifting messages:

> This is a wonderful day. I have never seen this one before!
> — Maya Angelou

> If the only prayer you said was thank you, that would be enough.
> —Meister Eckhart

> When eating fruit, remember the one who planted the tree.
> —Vietnamese proverb

Nicole stopped, allowing the rain to speckle the pages of her journal as she jotted down the affirmations. Perhaps these words might offer her some guidance.

Mary and a few of the healers were already at the Meditation Center, waiting to greet the women as they arrived at the door. Once all found their place, this time arranged in a "u" formation, Mary began to address them. Her voice, smile, and face were as luminous as ever.

"Good morning, my dearests. It is such a blessing for me to welcome you to day three. Thank you for being here on this joyous day. Thank you for giving yourself the blessing of your conscious effort. Thank you for being you and for allowing me the opportunity to share some insights with you this morning.

"Yesterday, we learned about the concept of self-awareness, essential in order to begin a process of personal growth and transformation. Being aware is about stepping outside of ourselves and viewing our actions as if we were watching our life play out on stage. Often, we're very quick to observe others but forget to look within. When we are aware, and observe ourselves with empathy, we can assess if what we observe coincides with the person we aspire to be.

"This self-reflection is intimate and deeply personal, and any decision is entirely up to you. By becoming aware of yourself, you harness the power to act by modifying or eliminating anything that does not align with the life you want to live.

"I want to emphasize that, in this context, I do not suggest labeling anything as 'negative'. Labels such as 'positive' or 'negative' and 'good' or 'bad' are judgments we impose on ourselves and our actions. I invite you to consider that, in essence, there are no inherently bad or good acts. Every experience contributes to our spiritual growth. Just as a teacher wouldn't mark a student's effort as a failure, or a mother wouldn't reproach her daughter for trying and not achieving something, we shouldn't judge or label ourselves. Each experience is a valuable lesson that nourishes our spiritual journey."

Mary fell silent, aware that her audience was being introspective and processing her words. She knew the women were ready for the next lesson.

"One of the most useful tools in our spiritual toolbox is that of being able to shift or lift heavy energy off ourselves," she continued. "It is crucial to let go of that which does not serve us well and, instead, allow pure loving energy to surge through us in its place. One of the most powerful tools we can use to generate that change is gratitude. By achieving and staying in a state of gratefulness, we can permanently shift the energy within us. Therefore, today, all day, we will direct our focus to gratitude."

There were some puzzled looks, including from Sofia, who thought what Mary had said sounded like a lot of New Age hooey. Nicole was frantically scribbling, trying to get down on paper every one of Mary's exact words. Stephanie, Olivia, and Jennifer sat avidly listening.

"It may surprise some of you to hear that the word 'gratitude,' which is a noun, in this case being used as a verb. We are using gratitude as an action word, and that is a preeminent spiritual teaching. Being grateful is one of the most powerful things you can do to change your life. It is a tool that can break the shackles that chain you and hold you back from happiness and contentment. Nothing can stand against it.

"Think back to yesterday's talk about vibrational energies and the levels of inner growth. What if I told you that gratitude is not just one of the stages of learning, it is also one of the express elevators you can take to reach the higher levels?

Mary stopped again to allow her words to sink in.

Then she continued, "A growing number of scientific studies report improved physical, mental, and emotional health, as well as improved social experiences and relationships, by those who practice gratitude daily. In this instance, science is just catching up with what folk wisdom has known for thousands of years.

"A grateful person lives in a mindset of abundance. When you are grateful, you see the world through different eyes. A grateful heart is never distracted by shortcomings or challenges but rather notices the beauty and the magnificence in all that she sees and experiences. You note the most delicate flower growing in the most inhospitable of places and you are grateful to the universe for its perseverance.

"When you are grateful, you raise the vibrational energy of your life. It is then that you connect yourself to the type of energy that powers greatness.

"And what should we be grateful for? Anything and everything.

"Start with things that come easily. At first, don't try feeling gratitude for those things still filled with hurt and pain for you. As you advance in your journey, I promise you, those, too, will yield to the power of gratitude.

"Begin being grateful for the beautiful gift of a new day, for breathing and being alive, for your amazing children, for the infinite love that you receive from your pets, for trees, for water, for the lessons you've learned along this journey.

"You can be grateful for being here and for being given an opportunity to look within and make changes that will serve to improve the life you are living.

"You can also be grateful for the absolute miracle that is your body. There are many things to be grateful for about your bodies: your blood, for example, and the job it performs of taking nutrients to every single cell of your fantastic organism or your kidneys and their job of cleansing your system of toxins. There are also 206 or so bones and 650 or so muscles in your adult body that hold all of it together and allow you to move. You can also be grateful for your eyes, your nose, your legs, and your arms.

"If you are truly stuck and cannot call things to mind for which you are grateful, recite the alphabet and name one thing for each letter. 'A' for air, 'B' for the ability to breathe it, 'C' for clouds or cats or candy, 'D' for dogs or dill pickles or the dirt of your garden. Continue on from there. Once you get rolling, you'll realize there are many blessings to list.

"Sometimes you will think that there are things that are not sufficiently important for an act of gratitude. It is at those moments that I always remember the words, 'I cried because I had no shoes, then I met a man who had no feet.'

"As you express gratitude, you will find yourself tapping into a force that elevates your vibration and, with it, creates all sorts of possibilities—for peace, for joy, and for self-love.

"Ok, my dears, now let us put this to practice. I would like to invite all of you to take a moment to go deep within yourselves. Dedicate this time to identify and give thanks. Don't think about it too much; in fact, I would say, don't think about it at all. Release yourself and simply begin giving thanks about anything and everything. Allow yourself to see this as a moving walkway that you are stepping onto and one on which all you have to do is be grateful for all that comes to mind.

"Begin with 'I give thanks for...,' and simply fill in the blank. I give thanks for my life. I give thanks for being here at The Orchid. I give thanks for these wonderful people around me. I give thanks for the rain. I give thanks for the time to look within. I give thanks for the lessons I've learned and am learning."

Feeling that the women now had a good basic understanding of the power of gratitude, Mary asked them to bring out their journals and spend the next twenty minutes writing statements of gratitude in them.

Olivia, who started every day with morning prayers, many of them giving thanks, found the exercise easy but vowed to herself to dig more deeply and think of other, overlooked things in her life for which she could also be grateful.

Stephanie realized she had much to be grateful for with the powerful awakenings of yesterday, including her unexpected meeting with Mary, opening up about her eating disorder for the first time, and her rebirth in the Watsu session. It was as though a veil had been lifted from her eyes and she now saw more clearly that, having been so submerged in her shame and self-blame, she had never truly appreciated her patient husband and loving children. Stephanie wrote about the tenderness and gratitude she felt for them.

For Nicole, Elena and Sister Consuelo were at the center of her world and were the recipients of her gratitude. "I give thanks for having Elena in my life, and for the love and support I receive from Sister Consuelo," she began writing. She then smiled when she thought of the students she taught, whose lives she touched and who enriched hers every day. She penned words of gratitude towards them too. She also gave thanks for her strong body but wished she could be grateful for an equally strong spirit. Nicole wished she were brave, but it was more of a desperate prayer than an acknowledgment of a missing personal trait. *But I am working on it*, she consoled herself.

Sofia seemed to have the most difficult time of all. Her life experience had forced her to be self-sufficient and she was therefore unaccustomed to giving thanks to anybody, especially some invisible creator or universe or whatever. She supposed she could pat herself on the back, but she knew that wasn't what was being asked of her. So she began, directing her writing to things for which she was grateful: "Thank you for my strength and dedication. Thank you for my business acumen. Thank you for my properties and bank accounts. Thanks for my brains and hard work. Thank you to my fam...." *Why would I thank any of them? They were aggressive, unloving, selfish, and made my life a living hell....* Then she stopped herself again. *Hold on, Sofia. Mary and the others at this place are trying to give you tools to use to tap into some greater energy. That is supposed to give you even more power to get what you want and make even your bigger dreams come true. What do you have to lose? Give it a shot.* And then she heard a voice in her head that sounded a lot like her own, but which she did not fully recognize. The voice said, *Stop being such a wise-ass and know-it-all and pay attention!*

Taken a little aback by the rudeness, Sofia barked out a laugh and said out loud, "All right already. I will."

Across the room, Jennifer was also having some difficulty. Giving thanks was not something she was accustomed to. In fact, it had been the opposite since Brian had left. She realized at that moment that she had stopped being thankful for what she did have, especially her children. A strong sensation of guilt for having neglected them, and even neglecting herself, was building in her. She started writing, "I give thanks ..." and filling in the blanks as Mary had suggested. "I give thanks for my life. I give thanks for health. I give thanks for Tommy and Michelle. I give thanks for my mom and dad. I give thanks for my job and for my bosses who insisted I come here. And then she tried to give thanks for her ex-husband and her marriage, but something stopped her train of thought as surely as if a boulder were dropped in her path. She felt anger rising up in her again! Pure rage. What was going on?

Mary allowed them enough time to themselves and then claimed their attention again.

"As with anything else, gratitude takes practice. And practice you will get, because being thankful and showing gratitude is something we encourage you to do daily. Eventually, it will become second nature, and you will do so constantly, during every moment of your existence.

"In this process of introspection, it is important for you to go within, and it is equally important to share externally whatever you identify. For that reason, I would like to create the space for any of you who would like to share any thoughts or experience from this exercise to come forward."

Mary became silent and waited for anyone to speak.

Olivia was the first to raise her hand. "Mary, since we are giving thanks, I just want to say thank you again, to you and everyone here, for your hospitality, your dedication, and your teachings. It's only been two days but I already feel different. The work that you do and the space that you hold here for us to learn and grow is very special. Thank you."

"That's very kind of you, Olivia. Thank you also," Mary said, closing her eyes slightly in a sign of heartfelt gratitude and humility. Then she asked, "Did you write anything in particular you want to share?"

"Oh, yes, um, thank you, Mary," Olivia responded, self-conscious now that her use of general flattery hadn't deflected Mary's attention from the more personal soul-searching Olivia had been asked to engage in before writing. Olivia felt hesitant to share now that she had begun to be aware that she had been superficial in her journaling, but she read what she had written, vowing to herself to dig deeper the next time. "I'm thankful for my personal journey, my career, my spiritual connection, and the opportunity to be here."

"Thank you, Olivia," Mary replied.

Sofia was next to raise her hand. "I had something weird happen to me. I began to thank everything as you suggested, and at some point, I almost thanked some people who caused me a lot of pain and trouble, and, seeing the ridiculousness of that, I stopped myself. It felt strange."

"What felt strange?" Mary asked.

"That I would want to thank them," Sofia said with some deep furrows appearing on her forehead.

"Thank you, Sofia, for sharing so honestly." Mary smiled at her with a slight bow, as though acknowledging Sofia as something of a star pupil for having handled such a thorny situation.

Sofia, encouraged by the unspoken praise, was a little surprised that she felt pleased at having earned Mary's accolade.

"Earlier, I mentioned that at some point, as you advance through your journey, painful and disturbing experiences would also yield to the power of gratitude. I believe that's what you experienced, Sofia. Something inside of you, perhaps your higher self, is pressing you to examine your past differently and see the enormous benefits that it has brought in your life. When you do that, there is nothing left to do but to give thanks. In your case, it seems you are not ready just yet, which is why you stopped yourself. That, my dear Sofia, is a sign that you are on the right path. I encourage you to go deeper within and explore that a bit more. Find some time to write and journal on the matter. Does that make sense?"

Sofia answered, "Yes," though it didn't.

For her part, Olivia felt Mary was speaking to her too when she said, "go deeper within." Mary looked around to see who else was ready to share.

Jennifer raised her hand. "I don't know how to explain it, but as I gave thanks, for a brief moment, I began to feel a little differently than I've been feeling for a long time. I realized I had been living with something like a weight on my chest, keeping me from taking a deep breath."

Mary, silently applauding, said, "That's fantastic, Jennifer. If you are comfortable sharing, please tell us, what was your experience yesterday while reviewing The Spectrum of Inner Growth?"

"I'm ok sharing it," Jennifer replied. "I found myself disappointed for having been in such a dark place, living in fear and loneliness, for such a long time."

"Thank you," said Mary, giving a slight nod to Jennifer before addressing the rest of the group. "I'd like for all of you to reflect on this. Yesterday, Jennifer was burdened by a long-standing despair. However, after just two days of exercises, introspection, writing, and expressing gratitude, that sensation has begun to shift, and she has recognized that this distress is a lingering burden she can release. This is truly remarkable, and it's just the beginning! Imagine what you can achieve with more time, practice, and dedication.

Jennifer had enjoyed Mary being pleased with her progress, but decided to shut her mouth about what else she had felt during the exercise. That unexpected anger thing kept coming up and confused her, but Jennifer knew it wasn't a good feeling. She'd keep that other feeling to herself and hoped it would just go away.

A woman named Claudia raised her hand. Mary acknowledged her.

"How do I know if this is working? I went through the motions, but I don't have any 'aha' moments to share. If nothing is happening for me, how do I know that I am doing it right?" Claudia pressed her lips together in frustration.

"What a fantastic question, Claudia. Thank you for having the courage to ask what others are probably thinking," Mary pointed out.

"This work of changing from within is at times lonely, difficult, and might even seem fruitless. You may find yourself feeling and seeing nothing. It will test you, and it will sometimes require that you are resolute to continue it. Do continue, though, because at the end of the tunnel, something great awaits you. Getting through that tunnel requires trust, faith, perseverance, and a suspension of judgement. Everyone is different. Some grow faster, some are late bloomers, but I promise you, at the end, you'll all get there. It is like filling a glass with water. If you are using a large pitcher, the glass will be filled quickly. If you fill the glass with an eye dropper, it will take longer, but you will eventually accomplish the same end. There are benefits to both methods. You needn't to judge which is more effective. Simply trust yourself and allow the moment and experience to continue."

After a few more shares and some additional questions, Mary asked the group to stand. Then, placing her hands in front of her heart, a symbol of gratitude, she offered a closing blessing.

> Oh, Great Universe,
>
> We are grateful for the many blessings we've received and for the countless more that have yet to reveal themselves. Through the days of this week, the months of this year, and the years of our lives, may we be continuously mindful of the beauty and abundance that surround us.
>
> Let the power of gratitude illuminate the path before us, brightening even our darkest moments with the light of thankfulness. Let its warmth become a signal, guiding us toward our shared path of growth, compassion, and inner peace.
>
> So be it.

Mary then addressed them again, "Thank you my sisters. What a pleasure it is when we share this amazing journey with each other."

She then glanced out the window to confirm that the drizzle had ceased. The faint rays of the sun had begun piercing the dissipating clouds, their warm glow promising a brighter day ahead.

"I encourage you all now to find a quiet place anywhere in the property and continue writing in your journal about gratitude, your experience this morning, and anything else that may come forth. Whether you felt something or nothing at all, both experiences are worth noting and writing about. I promise you they all contribute towards advancing you along the path of your transformation."

And, with that, Mary placed her joined hands on her forehead and said, "Namaste."

I Give Thanks

I'm grateful for

The Orchid

I'm grateful for

Chapter 24

The Energy in our Body

Tucked deep within the property and encircled by the embrace of the forest stood Heaven, The Orchid's spa facilities. As the path led her towards this retreat-within-a-retreat, Olivia congratulated herself for having carved out this time for herself and felt committed to the personal growth she envisaged unfolding.

The entrance to Heaven was adorned with a stone fountain, serving as a precursor to the calming interior. Inside, the space was flooded with natural light streaming through floor-to-ceiling windows offering uninterrupted views of the tranquil forest canopy. Plush seating beckoned visitors to relax and unwind, while rustic wooden accents and earth-toned décor beautifully echoed the sensation of being immersed in nature.

A petite woman was waiting at the door. "Hi Olivia, welcome to Heaven," she said, her voice dancing through the air, laced with the melodious cadence of an Indian accent.

Olivia chuckled a little. "I always knew I was an angel," she joked. "Thank you," she added. "Nice to meet you. How are you?"

"I'm great, thank you. Very happy to have you here. My name is Rani and I will guide you through your journey today," she said, her words exuding a gentle kindness.

"Please follow me." Rani steered Olivia towards a darkened room. It was lit only by glowing pink salt lamps. The sound of soft voices chanting "Om" was interspersed with bells chiming, played from an unseen source. The scent of sandalwood incense, the resin used for calming and clearing the mind, subtly perfumed the air.

"Would you like some water or perhaps a hot tea?" Rani offered.

The Orchid

"No, I'm alright. Thank you," said Olivia.

"Very well. In that case, let's begin. Today we have scheduled you for an energy-releasing, full-body massage. The session will last ninety to one-hundred-twenty minutes. You will guide me regarding the strength of my moves as well as the areas that you think require special focus.

"Unlike more traditional massages, I am connecting not only with your physical body but also your energetic field. By doing so, I can *channel* insights about you and what may be holding you back. Those insights may guide me to share certain things, many of which I don't necessarily remember after the session is done. They may also lead me to suggest a different approach to the bodywork or change focus. If that happens, I will ask you for your permission to make that adjustment for your highest good. You shall always be the one to decide whether we continue and how we do so.

"I would like to invite you to set an intention for your session focused on gratitude."

Rani stopped speaking and looked intently at Olivia. "Do you have any questions?"

"I have questions, but something tells me that I should relax and ask as I go. Is that all right?" Olivia asked.

"Yes, of course. We'll take it slowly and remain connected so that I am able to address any questions, discomfort, or concerns as we proceed," answered Rani.

"And here I was thinking that it was going to be one of those relaxing and uneventful massages," Olivia added, laughing.

"We would not be the place we aim to be if that was the case, my love," Rani said with a smile.

"Actually, one question did occur to me," Olivia interjected. "You used the phrase, 'for your highest good.' What does that mean exactly?"

Rani answered, "That's a great question. It means that we recognize that in our limited human capacity, we do not have the wisdom the universe has in knowing what is best for us. By adding that phrase, we ask it to guide us and lead us to do only that which it knows to be best. It is a great phrase or choice of words to include in any intention or meditation."

Rani paused again and then asked, "Any other questions?"

"No. Let's do this," Olivia said, excited to try something outside of her comfort zone.

"I will step out of the room while you undress. There are hooks for your clothing and a chair for your convenience. When you are ready, please lay face down on the table and cover yourself with the blanket. I will return in a moment." Rani then stepped out of the room and closed the door.

Olivia undressed and none-too-gracefully got up on the table face down and covered herself. A slight knock let her know Rani wanted to enter. "Are you ready?" Rani asked, through the door.

"Yes," replied Olivia.

Rani came into the room, adjusted a small foam triangle under Olivia's ankles, and floated her hands up and down her entire body, not touching but rather scanning it.

"Did you set an intention, Olivia?" Rani asked.

"Yes," Olivia replied, "to experience gratitude at a deeper level and let go of anything that is not for my highest good."

"You are a quick learner, dear," said Rani. "That intention encompasses a lot of wisdom. Mine is to be of service to you for the next couple of hours as you pursue your intention."

Throughout this exchange, Rani had continued to scan Olivia's body. "I am now passing my hands and connecting with your chakras. Do you know what chakras are?" she asked.

"Only somewhat," Olivia confessed.

"Would you like me to give you a quick summary?" asked Rani.

"Please," answered Olivia.

"Very well. In ancient spiritual traditions, particularly within Hinduism and certain branches of Buddhism, chakras represent integral energy centers. The word 'chakra' is derived from Sanskrit and translates to 'wheel.' They are essentially the centers of energy and emotions located at points along our body. I will speak to you about the seven main ones as per my Hindu tradition.

"The root chakra is the first," she continued, softly touching the base of Olivia's spine. "Situated in the tailbone area, it acts as our foundation, anchoring us to Earth. Its association with safety and stability makes it crucial. When imbalanced, it can incite feelings of fear and anxiety."

Moving her hand gently to Olivia's lower back, Rani continued, "The second, the sacral chakra, is here, about three inches below the navel. It represents our creative and sexual energies and imbalances manifest as repressed creativity or sexual dysfunction.

"The third is near the upper abdomen, right below the chest, and it is called the solar plexus. It plays a vital role in our sense of responsibility, willpower, and self-esteem. Imbalances can result in manipulative behaviors, misuse of power, or a lack of confidence."

Rani then placed her small open palm between Olivia's shoulder blades, "The heart chakra, the fourth one, rests here, around the chest area. It is intrinsically linked with love, kindness, empathy, and relationships. Unbalanced, it can lead to troubled relationships, an inability to heal emotionally, and a lack of compassion."

Moving her hand upwards, she reached Olivia's neck. "The throat chakra is the fifth. It governs communication and expression. If unbalanced, it can cause extremes of shyness or arrogance.

"The sixth chakra, the third eye, is between our eyebrows. It is the center of intuition, inner wisdom, and foresight. Imbalances can lead to a lack of direction, purpose, and clarity."

Finally, Rani moved her hand to the top of Olivia's head. "The seventh and last chakra is the crown chakra. It connects us to the divine and opens the doorway to higher consciousness, similar to how the root chakra connects us to the Earth.

"All the chakras, whether they are balanced or unbalanced, act as indicators of where you find yourself at the present moment, like a snapshot in time. Their condition is neither good nor bad. They just serve as a gauge. Having that information can give you guidance and insight on how best to address something misaligned. If you know that a particular chakra is not balanced, then you can be intentional about addressing such imbalance.

"As I have been speaking, I've been sensing and connecting with each of your chakras. I noticed that your fifth chakra, your throat, is a source of strength for you. Expressing yourself is not at all challenging, I see," Rani chuckled. "I can sense you use it to compensate for other areas in your life where you are not so confident.

"For example, I sense an imbalance in your root and heart chakras.

"Now, with this information, I have a deeper understanding of your energy and how I may be of service." As Rani spoke, she began to massage Olivia's body. Her touch was slow, firm, and deep.

This is no relaxation massage, Olivia thought. But it felt good and exactly what her body, and perhaps her soul, needed. With each stroke, Rani skillfully isolated the muscles that needed attention and was able to work them individually. Though small, she was strong and effective in her technique.

"My work is at both the muscular and energetic level. We store all sorts of energy in our body. More often than not, it's heavy energy and it tends to be about our early childhood and about our experiences with our mothers and fathers, though not always. Some people even carry the heavy energy of their ancestors."

Rani continued with longer passes of her hand from the top of Olivia's back all the way down to her calves. With each stroke, she massaged deeply, almost as if she were removing layers of unneeded material, as she created a transformative energy flow.

"Ouch," Olivia moaned. "That hurt."

"I'm sorry. You have some stored energies here, and they are proving a bit harder to remove." Rani continued massaging.

"I sense it is the result of a difficult time in your life," she paused.

Olivia noticed that Rani's voice had changed slightly. It was huskier, deeper, and slower in cadence than her earlier voice. *This must be what she meant by being a channel,* thought Olivia. *She sounds like a different person.*

"Between the ages of ten and thirteen years old was a traumatic time for you, and it involved your father." Rani fell silent for a few long seconds. "He was an aggressive man. Both with you and your mother. And that caused you a lot of pain."

Rani's words resonated within Olivia like a direct message from the universe, striking a hidden and deep wound. The outside world seemed to fade as she grappled with the internal maelstrom of feelings and emotions. That introspection felt eternal, as if each second stretched out, allowing her to process the deluge that had overwhelmed her.

Olivia was floored by the fact that Rani knew these things just by laying her hands on her body. Surely, she had researched Olivia's life and found out things about her. But even if that were true, what Rani was talking about was not public information. Her father's mistreatment of her mom and herself was not something many people knew about. The revelation was so shocking that she struggled to find her voice.

"How do you know these things?" Olivia demanded.

"We are all energy, and once we respectfully tune into that energy, the secrets of the universe are unveiled to us, my dear. It defies logical explanation. In essence, I've connected to you with an intention of providing healing, and as I do, I become a channel for the universe. When that happens, I am gifted with energy, information, visions, and feelings about you on all levels. The energy flows, and I simply become a conduit."

Olivia, a bit more composed, noticed that Rani's voice had returned to her previous lilting tone.

"Is there anything you want to share, Olivia? This is a safe space and you are in loving hands," Rani assured her as she continued to press different trigger points on Olivia's body.

"The situation with my father is something I've never spoken about, or at least not for a long, long time," Olivia said. "It was a source of a lot of pain, and the only way I knew to deal with it was to never speak of it again. I'm not sure that I'm ready to speak about it now either."

"I understand," said Rani. "Just know that that energy is with you. To heal, to truly leave that trauma behind, you must come face-to-face with it and make a conscious choice to remove it, to let it go from within you. The only person that can do that is you. You've already selected a powerful intention, continue to recite it as often as possible, commit yourself to the program, and then allow the transformation to take its course."

"Thank you, your words have given me a lot to think about," Olivia replied. "I'll reflect on them and on everything you've told me." Olivia meant those words.

She was still a bit shaken by Rani's uncanny ability and slightly unsure she was ready to come face-to-face with her trauma, but she would think about it seriously. Even that one small decision seemed to lift some of the weight from her shoulders. Olivia thought, *Maybe just pushing the pain down hadn't been the best idea, though it had seemed so at the time.*

Rani held up a blanket and averted her gaze so Olivia could turn over unobserved. She then worked on Olivia's neck, shoulders, and pectoral muscles. When the massage ended, Rani told Olivia she could get dressed and met her in the hallway when she had done so.

"We moved much energy around today, Olivia. I recommend you rest and recharge to allow your body and spirit to assimilate. Please drink lots of water and be mindful of your thoughts. You needn't fix everything in a day and the world really isn't on just your shoulders. We are all here to help. All you need do is ask."

"Namaste," Rani said and bowed slightly.

Olivia felt no self-consciousness when she bowed in return, saying, "Namaste and thank you."

She left the spa and walked somewhat aimlessly, lost in thought about what Rani had uncovered about her past. Her emotions roiling, Olivia didn't realize where she was walking until she found herself in a large vegetable garden.

She wasn't alone.

The Orchid

Chapter 25

Letting Go

Two figures were kneeling over a patch of spinach, examining the leaves, and talking quietly. A large straw hat obscured one of the women's faces, but the other, her own head wrapped in a bandana, was explaining that the lettuce was beginning to bolt as the days grew warmer, and that she had plans to expand the crop next spring.

"In the meantime, we will backfill this bed with organic compost, created from the kitchen's scraps, and then let it rest. We will concentrate on the warmer weather crops like the heirloom tomatoes in this bed over here," she gestured to a large plot of dirt to her left.

"We've already begun to add eggshells to the soil. Tomatoes, eggplants, and peppers love the calcium carbonate the shells produce. It helps them grow strong roots. It's like how seaweed is the potatoes' favorite soil dressing. I mound it over them as ground cover and they are delighted."

"Lucia, you and your team have done wonders with this garden, "the woman in the hat said. "Do you remember when this was just a barren patch of dirt, strewn with rocks and brush? I must admit, at the time I doubted we'd ever get all the land under cultivation, healthy, and ready for the plants and humans to co-exist."

Olivia then realized Mary was the figure in the hat and, not wanting to interrupt, waited for her to finish.

"And animals," Mary said. "We can't forget the animals."

Lucia laughed. "The bunnies will never be forgotten. We had to plant double the crops to satisfy the needs of our kitchen *and* the needs of the bunnies' stomachs. Early in the morning, I practically have to elbow them out of the way to get to the lettuce.

Mary joined in her laughter and then said, "I think it is wonderful what we are doing here. By not resorting to pesticides or chemical fertilizers, we have looked after the health of the people and all the wildlife, too. I think there are more birds here than even last year, and just a few days ago, I saw an eagle resting on a tree. It was beautiful."

"Yes, it is. We have restored the ecosystem to a very healthy balance. First the soil gets richer, then the plants are healthier, and, eventually, the animals return and everything thrives. We can always do more, but really at some point our job is to step back and let Mother Nature take its course."

"I am thrilled to see it. Really, thank you so much for all your work, Lucia." Mary said.

"You are welcome, Mary. I am delighted that I was able to help. It's a wondrous thing to be a part of."

"It is indeed. Well, I will see you later," Mary said, standing and brushing off her knees. "I hope you have a fabulous day." And, as she walked away from Lucia, Mary noticed Olivia.

"Oh, hello, Olivia," Mary said. "I didn't see you there. How are you today?"

"I'm sorry. I didn't mean to intrude," Olivia began and then answered truthfully, "I was sort of wandering around aimlessly trying to digest a few things when I found myself here."

"Don't worry. Your aimless walk isn't aimless and our encounter is not accidental. You needed someone, apparently me, specifically, and so you guided yourself here." Mary paused and extended her arm to Olivia. "Come walk with me. I have nowhere to go for a bit, and I would enjoy your company," Mary said.

Olivia grabbed on and couldn't help but appreciate how easily accessible Mary always was. They walked together as two old friends would, and as they did, Mary shared with her some of her favorite spots in the vegetable garden, like the rows of carrots, planted in lines as straight as soldiers' regiments. Olivia saw some holes in the lines, and Mary, anticipating her question, said, "Bunnies. They love digging up the carrots."

"Shouldn't there be a fence to keep them out?" Olivia asked.

"A fence might keep the rabbits out," Mary said, "but the voles would tunnel underneath it and snatch the carrots anyway. We don't want to be at war with Mother Nature but rather coexist with her and achieve, as in all things, a balance. Besides, there is enough to go around if we are good stewards of our land and the planet itself. The Earth is our home, but it is also home to the voles and rabbits. We must learn to share."

Olivia was moved by Mary's words. "That's a beautiful thought," she said.

"We humans have been taught that there isn't enough for everyone, that in order for some of us to have, others must do without. It's a '*me first*,' and too often a '*me only*,' attitude that leads us to act and behave in cynical and selfish ways. But it is changing and all of us can help that change along by being aware that we are not alone in the world. I have faith that the delicate balance can and will be restored."

Mary paused for a few moments and then spoke again. "So, Olivia, I sense some disturbance in your balance. Plus, you look a little troubled. What is on your mind?"

"To be honest, I'm not entirely sure," Olivia answered. "I was getting a massage with Rani and a few things, well, really, one main thing, came up. It was spot on, but it brought up some painful memories."

"Rani's massages will do that to you. She has a way of connecting with your energy and bringing forth that which is for your highest good." Mary smiled sympathetically and said, "Would you care to share what upset you so?"

"Well, I'm still processing it, but there is a lot of pain associated with it, and I had buried it deep within me for a long, long time." Tears began falling down Olivia's cheeks.

"May I ask you some questions?" Mary asked gently.

"Yes, of course."

"Is the source of the discomfort and pain clear to you?" Mary asked.

"Yes, it is," Olivia answered.

Mary inquired, "Are you ready to let go of it?"

"I want to, but I don't know how," Olivia answered.

"This may help you, as it did me when it was first explained to me," Mary began. "There is a difference in *wanting* something and *doing* something. I can *want* happiness, but if I am not careful in my intentions and choices, then all I ever will occupy is a space of *wanting* and *longing*, not *doing*.

"It's the same when you try to let something go. Saying 'I want to let it go,'

The Orchid

'I am letting it go,' or even 'I've let it go' are distinct in meaning. By making a conscious decision, you choose and act, and that's when you drive the change that propels you forward.

"So much of what we are and who we are is simply us deciding to be so. There is a very famous quote from Henry Ford that I love. The quote is, 'If you think you can, or if you think you can't, either way, you are right.'

"You see, you become what you *think* you are. It is not just that thoughts *guide* our decisions or our actions, it is that they *become* the reality that we live. You've understood this for some aspects—the professional aspects—of your life. But it is true for everything in our lives—love, health, happiness, peace."

The sincerity and depth of feeling in Mary's words was palpable.

All of what Mary said resonated with Olivia. She *was* ready to let go. She had hidden these tortuous emotions for far too long and they were no longer serving her. She believed this strongly. But…. There it is. There is always a 'but,' she thought, *that something got in the way and held me back*.

What is it? What am I afraid of? Maybe I'm afraid to dive deep to face these demons. Maybe I am not strong enough, and maybe by stirring up all the mud at the bottom of this river, the water would never be clear again. Maybe if I let all these painful memories go, I'll lose the only connection I'll ever have to my father. Maybe I don't know who I am without my pain.

Mary waited, watching the turmoil on Olivia's face, before speaking again. "There is an insightful poem attributed to a twelfth-century Persian poet, Hafez, called "Tripping Over Joy." May I share its wisdom with you?"

"Please," Olivia replied.

"The poem speaks of the contrasts in how people perceive their journey in life. It speaks of saints and how they see the world and their existence as a dance with the divine, a game where God's moves are so profound and filled with love that they are constantly overwhelmed with joy. Every unexpected turn, every challenge, is met with laughter, surrender, and a sense of awe. They have relinquished the need to control or predict the path and instead revel in the beauty of the present.

"On the other hand, many of us, consumed by our everyday concerns, believe we must strategize every step, foresee every challenge, and are constantly anticipating the next move, as if life were a game that we could win through sheer will and strategy. We're so caught up in our perceived seriousness of existence that we miss out on the sheer joy of living, the spontaneous laughter, and the surrender to the larger flow of life."

Mary then turned to Olivia to look into her eyes and said, "Sometimes, to find the answers, all we have to do is surrender." And she pulled Olivia into her arms for a hug before saying goodbye and walking away.

On the way back to her room, Olivia pondered what Mary had said. Holding onto the dark and tumultuous feelings about her father all her life *had* taken a toll on her. She was sure of it. But how was she to surrender? She didn't know.

Having reached the privacy of her room, Olivia turned to the one she always turned to when she didn't know what to do.

> "Lord, my path is dark and my vision is dim. I want to be free of this terrible burden. Please help me see what I am to do, and give me the strength to do it.
>
> Thank you, Lord.
>
> Amen."

The Orchid

Chapter 26

Letters of Gratitude

On the guests' schedule, it read only "Three Lessons in Gratitude" with no further description, so most of the women assumed the day's main class activity would be another talk by one of The Orchid's teachers.

When everyone arrived, waiting for them was Samara, who the morning before had shared the two writing techniques, journaling and free-style writing.

Mary was by her side, a reassuring presence at almost all sessions now.

Ugh, thought Sofia. *Are they going to make us write again?* Sofia was not fond of writing. It took too much time. She was made for texts—short, abbreviated, and immediate communications—barked like orders. One and done. All this digging into one's psyche and spirit gave her heartburn.

"Hello, everyone. It's wonderful to see you all again," Samara said in her clipped accent. "How is your day of gratitude coming along? Are you ready for this afternoon's exercise? She looked around as everyone was settling in their places. "If you haven't guessed it by now, we are going to spend some more time writing now."

She paused to let them absorb that notion and then continued.

"As I mentioned yesterday, words have power and can be used as actual tools to ignite change in ourselves, in others, and the world. Combine that power with other high vibrating energies, gratitude, for example, and you tap into something deeper and greater. You begin to transform from within.

"Today, we are going to use some of that alchemy by writing three letters of gratitude.

"The first is a letter to someone you love. The second is to someone you have difficulty expressing your love to, and the third is to yourself.

"You will have thirty minutes for each of the three letters, so in total you will have about ninety minutes for all your writing. We will pause for a few minutes in between each letter so you may clear yourself of any heavy energy that you may find is weighing down your pen. Mary and I will help you with that clearing if you have need.

"At the end of the exercise, you will pair with one other person, and you will select and read out loud one of the letters you wrote. Your partner will remain silent and will not comment or judge what you've said. This other person is there for only one purpose: to lovingly support you in your sharing. Then you will switch places, and you will provide that same loving support for her in return."

Samara asked for and answered some questions from those assembled.

"Are we sending these letters to the people we are writing to?" nervously asked a woman.

"Great question, and yes, we are," answered Samara. "But not the way you are thinking. Sending a letter to someone and releasing its energy isn't confined to putting it in an envelope with a stamp or an email. You see, your writing both releases and transforms energy. Since energy vibrates and travels through space, sending it to someone may be as simple as dedicating it to them, reading it out loud, or burning it on a fire while saying an intention. However, the choice to send it physically rests solely with you. If you like, you can wait until you write it to see how you feel about it. If you decide against it but wish to offer it to the Council Fire, be sure to bring it to our gathering later this evening.

"I remind you that the extent of your experience and transformation will depend on the extent of your effort. The deeper you decide to go in your writing, the greater the possibility of growth." Samara smiled. "And now, if there are no further questions, let's take a moment to center ourselves.

"Close your eyes and go within. Relax. Take a deep breath. And now another. Ask God, Source, the Universe, your Higher Self, however you refer to that higher power, to be present and guide you as you embark on this powerful exercise. Ask that you be granted the ability to write only that which is for your highest good."

There was silence in the room, and Samara paused briefly.

"Once you are ready, feel free to open your eyes, and, staying in silence, take up the clipboards or lap desks and supplies we provided, situate yourself wherever you are comfortable, inside or outside this room, and begin your first letter. I will ring the bell when each time period is completed."

Some women stayed in the room, while others sought spots outside, under the canopy of trees or on benches near the forest's edge, not far from the room itself.

Nicole was drawn to the beauty of a large oak. She sat on the ground with her back against the sturdy trunk and chewed on the pen's edge while she chose the words she'd use to write the letter to someone she loved. Since the subject was gratitude, Sister Consuelo would be the recipient. If not for her, Nicole thought, she might not even be here to write this letter. The old nun had saved her from a desperate act caused by a despair that might have actually claimed her life. She had literally been loved back to life by Sister Consuelo, who counseled her that there was hope—always.

As Nicole thought about how to begin, her eyes fell on a nearby affirmation painted on a sign. It read:

> Wear gratitude like a cloak and it will feed every corner of your life. —Rumi

She began to write:

> *Dear Sister Consuelo,*
>
> *As part of an exercise here at The Orchid, I have to write a letter of gratitude to someone I love. I, naturally, thought of you. I am grateful to you for so many things, but I've also realized that I've never formally thanked you for all that you have done for me, throughout the years. Every time I think of a difficult moment I experienced while growing up, and certainly more recently, I see your face, your warm smile, and feel your kindness. Thank you.*
>
> *Thank you for all the advice, all of the love, and all of the encouragement that you gave me. Thank you for helping me make sense of the world and at least some parts of myself. Thank you for not judging me, even though you knew what I was thinking and feeling. Your belief in me opened my eyes to the possibilities and the opportunities I never knew existed. You don't know this, but your presence in my life, your advice, your kind words, many times kept me from doing stupid things. One time, it even saved me from hurting myself.*
>
> *My dearest teacher and friend, thank you for all of the love, attention, and direction you have given me throughout my life. Today, I still feel the love you began*

The Orchid

sharing with me some twenty years ago, as I was learning to be the person I've become. You hold a most special place in my heart. I love you.

Nicole

**

On the other side of the building, overlooking a meadow of wild-sown tulips and daffodils, Stephanie was writing intensely, the words almost illegible due to all the erasures and tracks of tears falling from her eyes on to the paper. The first two days of the program had been intense. The defenses she had built up over a lifetime were starting to collapse and she was having to face all of her fears and traumas. The experience was freeing, but it felt like a thousand band aids were being ripped off her wounds all at once.

My Prince Charming,

It is Day Three here at The Orchid and I'm in the middle of some classes on gratitude. Apparently giving thanks is a very powerful tool and will help elevate me to a happier place. I hope so. I miss you. I love you. I'm sorry that I don't tell you enough. You and the kids are my life. Thank you for caring so much for me. ~~Thank you for putting up with me.~~ Thank you for your love. Over the years, your love has given me so much power to keep going. You are so kind, so gentle, and so forgiving. ~~I don't deserve you.~~

~~I'm so angry James. Not at you, but at myself for being so stupid. For allowing things to happen to me.~~ There are some things I still need to tell you. I have not been entirely honest about an incident during my time in Paris. I've kept things from you, James, because I've been ashamed. I think you know something. I see it in your eyes when I hide my body from you when I am getting dressed. I see it in your eyes every time we make love. James, in those early days of my modeling career, before I met you, ~~I was raped.~~ Somebody hurt me. ~~That event changed my life and I have never been the same. I have never been myself. There is so much of me, so much that I have kept hidden. Even from you.~~ I now know that because of this incident, I have been in a lot of pain and denial. It has impacted who I am and how I see myself.

I'm sorry that I have not been a most forthcoming and loving wife. I'm sorry that you had to carry so much of our relationship. I promise you that I will change. I feel like my time here is for a very good purpose and that I may be able to learn how to deal with my issues. I know I need to find the courage to be honest with you, my love. I see that now.

Thank you, James. Thank you for being you. Thank you for always standing by my side, ~~in spite of my shortcomings.~~

I love you, Stephanie

**

Olivia wrote on her lap and to someone that surprised even her. She began with the second letter, probably because it was the most difficult: writing to someone who hurt her.

Father,

I don't really know how to begin this letter. I have to give thanks to someone who I find difficult to express my love to. No sense beating around the bush, you were the first person that came to mind. Yours is always the face I see when I think of painful times in my life. In my eyes, you are not much of a man. If you were, you wouldn't have abused poor Mama or abandoned your family or chosen alcohol over us. Mama would have been spared the pain and suffering that she endured through her life and I wouldn't have grown up basically without a father.

I also wouldn't have such trust and abandonment issues and might have even been able to find a good man to become my husband, but for the shadow of you and what you did to us. No, instead, I tried to make up to Mama what you stripped off her. I worked extra hard to excel and make her proud. But no matter how hard I tried, I could never shake her free of her unwavering love for you and no matter how high I climbed, I couldn't ease her burdens or heal her broken heart.

I'm an educated woman. I know your addiction is a disease that took the choice away from you about what type of man you'd be. I know you might even feel badly somewhere deep in your heart about how it all turned out. Or maybe not...

But, in a twisted way, I am grateful to you. You gave me life. By your absence from it, you even forced me to make choices that made me the woman I am today and, make no mistake, I am a formidable woman—accomplished, respected, and powerful. I have you to thank for at least part of that. So, the grown woman in me thanks you. The hurt little girl may never be able to forgive you.

I am strong and resilient because you aren't. I am committed to helping people because you weren't. I keep my word because you didn't. Thank you for those hard lessons.

Olivia

**

Across the room, Sofia was still thinking about which letter to write first. Eventually she settled on the easiest. She would write a letter to herself.

Dear Amazing Sofia,

I am writing this letter to express my gratitude and admiration for all that you have accomplished, in spite of all the challenges you've had to face. You have persevered through difficult circumstances and have not allowed the poor examples of your mother, father, or brother to shape your life. You have remained strong and capable, even when the road ahead seemed unpredictable and uncertain.

I am grateful for your resilience and your ability to trust yourself. You have learned to rely on your own strength and judgment, rather than blindly trusting others. You have navigated your way through obstacles, and have come out on the other side, stronger and more confident. Thanks to that, you don't owe anything to anybody and you are able to stand tall and be the person you are, without any apologies.

I'm so proud of you for all that you have achieved and for the person you have become. I'm thankful for the great person you are. You are an inspiration to me and to those around you. Keep up the good work, and never forget that you are capable of doing anything you set your mind to.

In fact, I am certain that with your attitude and work ethic, coupled with the tools you are learning about here in this place, you will now be unstoppable.

With love,

Sofia

**

Jennifer sat on a bench near one of the paths leading to the forest and decided she would write a letter to her ex-husband.

Brian,

I'm to write a letter of gratitude to somebody I am having difficulty expressing my love to and, of course, that would be you.

I know that I have some things to thank you for—loving me at the beginning, our wonderful kids, and how we were a team, how you made me laugh, how you were a great friend… for a while…

Jennifer felt the tears that had been welling in her eyes as she wrote dry immediately as a white-hot rush of feeling roared like a plume of flame and took her completely over.

> *...until you decided to just walk out on us. You had to fucking leave and put your career and another woman before your family? I wasn't good enough for you. Our life wasn't good enough for you. Our kids were not good enough for you. You didn't see the value in having a family.*
>
> *And now our kids don't really have a dad and I don't have a husband, and I have to do everything alone. It's hard, Brian. It is hard as hell and I am fucking angry at you for wrecking my life. That whore whistled and you followed like a dog. She made you leave us and I hate her too. I hate you!*
>
> *You son of a bitch, if you didn't want to get married and have kids, then you shouldn't have. Nobody fucking forced you. You are the reason my life is a mess. It's all your fault and I hope you never know one day of happiness. You abandoned me and I want you to die like I am dying. I had a master plan for my life and you took me away from it. You convinced me that we were a team and made me believe that we could share a dream together. But you didn't want that. And now I'm trapped in this awful nightmare raising two kids by myself.*

Jennifer was trembling, her anger getting the best of her. But then something clicked inside of her. Her breathing steadied and the red glaze of rage cleared from her sight. She continued writing.

> *But, enough already! I'm done feeling sorry for myself. I need to grow up now. I can and will carve out a real life for myself and the kids. I'm not dying; these are birth pangs—I will become a new person, a better person. I'm tired of blaming everything on you, Brian. I can't make you love me, but I can let you go.*

That realization stopped Jennifer's pen for a moment and when she returned to her letter, she knew she had the answer to the roaring rage's origin: *The person I am so very angry with is me!* she thought.

> *I didn't know I had this terrible, black anger inside of me. But I can see now that, though I was disappointed in you, the truth is I was more disappointed in me for allowing myself to be in that situation. Now that I have written this letter, I understand that. But I'm done now, and I'm going to make my own way out of this mess.*
>
> *Jen*

Jennifer, near blinded by her tears—cleansing ones, not the scalding tears that would have burned her cheeks before she wrote the letter—started walking aimlessly and found herself in a clearing, where she practically stumbled into Mary's open arms. She cried and cried, but each tear felt as though it were washing some of her long-held pain away. Mary held her wordlessly, understanding that just being held was often a miraculous comfort.

Not far, the soft sounding of a bell was heard.

**

The exercise was repeated two more times as Samara had indicated.

The writing of each letter served a unique purpose, focusing on a different facet of their journey towards gratitude. Through each step, the women were progressively unburdening themselves, shedding layers of past struggles and experiencing profound emotional cleansing, increased self-awareness, and healing.

Then, once they all rested their pens, they came together in pairs, their hands clutching chosen letters. As they started reading them aloud, the room filled with their recitations of their raw, unfiltered emotions. It was a poignant symphony of shared stories, unspoken until this very moment. With roles exchanged, the process of emotional release carried on, deepening the catharsis. Amidst this exchange, a profound connection was kindled—a testament to the powerful, unbreakable bonds formed in the crucible of shared vulnerability and understanding.

Letters of Gratitude

The Orchid

The Orchid

Chapter 27

Activities

The conclusion of the emotional exercise marked the beginning of the individual afternoon activities at the center. Each woman followed a bespoke schedule, which had been meticulously tailored to address their unique needs and interests.

Sofia made her way to the art studio. During her application and interview, she had suggested that she wanted to engage in activities that would help her with her temperament. This afternoon she was to participate in a private watercolor painting session designed to calm her spirit and channel any anger issues into strokes of color and creativity. As she dipped her brush into paint, she found herself transforming her imbalances into a vibrant canvas of self-expression.

Stephanie, understanding the importance of continuing to focus on her health issues, found herself in the calm, comforting presence of Ruby, the dietary social worker Mary had recommended. The conversation revolved around the delicate subject of her eating disorder and the tools and strategies she could use to tackle and navigate her complex relationship with food.

Jennifer and Nicole were enjoying the soothing confines of Heaven, a well-earned reward for their bodies after the previous emotional workout. As they relaxed into the indulgence of facials and manicures, the tranquil ambiance facilitated a deep and engaging conversation. Theirs was a beautiful balance of self-care and newfound friendship.

At the Activity Center, Olivia met with a Pilates instructor for a private session. Having not visited a gym in quite a while and not being at all athletic, Olivia found the gentle yet firm movements to be a welcomed challenge. With each stretch and flex, she felt a surge of power, a testament to the strength within her waiting to be unleashed.

The Orchid

As the afternoon waned and shadows lengthened, the women finished their scheduled activities and made their way back to their rooms for a brief respite of warm showers, naps, journal entries, or the relaxing observation of the horizon.

At dinner, their conversations flowed freely. Laughter, subtle but genuine, mingled with nods of understanding and emotional moments marked by a few tears. As they savored their meals, the shifting energy within each became evident, a testament to the inner transformations they were undergoing. The third day was drawing to a close. It was a day filled with learnings and reflections and the understanding that becoming enlightened was no stroll in the park.

Shortly after, they gathered at the entrance of the Sanctuary, ready to participate in the day's closing activity: the Evening Council.

Chapter 28

Evening Council

The doors to the structure were still closed, and a member of the staff standing outside asked for a few more minutes while the final touches for the ceremony were completed. When the large wooden doors opened, Mary and another woman greeted them with their palms pressed together in front of their foreheads, symbolizing the shared respect, humility, and reverence for the souls entering the building. Mary wore a spectacularly embroidered white robe. The other woman stood out because of her shaved head and colorful brown and saffron cotton robe, a symbol of her chosen monastic life. Around her neck was a contrasting shawl and a traditional mala (a string of one hundred and eight beads used for meditation). Both women's appearance signaled their powerful energetic status.

As the women entered, each was asked to bow slightly so that they could receive a gift that would be placed around their necks—their very own white shawl and translucent prayer beads.

The Sanctuary was ceremonially decorated, and the light from hundreds of candles placed throughout accentuated its role as a place of contemplation. A mandala, a circular geometric figure in Hindu and Buddhist symbolism that represented the universe, had been placed at the center, adorned with colorful gold, red, and blue flowers. A strong and permeating smell of sage emitted from the incense burning around the room.

Once all found a place to sit on the floor, Mary began by greeting everyone. "Hello, my dears. What a day, right?" She smiled at the nodding heads and the whisper, "You aren't kidding," that she heard from one of the women seated in front of her.

"I am delighted to be here with you once again. Tonight's ceremony will be

The Orchid

held by another amazing teacher; we lovingly call her Sister D. She graces us with her presence, having traveled all the way from Bhutan to be here."

Mary beamed at the nun and then she and Sister D both bowed to each other, before Mary found a spot sitting among the women.

Sister D stood at the front of the group next to the mandala. She said, "Greetings, everyone and thank you, my dear Mary. I am grateful, and it's an honor to share this moment with all of you." Her luminous teeth showed as she smiled and made eye contact with all present while delivering her message.

"For me, gratitude is about appreciating the present moment and about giving thanks for all that I have. It allows me to focus and appreciate all that has been given to me by the universe and not at all on the things that have not. As a *bhikkhuni*, or female monk, my ultimate goal is to find inner peace and contentment through the teachings of the Buddha. I do that through meditation, humility, generosity, and reflection. Gratitude is also a major step in that journey.

"What Buddhists (and other spiritual teachers) have been practicing for millennia is now being supported scientifically. Recent studies have shown that people who regularly express gratitude have more fulfilling relationships and enjoy higher levels of social support. They are also more likely to experience healthy emotions and have a more optimistic outlook on life, which, in turn, has a whole range of mental and physical health benefits. When we express our appreciation and thanks, we strengthen our bonds and increase our feelings of connectedness with others. We also reduce stress and anxiety, improve our sleep, develop a stronger immune system, and lessen the risk of disease. Ultimately, gratitude helps us shift our focus away from the challenging aspects of our lives and towards the things that bring us joy and fulfillment, increasing our levels of happiness and well-being."

Sister D was then silent for a few moments. The span of time was brief but long enough to allow everyone to savor the high energy of the words she shared.

"So, how can we cultivate gratitude in our lives? One way is to do what we did throughout the day, to make a conscious effort to focus on the things for which we are grateful. This can be as simple as keeping a gratitude journal or sharing our appreciation mentally, verbally, or in writing with others.

"Another is practicing mindfulness. Mindfulness is being present and aware of our thoughts and surroundings. When we are mindful, we are more likely to appreciate the things that are happening in the moment and to be grateful for the experiences that we are currently having. Meditation, yoga, breathing, silence, and simply being conscious and present in our daily activities are common ways to practice mindfulness. By taking a few minutes each day to focus on these, we can cultivate gratitude and improve our overall well-being."

Sister D paused once again.

"This evening's exercise is going to be quite similar to what you experienced two nights ago. We are going to do a sharing exercise in which our partner will simply listen as we express our gratitude for something or someone in our lives.

"This will take place for about one minute. During that time, you will simply say, 'I am grateful for __,' and fill in the blank. Do that as many times as you can within the time, after which your partner will simply say, 'Thank you for sharing your thoughts of gratitude with me.' Then you will switch roles, with you listening and your partner sharing what they are grateful for, again for about a minute. Then you will go on to the next person and repeat the process again. We will do this until you all have the opportunity to express words of gratitude to at least half the group, and then we will ring the bell.

"Everyone will then have the opportunity to share in the larger circle. I understand that you have brought with you letters and/or journal entries that you wrote throughout the day. Later, during our collective sharing, if you so choose, you will have the opportunity to relinquish these writings to a fire, which will ensure that their energy is appropriately transformed.

"Before breaking into smaller groups, I would like to share with you a short prayer."

Sister D straightened her back and posture, placed her joined palms on her chest, and in a clear and profound manner, she said:

> All that I am,
> and all that I have,
> is a gift from the universe,
> and for that, I am grateful.

She then said, "Blessings to you all."

Following the blessing, the partners assembled and the exercise began.

The Orchid

As all the women came together, shared, and exchanged their words of gratitude, the process was repeated. The scene had the buzz and vibration of a beehive in full motion. There was a synchronicity now felt in their purposeful and intentional sharing.

The sound of a bell marked the end of the exercise. The hive quieted, and everyone was asked to join the circle again, this time with the fire lit, its flames wildly calling for attention and its voice whispering secrets to those who had ears to hear.

When all the women sat on the floor and arranged themselves in a semi-circle, Sister D began to speak.

"And now, we will go around allowing everyone to share whatever is in their hearts. It can be your day's experience, thoughts of gratitude, or anything else that is present for you at the moment."

Sister D directed everyone's attention to the fire. "At the end of the sharing, you will have the opportunity to relinquish to the fire any energy that requires transformation, all while maintaining a sense of gratitude. Gratitude is also a fire that burns brightly within us and which can serve as a catalyst for all other forms of energy, amplifying them and elevating them to new heights. Just as fire transforms all into heat and light, gratitude transforms our appreciation and thankfulness into a powerful force that can elevate all other aspects of our lives. Whether we are seeking to create change in the world, to build more meaningful relationships, or to simply transform ourselves from within, gratitude can be one of the most powerful vehicles to propel us forward.

"After relinquishing your writings to the fire, you will pick up some flowers from the vase," she said, pointing to a vase filled with spectacular-looking flowers of all colors and varieties. "Then you will continue to add to the mandala already here, expanding its size, symbolizing our roles in the expansion of the universe."

Sister D had a beautiful object in her hands, which she placed on a cushion at the center of the circle. It was a heart made of polished bronze.

She instructed, "Please, whoever wishes to speak first, take up this heart and with it the freedom to share."

Jennifer got up and, with a swift movement, picked up the heart and sat down again with a lightness not seen in her in days prior but now visible to all. "I am Jennifer and I just loved the words you shared. Thank you. I began this afternoon's exercise writing a letter to someone I had trouble expressing my love to. I wrote it to...." She had to take a deep breath as she said this, and soon tears accompanied her words. "I wrote it to my ex-husband, Brian. But my letter soon became a rant! I said some terrible things, and I was horrified at what was pouring out of me, but, once I spit that awful stuff out, it was like something caught fire in me and burnt away all that rage. As I finished the letter, I realized I wasn't letting go of him but rather freeing myself from my own chains."

Jennifer explained that she was so consumed by her letter to her ex-husband that she never got around to writing any of the others. She thought that it would do her good to burn the letter and release that dual love/anger energy and liberate herself from it.

Sister D thanked Jennifer for her emotional and moving sharing and continued.

"Sometimes our journeys take us through unforeseen paths, leading us to certain mental states, like anger. Anger can be startling, but I assure you, that it's an integral part of a healthy emotional process. It can help us uncover unrecognized facets of ourselves or suppressed feelings towards certain situations or individuals. It has a distinctive energy, contrasting with draining emotions like guilt, fear, or anxiety, which often arise when we're not fully aligned with our inner selves. When channeled correctly, anger can be a catalyst that propels us from states of emotional stagnation to proactive actions, or even be the onset of more enriching feelings, such as courage."

Jennifer understood why her tumultuous ride through rage had been both necessary and helpful. Had she not uncovered the rage she held, she would have remained a prisoner of grief, unable to move forward in her life.

Sister D invited Jennifer to get up and release her letter to the flames. Jennifer did so and walked to the fire, where she released the grief and anger that had been left behind by Brian's departure. As she did, her body felt a new sensation, the power of forgiveness.

She then grabbed a handful of flowers and placed them in the mandala and returned the heart amulet to its cushion.

Stephanie was next. She took up the heart and examined it before she began to speak.

"My name is Stephanie. My gratitude letter to someone I love ended up being a letter about being truthful, about being honest with my husband and trusting him with my darkest secret. I don't know that I will share the letter with him, but I'm really glad I wrote it. I feel a little lighter for having done so and it's given me lots to think about.

"My second letter was to my mother. She is the person I have difficulty expressing my love to. Today, while writing that letter, I came to the realization that I have strong emotions towards her, as it relates to the things that happened to me in my early years. I've had this feeling that I can't disappoint her, and because of it, I just kept doing whatever she told me. I am now realizing that I haven't really been listening to myself." Stephanie took a deep breath and composed herself. Gone were the uncontrollable tears. She now seemed clear and aware.

"Thank you for sharing, Stephanie," Sister D said. "As I said before, it matters little whether you share the letter with the person for whom you wrote it or not. The important thing is that you connected to that energy and to that awareness. You may not see the benefit immediately, but deep inside you are shifting and changing and experiencing the benefits, nonetheless. I encourage you to continue to meditate on these feelings and insights. Your higher self will clarify them for you."

The nun invited Stephanie to get up and release the energy. Stephanie walked towards the fire and relinquished all of her letters. Then she contributed her chosen flowers to the expanding colorful design of the mandala adorning the floor and returned the bronze heart to its place of honor.

Olivia was next to share.

"Hi everyone. I'm Olivia. Since I arrived here, I have begun to feel that my life has been less about what I was trying to be than about what I was trying to avoid being. I am not sure if anyone else relates to this, but I found the letter to myself difficult to write. I felt as if I could not easily express love to myself, as if I was not important, as if I could not give myself the benefit of my own love and attention. That began to make sense to me. Because I'm so busy with everything and everyone else, I can see I am placing myself second to just about everything in my life, especially my work. Don't get me wrong, I love what I do, but I've just realized that I seem to be loving that job more than I love myself."

Olivia fell silent for a moment, coming to terms with the depth of her revelation. After a deep breath, she continued.

"The next letter, the one to someone I have difficulty expressing my love to, was to my father. Ironically, I found myself thanking him for being a terrible father, because his behavior made me stronger and helped shape me into the woman I am today."

Mary, who was still among the seated women, was smiling as if Olivia had tapped into a very important lesson and she couldn't wait to acknowledge the breakthrough.

Sister D also showed signs of approval. "What wonderful realizations, Olivia! It sometimes takes a long time before a person can reach the understanding you came to while writing your letters.

"Regarding the letter to yourself, I'd say you've hit the bullseye. Often, in life, we are giving our energy, even our love, to other things, and we do so at the expense of the most important love of all—the love for ourselves. Finding that inner love is the only thing that matters. Ultimately, that is why you are here. That energy, in its most pure form, is not selfish. That energy cannot be relinquished, not to a job, not to another person, not to food or alcohol or any other form of distraction. Those things, material things, and also relationships, can and are likely to end. The love you feel for yourself, once discovered and appreciated, will be with you till your last breath.

"You may have heard Mary or others speak to this, but it is our belief that such love, the inner love, is not something that is found as much as it is something that is uncovered, for it is already inside of you. It simply rests under all sorts of layers—trauma, love of material things, codependency, unresolved feelings, and many other things we hide from ourselves. You, my dears, have just noticed the layers obscuring that inner love, and that is the first step in beginning the journey towards ridding yourselves of them."

Olivia felt the urge to ask, "How do I do that? How do I get rid of those layers?"

Sister D looked at her with the kindest eyes and said, "It varies for everyone. Potentially, you could do it in this very moment. We are all capable of it. For some, my dear, it takes longer. I, for one, am still working on it."

Olivia simply shook her head in admiration and respect for the shared honesty.

The nun continued. "With regards to your experience writing the letter to your father, there is a great book that comes to mind. As you may be aware, in Buddhism, rebirth is an important part of our existence. The book I speak of touches on this and discusses the agreements we sign with other souls as we are about to enter one of our lifetimes. In it, the author suggests that we, as unborn souls, decide on the curriculum that we want to learn and the lessons we wish to experience in the incarnation we are about to begin. Then we ask our partner souls, those who travel with us from lifetime to lifetime, our entourage, if you will, who among them would be willing to help us learn those lessons? One soul, or several, volunteer for that duty. 'I will lovingly help you, Olivia, or Stephanie, or Jennifer, or Mary,'" she said this as she made eye contact with all of them, "'to learn the lessons of gratitude, forgiveness, resilience, whatever lessons were pre-decided.' Then that soul, or souls, in their physical forms, act to ensure that we have the opportunities to learn those lessons. Sometimes those helpful souls may have to resort to painful or unkind behavior in order for us to be able to learn. It's a powerful and compelling idea about the extreme sacrifices other souls make for the sake of helping us learn invaluable lessons. What a wonderful depth of insights you had today, Olivia. Thank you for sharing. And if you don't mind me asking, who did you write your love letter to?"

"I don't mind," Olivia said. "It was to my Mama. That one was easy to write. It just flowed right out of me."

Sofia, still thinking about the book mentioned, remembered her morning thought about thanking her family and laughed. *My mom, dad, and brother, all colluding to help me learn some lessons. That's ridiculous!*

"Would you like to relinquish anything to the fire, Olivia?" Sister D asked.

With that invitation, Olivia, who now was wearing her shawl as a veil, walked to the fire, stood there for a few seconds, and then relinquished all of the papers she had in her hands. Standing there, fully dressed in white, she looked saintly. She projected a powerful image to all of the women watching her.

Olivia placed flowers on the mandala, returned the heart to its place, and then sat down to give the next woman a turn.

Sofia pushed herself to her feet and almost began speaking before remembering to retrieve the heart, which supposedly granted her the freedom to do so. She didn't feel she had much freedom about this task, but she went along with the program.

"My name is Sofia. I found it difficult to write notes of gratitude to others. For me, the easiest letter to write was to myself."

"Thanks, Sofia," Sister D answered. "It doesn't matter to whom you write the letter; the important thing is for you to enter into gratitude. You've started the ball rolling, spiritually speaking. You may or may not see the benefit of what you are doing, but deep inside, transformation is taking place. That said, Sofia, I invite you to revisit the reason why you are having difficulty expressing your gratitude to others. It may be an area that you might want to address. Perhaps it's even a source of great pain or resentment. Or maybe it's an opportunity for forgiveness. Ultimately, it may be a source of insight and an opportunity for growth and inner transformation."

Sofia was still holding the bronze heart firmly, her lips compressed and her brow furrowed.

"Would you like to share about your other letters or anything else that may be on your mind?" asked the nun.

"Yeah," answered Sofia. "With all due respect, I find the idea of other souls accompanying me in this life to help me quite stu … silly. Why? Don't they have their own things to figure out? Why don't they just mind their own business, and let people figure it out on their own? Who do they think they are…?" As she said those words, Sofia lost her composure and tears began to flow.

Sister D simply allowed the moment to unfold and held silence and love for Sofia. "Embrace the tears. They are energy that has begun to shift inside of you and now is requesting to be set free. Some of it will embrace you with love. Some of it will need to depart from you as it is not for your highest good and therefore no longer yours to keep. But all of the energy expended is for your healing. This is a great moment to release that which is stirring inside of you to the cleansing fire in front of you and within you. Find the courage to do so."

With those words and the support of the entire group, Sofia got up and threw all of the papers in the fire. As she did so, she let out a loud yell that was felt across the energetic world. The intensity of her scream was primal, akin to the wail of a wounded animal in deep pain yet seeking to rally its strength for survival.

She then grabbed one single flower and carefully placed it on the mandala and very gently laid the heart back on its cushion.

As she sat, Sister D's eyes fully on her, the nun simply said, "What a wonderful moment. Bless you."

The next to speak was Nicole. She took time to carefully look at the heart with reverence. Then, clutching it and the letters she wrote to her chest, she raised her eyes and spoke to the group.

"My name is Nicole." She composed herself, as she was still feeling chills from Sofia's share. "I used the opportunity to thank someone who has been a powerful light in my life," she said. "Writing to her just raised my spirits. I loved it."

"Thank you, Nicole. That's just wonderful," Sister D said. "I am pleased you had such a lovely experience. Is there anything else you want to share?"

"I also wrote a letter to my mom," Nicole answered. "She is the person I have the most challenges with. I want her to change so much. I need her to change. In my letter, I told her things I've been meaning to say for quite a long time. It's the only time I've been able to say something totally honest to her, for in real life, she and I simply don't see eye-to-eye and cannot seem to talk it out."

Sister D acknowledged Nicole and expressed some thoughts on her sharing. "I am so glad that you were able to give thanks to the lighthouse in your life. Perhaps you will one day see that the other, the challenge, is also a lighthouse, directing you through the lessons of this lifetime. And if I may, you spoke of real and not real. It has been my experience that the act of releasing energy through activities such as writing, chanting mantras, and offering prayers is as real and powerful as speaking directly to the person herself. I urge you to suspend your disbelief and allow the energy to take its course so that you may reap its benefits."

Sister D paused and looked, smiling, into Nicole's eyes.

"Anything else, Nicole?" she asked.

"No, that's all. Thank you," Nicole answered.

"My pleasure," the nun replied. "Would you like to relinquish anything to the fire?"

"Yes. All of it." So, Nicole did just that.

She then chose and placed a large bouquet of flowers on the mandala, which now was visibly growing. Then Nicole laid the heart down carefully.

Other women followed. They shared all sorts of stories about love and awareness as well as loss and confusion.

One woman spoke of her inability to write. "I just froze and could not for the life of me write anything. I am having a lot of difficulty with this process, with the idea of opening these vaults that I've shut so long ago." She stopped and placed her face in her palms, groaning softly while she wept.

"Thank you for sharing, my dear. I know it feels like this is not working, but I assure you, even what you just said, that awareness that allows you to acknowledge that which you just shared, is a sign that the movement within you has begun. Thank you for your sharing."

One by one, all the others took up the heart, spoke their feelings, consigned their letters to the flames, and added flowers to the expanding mandala.

Once all had had the opportunity to do so, Sister D stood up and recited a blessing, asking for the cleansing power of fire to purify and transform all the energy that was present in the room:

> With a humble heart, I express deep gratitude. For every breath, for every moment of love, and for the lessons learned, I am thankful. May this gratitude be a wellspring of peace for myself, a beacon of hope for you, and a gentle hand of kindness for all.

With that, Sister D, once again, acknowledged Mary and invited her to speak.

"What a wonderful experience tonight was. Thank you, my dear Sister D and all of you for allowing me to be present for it. Thank you all for your hard work and dedication to your growth and transformation," Mary said.

"You are all exhibiting the ability to experience awareness and gratitude. Because of that, you are changing. The next powerful step is forgiveness. This will be the focus of our day tomorrow. If you think gratitude was powerful, wait until you experience forgiveness."

And with that, Mary brought day three to a close.

The Orchid

Chapter 29

Trust Yourself

Sister D's talk about gratitude and the other women's sharing of the changes they were supposedly experiencing pissed Sofia off even more, to the point where she found herself observing the other women and judging them harshly.

There is no way they are changing as much as they say they are and in such a little amount of time. They must be faking it ... especially Jennifer. She wants us to believe that she walked in here completely shattered about her ex-husband, and now she is ok? What a bunch of horseshit. I don't believe it for a second. What a herd of sheep these people are, she thought to herself. At least she had clung to her individuality through this fog of spirituality that seemed to be blinding everyone.

For many reasons, Sofia had always thought that religion was not for her, and all this New Age talk struck her as much the same thing. She was so glad that she saw it so clearly. In spite of that clarity, Sofia was still very angry. *Who does Sister D think she is to single me out in front of everybody?* she thought, as she felt the tension of that energy throughout her body. *I need to relax,* she counseled herself as the group filed out after that night's Council. *It's time to have a little fun.*

As she walked, Sofia found herself next to Jennifer and grabbed her by the arm.

"Hey Jennifer, I just wanted to congratulate you. You seem to be making a lot of progress. Good for you," Sofia said, though Jennifer could not tell if she were truly happy or just mocking her.

"I know, right? Thanks Sofia." Jennifer answered, giving Sofia the benefit of the doubt. "I almost can't believe it really, but something changed inside of me. I feel so different, like I've dropped the thousand-pound boulder I've been carrying around. I feel lighter and happier and I can't seem to stop smiling."

"That's cool," said Sofia, now both angry *and* jealous.

"Hey, listen, I'm going to take a short walk before turning in for the night. Do you want to walk with me?" Sofia asked.

"Umm, sure, okay," Jennifer replied.

The two reached a path. After some time, when they had gotten far enough from the others, Sofia invited Jennifer to sit at the edge of a fountain they encountered. "I'm so glad you are getting so much out of this week," Sofia continued. "You seemed pretty sad when we first started here, but now you seem so different."

"And you, Sofia? How are you? Is the program working for you?" Jennifer turned the conversation onto Sofia.

"Nah, I don't think so. I just don't think this is for me, you know. I don't feel like anything is changing, and to be honest, I was fine when I first came, and even before I arrived. And I feel fine now," Sofia answered. "What I am is a little tense. I didn't particularly like tonight. You heard me in there. I just don't buy into a lot of the ideas they want us to believe."

As she said this, Sofia reached into her jacket. Out of her pocket, Sofia pulled a small round metal container. The label read "Artisanal Edibles, Clementine Orange Flavor."

"Want a couple?" Sofia asked, offering the tin to Jennifer. "They will help you keep that light feeling and the smile on your face."

"What are they?" asked Jennifer.

"Cannabis gummies. I carry them with me wherever I go," Sofia replied, "They take the edge off."

Jennifer said, "You know using those is against the rules, right?"

"Yeah, yeah, but rules were made to be broken," Sofia said dismissively. "They won't hurt you. All they really do is relax me. In fact, they may help me see something I can't see now. So, technically, they are probably helping me in my process. You've had them before, right?"

"Yes, but that was a while back." Jennifer answered. "Sofia, I am so much happier now than when I arrived at this place, and I think that change came about by doing all the things that I have been advised to do. But one of the things they specifically asked us *not* to do is to use any drugs or alcohol while we are here."

"We aren't children to be told what to do," Sofia protested. "And we aren't prisoners. We should be able to do what we want."

"Thank you but no, Sofia. I'm not taking those and I don't think you should either, but if you want to, go ahead. I won't judge you," Jennifer said.

Sofia opened her mouth to protest again but just then another voice was heard from the other side of the fountain, startling the two women.

"Good evening, Jennifer, Sofia," said Mary, looking at them both. "I was on my way to my room, and I overheard a bit of your conversation.

"Thanks for your vote of confidence, Jennifer," said Mary in her soft voice. "I am so pleased the program is working for you. It is your willingness to change that is really unlocking your joy. We just help you find that key for yourself. You are doing the rest."

Mary walked forward and wrapped Jennifer in a warm hug then stepped back and said, "Would you please excuse us now, Jennifer? I'd like to speak with Sofia alone if you don't mind."

"Sure. I think I'll head to my room," Jennifer said. "I hope you both have a great night," and she widened her eyes at Sofia as she blew her a kiss before she turned and left.

Sofia was unaware that she had squared her shoulders and clenched her fists in a defensive posture as she faced Mary. *Here it comes,* she thought. *Mary's going to drop her serene little mask and scream at me.*

But that is not what happened.

Mary smiled sweetly at Sofia and said, "Let's sit and talk a moment, shall we?"

When both had sat at the fountain's edge, Mary began speaking, her voice still low and calm.

"Your name is an ancient and lovely one ... Sofia, from the Greek *Sophia,* meaning 'wisdom,'" Mary began. "Had you heard that before?"

Sofia nodded, and Mary paused and then continued, "Can I ask you a few questions about your conversation with Jennifer?" Sofia nodded again.

"Do you believe our program is seeking any financial gain?"

"No, it doesn't appear you make any money doing this," Sofia admitted, recognizing that the program was truly free of charge for all who attended.

Mary continued, "Do you believe we are honestly trying our best to help the women who come here to lead happier and healthier lives?"

Sofia admitted that seemed to be the case.

"And lastly, Sofia, speaking of myself and the staff." Mary's eyes were laser focused on Sofia's, but her tone remained gentle and loving. "Do you think we actually believe all the things we say we believe in or are we just spouting…," she paused briefly, "horseshit?"

Sofia was taken aback by Mary's use of the word "horseshit." It seemed too incongruous to be coming out of Mary's mouth, and yet it was the very word plucked straight from Sofia's mind when she thought about the program's teachings.

A little flustered, Sofia admitted, "Umm, yes, I believe that you believe it all."

"So, to your knowledge, we are not benefitting financially, we are honest, we are caring, and we do our work here selflessly and with integrity, always aiming for our guests' highest good?" Mary asked.

At Sofia's answering nod, Mary continued. "Given that you now know that our experience, gained over decades of perfecting this program, is being used in such helpful ways, I think it is fair to say that it fits the definition of 'wisdom' with which we began this conversation. I believe 'wisdom' is the ability to apply experience, knowledge, and good judgement to one's actions and decisions.

"I invite you to reflect on your experience and what you know about our work here and apply it to the decisions you're making. The rules were set up to support your journey. One of these rules is abstaining from any mind-altering substances during your time here to ensure a conducive environment for your transformation. You agreed to this rule at the outset. It would be beneficial for both you and everyone here for you to reconsider the significance of that guideline."

Sofia thought a moment and said, "I don't know if I am being transformed, as you call it, Mary" she said. "I just don't feel it. What I have felt is annoyed and impatient most of the time since I got here, actually."

"That's exactly our intention. We are placing you in a place outside your normal comfort zone," Mary said. "Your strength is one of your greatest character assets, Sofia, but instead of using your great strength to build a wall between us, I invite you to use it to tear down the wall that stands between you and your growth. Trust and follow the rules which were put in place to help you. Trust me. Trust the others. We are all travelers on the river of time, learning as we go."

Sofia grimaced at the description of "the river of time," and Mary noticed.

"Sofia, we are made of the experiences we've had in the past, the present-day ones we are experiencing now, and the future ones before us. We cannot see around the bends in the river in front of us. Our vision is limited. But there *are* bends in front of us, as real as those we've left behind. If we open our minds one tiny bit, miracles can happen, and we can see further downstream and steer ourselves to better choices. That's what I mean when I say we are all travelers on the same river."

Mary paused a moment in silence and looked distracted as if she were receiving inspiration. Then she turned to Sofia and said, "Something came to me just now, and I want to propose it to you for your consideration."

Sofia narrowed her eyes a bit at that revelation but answered, "Yes, what is it?"

"Would you be willing to suspend your disbelief long enough for me to show you that there are more mysteries and wonders in the universe than our logic or philosophy can grasp? Would you allow me to show you the truth of that statement?"

Sofia was looking intently at Mary. "Sure, Mary, I'll let you take a shot," Sofia answered, and then she asked, "How are you going to do that?"

"Tomorrow, my dear, you will have a tarot reading. Prepare yourself for what will be a very personal and powerful experience."

With that, Mary warmly hugged Sofia and got up to leave.

At that moment, Sofia said, "Mary?"

"Yes, Sofia?" Mary replied.

"Here, take these with you," and Sofia extended her hand and offered the tin can.

"I don't need to take them, my love. You have the power. Trust yourself."

The Orchid

Part V
Forgiveness

The Orchid

Chapter 30

Morning Reflections

Having spent a handful of days in this tranquil haven, the guests had gradually synchronized their rhythms to the natural and melodic alarm of the symphony of birds and the accompanying sound of the bell. With the first sleepy stirrings, each guest noted the soft luminescence peeking through the dark tree canopy announcing the fourth morning of the program. A palpable sense of anticipation hung in the air, an unspoken shared understanding that a new day, full of promise and discovery, was preparing to make its grand entrance.

This day, like the previous ones, promised many new lessons for the guests. The difference now was that each person was starting to notice the changes in herself and the activities that at first had made them feel self-conscious, uncertain, and uncomfortable, now felt inspiring and intimate.

Mary and her team had made a lasting impact with their singular, unwavering commitment to elevating and transforming energy. The Orchid's philosophy, rooted in the belief that all that was needed was a safe space, genuine attention, and the support of dedicated and skilled hands, was manifesting its transformative power.

**

Jennifer had taken a hot shower and was readying herself, flying high on the experiences that came with the release of the anger she had been holding inside.

She remembered the feelings that washed over her and the vision she had been gifted the day before while writing the letter to Brian. She was a little surprised but smiled at the thought and then said out loud, "I forgive you,

The Orchid

Brian. I forgive you." Jennifer took a moment to enjoy the feelings she was experiencing. It had been a long time since she had felt as free as she did at that moment.

Still, Jennifer felt a lingering guilt about her kids and was having trouble shaking off the feeling that she was a bad mother. She needed to decide what to do with it and perhaps even speak with someone about it. The good thing is that she really wasn't alone. Her time at The Orchid had shown her that.

**

Stephanie continued to feel better, which seemed a tad miraculous given the state she was in when she'd first arrived. Being confronted by Mary and experiencing Watsu had been revelatory and life-changing for her. She had not forgotten the traumatic things that had happened to her and she was sure she never would, but she felt like she had escaped from a cage. For the first time ever, Stephanie felt a significant shift in her emotions and her situation. She looked forward to whatever the day would bring.

**

In the insularity of her cave, Nicole had placed a yoga mat on the floor and was doing some stretching exercises, feeling as though something within her was stretching as well. She was enjoying and getting so much out of the program and appreciated the fact that the other women, strangers all, were so supportive. It made her feel cared for, just as Sister Consuelo's support had made her feel all those years—like she had reached a port in a storm.

But the storm was still raging inside of her and was waiting for her beyond the safety of this cave and the gates of The Orchid. Nicole knew that very well and she didn't look forward to stepping out into it again.

Why can't Elena just be happy with what we have, she whined to herself. *I love her and treat her well and tell her how much she means to me every single day. Why isn't that enough for her? Why aren't I enough for her?*

Nicole immediately answered herself in her mind. *Well, you would be enough for her if you had a spine. How do you think Elena feels every time you deny who she is to you? In public, at work, with your family—you negate her. By doing that, you are saying that you value the opinions of others more than her presence in your life. It is clear that you are ashamed of her.*

Nicole felt as though she were in an old movie with a devil on one shoulder, whispering in her ear, and an angel on the other, both countering each other on the topic.

I am not ashamed of her.

Yes, you are.

No, I'm not.

But you are.

No, I am not ashamed of Elena ... I am ashamed of me.

There it was again. That big ugly truth right in front of her. *I am a freak of nature, and I'm not doing what God wants of me.*

Then you should cut Elena loose, one of the voices on her shoulders said, though Nicole couldn't decide if that advice was good or evil.

I can't cut her loose. I don't think I'd make it without her.

You'd better decide soon. Time is running out.

Nicole knew that much was true. It had been two months since that awful dinner when her mother tried fixing her and Elena up with the two men from church. Elena didn't appreciate the ambush but was even more furious that Nicole always expected her to go through with such charades. The look on Elena's face and the words she said made Nicole think that the incident had truly been the last straw. Even when Nicole spoke to her a couple of weeks ago, she had felt Elena cold and distant.

Have I lost her for good?

Why can't my mom just mind her own business? I am thirty years old, I live on my own, I pay my own bills, and still she wants to control my life. "Just leave me alone," Nicole screamed out loud. Then, just as fervently, she said, "I'm sorry, God, I didn't mean that. I don't want them to leave me alone, so please don't take them from me. I will try harder to honor my mother and father like You command us."

But one of the voices again, Nicole wasn't sure which, whispered back, *The Bible also says you should leave your parents and cleave to your wife, you know. Elena should be your wife.*

"Arrrrggg," Nicole growled, her thoughts once again tangling and tripping her. *I can't do both things. What am I supposed to do?*

The Orchid

**

Olivia, with the benefit of age, was sitting and thinking over the revelations that had come to light during the past few days. She wasn't sure what to do with what she'd learned. She wasn't angry or sad, just a bit wistful as she sipped her steaming mint tea. *No point wishing things had been better growing up.* As her mama used to say, "Don't cry over spilled milk Livy," and she agreed, there was no point getting all upset about things you could do nothing about.

It would have been wonderful if my father had been a good man. No, she corrected herself. *If my father had been a well man, instead of a sick one. Mama and I would have had a different life. There was a lot of joy and happiness wasted and too much pain for all involved and that was a fact. Still, that is now all water under the bridge and I need to learn to live with it in a way that is, as Mary would put it, for my own 'highest good.' Well, that would be a new approach for me, that's for sure,* thought Olivia, taking another sip.

**

Sofia woke up still thinking about and reacting to her run-in with Mary the night before. Truth be told, Sofia kind of enjoyed arguments, even ones taking place in her mind. *Oh well, at least it will give me something to do on the silent morning walk.* She was looking at the schedule before her. *I can use that time to think up all the sharp-witted comebacks I could have said to Mary if they'd only occurred to me at the time.*

Despite the unresolved argument churning in her brain, Sofia was beginning to reevaluate some things she'd never given much thought to before now. This was a marked departure from her usual approach. Instead of just doing things her way or, as she most often did in her business, barking orders for others to do things her way, Sofia was considering her position. It was a subtle shift but one that let in a glimmer of new perspective, much like a crack in a window allowing a sliver of sunlight to filter through.

Sofia laced up her walking shoes tightly and headed for the door.

Chapter 31

Asking for Forgiveness

Flashlights were seen from all corners of the property as the women made their way through the darkness of the early morning to the gathering area in front of the dining hall for the day's first activity.

As they walked towards the central campus, they read the daily messages and quotes that had been placed by the staff throughout the paths and were illuminated by subtle accent lights. It was clear what today's main focus was all about, as the messages all revolved around forgiveness.

> To forgive is to remove a block in your awareness and to open to love's presence. —A Course in Miracles
>
> When you choose to forgive those who have hurt you, you take away their power. —Anonymous
>
> The act of forgiveness is all about you and nothing at all to do with others. —Louise Hay
>
> Forgiveness is not an occasional act; it is a constant attitude. —Martin Luther King Jr.

Jennifer caught up with Stephanie, who was reading the signs. She decided it was a good idea to approach Stephanie with what was on her mind.

"Hi Stephanie. Good morning," she said.

Stephanie turned and smiled, saying, "Good morning, Jennifer. How did you sleep?"

"Good, thank you. Can I walk with you? I'd like to ask you a question," Jennifer replied.

"Of course. But only one," Stephanie said, grinning.

Jennifer laughed too. "Well, when I first saw you here, you looked kind of perfect to me—beautiful, thin, elegant—and I confess, I was a little intimidated by you. But now...."

"But now what? Now you don't think I am perfect, beautiful, thin, and elegant anymore?" Stephanie winked at Jennifer so she'd know she was teasing her.

"It's not that," Jennifer quickly clarified, laughing slightly. "It's just that after hearing you share your own experiences, I realized you face challenges too, just like all of us."

"Pedestals are never a good thing, that's what I've found," Stephanie remarked. "You can only look down on others from there. And sooner or later, you're likely to fall off."

Jennifer chuckled. "That's true, I guess."

"What did you want to ask me?" Stephanie said.

"Since you are a mom too, I wanted to know how *you* managed."

"Managed what?" Stephanie asked.

"How you kept your daughters from seeing your pain?" Jennifer replied.

"Oh, well, I didn't," Stephanie stated flatly. "I'm sure my daughters saw right through me. You can't hide anything from kids. They may not have known details, but they knew something was not right. After reflecting and meditating these past few days, I've come to realize that all I was doing was keeping myself distant, but I wasn't hiding any of my secrets from them or from my husband, really. I've been excessively emotional, frequently crying, and constantly on edge. I've been unhappy and irritable, and despite their young age, it's only natural that my children would have sensed that."

"Jeez, you've been getting some insights, huh?" said Jennifer, slightly awed.

"Yes, I guess I have. I'm really trying. I don't want to waste the opportunities this place is offering me."

"Yes, me neither," said Jennifer.

"Anything else you wanted to know?" asked Stephanie.

"You pretty much answered it," Jennifer replied. "My kids definitely noticed how bitter, angry and sad I was. I trash-talked their dad, I drank too much, and I was entirely self-absorbed. I was supposed to be the grown-up, but I was the one who sucked up all the attention that should have been theirs.

Now that I see that, I can't help but feel guilty about it. Are you feeling guilty too?"

"Totally," Stephanie answered, "but I now know that I can't do anything about the past. So, when I get home, I'm going to have a long talk with my husband and another heartfelt one with my daughters, and I will tell them Mommy is sorry for not listening to them when they needed her and for having been sad and mad so many times. I'll make amends to them as best I can."

"I need to do the same," Jennifer declared. "But I've been toying with how I should say that I'm sorry."

"I'm sure you'll find the right words," Stephanie said, "but I think the most important thing is to make sure you aren't saying you are sorry just so they will forgive you, and you can be done with a difficult conversation. I'm keeping careful watch over myself to make certain I'm not just trying to make myself feel better but to really make changes in my life and improve my relationships."

"Yeah, but instant forgiveness would be nice and easy," Jennifer added, with a mischievous grin.

"It would, no doubt, but it probably isn't what we need," Stephanie pointed out.

"You know, Stephanie," Jennifer said, smiling at her. "When it comes to giving advice, you *are* pretty perfect. Thank you."

"You're quite welcome, Jennifer," said Stephanie as they arrived at the gathering place.

They hugged and then turned to the others, who were helping themselves to hot beverages to beat back the morning chill before the scheduled walk began.

The Orchid

Chapter 32

Silence

Mary and a few others were engaged in conversation. The "not morning people" kept to themselves, while some others stood in small groups but remained quiet, readying themselves for the Silent Walk Meditation.

When the last person arrived, Mary addressed the group.

"Good morning, everyone. I trust you all had a wonderful night's sleep." She smiled, looked around, and waited for the chatter to die down.

"Last night's Council," Mary continued, "was such a privilege to experience. Your presence and openness made it all so special. I know such energy movement can be tiring, so thank you all very much for showing up so early this morning.

"This morning's activities," Mary continued, "provide an opportunity for each of us to become aware of and connect with another amazing power—forgiveness. We'll do that through silence, being present and in the *now*. We will be allowing ourselves to feel, sense, and experience our connection with the Earth and all that surrounds us, finally letting go of that which doesn't serve our highest good. As we go through these exercises, it also helps to have an intention."

As Mary said these last words, she looked and motioned for Silvia, who had led the morning meditation the first day, to take over.

Silvia took a few steps to get closer to the center of the group, and, placing her right hand on her heart and her left on her stomach, said, "*Gracias*. Thank you, Mary, and good morning, everyone. Today, it is my honor and pleasure to be with you again and guide you through this beautiful exercise.

"This activity will take you through the stages of silence, connection, and release.

"There is incredible power in silence. Silence is an opportunity to reflect, to listen, and to experience the wisdom that is inside each of us and in all which surrounds us. When we are silent, the messages of the universe present themselves, becoming clear and apparent.

"Next, we will concentrate on connection, first with our breath, then with our physical bodies, and finally with the natural world surrounding us.

"When we focus on our breath, our mind is present and cannot wander."

Demonstrating as she spoke, Silvia then said, "We will inhale deeply and slowly, pause, and then exhale just as gently and for a slightly longer moment. We will do that a few times, until we are fully present and in the now. Then, once that has been achieved, on our next exhalation, we will take one step forward. Every step is to be completed with the utmost mindfulness." Silvia demonstrated how slow and deliberate each step should be, raising and lowering her feet as though walking through heavy syrup.

"Feel the soft, solid placement of your foot as you place it on the ground and the connection to *Pachamama*, the name my Quechua people, descendants of the Incas, gave to Mother Earth. Feel every muscle in your body as it contributes to your movement. Feel the weight of your arms at your sides, the weight of your head on your shoulders, and their roles in balancing your body. Observe yourself with awareness and purpose.

"Finally, we will connect with nature—the beauty and majesty that is all around us. Begin by simply observing, intentionally and mindfully, all which you see: trees, birds, rocks, and flowers. Admire it all. If you have trouble focusing, give your mind something to momentarily concentrate on by quietly naming the things with which you are connecting. When you are focusing on a tree, call it by its name—tree. When you see a bird, call it—bird. A rock—rock. A plant—plant. By doing this, you keep your minds intentionally occupied and grounded in the present.

"In silence and through these connections—breath, body, and nature—you open the door for your inner self to manifest, and then, using its infinite wisdom and power, you can advance to the next step—release."

Silvia repeated the word "release," pausing intentionally.

"I want all of you to pick up a rock, any one that catches your attention. At that moment, with gratitude in your heart, give thanks to the rock for the service it is about to provide. You will walk with that rock in your hand, and every time you have an unhelpful thought, you are going to blow that thought into the rock, releasing all energy associated with that thought."

Silvia blew softly on the rock she held in her hand.

"Do that as many times as such thoughts present themselves. At the end of the exercise, you will leave the rock behind and, with it, all that heavy energy you will have released into it.

"If at any time you find that your mind is wandering to other places and thoughts, do not despair, and don't give it too much attention. Lovingly, just return to your intention and begin the process again.

"Remember, this walk is meant to be conducted in complete silence. I know it sounds unnecessary to say this," she smiled, "but please don't name out loud the things you are seeing along the way." The women laughed at the thought. "The goal is for us to be in complete silence, and through that silence, to go deep within and hear our inner selves.

"To facilitate this, please keep about ten feet or so apart from one another on the path."

She paused, "Any questions?"

Nicole raised her hand.

"Yes?" Silvia acknowledged her.

"What if I don't have an intention?" Nicole asked.

"Thank you for the question," Silvia responded. "I suspect that if you don't have an intention on which you are focusing by now, it is not because you don't want one, but rather because you are not yet clear on what that intention should be. What that needs to be will be revealed to you when you are ready. For now, I recommend that your temporary intention could be to be clear on what is for your highest good as it pertains to forgiveness. Does that make sense?"

Nicole nodded, "Yes, it does."

A second woman raised her hand to ask another question.

"Yes?" Silvia said, looking at her.

"Mary spoke of activities, but you have only spoken of one. Are there others?" the woman asked.

The Orchid

"Yes, thank you for that. There are actually three parts to this activity. The first is the walk towards the top of the hill, the second is a moment of contemplation at the top of the summit as we appreciate the magnificence of the sunrise, and the third is walking the labyrinth. We will do all three in silence.

"The walking of a labyrinth," she continued, "is an incredibly powerful experience. Something special happens when the energy of a labyrinth intertwines with the energy of a soul. As the two interact, they create a spiritual union that manifests itself in the form of peace, harmony, and a knowing you may not have ever experienced before. It is there, at the powerful center of the labyrinth, where you will leave the rock, with all its heavy energy, to be lifted, cleared, dissolved, and transformed.

"Let me just add that there are no words that can fully describe what you will experience this morning, but I promise, you will understand it after you've completed the exercise."

Silvia looked around to see if there were any other questions and, seeing no hands raised, looked to Mary to see if she wanted to add something.

Mary simply thanked Silvia and, looking at all the women, said, "As you go about your walk, keep the power of forgiveness present within you, and if you can and are willing, integrate it into your intention. We will speak a lot more on forgiveness later today."

Mary smiled as she motioned for Silvia to continue.

"Ok then, let's get on with it," Silvia said as she led the way towards a path to her left, barely discernible in the darkness. The lights from the flashlights lit the way as the group followed single file, keeping a distance between them. A member of the staff walked at the tail end of the group to make sure no one was left behind. Soon, they all disappeared into the heavy foliage.

Chapter 33

Releasing Heavy Energy

All the women scanned the ground for the rock they would carry for the walk. Nicole, who was towards the rear of the group, was thinking that she picked the perfect rock. It was round, polished, light, and small, fitting perfectly in her right hand. It was still cold and damp from the early morning dew, and she held it tightly as she kept her hands inside her jacket's pockets. *Wow,* she thought, *Is spiritual insight really this simple? All that's required is a rock, an intention, connection, and silence?*

As they continued on, the group established a pace and rhythm. Though quite slow, the walk was steady. The calmness and serenity of the moment was palpable through the silence. As they ascended, the pink clouds stretched across the golden sky, soon to welcome the rising sun, the birds all joining in the now familiar symphony.

Nicole started to obsess, her thoughts returning to her situation with Elena and her parents, rolling the same arguments over and over in her mind like a gerbil on a wheel. She remembered Silvia's instructions and began naming the things she saw and heard. *Dirt, bamboo, birds, rocks, mountain, flower,* she recited in her head. Doing so distracted her from the thoughts that were plaguing her, and she soon realized the purpose and power of the method.

Nicole was very conscious of doing the exercise correctly, remaining at the proper distance from the woman who preceded her. She didn't want to disturb the woman's concentration. *Why do I always follow every rule so strictly?* she thought to herself. The next instant, she got her answer as she heard her mother's voice, shrill in her mind, "*Be a good girl, Nicole. Don't get dirty. Good girls don't do that. What will people think? You are breaking your mother's heart. God is going to punish you, Nicole.*"

The Orchid

The idea that she had to be a good girl, earn her mother's pride, and please God, had kept Nicole following the rules all her life. *If I am doing the right thing, why do I feel so miserable?* Nicole tightened her grip on the rock and blew long breaths into it. With a deep sigh, she took up the recitation again. "Shoes, rock, rabbit, tree, rooster." Her mother's scowling face looked on in her mind, disapprovingly.

Chapter 34

Silent Meditation

As she walked near the tail end of the group, Olivia noticed the natural beauty surrounding her and felt her shoulders relax from their usual tensed condition. She was, albeit briefly, in the moment, aware only of the chill morning air, the changing colors of the sky, and the shadows retreating from the foliage, their night shift over.

But the habits of a lifetime soon took over, and she found herself anxious about the other women walking with her. *Are they getting everything they need out of this walking meditation? Is there any way their week here could be more productive? Is Stephanie eating enough?* And then she stopped herself. *No!* she all but said out loud. *How the other women are doing is not my responsibility but my own well-being is. Time to concentrate on how you are doing, Olivia, you old busybody,* she chided herself.

Ok, Olivia, pay attention to just you for a while. As that thought crossed her mind, she realized she had a tool to help keep herself focused, and she literally had it in the palm of her hand. She started a mental conversation with her companion. *Hey rock,* she said, feeling a little silly, *I'll start out thanking you for sort of volunteering for our mission today. I am going to breathe onto you any unhelpful thoughts that do not serve me well. I think it's kind of a raw deal for you, but I want you to know that I really appreciate your service. Thanks for lightening my load.*

Another voice, *Maybe the rock's,* she thought wildly, asked, *The same way you lightened the load for your Mama?*

Well, I tried to do everything I could to be helpful, Olivia thought. *I loved her so.*

And she loved you too, the voice said, and, just then, a hummingbird flew very close to Olivia's face, hovering in the air just in front of her.

Wow, what a lovely bird, and how close it is flying, she said to herself, admiring the emerald-green breast and the wings fluttering so fast she could hear them buzz. And then, it hit her. It took her a second or two before she realized that this was not any bird. *It was a hummingbird! Mama's favorite!*

The sounds of the forest and her fellow walkers faded away. The air grew still and started to shimmer like a heat mirage rising from the highway on a summer's day. The light became opalescent and Olivia caught a light scent on the slight breeze that rose up, caressing her face like loving fingertips. It was familiar, *oh so familiar,* and Olivia was transported to those Sunday church services with her Mama. Only on that day would her mother use a few drops of the precious bottle of eau de cologne her husband had bought her when they were first married. Olivia remembered the sweet floral fragrance surrounding her like a hug. *Mama?* she whispered. *Mama?* Suddenly Olivia sensed her mother walking beside her. The sensation was so real she stopped breathing and felt a deep sense of gratitude that reverberated throughout her body. Olivia felt if she just turned her head, she would see her mother, but she found herself frozen with intense emotion and blinded by tears. *Hey Mama,* she whispered. *I really miss you. I wish I could talk with you; there's so much I never had a chance to say.*

Say it now, child, the voice said.

I am so sorry that I couldn't save you from my father, Mama. I'm sorry I couldn't throw myself in front of you and take the punches on myself. I caught enough of them; I could have taken more. I wanted to shut his lying mouth every time he talked his way back into our home. I wanted to kill him, Mama, for leaving us and for coming back. I wanted to rescue you, and I wanted him dead.

There it was, as honest a declaration as Olivia had ever heard, and it came from deep within herself.

As she spoke, the loving emotion that she had felt just a few seconds ago was replaced with growing anger. Olivia tried blowing into the rock as she'd been told. The anger seemed to have a life of its own though, the pressure building like a volcano on the cusp of erupting. She started feeling a tightening around her chest as if its walls were collapsing in all directions. Gasping now for breath, Olivia felt her heartbeat speed up like a trip hammer, and her face flushed with hot blood that emptied as she broke out in a cold sweat. The world tilted. Confused, dizzy, and disoriented, Olivia leaned against the mountain wall, slowly sliding down to sit on the ground as she tried to catch her breath.

Nicole was closest to her and ran to her side. One of the staffers joined them, too. Nicole reached her first, tilting water from her bottle into her hands and tapping Olivia's cheeks.

"Olivia, Olivia, can you hear me?" Nicole asked calmly. Olivia, breathing irregularly, gave a slight nod. "I'm a trained paramedic. Please try not to move," instructed Nicole. Quickly but gently, Nicole checked Olivia's pulse by holding her wrist. It was fast but strong. Then, she observed her breathing and coloring. As Olivia began to stabilize and color returned to her face, Nicole asked, "How do you feel?"

Olivia took a few moments to respond. "I'm better now," Olivia said, taking several deep breaths. "Thank you. I think I just had another panic attack. I have been having them recently."

Mary, who was not too far away, ran down the mountain to Olivia's side.

"My dear, Olivia. Are you alright?" Mary asked, placing one hand on her shoulders as she knelt next to her.

"Yes, thank you. I'm alright. I'm much better now. I guess I didn't blow all my harmful thoughts into the rock fast enough," Olivia said, trying to lighten the mood some and retrieving the rock that had rolled from her palm. "It was another panic attack."

"How many does that make?" Mary asked.

"Too many," replied Olivia, a little shaken still.

"Olivia, you need to be checked out at the infirmary immediately," Mary said.

"No, not now please," Olivia answered. "I have to continue this walk. I'll take full responsibility, but I'd like to continue the walk. I promise to report to the infirmary the second we get back. Please Mary."

The two women's eyes locked, and Mary nodded.

"Ok, but one of the medically trained staffers will be walking behind you."

They all assisted Olivia to her feet, and turning to Nicole and the others, Mary said, "Thank you so much for your amazing help, Nicole. Olivia wants to continue. We'll be keeping a close eye on her, the rest of you please continue with your exercise."

Watching while Olivia took some sips of her water bottle, and, with a final embrace, Mary asked one of the staff to remain behind and attentive to Olivia, as she, Mary, headed to the front of the group again. Gradually, Olivia resumed her walk and the conversation she'd been having. *Was it with myself or the rock?*, she wondered.

She couldn't say, but she knew what she saw as her anger had built just before she had the panic attack: the face of her father, as clear as day, looking at her with a world of sorrow in his eyes. He was crying. She heard his still familiar voice say, "I'm so sorry, Livy. I didn't mean to hurt you or your mother. I loved you both, best way I knew how. I'z a sick man, not a bad man. Forgive me, Livy."

As Olivia heard her father use his childhood nickname for her, Olivia felt her heart open.

"It's ok. I know you didn't mean to. I forgive you, Daddy," she whispered, and blew all the pain and anger and sorrow into the rock, which grew heavier in Olivia's hand as her spirit grew lighter.

Chapter 35

A New Day

The pink rays tinged the golden sky, ready to welcome the sun as the women reached the summit. They were silently directed to sit, facing the eastern horizon. After the intensity of the walk and the profound introspection that some of the women were experiencing, the energy of the sunrise brought about a huge sense of gratitude. The entire world and all its living creatures—people, animals, plants, fungi—seemed to be kneeling in homage to its power and might.

As the sun lit the upturned faces of the seated women, Sofia looked at each, searching for insincerity and could find none. Every face was aglow with serenity and looked on the sunrise with rapture.

Sofia turned to watch the solar disk as it rode the sky. It was magnificent, and Sofia was struck by how she was only a small part of something so much larger. Perhaps there *was* a higher power, like they all talked about, a Creator of all this—a force that had created her. And maybe that power didn't stop after creating her. *What if that power still looks out for me and is available to guide my life? Maybe I don't have to go it all alone,* Sofia thought. *Maybe I've never done it alone.*

Turning the concept over in her mind, Sofia whispered, "Ok, I am listening. Tell me what I need to know."

**

Olivia, watching the sunrise, had a deep sense of gratitude. *I'm thankful for the opportunity of being alive,* she thought. These words, in particular, had a deeper meaning, especially after the scare she had just experienced. *Thank you for the opportunity to be here, for those special moments, for being able to be with my Mama and for finally being open to the pain I have carried inside of myself for so long.* She knew that facing the pain was the beginning step to being truly rid of it.

As the first rays of sunlight caressed her face, she thought of how beautiful the Earth was and how rarely she was able to experience it in all of its glory, with such gratitude and calm. She reached for the rock in her pocket and once again breathed into it, this time letting go of the guilt of not having dedicated more time to herself and allowed more moments like this in her life. She promised herself that she would be sure to include them more often from now on. As she did, she closed her eyes and enjoyed the sensation of the sun's warmth on her skin. She took a deep breath and then another and felt a peace wash over her.

At that moment, and for what seemed the first time in her life, Olivia was able to connect with and be acutely aware of her other senses. With her eyes still closed, she heard the choir of birds that accompanied the arrival of the day and felt the life force of grass as she lightly caressed it with the back of her hands. She still held tightly to the rock but noticed that it was no longer heavy.

She thought about her father. She searched her heart and knew that the anger and animus was gone. Now she felt only sorrow that, because of his disease, her father had missed so much. He never felt the support and comfort of a loving family. He never got to truly know her as a little girl, never got to see her grow and become the woman she was today. She had missed having a father in her life, but he, too, had missed out on having a loving daughter in his.

The thought made her sad. In her mind, she sent him off with one final message: *I do love you, Daddy, and I always will.*

Olivia opened her eyes, and, as she did, she saw that Mary was sitting next to her. Mary had never ventured too far from Olivia after the panic attack. She had also sent word to Leyla, The Orchid's physician. The doctor had made the climb to the mountain and was also sitting nearby, observing Olivia quietly, not wanting to disturb her process.

Olivia was pleased to see Mary. Any other time and she may have felt crowded and encroached upon, but not here and not now. She knew Mary's concern for her stemmed from a place of love.

Mary asked in a low voice so as not to distract the others, "I'm sorry for disturbing your silence and meditation, but I must ask. How are you feeling?"

"Good. Thank you. The panic attack seems long and far away," Olivia said. Then she quickly changed the subject. "I've had some very profound insights."

"Anything you want to share?" Mary asked.

"I feel as if I have relinquished a heavy burden," Olivia replied. "My mom was here, and I think my dad was too."

"Yes, I could sense them as well," Mary answered.

Olivia's eyes welled up again, and tears rolled down her cheeks. "Thank you," she said simply.

"You're welcome. But I didn't do anything. I simply held the love, and you did all the work. Forgiveness is a powerful thing." Mary grabbed and squeezed Olivia's hand before letting go.

Then, just as Mary started to rise, Olivia grabbed her hand again and whispered, "Why did you mention forgiveness?"

Gently holding Olivia's hand, Mary replied, "Because forgiveness is the key that unlocks the door to healing and I can see you're on that path." She then stood up and walked away, leaving Olivia lost in her thoughts.

The Orchid

Chapter 36

Labyrinth

Olivia's walk down the mountain was different than the one going up. Gone was the pain and heaviness that she had felt earlier. Venturing into the labyrinth, Olivia was filled with a sense of purposeful tranquility. The circuitous path symbolized her own journey, each turn echoing the decisions that had shaped her life, the joys and sorrows interwoven to create her unique tapestry of experiences.

As she reached the center of the labyrinth, Olivia felt a deeper harmony with her inner self and a serene reconciliation with her past. She felt for the rock in her pocket, now the vessel of her anguish, resentment, and harmful emotions. She then kissed it, thanked it, and placed it on the ground, releasing that darkness that she had carried for nearly all of her life back into the nothingness from which it came.

One by one, as all women completed their respective journeys through and into the center of the labyrinth, they made their way back to the area were Mary and Silvia were standing. All still observed the silence. Their faces variously reflected joy and sadness, awareness and denial, tension and acceptance, but none remained unchanged.

As the last one joined the group, Silvia began to address them.

"How powerful it is to be in silence and to receive the strength of that encounter. The poet Rumi wrote, 'In silence there is eloquence. Stop weaving and see how the pattern improves.'

"It is a reminder that when we take a deep breath, and when we allow ourselves to relax, to be still, silent, in reverence, when we put aside all of the things that distract us, we open ourselves to the frequency, to the knowledge, and to the most powerful experience in the universe. We open ourselves to the power and perfection of love."

She continued, bringing the women's focus back to the present moment. "I can see that many of you are still processing all of it. I know that there are thoughts, images, feelings, and emotions that have surfaced. Allow yourself the time to let those simmer and provide you with a rich soup of wisdom, full of insights you never knew you hungered for."

She paused again and smiled, placing her right hand over her heart.

"It is important that when you are in such a place, you remember to be kind to yourself; to bathe in absolute self-love; to forgive yourself for the feelings of guilt, shame, grief, and fear that may be present and which may bring your energy down. You are not your thoughts. You are not your actions. You are not broken. You are wonderful. You are perfect. You are divine."

Silvia turned then to Mary.

Mary said, "As it has been written and repeated many times, 'We are not human beings having a spiritual experience; we are spiritual beings having a human experience.'"

She paused and then repeated it, gesturing for the women to join in, "'We are not human beings having a spiritual experience; we are spiritual beings having a human experience.'"

"When you understand the depth of that statement, you realize that you are not the fear, the hate, the guilt, or shame that you carry. However, and this is critical to also realize, if you find yourself wrapped in those thoughts, they still have an effect. They will bind your spirit. You all learned about energy, vibration, and the power of attraction and resonance. That which you are attracts more of the same. If you are bound in shame and guilt, you will attract that. If you are in forgiveness, acceptance, and love, you will attract that too. It's really that beautifully simple."

Mary continued. "For now, as you head back to your rooms, remember to be kind, loving, and forgiving with yourself. When you find you are having an unkind thought, simply place your hand on your heart and say, '*I forgive myself* for this idea, this unhelpful thought. *The truth is*, I am a spiritual being having a human experience.' Repeat this as many times as you need to access your inexhaustible reservoir of self-love.

"Search within to determine which forgiveness and truth statements most resonate with you." She then went on to share a few examples.

> "I forgive myself for the idea that I cannot trust people. The truth is, I am fully capable of trusting myself and others.

"I forgive myself for the idea that it's my job to carry the weight of the world. The truth is that each person has their own path and learning.

"I forgive myself for the idea that if I honor who I truly am, others will not love me. The truth is, I have every right to be exactly who I am or choose to be.

"I forgive myself for the idea that it was my fault. The truth is that I did the best I could with what I had.

"I forgive myself for the idea that I cannot be happy. The truth is, I am both deserving and fully capable of feeling joy."

Mary paused and was quiet for a moment, she knew it was best to give everyone time and space to process.

After a few moments she spoke again. "And now, continue your journey. Keep searching deep within for the answers. I promise you they are all there.

"A suggestion for your consideration: try to remain in silence for a while longer. Use this opportunity to journal your experience, following the guidance we gave before. It will be incredibly powerful to purge some of the feelings and experiences that may be present, and writing is a most powerful tool.

"Remember to light a candle, write for fifteen to twenty minutes, do not read what you wrote, and burn it afterwards. Simply get it out of your system and release it back into the energy of the universe from which it came."

Mary placed her two hands crossed over her heart and beamed at them with admiration for the work they were doing. "And now, my loves, we will see you later this morning. Much light and love to you all."

The Orchid

Chapter 37

Tarot

Mary had arranged for Sofia's tarot reading to take place at the Observatory, a small, singular domed structure settled on a hill deep within the property. The building rested in a clearing, providing wide, unblocked vistas of the sky. Crafted in a unique blend of modern and traditional design, its exterior of reflective glass and polished chrome captured the movement of sunlight throughout the day, casting a bewitching play of light akin to a mystical dance. Hanging above its door was the same legend that greeted visitors to the Temple of Apollo at Delphi, where the famous oracle once spoke to visitors: "Know thyself."

Sofia, still reflecting on her encounter with Mary, thought she did know herself, but her old self would have snapped right back at Mary's criticism and then forgotten the entire incident. That wasn't Sofia's reaction this time and that change confused her. She respected Mary, thought she had integrity, and didn't appear to be after anything other than sincerely helping the women achieve some level of transformation.

Sofia believed Mary might only be trying to help her, too. She started to question why she always had to rebel against authority, to be so combative and arrogant. *Maybe*, a voice in her mind niggled her, *if you just shut up and listen with an open mind, you might just learn something.*

Annoyingly, Sofia recognized the voice as her own and decided to heed the advice.

She knocked on the door of the Observatory, reluctant to just barge in, and it slowly opened to reveal a dim interior shot through with sunbeams from the many tiny windows encircling the dome. Greeting her in the doorway was a woman of indeterminate age—not young nor old—with jet black hair; a swarthy complexion; and large, luminous eyes. Those eyes looked into

Sofia's, and it felt as though they were reaching into her soul. Sofia gave a small shudder, and the woman answered it with a warm smile.

"Welcome Seeker," she said as she stood aside to allow Sofia to enter.

"Hi, my name is Sofia," Sofia offered.

"I know. Welcome. I've been expecting you," she replied.

The interior of the building had several rooms projecting from a central area marked by a mosaic of a crescent moon created through sparkling tiles and semi-precious gems—amethyst, jasper, garnet, lapis—, with the moonbeams themselves made from golden citrine. Sofia stopped for a moment, mesmerized by the beauty of the piece.

"The moon is sacred to the goddess and we, who bleed every month according to her cycle, are daughters of the moon, daughters of the goddess. This is a sacred place, where we ask her to help us see into ourselves," the healer said. "Please follow me."

She led Sofia to one of the rooms. It was dim, but Sofia could still see that the walls were hung all round with royal purple velvet and lit by candles to chase away any shadows. In the center was a small round table covered by a draping cloth, navy blue with metallic stars, and drawn up to it were two high-backed chairs with embroidered cushions. Inviting Sofia to sit in one of the chairs, the woman took the other and spoke again.

"Would you care for a cup of tea before we begin?"

"Yes, thank you," Sofia answered. The woman leaned to her side and, from a low table there, poured Sofia a fragrant cup of cardamom tea that smelled so lovely Sofia thought the amber liquid could be used as a perfume.

"Aside from your first name, Sofia, I know nothing more about you. I asked Mary not to share anything so that my interpretation of our reading wouldn't be tainted with any pre-knowledge I would have. But to make you feel comfortable, I will share with you some things about me and what we will do here together.

"My name is Magda and I hail from Ireland, though I am not Irish. I am of the Roma, what the Irish call 'Travelers' and what the rest of the world calls 'Gypsies.' We live in caravans and travel the land as we have for thousands of years, keeping our own culture—a rich one filled with mysticism. I learned to read palms, tea leaves, and Tarot from my grandmother, who had learned it from hers, who had learned it from hers. Our culture stretches back through the mists of time, perhaps to ancient India; no one is certain. What is certain is that many of us, me included, have the gift of divination, and I dedicated mine to helping women here at The Orchid, at Mary's invitation, from the moment it opened its doors more than twenty years ago."

Magda continued, "Do you know of Tarot and the reading of the cards?"

Sofia shook her head and said, "I've heard of the Tarot but don't really know anything about it."

Magda went on to explain. "In the middle of the fifteenth century, Bonifacio Bembo, a painter for the Visconti family of Milan, created a deck for an Italian game called *Tarocchi*, which may have been a gambling or parlor game. The deck contained images used in esoteric or magical practices of which Bembo himself may have been an initiate and," Magda winked at Sofia, "if that was the case, he may have been passing along knowledge as old as humanity.

"One of the suggested coincidences in Bembo's deck is that it contained twenty-two major cards, corresponding to the twenty-two Hebrew letters of the alphabet, an alphabet which is used in the mystical symbolism of the Kabbalah, the occult branch of the ancient Jewish religion. Bembo's deck could have been a pictorial representation of the Kabbalah. There is even talk that there was a gathering, a conference of Kabbalists and occult masters in Morocco in 1300, where the deck was created, but that may be a fable. Then, in the nineteenth century, a Frenchman, Antoine Court de Gebelin, pronounced the deck to be a missing part of the *Book of Thoth*, the ancient Egyptian *Book of the Dead*.

"Whichever of these tales is true, or even if none of them are, is unimportant. We may even think of Tarot in modern terms. Carl Jung, one of the founding fathers of psychoanalysis, taught that there are basic spiritual archetypes built into the human mind that govern our subconscious and so affect our consciousness and therefore our actions. Perhaps Bembo was just illustrating those archetypes.

"Whatever is the true origin, we now use the Tarot as a tool of spiritual growth to help us understand ourselves. That is why the quote over the door as you enter reads, 'Know thyself.' Knowing ourselves is the path not only to wisdom but to freedom.

"Are you finished with your tea? If so, let me take it from you and we shall begin."

The Orchid

Magda asked that Sofia give her both her hands, and, as she held them in her own, she said:

"You should know that the words you are about to hear are not my own. I am merely a conduit for the wisdom of the universe. The messages you are about to receive through the cards are reflections of the energies and forces that currently surround you. They are not fixed predictions of the future, but rather guides and perspectives that can help you navigate your path. The cards can reveal tendencies, challenges, opportunities, and lessons, but at the end of the day, the power to decide and act lies with you. The true magic is not in the cards, but in how you choose to respond to the messages they present. So, as we proceed with this reading, I invite you to keep an open mind and to listen with your heart."

Sofia could have sworn she felt a jolt of energy. Startled, she looked at their clasped hands as if she could see an actual spark. Then she looked up at Magda, who was smiling ever so slightly.

Magda closed her eyes and bowed her head as she said,

> "Please, Mother Goddess, ancient spirits of the earth and wind, guide my hand, my words and my sight on this journey. May the cards speak the truth of the universe, and may their message illuminate the path of the seeker. For her highest good. So be it."

Then she let go of Sofia's hands and opened a carved box set to the side of the table. In it was a slightly oversized deck of cards with bright colors and fascinating images, the likes of which Sofia had never seen.

"Today, there are countless adaptations and variations of the tarot. Most have their roots in the Rider-Waite deck, which was created in 1909 by Arthur Edward Waite and illustrated by the artist Pamela Colman Smith, also known as Pixie. Mary herself gifted me this particular deck I hold in my hands when I first joined the team two decades ago. It is also inspired by the Rider-Waite deck, but it incorporates Egyptian design and symbolism and of course, orchids. I've used it for two decades now, and it has accumulated a lot of wisdom with each reading. I'll guide you through the process, explaining each step, allowing our energies to merge for an insightful interpretation."

Magda took the deck and with her left hand tapped it hard, three times, on the top card.

"This is to clear any energy still left in the deck from someone else who has had a previous reading. We don't want to mix up your future with someone else's, now, do we?" she said with a playful laugh.

After shuffling them briefly, she extended the deck towards Sofia. "Now, I want you to tap the cards three times and shuffle them. This way, the cards will start to tune into your energy."

Sofia, slightly nervous, did as Magda instructed. After shuffling, she handed them back.

As Magda took the deck again she asked, "So, Sofia, what is it you want to know? And please keep in mind that the Tarot gives the best answers when we ask specific questions. Try to be as precise as you can."

After some thought, Sofia said, "I guess I want to know what is going to happen to me and my business when I leave The Orchid."

"Excellent," Magda replied and set the pile of shuffled cards on the table. "Please cut the cards as many times as you like, keeping them face down."

Sofia cut the deck three times (never realizing that was the sacred number of many metaphysical practices) and then sat back.

Magda reassembled the cards and began laying them out.

"I'm using a layout called the Celtic Cross, which consists of ten cards. The first six cards are arranged in the shape of a cross: one in the center with another crossed over it, one above, one below, one to the left, and one to the right. The remaining four cards are placed in a vertical line to the right of the cross, often referred to as the staff." Magda paused for a moment to study the spread and then began to explain the different cards and what their positions meant.

QUEEN OF SWORDS

"The first card, in the central position, represents your General Situation. It's a reflection of your essence, your center. Here, the cards show us the Queen of Swords. This card symbolizes strength, independence, and courage in the face of adversity. It suggests that you've faced challenges, but just like this queen, you've shown resilience. There's an energy of intelligence, determination, and unwavering will in you. While you display a strong inclination towards professional ambition, the cards also reveal an inner desire for connection and romantic love.

KNIGHT OF CUPS

"The second card, covering the first, is the Opposing Influence card, which indicates how you act. Here we see the Knight of Cups, representing your current actions and influences. As you can observe, this knight isn't in motion; he's contemplating the contents of his cup. He's neither drinking it nor discarding it. He is simply considering it. The cards tell us that you're in a stage of reflection. You're thinking about your past, somewhat confused about your present, and concerned about your future. It's a time of deep introspection and consideration for you."

Sofia's eyes widened as her mind sped back to the conversation she had been having with herself at the door. *That's exactly what I was thinking a little while ago. I didn't say anything out loud. How did Magda know what I was thinking?*

XIII DEATH XIII

As Magda revealed the third card, Sofia felt a chill go up her spine. Anubis, the god of the afterlife, stood majestically next to a sarcophagus. The card bore the name Death.

Magda stopped momentarily and looked into Sofia's eyes. "This third position is the Basis card, and it is what has caused your current situation. Death, in this instance, does not mean something or someone dies. It doesn't speak of a literal end, but of transformation and change. The cards suggest that in your past, you faced many emotions related to your parents. You've pushed them out of your life, and there's a sense of abandonment that you've held deep within for a long time."

Sofia struggled to contain her emotions. A tear rolled down her cheek as a pang of pain resurfaced from her childhood memories. She wiped her eyes with the back of her hand and continued to listen.

Magda went on: "The cards suggest that you've developed ways to cope with and overcome pain over time. These strategies, which once provided support and are part of your essence, have shaped your current reactions. However, the cards also indicate that some of these tactics, like being defensive or individualistic, might not be as relevant in this current stage of your life. It's an opportune time to reflect on what truly benefits you and consider the possibility of refreshing what no longer resonates with you.

IX

"The fourth card, the Nine of Swords, reflects the Recent Past and evokes memories and feelings of pain and grief, especially related to your parents and your brother. It seems you've felt their absence weighing on you, like the swords depicted in this card, for a significant portion of your life.

The Orchid

"But what this card also reveals is that you've recently undergone a rediscovery and deep introspection about your self-perception. In the past, you had a specific approach to facing challenges, based on your previous experiences. But what once provided you with security and certainty no longer works for you and appears to be transforming. However, the Base card indicates that you're in a phase of acknowledgment and adaptation, exploring new ways to interact with the world and yourself.

III

"The fifth position represents Possible Outcomes. The card drawn for you is the Three of Pentacles. While it has a spiritual undertone, Pentacles are often associated with material aspects. The image illustrates collaboration between a priest, an architect, and a builder, symbolizing the union of skills. It suggests an upcoming partnership where your abilities will be enhanced in conjunction with someone else's. This association will bring you satisfaction, and with effort, you're likely to achieve your goals. The spiritual aspect of the card serves as a reminder to show gratitude towards the higher forces that have endowed you with your talents."

Still moved, Sofia's mind couldn't help but wander to the idea that the cards were hinting at her desire to form a partnership with her friend Monica. With that thought in mind, she paid even closer attention to what followed.

V

"The sixth position is the Near Future card. The image depicts individuals in conflict, but it's not a violent confrontation as they use wands or tree branches instead of swords. It seems to be a situation with your family, where there are differences to be resolved. While there have been tensions in the past, the card suggests that future interactions will be more constructive. Notice how the branches show new sprouts, and some cross to form a 'V',

The Orchid

symbolizing 'victory.' A period of growth and mutual understanding among you is anticipated."

Sofia, who was experiencing a more profound connection with the Tarot reading, thought: *Maybe, I'll have to be the one to make the first approach with my family. Me! A peacemaker! Who would have thought? I guess that death card is right about transformation happening.*

IV

"In the seventh position we find the Self card," Magda continued. "It's helpful to consider this card in relation to your overall situation rather than in isolation. As I mentioned earlier, Pentacles are often associated with material aspects. Looking at the card, it's evident that the figure seems to have an abundance of Pentacles, but he clings so tightly to them that he can't move his hands and feet. He fears they are being taken away. His mind is also consumed, as money is on his thoughts. Sofia, the message for you is that you have valuable resources, but the card suggests you might be holding onto them with some reservation.

"It could be beneficial to reflect on how you relate to your resources and emotions. The card suggests that by opening up and sharing, you might experience broader growth. Caution is natural, but it's essential not to lose sight of the beauty and the opportunities surrounding you. By expanding your horizons, you can find new sources of inspiration and vitality."

At that moment, Sofia felt an internal shiver and became aware of her attachment to money and possessions, and how, at times, this attachment blinded her, preventing her from appreciating the beautiful moments life offered her.

III

"The eighth card represents the Environment, showing the external influences in your life. In the Three of Cups, we see figures joyfully celebrating. This card suggests an environment of support and emotional well-being. It indicates that, surrounded by these influences, you feel appreciation and value. Even though you've made progress, the journey of personal growth continues. The figures in the card might represent companions and guides on your path. It seems you're at a point of expansion and self-discovery, and these influences will be crucial in your evolution. They might be related to people you've met at The Orchid. But, to get a clearer insight, let's look at another card."

With that, Magda pulled another card from the top of the deck: the High Priestess.

"Ah, there she is," Magda added.

|| THE HIGH PRIESTESS ||

Sofia with a mixture of awe and respect in her voice said, "Mary. That's Mary, isn't it?"

Magda nodded, "Look at her crown: the full moon in the center. The High Priestess represents spiritual knowledge, wisdom, and feminine intuition. Behind her, a curtain suggests that not all lessons are revealed at once. However, through reflection and meditation, you can trust that the way will be shown to you. She invites you to introspection and to seek calm as you uncover internal answers. Her light will guide your path, and yes, Sofia, I agree that she could be a representation of our Mary.

VII THE CHARIOT VII

"The ninth card symbolizes Hopes and Fears. Notice it's not hopes or fears, but both simultaneously, and in your case, Sofia, it's easy to see that it addresses a balance between what you fear and what you hope for. The Chariot highlights the tension between your desires and concerns, and the challenge of steering and balancing those internal forces, as if you were guiding horses wanting to pull in opposite directions. It's a call to understand your impulses, neither suppressing them nor letting them sweep you away. Seeking balance is key; it's not about extreme reactions, but about channeling energies constructively. While conflict can be a catalyst for growth, it's vital to act thoughtfully, avoiding unnecessary harm. Even though you might feel insecure at times, there's also a latent hope for overcoming. I see in you the ability to face these challenges with wisdom and determination, Sofia.

XVII THE STAR XVII

"The tenth card symbolizes the Outcome, offering a consolidated view of the preceding cards. For you, Sofia, this card is the Star. It represents rebirth, renewal, and a beacon of hope. Despite facing challenges, you've shown resilience and have kept hope as your guide. This light is becoming the beacon illuminating your future. Signs indicate that things are starting to align in your favor, giving you reasons to be optimistic. Fresh opportunities and a renewed sense of purpose are on the horizon. Approach these experiences with an open mind and move forward with confidence. As you continue on this path, the shadows of the past will fade, leaving a radiant clarity, much like the glow of the Star."

As the reading finished, Magda looked up at Sofia, who met her gaze with a new sparkle in her eyes. "That was amazing," Sofia said. "Simply amazing. It's like you've known me my whole life!"

"I am so pleased, and yes, these readings often are," said Magda. "I have dispensed a lot of information. You might want to take some time to reflect and allow all of this to sink in. This may take days months or even years, so please do be patient. It will all be revealed in due time.

For now, do you have any questions?" Magda asked.

Sofia thought for a moment and answered, "Yes, I do. I have many, but I think I should take the time to process all that you have shared. Perhaps another time, if that's alright."

"Of course, it is," answered Magda.

"How can I ever thank you?" Sofia asked as she stood up and spontaneously hugged Magda.

"If you find value in the cards and the messages they've conveyed to you, I encourage you to reflect on it. Consider reconciling the conflict with your family, reevaluating your responses, and seeking balance in your interactions. Collaboration, trust, and affection can enrich your life. Follow a path that allows you to live fully, that dear seeker, is thanks enough for me."

The Orchid

Chapter 38

Blue Tape

After lunch, the women met at the Sanctuary to attend the afternoon lesson. The schedule showed that the session was expected to last five hours, as the work would be intense and required time to unfold properly.

They were greeted by Mary and many of The Orchid's teachers and healers. Familiar faces like Wakinyan, Silvia, Sister D, Flavia, Teena, Rani, Samara, Isabelle, Lucia, Magda, Aisha, and Leyla were present, along with some new people, apprentices to the veterans. It was quite a large gathering, and the guests wondered what would happen at that afternoon's session that required so many supporting hands on deck.

Jennifer led the way as the group took their seats on the floor mats. Around the room's perimeter were whiteboards on easels, one for every attendee. Besides markers of various colors, each easel also sported many pieces of blue painter's tape, each cut to about a foot long.

"Welcome, my dear sisters," Mary said when everyone had settled. "Today we have a special activity planned—a powerful and moving one which is in line with the theme of forgiveness. You have reached the mid-point of your journey with us, and it has come time to dig even deeper to help you grow along your spiritual path.

"As you have been learning throughout the day, forgiveness will help you do that. Like gratitude, forgiveness has also been found to improve health, reduce anxiety, and, especially, to lead to inner peace and spiritual advancement.

"Some of you will find today's activity uncomfortable, while others may find it liberating. Know that regardless of which group you fall into, it will definitely challenge and stretch your spirit. As you can see, many more of our team have joined today's session. They are here to provide you with any added support you may require during today's journey. I ask that you trust all of us. Collectively, we bring more than 450 years of shared expertise in our individual healing modalities and many years of experience having helped others through this very lesson. Relax, knowing we are all working for your greater good, and that is exactly what awaits you on the other side of this experience—a new perception of yourself, a clarity about who you have been, who you are, and who you are meant to be."

Mary paused and called upon a woman, Jana, who had raised her hand.

"This exercise sounds a bit overwhelming," Jana said in a tremulous voice. "Do I have to participate if I don't want to?"

"No dear, of course not. The choice to participate or not is always yours," Mary answered, "but, having said that, I would encourage you to join in this process of self-exploration. Over the years we have found this exercise to be one of the most life-changing for participants, well worth any momentary emotional discomfort you may feel during it."

Jana nodded her head and dropped her eyes. She didn't want to let Mary, or herself, down because of her lifelong reluctance to take chances.

"As we have said, our thoughts are powerful forces. They awaken emotions, and those emotions become the force that drives or stops our actions. In this manner, our emotions either empower or restrict us. We feel bold, brave, and confident enough to take action or we are stopped in our tracks with self-doubt, trepidation, or outright fear. When we find ourselves in the emotional storm of the latter, we are held back from reaching our full potential. Instead of being empowered, we are disempowered. These are our 'limiting beliefs.'

"When we spoke about awareness a couple of days ago, we touched on how these limiting beliefs were learned from our parents and family, our environment, from our society, and from our individual life experiences. All of those beliefs literally become the set of instructions, the user manual telling us what is possible or not in our lives, even if we aren't aware that we are following such instructions.

"Today's exercise invites you to explore and better understand those beliefs you carry with you. It will assist you in recognizing and reflecting on those thoughts and emotions you feel are holding you back. The goal is to identify them, understand them and if you wish, rewrite that internal guidebook so you feel more liberated and in tune with yourself."

Mary cast a glance at the faces surrounding her. Most were attentive and seemed eager to start on this new exercise.

Mary said, "We will begin with a short meditation asking the universe to bless us and empower us to go within and to discover only that which is for our highest good." She bowed her head and placed her palms together in front of her chest. Then she called for a few moments of silence, and, after each woman grew quiet, she began the meditation by saying:

> Dear Universe, Higher-Self, Infinite Source, Spirit, God,
>
> We humbly come before you today with open hearts and minds, seeking inspiration and guidance. We ask that you help us to bring forth all limiting beliefs, held pain, hurt or hurtful feelings, cutting words, and any heavy energy that we may hold within us and against ourselves and others. We ask to see them clearly and become acutely aware of them.
>
> We ask for the strength to forgive—to forgive ourselves and forgive others—and to release any heavy energy that may control us and which is not for our highest good.
>
> We are grateful for the power of love, awareness, gratitude, and forgiveness, and we thank you for guiding us on our journey of self-discovery and growth.
>
> To that we say—so be it and so it is.

Mary then raised her head again and said, "Now, please, everyone claim one of the whiteboards as your own."

When each person was standing next to an easel, Mary continued.

"Holding the highest good as your only intention, take a marker, and, on each piece of tape, print in big, clear letters what comes to mind when you imagine the thoughts and beliefs that may be holding you back. Write whatever you think is limiting you.

"Don't over-think your selections or argue with yourself about whether what you write is true or not. Allow yourself the freedom to write what springs to your mind, any belief that might be restricting you from living your best life. Add to the list your sources of pain and anxiety, including the names of people that you believe have hurt you and the situations you've experienced that you feel have left a disappointing mark on your life. Write also things for which you feel guilty or ashamed or blame yourself for, those things adding weights to your soul and preventing you from soaring to your highest heights.

"Scan your recent past, your childhood, even the fears you have for the future. Put each thing on a separate piece of tape. If you run out of pieces, our staff will provide more. Some of us may carry more than others," Mary said, smiling sympathetically, "and that's quite alright.

"I know this can sound like a tall ask. I remind you to be gentle with yourself but to be vulnerable and go as deep as you possibly can for the greatest level of healing. This is a safe space, and we are all here to support you.

"You will have ample time for the exercise, but keep in mind that this part of the exercise is meant to be quick. Get things off your spirit just as you pull lint off a sweater. Don't dwell on each thought. Just write it out onto the tape so you don't become overwhelmed. This is not a competition or a race—it is a clearing of the air of your soul."

Several of the women looked at each other quizzically, but others were already reaching for their markers.

Mary sensed some anxiety among those present and said, "If there are no questions about this exercise, let's begin with a short meditation. Let's take a moment to connect with our inner selves. Please, close your eyes and take several deep breaths.

"Imagine that with each inhale you are drawing in light and clarity into your being, and with each exhale you are releasing tensions and doubts. Feel how your feet connect with the ground, grounding you to the earth. Visualize a warm light descending from the universe, passing through the crown of your head, and flowing through your entire body down to your feet. This light brings you tranquility, safety, and clarity. By doing this, you'll center yourselves and reach the depth of introspection needed to approach this process from its deepest level.

"When you feel ready, open your eyes and we'll begin."

Olivia was impatient to do some deep work on herself. Her recent panic attack had shown her quite clearly that her body and spirit needed introspection, which helped her become clearer about the importance of doing the work. *I really need to stop hitting my head against brick walls,* she thought. Unless I'd like a future of passing out and racing heartbeats, I'd better just get on with it.

She wrote her name in caps across the top of the whiteboard—OLIVIA…—with three dots following it to begin her descriptions. The marker flew across the pieces of tape, enumerating many ideas that she thought might be weighing on her spirit.

> My father was abusive and abandoned me.
> I'm afraid of repeating my mom's mistakes.
> The color of my skin limits me.
> Being a woman limits me.
> I have to work harder to compete with men.
> I'm not capable enough.
> I'm failing at my job.
> I can't show weakness.
> I'll never have enough money to create the life I want.
> I'm not responsible enough.
> I don't trust people.
> I have to do everything myself.
> I don't have time for myself.
> I'm afraid of ending up alone.
> Many people's lives depend on me.
> I can't cry. Crying is for the weak.
> I'm surrounded by incompetent people.
> I'm not honest.
> To succeed, I can't have distractions.
> I don't have time for a personal life.
> Too often, selfish people are in power.
> Our inhumanity sometimes defeats me.
> I'm fat and unattractive.
> I'm always tired.
> I can't change.
> I wish I were twenty years younger.

Next to Olivia, Jennifer was very intently scribbling on the blue pieces of tape. She had a long list already:

I'm trapped.
I'm nothing without a husband.
I don't have enough money.
I'm fat.
I'm no longer attractive.
I'm lost.
I hate my job.
I'm not good at my job.
I'm scared.
Why did he abandon me?
No one will ever love me again.
Drinking helps numb my pain.
I'm mediocre.
Sometimes I don't want to live.
I'm not a good mother.
I'm not a good daughter.
I'm alone.
I don't deserve my children.
Everything is hard.
Life isn't fun.
No one wants to be my friend.
I'm always tired.
My life is sad.
I hate my house.
I can't trust men.

While writing these phrases, Jennifer realized some of them were old habitual thoughts that had begun to fade away through her time in the program, but she knew old habits die hard and wanted to root them out of her consciousness forever. She realized now that they were chains holding her down, and she had to break free in order to create a different future for herself. When she put down the marker, Jennifer felt like she'd just done ten rounds in a boxing ring, and the boxer punching her was herself.

Stephanie had taken the board off the easel and was sitting on the floor writing on her pieces of tape:

I am broken.
My abuser was a piece of shit.

It was my fault.
I want him to pay for what he did.
I don't have a problem with food.
I have to be a good daughter.
I'm not smart enough.
I'm a victim.
They only see me as a sexual object.
I can't trust anyone.
I'm not thin enough.
No one cares about what happened to me.
No one will believe me anyway.
I need to be perfect.
I have to keep my secrets.
If I gain weight, no one will want me.
I can't let anyone down.
My father didn't protect me.
I can't tell my husband.
I need to be thin at any cost.
I'm not brave.
I'm not a good mother.
I'm weak.
I have to be a better mother than mine was.

As she finished, Stephanie was quietly reading the list and was surprised by the thoughts she had repeated to herself so often they had cut grooves in her brain. She now could see these were distortions. She was determined to do the work that would help her stop looking at herself as though through a fun house mirror.

Nicole paced back and forth, the marker clenched between her teeth. She made jabs at the white board, writing on a piece of tape and then stepping back quickly as though the words she wrote burnt her:

I'm not a good teacher.
I'm not attractive.
I need to hide.
I have secrets I must keep.
I'm scared.
I'm a sinner.

The Orchid

> God will punish me.
> I don't trust myself.
> No one understands me.
> I'm afraid of being judged by God.
> I'm afraid of being judged by others.
> I'll disappoint my parents if I tell them the truth.
> I'm a bad daughter.
> My mother doesn't love me.
> I can't be transparent.
> I might lose my job if I'm honest.
> Being gay isn't natural and it's something I'm ashamed of.
> Life is easier if people don't know I'm gay.
> Sometimes I think I don't deserve to live.
> I'm not brave.
> I don't deserve Elena's love.
> I'm a disappointment to myself and others.
> I don't deserve to be happy.
> I'm afraid of being alone.

Reading what she had written showed Nicole, quite clearly, that her outlook on life was bleak. A small niggling thought bloomed in the back of her mind like a dark rose: *Surely God didn't create me to be miserable. Could that be true?*

Sofia, still raw from her experience with Magda and having accepted that indeed there was more to this place than what she had previously admitted, was feeling more sensitive and aware than before. She also looked around and saw the ferocity with which the others were writing on their boards. Inspired to use the exercise for her highest good, she chose a red marker and wrote decisively on the pieces of blue tape.

> I can't trust anyone.
> Everyone is trying to take advantage of me.
> My father is a liar.
> My parents don't care about me.
> I don't trust my brother.
> People think I'm stupid.
> No one will protect me.
> Only the strong survive.
> You can't be ethical and expect to succeed.

Men only want me for sex and money.
If I'm not the center of attention, I'd be invisible.
I need to protect myself.
I'm ugly and fat.
The good ones always finish last.
If you don't cheat, you won't get ahead.
I can't forgive.
I need to hold a grudge.
There are no good men.
Romantic love isn't for me. It doesn't exist.
No one will ever help me.
No one will ever love me.
Knowing how to lie well is a vital skill.
Everyone is dishonest and only looks out for themselves.
I'll never have enough money.
The rules don't apply to me.

Sofia was surprised by her own list. It made her sound suspicious and cynical and showed she took a hard-eyed view of the world. She compared herself to the women around her who seemed to live their emotions with greater intensity and fluidity. She was more of a concrete block, with these ideas and attitudes solidifying within her and becoming an immoveable mass. *I'm going about things the wrong way, aren't I? I need to make some changes in my life.*

All over the room, women were writing furiously, chronicling lifetimes of bottled-up emotions that had become a prison of limiting beliefs. When Mary announced that the time was up, most laid their markers down, but a few kept right on writing, banishing these damaging thoughts to the blue tapes, as though by writing them down they could instantly be rid of them.

It had been an intense session, and Mary saw tracks of tears on some cheeks and looks of relief on almost everyone's face that the exercise was done. For most, it was like going to the dentist. It was great to have the sore tooth gone, but the extraction had been painful.

Mary asked them all to take one more moment to go within again and congratulate themselves for a job well done. "You have all just practiced extreme self-love," she said. "I now recommend three things. Drink a large glass of water, head to the restroom and urinate to allow the energy the exercise has stirred up to exit your body, and, lastly, wash your hands." She encouraged them not to speak but to do those things in silence and then return to the room.

The Orchid

After all were back, Mary began speaking again.

"Now, let's continue with the next part of the exercise. Once again, I ask that you trust the process and us.

"Please stand in front of your respective boards, and a member of our team will come and stand with you," Mary explained. "The team member will take every one of the pieces of tape on which you have written and place them, like name tags, all over your body."

Mary waited until the twittering and nervous giggles subsided before speaking again.

"These beliefs that you have written have covered your lives as surely as the pieces of tape will now cover your bodies. They are thoughts and ideas you have repeated to yourself over and over, some for decades, and they have restricted your emotional and spiritual movement. They have acted as weights on your very souls. They are barbed words that have never lost their sting and have only grown in power through repetition. Some of the experiences or people who hung these limiting beliefs on you are no longer living or the situation took place in the past—a dead parent, a failed marriage, a cruel spouse, a teacher from long ago—yet those feelings, thoughts, and words still live in you and hold you back. You have given them your power and continue to give them safe harbor and absorbed them into your inner being."

Mary waited until all the pieces of tape were applied to the participants, and then she said, "It is time to free yourself from these harmful notions at last. Form a circle, please.

"I have asked one of our team members to also write out her limiting beliefs on blue tape and have them applied to her own body so that she may demonstrate what you are all about to do. Thank you for volunteering, Isabelle. Please step into the center of the circle."

Isabelle, the healer who led the breathwork exercise on the second night, stepped into the center. Her red hair and the large crystal hanging from her neck stood out against the pieces of blue tape stuck everywhere on her white robe.

"Now I will ask Isabelle to extend her arms and close her eyes," Mary instructed. "All the rest of you, please take a step closer to Isabelle, and, when I tell you to, read one of the pieces of tape she has stuck to her body and yell it at her."

"Aim the message like an arrow. Make it an accusation. So, if the message you have selected reads, 'I'm a victim,' rephrase it and yell, 'YOU are a victim.' If it says, 'I cannot change,' rephrase it and yell, 'YOU cannot change.'

"Don't be afraid to yell. These messages have been screaming loudly in that very same manner inside Isabelle's head and your own heads for years. It is time to see them for what they are and push them out.

"Isabelle will remain in the circle for a few minutes. One person will yell the first limiting belief, and then the person to her right will continue to do the same and so on until we have gone all round the circle or until the time is over. At that point, Isabelle will step out of the center, and I will select the next person unless, of course, someone wants to volunteer." Mary looked briefly around the room and acknowledged Olivia when she raised her hand.

"After that, Olivia will step into the center, and we will begin the exercise reading the limiting beliefs written all over her. Remember to yell them back at her like they are accusations. After the time is over, Olivia will return to her place in the circle, and the person to her right will step in. We will continue until everyone has had their turn."

Mary answered a few questions, and, when there weren't any more, she said, "Let us begin."

Isabelle extended her arms and closed her eyes, and Mary nodded to a woman named Grace to begin. Clearing her throat, Grace read one of the tapes adhered to Isabelle's body and yelled, "You are not pretty." The woman to Grace's right yelled, "You are not enough." The others joined in turn, their voices harsh and loud: "You are afraid. You are not powerful. Your ego runs your life. You have a dark secret. No one will forgive you."

This went on for a few minutes and nearly two full turns around the circle. When everyone had yelled the messages and their voices died away, Mary asked Isabelle to check in emotionally. "I am all right," Isabelle assured them all, but some of the participants looked rattled.

Once Isabelle had exited the circle, Olivia took her turn in the center. As she extended her arms, Mary directed the women to read and yell out what Olivia had written on her blue tape.

"You can't afford to fail. Your father was abusive and abandoned you. The color of your skin and being a woman limits you. You're fat and you are not attractive. You'll always be alone. You can't trust people. You are not capable. You are weak if you cry. You are irresponsible. You will never change."

The force of the words thrown at Olivia at top volume underscored their ugliness and left Olivia visibly shaken and in tears. Most of the women in the room had been sure Olivia was the strongest among them. Educated, accomplished, motivated, important—that is what they thought of her. It was stunning to hear how much less Olivia thought of herself.

Stephanie, trembling a little, was next. She took a deep breath, closed her eyes, and extended her arms. As they did before, the women in the circle each took turns yelling what Stephanie had written:

"You are broken. You are a victim. Everything was your fault. No one will believe you anyway. No one cares about you. You are weak. You are not brave. If you gain weight no one will love you. You can't trust anyone. Your father didn't protect you."

On and on the voices went, and Stephanie was weeping from the first sound. *How awful the messages are,* she thought. *How could I constantly spew such poison all over myself? I am killing my own spirit.*

Before Stephanie could answer Mary's question about her emotional state, a sob broke out of Jana, the woman who had earlier expressed her misgivings about the exercise. Stephanie recognized her as the same woman who at the first Council had held Wakinyan's ceremonial stick in silence, unable to speak. Now Jana broke the circle and ran from the room. At that very instant, almost as if she were expecting it, Mary looked at Sister D, and, without words, Sister D acknowledged the unspoken request and immediately went to look after the woman.

The incident caused a ripple of shock and uncertainty in the room. Mary quickly addressed the energy shift and said lovingly, "My dears, while it may appear unfortunate, this is not an uncommon reaction, and it is exactly as it needs to be. Sometimes, the forces and energies that hold us back are strong. Until we are able to see beyond them, they will continue to exert a powerful control over us. That said, remember, change will happen in us when the time is right, and that timing is different for each of us. You do more for Jana by sending her love than by worrying about her. The love you send her will reach her and help her to heal, hastening the time when she is able to break free of fear and torment. The energy of love is the greatest force in the universe, and it will wrap Jana up and keep her safe, so you mustn't worry. May I ask that you all please return to the present moment and continue our work together in the here and now?"

Mary checked on Stephanie to make sure she was alright, which Stephanie confirmed.

Sofia then followed.

Hesitant but determined, Sofia stepped into the center, and the women began yelling her limiting beliefs at her:

"You cannot trust anyone. Everyone is trying to take advantage of you. No one will protect you. Your parents don't care about you. Nice people finish last. If you don't cheat, you won't get ahead. You can't forgive anyone. No one will help you. Rules don't apply to you."

Sofia didn't cry, but she did feel ashamed of how her beliefs made her sound—hard and cold. *No, not made me sound,* she realized. *If these are my beliefs, they are who I am and they dictate my actions. I am hard and cold.* She stepped back to her place in the circle, looking pensive and staring only at the floor.

As the exercise progressed, the energy in the room became quite heavy. The women were not laughing; they weren't enjoying the exercise. They even began hesitating when yelling out the words being read from the tapes. A heavy feeling was palpable throughout the entire room. What they didn't realize was that Mary, the healers, and the apprentices had formed an exterior circle. This circle was serving as a powerful force field that protected those inside of it by isolating the heaviness and injecting it with a large dose of love. It was this protective field that allowed the exercise to continue without permanently harming the participants while ensuring that the lesson was learned.

And so, it continued.

Next up in the circle's center was Jennifer, then Nicole, and, eventually, all other women.

Throughout the rest of the exercise all sorts of limiting beliefs were yelled out. "You need to stay at home with the children. You have to work even if you don't like what you do. You will never make enough money! The divorce was your fault. You are too old to run a marathon. You don't have control over your life. He's out of your league. You are not pretty enough. No one loves you. You don't know what love is. You are awful. You are not in shape. You are a loser. You are not enough. You are not strong enough. You are not rich enough. What will other people say? You can't do it alone.

◉ The Orchid

You are no fun. She won't love you. It's too late for you to go to college. You can't trust yourself. It's a man's world. You don't have time for that. You will only be complete when you are with someone. You need a man to be complete. You are not lovable. You'll never have what they have."

By the time they all had had their chance to be in the center of the circle and felt the weight of their limiting beliefs, each person in the group was exhausted. When they all had resumed their places in the exterior circle, and the center was empty, the second part of the exercise came to an end.

Chapter 39

I Forgive Myself

Mary repositioned herself at the center. "Let's take a deep breath. Inhale, counting to four: one, two, three, four. Now, exhale through your mouth with a pronounced 'ahhh', counting to five: one, two, three, four, five. Let's repeat.

"Now, dive deep within yourselves and acknowledge with immense love and kindness the brave and remarkable work you've just done.

"Confronting these beliefs is exhausting, I know. Even if you've only felt their weight for a few minutes, it's nothing compared to the years they've been present in your lives, influencing every thought, word, feeling, and action. The first and most crucial step to freeing yourself from them is awareness. It's essential to recognize the ideas that limit us, like the blue tapes symbolizing these beliefs. They not only affect our essence and well-being but also shape our self-perception. It's vital to free ourselves from them to prevent them from continuing to limit our true selves."

Pausing for a moment to allow her words to settle with the listeners, Mary then said, "Please lay down on your backs on the floor, as we will now begin a cleansing ceremony which will give you the opportunity to remove all of those limiting beliefs from your body and your spirit."

At Mary's words, a powerful drum began beating rhythmically in the background, the deep and steady sound resonating with each woman's heartbeat.

Tum, tum. Tum, tum. Tum, tum.

The rhythm was hypnotic, calling to something deep within each woman's consciousness, stirring their emotions.

Tum, tum. Tum, tum. Tum, tum.

The Orchid

As the beat went on and on, the women's breaths seemed to join each other. Mary's voice could just be heard riding the rhythm like a wave.

"Now, I invite you to follow the beat of these ceremonial drums and go within your consciousness. Ask yourself, why do I allow these ideas and beliefs to rule my life? When did I first start doing so? How and by whom was that belief implanted in me? Was it something I saw? Something I did? Something someone told me? Do I truly believe that thought to be a fact, or did I simply allow it to be true and have been acting as though it were ever since it first appeared in my mind?"

Tum, tum. Tum, tum. Tum, tum.

Mary was silent to allow for introspection. The penetrating sound of the drum became stronger, more insistent.

Tum, tum. Tum, tum. Tum, tum.

"But no matter when and where such ideas began, it is important that you are now aware of their existence and that you can root them out. You, you are in control of your thoughts and, as such, can change the way you think. It is your choice, and you have the power to change it. At any moment, you may make another decision—to release those warped ideas and distorted thoughts which have wreaked such havoc in your life. You can release yourself from the bondage of such limiting beliefs by using forgiveness. Forgiveness is a most powerful and cleansing force. As you begin this next part of the exercise, use that force on yourselves and others that you think have wronged you. Forgive. Forgive. Forgive.

"So, I ask you now, place your right hand on your heart and begin repeating the following: 'I love you,' and say your name. 'I forgive myself for the idea that I am not enough. I forgive myself for the idea that I am not attractive. I forgive myself for the idea that I need a partner to be complete. I forgive myself for the idea that I am a victim. I forgive myself for judging myself as unlovable. I forgive myself for anything else that burdens my soul and stifles my joy. I forgive my mother for not loving me in the way that I needed. I forgive my father for his inattention or inability to express his love. I know my parents did the best they could with what they had.'"

Mary's voice was louder now and had a new power and intensity. "Speak out," she said, her voice rising to a yell. "Speak out so you can hear yourself. Speak out so the universe can hear you. Speak out your new truth. Begin now."

Tum, tum. Tum, tum. Tum, tum.

"I forgive myself for the idea that I am not enough. I forgive myself for judging myself as not capable. I forgive myself for the idea that I'm broken. I forgive myself for…," and, one by one, the women brought forth all of the limiting beliefs that they had identified throughout the afternoon. The women, grounded on the floor, continued speaking the mantras of forgiveness for themselves and for others. And as they did, the energy in the room lightened and the heaviness rose up and away like souls released from darkness.

"Now get up from the floor," Mary intoned, "and announce what you no longer are: You are *not* weak. You are *not* broken. You are *not* alone. You are *not* to blame. You are *not* incomplete. Forgive yourself. Love yourself. Look around into your sisters' eyes and share that you love her, too. Acknowledge that you can change. Acknowledge that you have changed. Right here, right now, you have been transformed. Feel it. Know it. You've liberated yourself of your chains and your spirit is free to fly."

An intense and powerful force was present in the room. When the women had finished hugging each other and wiping each other's tears, Mary ordered the fire to be ignited and spoke yet again.

"We have lit the sacred fire so you can rip every one of those limiting beliefs from your body and throw them into it. As you do, counter each statement with its opposite, which is the only statement that is *true* and *real* and speaks of your authentic self: 'I am not alone. I am enough. I am love.' Drag those limiting beliefs from the shadows into the sunlight of your spirit. Rob them of their power. Then cast them into the fire so their energy can be released and transformed into something greater. As you do, hold the feelings of love and forgiveness, for that is all you are."

With her own arms extended, Mary pivoted in place, looking around the room. All the women were in an emotional trance, ripping the tapes off their bodies, while the rest of the healers still stood in a circle formation, holding the space and the love around them.

Some sobbed and fell on their knees as they removed those painful and numbing limitations and countered them with new hopes and ideas. It was a cleansing exercise like none of them had ever before experienced. All stared at the fire as the pieces of blue tape dissolved.

Tum, tum. Tum, tum. Tum, tum.

"Beautiful souls, powerful women, sisters, rise and claim what you truly are and have always been: you are brave, strong, insightful, beautiful, brilliant and loving. You have choices and are in control of your life. Embrace your awareness and the freedom it brings. Embrace all you are with compassion and forgiveness and love."

Tum, tum. Tum, tum. Tum, tum.

"From now on, before you allow anything to take up residence within you, ask yourself: What do *I* believe? Ensure that the thoughts are your own and not imposed on you by someone else no matter how powerful, charismatic, or persuasive. Ask if your beliefs are empowering you or restricting and limiting you. Adopt only the beliefs that you know to be true for you, as those thoughts will come to help define you. And, when you are ready … say to yourself: 'I am not my thoughts. I am not my words. I am not my feelings. I am not my actions. Yes, they exist and they pass through me. At times they even reside in me, but they are not me. They do not control me. I am in control of my choices. I choose my thoughts. I choose my words. I choose my feelings. I choose my actions. I am in control of my life, and, through my choices, I will make it a valuable and beautiful one.'"

Mary directed the women to turn towards each other, and repeat, "I love you. I love you. I love you," and wrap each other in a warm embrace.

"Tell each other how powerful you are. Feel free to be vulnerable enough to share your feelings. These are your sisters, this is your family and this is your community."

The energy in the room was rising and shifting. The women laughed and wept and held each other as the drums became softer in the background. Wakinyan then walked into the circle and clasped Mary's hand to invoke the blessing:

Great Spirit

We come to you in gratitude for the guidance and protection you have provided to us. We ask that you clear any heavy energy that may still linger and fill this space with only love and light. We are grateful for the power within each of us to choose our own path, to release our fears and limiting beliefs, and to open ourselves up to new possibilities. We thank you for your presence in our lives, for the oneness of us all, and for the wisdom you have shared. We ask that you bless us and guide us on our journey in this life and beyond.

And with that, the Blue Tape Session was closed.

The Orchid

Chapter 40

Celebration

The women stayed in the room talking excitedly, sometimes right over each other. Recognizing that their excess energy needed channeling or there would be no sleep for any of them that night, Mary signaled to Flavia, who leapt to her feet, blew a whistle reminiscent of old disco days, and shouted out loudly, "Come on, you gorgeous women. Dance with me!"

A contagious rhythm emanated from the speakers, evoking familiar melodies. Flavia began to move with innate grace, her feet and hips in perfect harmony with the beat.

"Dance out your joy. Dance to release all that energy that just moved through you like a strong breeze. Dance to release your fears. Dance to celebrate the power of choice. Dance to show yourself some love! Dance like your life depends on it. Shake it out. Dance with me!"

Up they jumped, screaming, spinning each other like tops, and inventing new dance steps straight from their jubilant spirits. Those who didn't join in were soon dragged to their feet and enfolded into the raucous celebration.

After a long while, the women, weary to their bones but happier than they had felt in a very long time, dropped to the ground, holding each other's waists and shoulders and hands. They instinctively formed a circle.

Mary stood again in the middle to address them all. "Thank you, thank you, thank you for all your hard work and the courage you displayed today. You were vulnerable and fierce and authentic, and we are proud of each of you. You helped yourselves and helped each other. It was a blessing for all of us to be part of today's session."

She smiled at them all with her heart in her eyes and then said, "Before our evening meal, I'd like to ask if anyone feels moved to share anything with the group about today's experience?"

Sofia almost didn't let Mary finish her sentence before she spoke up.

"I feel so light and free," she said, and almost immediately the tears came. "Like a blank canvas ready to be painted on with the most brilliant colors imaginable. I feel—no, I know—that I can choose to be successful and kind at the same time. I don't have to be hard or cut-throat or cheat for my business to grow. I can't wait to conduct myself and my business in a different way."

Sofia's smile was wide, mixed with tears and powerful emotion, as she turned to Mary and said, "You showed me how that could be done by the way you are and the way you run this place, Mary. The rest of you all taught me that I can look at life differently and that my life can change for the better because of that new way of seeing things. Thanks to you all for loving me until I could learn to love myself enough to shed my tough old skin and grow a new heart. I didn't know I had it in me."

Olivia was smiling at Sofia with approval and then she spoke up. "I realized some things about myself today, too. I know now I have been carrying a lot—too much. By taking myself too seriously, I've been missing out on the joys of life, including the truly satisfying parts of the job I love. I lost sight of who I am and endangered my health while doing that. I've come to see how I need to release the heaviness so I can see more clearly and live a balanced life."

Olivia was visibly moved, yet she wore a broad smile. Tears glistened in her eyes not from sadness but from deep understanding and renewed hope. Her chest rose and fell with lighter breaths, as if she had released a burden she had been carrying for a long time. It was evident that even though she still had a journey ahead, she had found the starting point towards self-compassion.

Nicole was next. "Today's exercise was the scariest and most difficult thing I've ever done in my life," she said, and a chorus of "oh yeah" and "yes, sister" came from the women around her.

Tears filled Nicole's eyes as she continued speaking. "I am so grateful to be here and share this moment with you all. I see now that I'm not alone, and it gives me courage to continue with this process. I can see more clearly how I have been sabotaging myself, how I have been allowing others, my mom especially, to dictate how I live my life. But I also see that my mom is doing the best she can. That she can't help herself. I still feel confused, and wish things would go faster, but I feel—I know—that I am moving towards some big thing in my life. I don't exactly know what it is, but I can feel it headed my way." She sat down again with a huge smile on her face.

"Oh my, I see that too," Stephanie jumped in, her own cheeks wet with tears. "For far too long, I have allowed others, directly and indirectly, to dictate how I live. I can see now how many obstacles I've created or allowed others to place in front of me, and all because of my shame and guilt for something that I was not responsible for. I now understand that I could not have done anything else. I did the best I could at the time. My past experiences don't define me and only who I am now, here, at this very moment, is what matters. I now get what being 'in the now' really means.

"I'm beginning to see my life filled with possibilities rather than with fears and self-imposed limitations. I thought those barriers were protecting me, but in reality, they were limiting my potential. I've even been making myself sick, as if I deserved punishment for my imagined wrongdoings. But now I understand that I can heal and that I need to give myself care and treat my body with love, kindness and respect." In spite of the tears still glistening on her cheeks, Stephanie's smile lit up the room like a blast of sunshine.

Jennifer was next to speak. "I felt, for the first time ever, in an absolute and powerful way, that I am not broken, that I am stronger than I have allowed myself to believe, that I can do all I need to do and more. I am capable. I also realize now that I am not alone. There are many people who support me: my parents, my friends, my bosses, my colleagues, my neighbors, and all of you. Thank you," she said, looking around at all the women and at Mary and the other healers. "Thanks for helping me put my head back on straight," and her laughter pealed like a bell.

As they went round the circle, the rest of the women shared their own stories, in which they were now the heroines, as they acknowledged their strength and power and their precious ability to choose.

"I have never given any thought to the limiting beliefs and ideas I carry," said one.

"It certainly was eye-opening," said another.

"I feel like I really saw myself for the first time in my whole life," said a third. "And I'm not so bad! I mean, I'm not bad at all."

The Orchid

Everyone laughed with her as they all took turns and shared their joyful discoveries. After all had shared, some a few times, Mary asked them to stand and repeat after her. She said the words with her hands raised.

"I am clear and focused," said Mary.

"I am clear and focused," they repeated.

"I am aware of my thoughts and actions.

"I live in the present moment.

"I act with intention and purpose.

"I have balance and harmony in my life.

"I am the love of my life.

"I AM love.

"I AM love.

"I AM love.

And then, as she lowered her hands, she announced, "Come, everyone, we have a surprise for you."

She led them to the front doors of the Sanctuary, last opened five hours before, and flung them open to the gathering dusk to reveal long tables set with snowy linens and adorned with hundreds of candles. Overhead, hanging from the trees, were fairy lights and paper lanterns illuminating a feast fit for what they all were—queens of the universe.

Silver bowls of jeweled fruit, samovars steaming with fragrant teas, dumplings in bamboo steamers, and mounded hills of salads, grains, and tubers of all shapes and sizes graced the tables. Raw vegetables, fresh from the organic garden, with dipping bowls of hummus and tzatziki shared space with grilled tomatoes, peppers, and eggplants. Wheels of golden cheeses sat next to homemade breads fashioned into braids and stars and fanciful shapes. It was a Valentine—an edible expression of love from The Orchid's staff to their wonderful, and now more powerfully aware, guests.

Part VI
Acceptance

The Orchid

Chapter 41

A Place to Love Themselves

The early morning fog flowed across The Orchid like love pouring from an open heart. Walking to the mountaintop, Mary passed the site of the previous night's feast and smiled. The guests had been so surprised, and Mary enjoyed delighting them. It was a well-deserved celebration after all the hard work they had done.

Mary had retired early, so everyone left could let their hair down and truly enjoy themselves without the pressure of her presence. She knew from experience that the guests sometimes held her up on a pedestal and were more comfortable with her in a formal teaching setting than in a social one. Some were either too impressed or too intimidated by her. While such stature was useful in running the operations at The Orchid, it sometimes had the effect of making many of them apprehensive around her. Everyone kept one eye on her. Mary didn't want the women stifled at all, even out of respect for her, but rather wanted them to let it rip and let their inner wild women run free at the feast. So off Mary went, wishing everyone a wonderful night and mentally blessing them as she did so.

Mary continued her walk and made her way to the top of the mountain for her solo meditation. She could have hiked the trail blindfolded, her feet following the well-worn path. She knew every rock, every tree, every plant—they were all as familiar to her as the back of her hand.

She remembered the first time she toured the grounds on which The Orchid now stood. It had been love at first sight. She had been on the road for weeks visiting properties around the world, looking for the perfect spot to build the

The Orchid

center, but it was this one with which she connected. All it took was a look at its green hills, shadowed mountains, and breathtaking vistas. Both sunrise and sunset could be viewed from here, and the small valley nestled between the mountains provided an ideal setting for all the structures and areas she envisioned.

Mary had asked the brokers showing her the property for some time alone to meditate and feel the energy of the place. She had chosen to hike to a nearby mountaintop, the very mountaintop on which she now stood, and it was here that she received the message. "This is the place," the voice said, as clear as a bell piercing the crystal silence surrounding her. "It will attract healers from many nations to come and share their wisdom with guests from all over the world, so that they can learn the most important lesson of all—to love themselves."

She smiled, recalling the clarity and profound energy of that moment decades before. She knew that her mission had been defined that day, and she took up the challenge to make her vision a reality, to make The Orchid, an oasis of love, to make it come to life.

Though she had experienced the climb thousands of times over the years since she'd heard that voice, she always felt excitement deep in her gut as she headed towards her morning meditation. Still, some days were more special than others, and the fifth day of the program, as the guests approached the end of their stay, was one of those.

By this time, the women had already been through some powerful exercises, in which they had released large amounts of the energy trapped within themselves. Mary was constantly consulting with the team to ensure the exercises they chose would yield the greatest results. She was especially pleased with the Blue Tape Exercise. It had been in place for several years and was powerful in achieving its desired objective—to access the power of forgiveness by helping the women free themselves from the heaviness of their limiting beliefs.

Another reason this stage in the program was cause for celebration was that participants were now more accustomed to the rhythm, more open to the exercises, and, therefore, generally happier. They now saw evidence of what Mary already knew: that the transformation had begun. Each woman was beginning to get in touch with and to embrace her higher self. More aware and better acquainted with gratitude and forgiveness, they began to experience more power and acceptance in their lives. They could see it in themselves and in each other. Now all else would continue falling in place with greater ease.

Mary made a conscious effort to recognize and be grateful for the role she played in this transformation, but she was ever mindful to keep a tight rein on her ego. It wasn't because of her, or even the efforts of the other teachers and healers, that thousands of women who passed through the gates of The Orchid had experienced their soul's awakening. Mary understood that she and her team were simply contributors to a far grander plan set in motion by the universe.

> "Oh, Powerful One," she whispered as she approached the mountain top. "Let thy will be done."

She repeated the words over to remind herself (and her ego) of their minor role in this grand scheme.

Reaching the summit, Mary found her usual place and sat on a large boulder that overlooked the eastern horizon. Even before the first signs of light appeared, Mary had adopted the lotus position and opened her heart, body and mind to receive that which could only be received in silence, gratitude, and love.

After her practice, Mary descended to begin the day's activities.

As she walked by, a staff member greeted her. "Good morning, Mary."

"Good morning, Jessica. How are you today?" Mary said as she stopped to make eye contact with the young woman who was part of the crew tidying up the grounds. Jessica's task was to change the signs adorned with affirmations and quotes posted throughout.

Jessica had just installed one sporting the powerful "Serenity Prayer"

> —God, grant me the serenity to accept the things I cannot change, the courage to change the things I can, and the wisdom to know the difference."

Mary smiled as she passed the sign. She would be speaking to the group about acceptance later that day.

Answering Mary's query, Jessica replied, "I am just excellent. Thank you."

The Orchid

"That's great to hear," Mary responded. "Thanks for your work changing out the signs. I love the messages. They have a way of always finding the right person to speak to at exactly the right moment."

Then Mary bid farewell with a smile and continued walking the grounds. All around, the ground crew was trimming and tidying the property. *Polishing Paradise*, she thought, and she went to prepare herself for her day.

As Mary walked away, the calming duet of the Tibetan bell and birdsong could be heard throughout, as it announced the morning of the fifth day.

Chapter 42

I AM

Today, the doors to the Meditation Center would open an hour later than usual to allow whoever needed it more time to recover from the prior day's activities.

The women, now more accustomed to the pace of the various activities, seemed to climb the mountain top with greater ease than in previous days. Once they had gathered in a circle around Mary, she greeted them warmly. "My dears, it's wonderful to see you all again this morning. How is everyone feeling?"

Different answers were heard from the group, but almost all sounded happy and enthusiastic.

"I'm so glad to hear that you are enjoying yourselves. Nowhere is it written that enlightenment has to be dreary."

"Dears," Mary said. "Before we begin, I wanted to share with you a quick update.

Sister D and I shared some time with Jana after she left the activity yesterday. We comforted her and offered whatever help she needed. After a very emotional and candid discussion, Jana concluded that she would rather depart than continue with the program. We, of course, respect and uphold her decision."

Upon hearing this, several women began to exchange glances and shake their heads. A few whispers and murmurs began among them, discussing how Jana's situation could have happened to any one of them.

After a brief pause, Mary continued. "Our philosophy is that growth and transformation must happen at the speed that is suitable for each of you. We believe that everyone must navigate their unique journey, following their own rhythm and timeline.

"We can only plant and water the seed. We cannot accelerate its natural growth. So, we ask that you all join us in sending Jana our love, blessings, and prayers, so that she finds what she seeks and what she needs in her own time. Thank you."

Mary then opened the morning session.

"Yesterday's exercise was very effective in creating the space for you all to release large amounts of the heavy energy stored throughout your bodies. I'm not sure if you are aware of it, but there is a lightness in the room today. I can sense it energetically, and I can see it in each of your faces, which look like flowers opening to the sun.

"Let me begin by calling for spiritual guidance and support. After that, we will open the floor for some sharing. Please join me by closing your eyes."

She began:

> Spirit, God, Universe, Higher-Self,
>
> It is with great humility that we present ourselves to you this morning. We ask that a blessing of love, light, and wisdom be present with us all as we embark on this wonderful day and learn about and experience the power of acceptance.
>
> May we have the courage to accept ourselves, just as we are, with all of our flaws and imperfections.
>
> May we have the wisdom to accept all others, with their own unique differences and quirks, and to treat them with infinite love, kindness, and understanding.
>
> May we learn to accept everything that is out of our control, letting go of any resistance or frustration and surrendering to the trust that everything that happens is divinely guided and for our highest good.
>
> We know this to be so. We feel it, and so it is.

Mary opened her eyes and smiled at all the wonderful souls occupying this morning's circle. "And now, I would like to open the floor for some sharing. Tell us, what is present for you this morning?"

Sofia initiated the sharing. "I'm still processing everything that happened yesterday and all that has occurred since my arrival," she said. "Yesterday was such a revelation. I saw each of you embrace total vulnerability. Thank you," she glanced at the women encircling her. "It was very impactful to voice aloud our limiting beliefs, acknowledging how we unnecessarily burden our minds with these notions. For far too long, I've been controlled by countless ideas and restrictions imposed on me. I recognize that now. The act of writing them down, attaching them to my body, audibly acknowledging them, and ultimately discarding them into the fire was transformational. I arrived here full of skepticism, ready to dismiss the whole program, but now, there's a shift happening within me. I can't quite put it into words, but I am acutely aware that I am changing," she concluded as she sat down.

"Thank you for such a beautiful sharing, Sofia," said Mary, placing both her hands on her forehead and bowing slightly to acknowledge Sofia's growth.

Stephanie raised her hand, and, when acknowledged, began to speak. "Yesterday was a very difficult day for me. The vulnerability was almost too much to bear." She choked slightly as she said these words. "But I agree with Sofia, it was so liberating. And I agree with you too, Mary. I feel lighter. In fact, I feel lighter than I've ever felt before. I also feel capable, hopeful, and maybe even a little courageous—like I can handle whatever may come my way. I know I have a lot of work in front of me, but I've never, ever felt this way, and it's nice to experience it, so I'm going to enjoy this small win."

"Thank you, Stephanie," Mary offered. "I'm so happy for you for embracing your vulnerability and turning it into strength and courage. That lightness you're feeling means you have arrived at acceptance. The path ahead may at times be challenging still, but every journey begins with a single step, and this, what you call your 'small win,' is not small at all, it is significant, so do enjoy it. In fact, celebrate it," said Mary with a beaming smile.

Olivia followed Stephanie. "Exposing myself as I did yesterday isn't something I typically do. I usually hide behind this towering persona—this *Madam*—who places herself above all, even though I had no specific set of goals to which I was aspiring. But today I'm aware of my own insignificance and the unnecessary burdens I've shouldered under the misconception that everything depended solely on me. It's become clear that I don't have anything to prove, and that I need to let go. This week, especially yesterday, has made me recognize much of the resentment and anger I've harbored pertains to things that no longer matter or are reactions to memories that aren't necessarily accurate. My perceptions were skewed."

"Thank you, Olivia," said Mary, bowing slightly. "I congratulate you. Acknowledging your own insignificance, understanding the needless weight you've carried, and seeing that you don't need to prove anything are major milestones in self-awareness and growth."

The Orchid

Nicole was next. She looked a bit serious. "I've got to admit that I'm feeling a bit jealous this morning. I'm sorry." She paused, feeling embarrassed.

"You don't need to apologize for such a feeling, Nicole, or for any feeling you have," Mary assured her. "Do you want to share why you feel that way?"

Nicole sighed and seemed to gather herself to go on. "It's just that everyone seems to be making so much progress and I ... and I feel like I haven't made any progress in the things that matter. On those issues, I'm still stuck in the same place I was when the week started. I feel like God is still punishing me." Nicole put her head down to avoid eye contact with the others.

After a silent pause, Mary stood and spoke softly.

"I understand that you feel that way, Nicole, but you must remember feelings aren't facts."

That phrase got everyone's attention, and you could have heard a pin drop in the silence that followed Mary's words. Everyone leaned forward just a bit to clearly hear whatever wisdom she would share next.

"That conception of God as punisher is not the God I surrendered my life to and have experienced every day since. The power I know doesn't require us to feel shame or guilt. It doesn't judge or punish us. It doesn't separate the good from the bad or favor one child over another. This amazing power is always present and always available to us, at anytime, anywhere. It simply loves us unconditionally.

"From my experience, one that encompasses witnessing thousands of women like you walk a similar path and encounter diverse forms of spiritual power, there's one common thread: God, Spirit, the Source, the Higher Self, the Universe, or any other name or term one chooses to use, embodies the purest form of love, one that transcends human comprehension. This love accepts you, Nicole, just as you are. Love is the most potent force in the universe, certainly strong enough to conquer shame, guilt, and our perceived imperfections. In the eyes of this higher power, we are all perfect. We simply need to perceive each other as this divine spirit does."

Mary bent to Nicole and offered her a tissue so she could wipe her tears away.

"Nicole, your bravery in expressing your feelings of inadequacy and suffering is admirable. By doing so, you've rallied a legion of angels to support you in this challenging time. Look around." Mary motioned towards the other women in the circle. "These are your pillars of support, ready to embrace you with comfort, prayers, profound dialogues, and soft whispers of affirmation. We will stand as your examples of strength when weakness threatens to overwhelm. We will shoulder your burden when the path ahead feels unbearable. Remember you're never alone, and that feeling of solitude will never haunt you again. Our love for you is unwavering.

"Yet, even as we support each other, there's one task no one can do on anyone's behalf, and that's learning to love yourself. That's a journey we all have to embark on by ourselves. Everyone in this room is learning to do just that."

Nicole was sobbing now, and the circle broke momentarily as the women gathered near to hold her or pat her hand and murmur endearments. When Nicole's tears subsided, everyone returned to the circle, and Mary spoke again.

Mary again addressed the group. "There is a book I love in which a boy befriends a mole, a fox, and a horse. At one point in the story, the boy asks the horse, 'What is the bravest thing you've ever done?' The horse answers, 'Ask for help.'"

Nicole laughed through her tears and asked, "So, I'm a horse?"

"No, my dear, you are brave," Mary replied.

The sharing continued as some women spoke of their increasing awareness and others of their yet unmet expectations. Mary was thrilled. She could see growth in them all.

Once the sharing was finished, Mary met everyone's eyes round the circle and said, "The focus of our work today is acceptance, one of the most important lessons you will learn in your life. All the lessons you've learned here have acceptance at their core.

"It is ultimately through acceptance that you become aware of your power and your connection with all that surrounds you. When you live in acceptance, you are saying, I accept who I am, all of me, warts and scars and wounds included. I believe and know, with every part of my body and soul, that I AM not broken, I AM complete, I AM perfect and I AM love.

"In the Bible, God identifies himself by name to Moses, speaking through a burning bush. When Moses asks God, 'When the people ask me, "What is his name?" what should I say to them?'

"God answered, 'I AM Who I AM.'

"Our answer should be the same: we are who we are.

"Our meditation for this morning is simple, but at its center is a most formidable power. We are going to fill the space left by the energy released so far this week with powerful words—the words 'I AM.' You will be thinking about and repeating nothing but this mantra, adding whatever ending you deem appropriate:

"I AM love. I AM peace. I AM abundance. I AM smart. I AM happy. I AM strong. I AM capable. I AM free. I AM complete. I AM bliss. I AM light. I AM perfect. I AM truth. I AM grateful. I AM gentle. I AM gracious. I AM beautiful. I AM divine. I AM powerful. I AM giving. I AM surrendering. I AM joy. I AM forgiving. I AM a spiritual being having a human experience. I AM doing the best I can with what I've got. I AM love."

As Mary spoke, her arms reached, palms upward, towards the heavens. She appeared connected to a higher energy. The space she and the women occupied appeared so too.

Each of them began softly repeating the mantra, but the volume of their chanting swelled as they continued, the words seeming to catch fire as the women poured passion into them. The rhythm, the cadence of the I AM mantra, grew in power and soon shook the very heavens, transporting the speakers from the mundane to the divine.

When the energy had peaked, Mary clapped her hands lightly to regain their attention.

"It is important for you to be aware of the immense power of creation and manifestation that lies in your words. Repeating these mantras here and now, in this powerful setting, is sending a clear message to the universe of who we are. Own it. Feel it. Believe it. Accept it. Through acceptance, you become whole, and, by being whole, you are claiming the power that is your soul's spiritual birthright. With that power, you can attract anything you want. You can create your own reality. Feel it in every cell of your body. It is happening *now*."

Music, soft and compelling, began to play from speakers. A violin accompanied the singer, whose angelic voice helped raise the vibration in the room even further. The lyrics, a mantra of their own, filled the listeners with serenity and peace.

I am one with my spirit;

I am radiant, I Am.

I am the glow of my spirit;

I am powerful, I Am.

I am peace; I Am, I Am.

The song continued, and, as it did, all who listened were transported, in their mind's eye, to the highest realms of the universe.

"I am the glow of my spirit; I am powerful, I Am." Each verse of the song deepened the connection and inspired the women to continue to repeat and feel their own mantras in the silence of their minds, bodies, and souls.

The energy in the room had strengthened and the women's vibrations with it. Mary smiled proudly, knowing that change was taking place. They were being transformed from within and that spiritual rebuilding would serve them the rest of their lives.

After some time, Mary slowly brought them back from the depths of their thoughts.

"I now invite you to savor this moment through quiet reflection. Please take your journals and record your experiences," Mary encouraged. "Capture the essence of your feelings, the depth of your thoughts, and any revelations or insights that surfaced during our session. Allow your pens to map the contours of this journey we shared today. This written testament, one we shall not burn, will serve as a valuable tool for further self-exploration and growth."

After allowing some time for the journaling, Mary concluded by folding her hands in front and bowing respectfully to the group, saying, "Namaste. Thank you all for your hard work and dedication this morning."

As the women filed out, Mary approached Nicole and quietly asked, "May I invite you to take a walk with me, Nicole?"

"Yes, of course," Nicole answered, assuming it had to do with her sharing.

The Orchid

Chapter 43

Find Your Truth

Mary and Nicole's path took them into the bamboo forest, where they took seats on a bench surrounded by the tall, tree-like plants.

"I love bamboo." Mary shared. "Do you know some species can grow more than an inch per hour? How amazing is that? But then I am also fascinated by the Saguaro cactus, which may grow only an inch in its first decade. But even that is eclipsed by the *Puya raimondii*, the Queen of the Andes, a bromeliad that is a distant cousin of the pineapple, which can take the length of a human life, eighty years or more, just to bloom at all."

Nicole caught the drift of Mary's message and said with a wan smile. "Thanks, Mary. I get what you are saying to me. I know this spiritual awakening is not a race, and I know everyone has their own timetable. It's just that … well, I'm sorry."

"What are you sorry about?" Mary asked.

"Oh, about a lot of things. I'm sorry about not advancing like the other women seem to be advancing. I feel stuck. I am sorry for disappointing everyone and not living up to their expectations. You, the other women here, my parents…," and then, with a heavy sigh, Nicole barely whispered the last name. "Elena. I am so sorry to disappoint Elena, too."

Mary took Nicole's hand in hers.

"Nicole, be careful not to compare your journey to anyone else's. We are all walking different paths and doing the best we can with what we've got. Sometimes we seem to be ahead and sometimes we seem to be behind, but this is not a race.

"Moreover, you are not disappointing me or any of the other people here.

All of us have stood or are standing where you are now, unsure, frightened, confused, and we are all here to help each other. You are not *less than* in anyone's eyes. You are *more than*."

"Ah, Mary, if you only knew what I really am, you might write me off as a lost cause," Nicole said, eyes downcast.

Mary remained in silence, waiting for Nicole to raise her chin again. Mary then pressed, "Tell me, Nicole. Tell me who you really are."

"I am a coward is who I am." Nicole's voice took on a tone of condemnation. "I am too scared to go against my parents' wishes or to give Elena what she needs, what she deserves from me. I am even scared of God and what he has waiting for me."

"From that list, let's start with your conception of God," Mary said. "I know what you were taught as a child about a punishing God and how he deals with sins. But is that what you have seen with your own eyes? Has that been *your* experience?"

Nicole considered that for a moment and answered, "No, not really. I went to Catholic school and there wasn't much talk about punishment. It was more about redemption and helping others. And then I met Sister Consuelo, who has been supportive and compassionate and listened to me even when I was sick of hearing myself."

"So where did you get the notion about God as punisher-in-chief if not from your own experience?" Mary asked.

"Well, I guess my parents—my mother, really. My mother got that notion, I assume, from my Nonna, my grandmother. As a child herself, my mother grew up with a lot of very strict rules of what she could do and couldn't do or else she risked being cast into the eternal fires of Hell, and that's what she passed on to me."

Mary nudged Nicole to continue, "And what have you done, in your mother's estimation, to be cast forever into hellfire?"

"I am … I am a sinner because I am a … I am a lesbian," Nicole stammered. "My relationship with Elena is a sin."

Knowing that the best approach was to urge Nicole to search inwardly for answers, Mary made a suggestion. "If you're comfortable with it, how about we take a moment right here and now for some introspection? A few deep breaths can often provide a fresh perspective."

"Yes, let's," Nicole answered.

Mary began softly, "I'm going to invite you to go within for a moment. Please, close your eyes. Breathe in deeply. And again. Now, set aside any preconceived notions and judgments for a moment and answer this question. If you could design any God, any higher power you wanted—no rules, no limits—what would that God look like?"

Nicole thought in silence for a few minutes, and, with her eyes still closed, said, "Well, I guess that God would be kind, loving, and accepting. He would be wise, too, and always present. When I didn't know what to do, I could go to him for advice. He wouldn't judge me, but would always listen and guide me."

"Continue with your eyes closed. Breathe in deeply again," Mary instructed. "What does this God look like? See him in your mind and describe him to me, please."

"Well," Nicole began. "He resembles those familiar depictions of Christ: a young man with long hair and a beard, graced with a genuinely warm smile." She took her time, fully immersing herself in the mental image she was painting.

"He is seated but not on a throne, more like in an armchair," Nicole giggled. "It might even be a recliner, because he looks pretty comfortable. His arms are open. He is standing now and inviting me in for a hug." Pausing momentarily, Nicole's body relaxed noticeably, surrendering to the profound serenity of her vision. Her voice, too, resonated with the intensity of the moment. "It's not a mere polite hug. It's a profound embrace, one where he pulls me close, allowing me to rest my head against his shoulder. I feel safeguarded, cocooned in divine warmth, as if he's gently rocking me, enveloping me in his boundless love and care."

"Does he speak?" Mary prompted.

Nicole's eyes remained closed and she tilted her head a little, as though she were listening. "Yes, yes, he is speaking, softly, into my ear as he holds me."

"What does he say?" Mary softly probed.

"'Welcome, my child. All will be well. You are perfect just the way you are. You are a reflection of me, and I love you,'" she replied. Upon completing her sentence, Nicole's eyes flew open, revealing her awe and shock. Her eyes teared, and she swiftly covered her mouth, speechless. Mary waited patiently for Nicole to gather her thoughts.

"He spoke to me!" Nicole's voice quivered as she extended her hands towards Mary. "He spoke to me!" she repeated, her voice a mix of disbelief and joy. "It was so incredibly real. His warmth, his kindness was boundless. I've always felt unseen, unheard ... until now," she confessed.

"Nicole, the God you described, brimming with love, acceptance, compassion, and free of judgment, is the God I recognize," Mary reassured her. "He doesn't distinguish between us. He accepts us all. He loves us all just as we are."

"I ... I had never felt that before," Nicole admitted, still visibly shaken.

"Why, do you think?" Mary asked.

"Because that's not the God my parents introduced me to," Nicole responded. "Oh Mary," Nicole said, shaking her head, "You've never met my parents, especially my mother. If you had, you'd understand why I've never told them the truth."

"You are right. I haven't met them, Nicole," Mary acknowledged. "But let me share the following for your consideration: your parents, like all of us, are wonderful human beings with their own flaws, imperfections, and areas of opportunity. I suspect they have only done the best they could all their life to protect you. I'm sure they never intended to cause you any pain with their teachings." Mary explained.

"Nicole," Mary continued, "how will you know their true feelings unless you give them an opportunity to express them? They may surprise you. And, even if they don't, or can't, you still have the power to decide how you want to lead your life. The choice, ultimately, will always lie with you.

"That being said, no matter your choice, send your parents love. Remember, when God made time, Nicole, he made plenty of it and things can change over time. As you yourself have been witnessing here, love is a powerful force. Because of it, your parents may come around someday."

"Why do you think so Mary?" Nicole said, glumly.

"Because at the end, all we are is love," Mary whispered.

Hope flickered across Nicole's skeptical face like a candle flame. Mary saw it and ushered a prayer for it to burn brightly for Nicole's highest good.

Mary then stood up and said, "I know your path ahead seems murky and unclear to you at this time, but I assure you, the answers you seek are all inside of you waiting to be uncovered."

Nicole was listening intently.

"That infinite force, the one we call God, or Spirit, or Source, or Universe, is always present, around and within us. It is we who distance ourselves from her. But from the look of things, particularly your powerful vision, I'd say you, my dear, have finally found your connection again. Perhaps this is a good moment to continue that conversation.

"That bench you are sitting on, surrounded by the company of these wonderful plants, has been a place in which I personally have found many answers before. Perhaps you want to remain here a while."

Energized by her time with Mary and the incredible encounter with her God, Nicole felt suddenly braver, more hopeful, and less shameful. *Maybe there is another path. Can I be open with my parents about who I am and not lose their love? Perhaps I can accept them just as they are, and they can accept me just as I am?*

Nicole drew herself back from her thoughts long enough to reply, "Thank you, Mary, for your time, support, and suggestion. I think I will go back to my room instead and continue the conversation there."

Mary replied, "Follow your intuition, my dear. I'm sure your journey within will be incredibly fruitful and fulfilling. I will see you later."

They wrapped each other in a warm hug and left in separate directions.

The Orchid

Chapter 44

Unconditional Love

Nicole was so deep in thought she barely remembered her walk back to her room, until she reached the waterfall at its entrance. It was as though she were dreaming and yet she had never felt more awake.

She longed to continue her conversation with Christ but was unsure of how to reach him again. Just then, she remembered Mary's words. "That infinite force that is God is always present, around and within us."

Nicole smiled at the memory of how she longed to have such a personal connection with God. Now, after her vision, it seemed she was being offered just such an opportunity.

Where to begin? Nicole wondered. She turned back to her childhood training and brought out the rosary her Nonna had gifted her, a talisman she carried everywhere.

As a child, she'd played with the rosary during Mass, counting each bead and paying scant attention to the prayers that were enumerated by them. Little did she understand then that this simple act was her initiation into a meditative state. Now, Nicole used the familiar rhythm of the rosary to calm her bustling mind, hoping to pave the way to another divine connection.

She found a spot beside her bed, kneeling on the soft carpet, her eyes gently closing. She pressed a small silver crucifix against her forehead, her heart, and then each shoulder, the symbolic Sign of the Cross that marked the commencement of prayer.

She started with a prayer of honor and glory, praising the Father, the Son, and the Holy Spirit, acknowledging the eternal divine presence. Next, she began her whispers of veneration towards the Holy Mother in the "Hail

Mary," a conduit to the feminine divine. Following this, she said the "Glory Be," acknowledging that God had been there from the beginning of time and would be there till the end. Then she started a heartfelt conversation with the heavenly Father.

Her plea for divine guidance reverberated within her, filling her with a profound longing for spiritual direction. *Lord, let your will be done. Please, please show me what your will is so that I can follow what you want me to do.*

In her silence, Nicole continued her cycle of prayers, each word echoing in the thoughts of her tranquility, providing a rhythmic solace to her agitated mind. Her words flowed naturally, a testament to her faithfulness even as her heart wrestled with its turmoil.

I am a sinner, Lord, and I've broken your laws. I don't deserve your love, because I can't give up my sin, my unholy love for Elena. I am so scared, God, of eternal punishment....

> "Nicole, my beloved child," a voice, rich with divine warmth and affection, seeped into her thoughts like golden sunlight on a spring day. "I find immense joy in your decision to continue our dialogue." The voice, tender and gentle, remarked, "I see that guilt is crowding your heart, and it feels to you as though you are carrying the weight of the world."

Nicole was sure that these words were not her own. Once again, she was being given the privilege of engaging in a sacred dialogue with Christ himself! Overwhelmed, she felt an urge to kneel only to realize she already was. In response, she lifted her hands to cover her face, a timeless gesture of awe and humility before such divine presence. Yet, the voice lovingly reassured her.

> "Nicole, there's no need to hide any part of yourself from me. I cherish you, completely and wholly, just as I have told you before."

In the sanctum of her mind, Nicole visualized Christ. Seated initially but now bending forward, his arms rested on his knees as he lowered his radiant visage closer to her.

> "There is nothing required of you to secure my love or to prove your worthiness of it. You don't need to distort your true essence in a bid to secure it. My love for you is inherent, unequivocal, and everlasting. Nothing can estrange you and I. We are bound to each other, forever. I breathed life into you, gifted you free will, and, during my sojourn to your world, I left unambiguous guidance on this matter: 'So now faith, hope, and love abide, these three; but the greatest of these is love.'

> "Do you understand what the word 'abide' means, Nicole? It means 'eternal.' My love for you is eternal—everlasting, undying. It can't be retracted or annulled, and its existence can't be denied. So set aside your worries.
>
> "I am the personification of love, and you, my dear, haven't committed any transgression by loving someone. There is no impending divine retribution for experiencing love. Your affection for my child Elena isn't an error or a source of shame. Rather, it is a joyous celebration of love."

"But, Lord, my mother...," Nicole managed to utter, her voice laced with despair.

> "Ah yes, your mother. She, too, is a cherished child of mine, and I hold infinite love for her. She is walking her own life path, doing her best in her personal journey. However, Nicole, this interaction isn't about your mother or anyone else, for that matter. It's about *you*. Your purpose, the reason for your existence, is to manifest your truest self. I didn't grant you this life to conform to the expectations of others. I placed you in this world to realize your unique potential, and, most importantly, to embody love."

Suddenly Nicole heard the voice proclaim with celestial authority,

> "Love ye one another is the whole of the law."

When the heavenly echoes receded, Nicole whispered a question, "But what do I say to my mother? What words do I use?"

The voice responded:

> "When the time comes for you to have that conversation, Nicole, seek divine guidance in prayer. Be truthful, be genuine, and above all, be love.
>
> "Remember, I am eternally present with you. In times of difficulties and joys alike, come to me. I assure you, Nicole, happiness will embrace you when you're ready to receive it. Your season of sorrow can end when you choose to move beyond it. Your joyful morning is on the horizon and as you witness the sunrise, know that my love for you is limitless."

As the divine voice gradually receded, Nicole experienced a fleeting sense of loss and solitude akin to a child suddenly missing the comforting presence of a parent. However, this void was swiftly replaced with a knowing. Her soul echoed with the deep and profound wisdom imparted to her about her choice and the eternal, unwavering love of the divine.

When she looked down at her hands, she saw that she had reached the rosary's end. Blessing herself once again, she said, "Thank you, Lord. Thank you so very much."

She could have sworn she heard him say,

> "No worries, my child."

Chapter 45

The Power of Acceptance

As the women entered the Activity Center, they noticed that there were individual chairs arranged throughout the room. In front of each was a small table upon which rested a single mirror. These mirrors were all of different shapes and sizes, ranging from fifteen to eighteen inches tall with frames made of polished silver, brass, or pewter.

The first women to arrive took their usual places on the floor and so the others followed suit.

There was some sense of relief in the room when Mary walked in with only Sister D and Teena. The women assumed, since there were only the trio of them, that the day's lesson wouldn't be as demanding as the exercises the previous day.

Noticing that everyone was ready and attentive, Mary wasted no time in starting the activities.

"Good afternoon, beloveds. As I mentioned this morning today, the power of acceptance is one of the most important lessons you will learn all week, and, I dare say, all of your life.

"When you are in the energy of acceptance, you are at peace with yourself and with all around you. When we accept, we enter into a communion with the world. You and the world conspire, co-create, and co-exist in complete and seamless partnership. As such, there are no surprises, no coincidences, all is received and welcomed, and all that occurs, regardless of its effect on us, is understood to be for our highest good.

"In the vibratory energy of acceptance, things don't bother you and people don't irritate you. In acceptance, you begin to see the world as a classroom and those around you as teachers. These teachers all provide you with experiences and lessons that enrich your life and advance you towards the highest vibrations. In acceptance, there is no judgement and there is no resistance.

"I am not saying that the external factors and those triggers disappear. They will continue, and you will face them as you always have. What changes is *you*. The way you experience them and the way you relate to them will be different, lighter, and simpler. This is when your true liberation begins.

"Eventually, when your consciousness grows to an even higher level, you will come to realize that nothing and no one can touch you because you are one with the most formidable power in existence. When you tap that power, you have achieved total acceptance. Acceptance acts both as a filter and a shield, allowing everything and anything to pass through you without having an impact. Nothing is able to touch or hurt you, because you are protected. You are immune and you are free.

"And what must you accept?

"Well, to experience the highest level of acceptance, you have to accept two things—yourself and everything around you. And those, my dears, are the two things we'll aim for today with our exercises.

"So, are you ready to practice more acceptance?" asked Mary. When all the women had nodded or answered "yes" out loud, Mary continued speaking.

"This morning you learned the first lesson: accepting your power. When you place qualities like 'peace,' 'free,' and 'love' as the ending of the phrase, 'I AM,' you are claiming and affirming what you say to be true. I AM peace. I AM free. I AM love."

Mary's gaze moved over all the women seated before her, measuring their understanding of her words.

"And now, for the next three lessons," Mary continued, "loving yourself, accepting yourself, and, finally, accepting others.

"It is our experience that most people go through their whole lives without ever saying to themselves, 'I love you.' If that is the case for you, in a few minutes you will have the opportunity to change that. By saying 'I love you' to yourself, you take another major step in acceptance."

Mary strode towards the tables and said, "Now, please claim a seat in front of one of the mirrors positioned throughout the room."

The women each found one of the tables to claim. Once they were all in place,

Mary continued with the instructions.

"Now, face the mirror, and, as you do, notice the image of the person reflected in it. This person is the most important person in your life. You are deeply connected with her. You know her intimately, and you love her, although perhaps not as fully as she deserves. She deserves that you love her unconditionally.

"Loving yourself is the next lesson in acceptance."

The women knew that no matter what was about to be asked of them, it was being asked with the best of intentions. They trusted that and they knew that trust to be well-placed.

"In this first part of this exercise," Mary continued, "you will repeatedly tell yourself 'I love you.' One-hundred-eight times, to be exact. You can keep count using the mala beads—those circlets of beads—that we've placed on the table. Using them saves you the stress of losing count.

"If there are no questions, please begin."

As they started, the first few tries were awkward for most and challenging for some.

"I love you. I love you. I love you. I love you. I love you," they kept repeating. After about twenty-five or so repetitions, some started to realize and remember all the instances in which they had not been kind or had said harsh and unpleasant words to themselves. They felt and recognized the pain and energy associated with those moments. The weight of those memories caught up with the raw emotions of the past few days and soon the tears flowed. It was then that the exercise took on more meaning.

After they had reached their assigned count and the room became quiet again, Mary, acknowledged their effort and asked them to take deep, cleansing breaths to clear the energy. The deep breaths were repeated a few times.

Mary spoke with great empathy, "We tend to forget the power our words wield. We forget the energy contained in them. Our words can raise and construct or lower and destruct. Unfortunately, because we are not aware of the power of our words, we often allow the latter.

"Please take a moment to forgive yourselves for all those times that you were unkind with the most important person in your life—*you*. You didn't know better. Now you do, and so, moving forward, you can make things different.

The Orchid

"Repeat the words: 'I forgive myself because I didn't know better. I forgive myself because I didn't know better. I forgive myself because I didn't know better.'

"For some of you, it might be a welcome change. For others, it might seem difficult, perhaps even impossible. Through repetition, this exercise will become easier and more helpful. You will begin to normalize it so that soon it won't even feel foreign to tell yourself how much you love yourself. As you can probably tell, the act of repeating these words is a powerful step in unlocking your self-love and self-acceptance.

"Now, I ask that you please stand up for a moment. Let's shake this energy off to the rhythm of the music. Walk around, smile, jump, release anything that is not serving your highest good."

The women stirred, shaking their hands and raising their legs, their bodies humming with anticipation. As empowering melodies filled the room, they found themselves caught in the rhythm, dancing uninhibitedly. Each beat was a testament to their self-love, each note uplifting their spirits. They swayed and twirled, their laughter mixing with the music, creating an intoxicating atmosphere of shared joy and unity.

As if guided by an unseen force, they began to slow down when the music softened, and the energy shifted. Their dance became a serene sway, their bodies resonating with the echoes of the music. It then concluded, leaving the women basking in the afterglow of their shared experience.

As the dancing gradually concluded, Teena came forward and took over the session. She sounded eager as she announced, "Now we're moving on to the next lesson—self-acceptance. It's a common experience for us to be our harshest critics. When we gaze at our reflections, we often focus on our perceived flaws, pondering ways to change or conceal these so-called imperfections.

"For the upcoming exercise, you'll stand before the mirror and speak to your reflection, reciting affirmations of love, encouragement, and acceptance. Should you need a spark of inspiration, we've placed a list of uplifting phrases on the desk. Feel free, however, to use any words that resonate with you personally. The only guideline for this exercise is to say your words aloud and ensure they are imbued with love, appreciation, and encouragement towards yourself.

"That is all. It's pretty simple. When you are ready, please begin."

The women again sat in front of the mirrors. Each looked at her own face and all of its features and, in the spirit of accepting themselves just as they were, repeated these powerful messages to themselves:

> I love you.
> You are beautiful.
> You are the most important person in my life.
> I love the shape of your eyes.
> You have an enchanting smile.
> I love the color of your skin.
> Your eyes are so expressive and lovely.
> Your dimples add so much personality to your face.
> Your freckles are adorable.
> I love the shape of your head.
> Your hair is so shiny.
> Your curls are beautiful.
> I love every inch of your body.
> Your skin and wrinkles tell such beautiful stories.
> Your smile is so very infectious.
> You are perfect.
> I love your grey hairs.
> The lines in your face are a work of art.
> I love the shape of your body.
> You are enough.
> I love your graceful neck.
> I love that your eyes are slightly different.
> Your nose is perfect.
> Your skin is so healthy.

Mary, Sister D, and Teena circulated around the room, offering their support to each woman. As the air vibrated with repeated affirmations of love and appreciation, a palpable shift in energy swept through the space again, each woman experiencing her own unique and personal transformation.

Sofia was smiling. It was her smile that surprised her the most. She saw it so rarely. She spent most of her time being serious, angry, and closed off. She acknowledged now that her teeth were beautiful and quite straight. *Odd*, she thought, *since I never had braces.* Her dark brown eyes were also quite stunning. *I'm going to use mascara more often to accentuate my eyes,* she thought. Then she said aloud, "You are so beautiful, Sofia. Any person would be lucky to have you as a friend, or a girlfriend, or wife." *Wow, slow down girl! Take it easy. I tell you that you are beautiful and you go crazy on me*, she thought. She was enjoying the dialogue with herself. "I love you, Sofia. I love your new attitude in life. I love that we are friends. I have been very tough on you over the years, and, for that, I'm sorry."

Olivia was a bit more serious, perhaps feeling a little uncomfortable with the exercise. She had never in her entire life spoken to herself in this fashion, but she pressed on. "You are not so young, Olivia," she said out loud, unsure if this was a compliment or criticism. She decided that she was complimenting the wisdom of her years. "You are a sexy woman, Olivia, years and all. I love you, Livy, and I like the way you look. Your smile transmits respect and reassurance. I love the color of your skin. It's dark, vibrant, and so very attractive. You have penetrating eyes. You are smart and intelligent. I love you, Olivia."

Jennifer was having a little more difficulty. It had been many years since she had been in any situation that required her to sit in front of the mirror and admire her own beauty. In fact, she couldn't remember the last time that actually happened. Since the divorce, she had gotten accustomed to calling herself stupid, fat, and ugly. The extent of her entire beauty routine had been combing her hair and brushing her teeth. But she bravely waded in and said, "You are pretty, Jennifer. Your lips are nice. Your lips are full, actually. Your teeth are clean. Your eyes are naturally beautiful. Your nose is a little pointy but cute." Little by little, she continued to say lovely things to herself until it became more natural and less painful. "You are a catch, Jennifer. You are beautiful. You are amazing. I love you, Jen. I love you, babe."

Stephanie had the experience of being paraded in front of mirrors many times before and of having heard every single compliment (and insult) about her looks imaginable. For her, it wasn't so difficult to find the words, as much as it was to allow them to come out of her mouth and for them to be heartfelt. She stood motionless in front of the mirror for some time without uttering anything at all. And then, as if directed by an inner knowledge, she began to call out both her interior and exterior beauty. "You are so lovely. Your skin is flawless. Your heart is so pure. Your smile is picture perfect. Your eyes are penetrating and loving and the look in them speaks a thousand words. I love you, Stephanie. I love you, little Stephanie. You are so amazing. You are so brave."

In a corner of the room, and, still feeling moved from the time with Mary and her conversation with her God, Nicole was making an effort to admire and praise herself. She made use of the lessons she had so recently learned. Quietly, she said to herself in the mirror, "You are such a beautiful woman, Nicky. I love your hair and how it falls on your shoulders. I love everything about you. Your smile is so amazing, Nicole. Your eyes are so beautiful. You are so attractive. Elena loves you just as you are, Nicole. You don't have to hide. You are perfect just as you are." Still, she felt twinges of disbelief as she said those words to herself.

After some time, Teena gave notice that the exercise was ending momentarily. As it did, all were now more at ease and somewhat more accepting of themselves, their bodies, and their persona.

After they had taken a few moments for a drink and a bathroom break, it was time to begin again. Sister D took the lead this time, setting the stage for the next lesson: accepting others.

"At times," she began, "this task may seem challenging, especially when we're confronted with those whom we believe have hurt us through their actions, words, or behavior. That is precisely what we'll be addressing now. We'll tackle this by voicing our feelings. Then we will attentively listen as a partner, standing in the shoes of those who have wronged us, responds to the feelings we voiced.

"First, I invite each of you to identify someone in your life—be it a parent, a spouse or lover, a child, a longtime friend, a recent acquaintance, or even someone you once considered a friend—towards whom you carry feelings of hurt or resentment because of their actions. Over the next few moments, you'll be given the opportunity to express whatever you wish to say. This might include explaining how their actions, words, or behavior caused you distress. Once you've had a chance to share, your partner will step into the role of that individual and respond to your words. However, their responses must adhere to one of the three following statements:

> 1. "I'm sorry. Please forgive me. I love you. Thank you." You may recognize this. It is the "*Ho'oponopono,*" an ancient Hawaiian prayer that focuses on radical responsibility through the offering of repentance, forgiveness, love, and gratitude.
>
> 2. "I'm sorry. Please forgive me. I am a spiritual being having a human experience." This is from the phrase originated by the French philosopher and Jesuit priest, Pierre Teilhard de Chardin.

3. "I'm sorry. Please forgive me. I did the best I could with what I had. Now that I know better, I'll do better." This is a favorite of mine, and endless variations of it have been repeated by many.

"When our partner offers these replies to our spoken pain, it allows us to plant new ideas in our subconscious. This helps us reprogram our brains with empathy and understanding that eventually allows us to forgive. Forgiveness, in turn, leads us to the higher energetic vibration that lies in the state of acceptance.

"After the first person has had her turn to express her feelings, we will take a short break and then we will switch places and repeat the exercise," Sister D concluded.

She answered a few questions, and then the women selected their partners.

Olivia, who partnered with Stephanie, looked directly into her eyes and plunged straight into the deep end, selecting her father as the object at which she aimed her deluge of words and thoughts. They flowed from her like a fast-moving river.

"You came home drunk so many times," Olivia said right off. Not quite able to call her father "Dad" while talking about his abusive behavior, she simply went on to say, "You were abusive and hit Mama and me and you hurt us badly. You never helped me financially. You disappeared so many times. Where did you go? You did not see me grow and you missed so much of my life and our life as a family." This one statement seemed to impact Olivia more than the others so she paused, choked with tears.

Stephanie, taking the opportunity created by the momentary silence, answered, "I'm sorry, Olivia. Please forgive me. I love you. Thank you. I was a spiritual being having a human experience, Olivia. I'm so sorry. Please forgive me. I did the best that I could with what I had."

Olivia and Stephanie repeated this exchange a few times, and both soon began to recognize the inherent power of the exercise.

Elsewhere in the room, Sofia was unloading her pain onto her partner, who stood in for her brother. "Why did you have to follow in dad's footsteps? Why did your actions towards me always border on aggression? You were so selfish!" Her voice was charged with anger yet swiftly turned mournful as she continued. "I felt so exposed and so unprotected every time I was around you. Thanks to you, I was in a constant state of fear and loneliness."

She faltered, choking on the raw emotions her words stirred up, pausing to collect herself. As she resumed, an added depth of grief tinged her words, "You left a void, a vast and echoing void where the warmth of a brother's love should have been." As she spoke, the profound depth of her sadness was palpable, filling the space around her.

Jennifer responded, "I'm sorry. Please forgive me. I love you. Thank you. I'm sorry, Sofia. Please forgive me. I love you. Thank you. I'm sorry. Please forgive me. I love you. Thank you." As she repeated the message, Jennifer realized that the exercise was also for her, and that, though she was simply replying, she also was benefitting from the exchange.

Nicole had partnered with Lisa, a woman to whom she had spoken a few times during the week. "Mom, you are so hostile, even though sometimes its passive and you don't always say it in words. How you look at me speaks volumes. Why are you always so damn judgmental? I know that you know, deep down, that I am gay. Mom, can you not love me just as I am? Sometimes I don't think you love me at all. You are always reminding me of all my sins. I don't want to sin anymore, but I am not going to hide anymore either, Mom."

Lisa spoke the prescribed replies while holding both of Nicole's hands and offering a heartfelt smile. "I'm sorry. Please forgive me. I love you, Nicole. Thank you," she said. "I'm sorry. Please forgive me, Nicole. I love you. Thank you. I'm sorry. Please forgive me. I am a spiritual being having a human experience."

Following the first cycle, Sister D asked everyone to take a moment so that the person who had just shared her sentiments could have a space to assimilate and process the exchange. Then it was the other person's turn.

Stephanie focused her words on her mother. "You pushed me so hard to be a model, mother. I think you wanted to be a model more than I did, and, because of it, you were blinded; blinded to my pain and to my needs. I was only a little girl. I remember you pushing me to not eat, to stand up straight, and to hide from the sun. But I don't remember you ever expressing your love to me or saying that you accepted me just as I was. I was so scared that day you were laying on the floor unconscious. I thought you died and I always thought it was my fault." Stephanie's voice was solemn. She wasn't crying and she wasn't angry, but she sounded devastated.

Standing in front of her, Olivia waited for her turn to reply. "I'm sorry, Stephanie. I'm sorry, my beautiful, smart, and strong little girl. Please forgive me. I did the best I could with what I had. Now that I know better, I'll do

The Orchid

better. I'm sorry, Stephanie. Please forgive me. I did the best I could with what I had. Now that I know better, I'll do better." Stephanie felt the power of the message deeply. She reached out to Olivia and hugged her. "Thank you, Mommy, thank you. Your words mean so much to me."

When it was Jennifer's turn, it wasn't who hurt her to whom she wished to speak—it was two people she believed *she* had hurt. She chose to speak to her kids. She wanted to apologize. "My darlings, Michelle and Tommy, I am so, so sorry. Sorry to let you down. Sorry to have allowed the divorce from your dad to make me mad and ruin our times together. You are only kids. I shouldn't have dragged you into the middle of an adult fight. I was lying to myself about the job I was doing with you two. Now I know that I was screwing up everything. You two are so precious to me, and I was so angry that I lost sight of that. I did the best I could at the moment. I know I have a lot of work to do. But I promise you, from now on it will be different."

Sofia, while listening to her partner, also couldn't help but to think of her own mother and the challenges she had faced. A faint echo of her mother's voice whispered in Sofia's mind. It seemed her mother was asking Sofia for forgiveness for all the times she had disappointed her.

Sofia found herself answering both her own mother and Jennifer. "Mom, you don't have to apologize to me. I forgive you. You did the best you could with what you had. If you had known better, you would have done better. But you didn't know what you didn't know, so you don't have to be sorry, Mom. I forgive you. I love you and thank you for all that you gave me."

At that moment, Sofia and Jennifer, both moved beyond words, embraced each other and gave in to the power of forgiveness that both had felt during the exchange.

All over the room the women were engaged in these interactions. One half of each partnership was digging up the bones of those long-buried grievances and the other half offering the only words that truly mattered—sincere apologies for the harm they had done and giving voice to the love they felt. Hearts were healing all over the room.

"I'm sorry. Please forgive me. I love you. Thank you."

"I am a spiritual being having a human experience."

"I did the best I could with what I had. Now that I know better, I'll do better."

The Orchid

Chapter 46

The Power Within

Hundreds of candles and torches had been lit to welcome the women to the Evening Council.

Unlike previous nights, the Council ceremony was being held in the heart of The Orchid, the Central Plaza, right outside the Sanctuary, the same place the banquet had been held.

At the center of that space, the wood for a ceremonial fire was already set up for later use. The clear night sky was illuminated by a million stars and by silver moonlight.

Slowly, all the women filled the area. Dressed in their white gowns, they looked like a legion of angels. They walked lightly, smiling. Gone was the heaviness they carried during their first few days of the program. Now, experienced and self-aware, they walked with a sense of spiritual maturity. They had begun to see the power they held even if they didn't yet know how to wield it.

All of the healers were present. Dressed in their finest with their crystals, jewelry, and amulets on display, they resembled an assembly of super women and goddesses, armed for a powerful encounter. Infectious drum rhythms were playing in the background. Everyone was smiling, cheerful, and engaged. The energy present was at the highest level it had been all week. It was vibrant and strong and could be felt by all.

Mary stood and motioned for attention. Her warm voice, loud and clear, filled the space.

"My dearests, we are all so grateful to be here with you. Thank you for the amazing effort that each of you has given and for the opportunity for us to be of service, helping with your growth and development. You have now been here five days. Throughout that time, we have shared with you insights and information about some of the most important forces in the cosmos. Moreover, you have come to experience and observe their power.

"You have learned about:

Awareness: The ability to step back and look at all that is happening to you and around you, with a sense of detachment. You become the observer of your own life.

Gratitude: The force that allows you to view everything that happens with optimism and which compels you to live in the present moment and fully appreciate all of your current circumstances.

Forgiveness: The power that comes from liberating yourself from the pain and trauma associated with past experiences because you understand they are only lessons for your growth and transcendence.

Acceptance: The certainty that comes with knowing all that you are experiencing and everything unfolding around you is exactly as it should be.

"And, of course, there is always…

Love, the most infinite and grandiose force there is.

"You have learned to access and tap into each of these powerful forces. Any one of them, and certainly any combination of them, can transform your life. Accessing them raises your vibration, brings happiness, promotes health and healing, grants you empathy and compassion, and, ultimately, liberates your spirit.

"Combine these with the other tools with which you are becoming familiar like meditation, journaling, self-love, silence, energy practice, breathing therapy, and sound healing, and you'll have the ability to access, in a manner you didn't quite understand before, the divine power that resides within you."

Mary paused to allow her words to sink in.

"Stand up, my dear sisters, and join me as we ask the universe to grant you your rightful access to these forces. They are yours for the asking. Love is already freely available inside each of you. You just have to embrace it and allow it to shine forth from within you."

The other healers and teachers all took positions on the perimeter, just as they had done the night of the previous ceremony. But this time they were not corralling heaviness. Today, they were in the presence of love, and their intent was to become powerful antennae to magnify the activation that was taking place at that moment and in that space. They all joined Mary as she raised her hands as if invoking the heavens to open.

"Echo my words with the 'I AM' phrase," Mary began. "In doing so, you claim your rightful place in the universe.

"I AM love," her voice resonated through the room.

"I AM love," the women echoed back.

"I AM aware. I AM grateful. I AM forgiving. I AM accepting. I AM love."

With a determined look, Mary encouraged the group, "Now, continue independently. Feel the words. Realize, accept, and embrace your inherent power and magnificence."

The women confidently proceeded, their voices amplifying with each repetition. "I AM love. I AM aware. I AM grateful. I AM forgiving. I AM accepting. I AM love," they affirmed.

"Internalize these words and believe them," Mary instructed. "Invite the highest vibrations into your being by invoking and embracing these powers."

In unison, they repeated the affirmations, their voices resounding through the air. "I AM love. I AM aware. I AM grateful. I AM forgiving. I AM accepting. I AM love."

"Repeat it and feel it," Mary guided. "In doing so, you are ushering in a new reality where you acknowledge your immeasurable power."

The group repeated the affirmations once more. As they did, a member of the staff ignited the fire. Mary gestured towards the group, inviting them to continue.

"As you speak these words, look into each other's eyes," she instructed. "Connect with the spirit of your sisters and discover the depths of your own being."

The women recited the affirmations several times until Mary advised them to choose a partner. "Repeat the affirmations to your sister. Once finished, the listener will affirm, 'Yes, you are. Yes, you are.' Then switch roles and repeat the exercise."

The air became a symphony of affirmations and acknowledgments as the women all took turns. They connected, and, as they did, their eyes reflected the power and transformation each was experiencing.

The Orchid

"Today, you've accessed ancient wisdom and opened your minds to new perspectives," Mary announced. "You've transformed, become entirely new beings. Remember this day, for today you've been reborn."

The women felt the energy within the circle and in themselves. It shot through them like a lightning bolt. At Mary's direction, they threw their arms towards Heaven and directed the love upward and outward to add to the invisible web of love that circled the Earth just like the healers encircled them. Their gift was accepted and returned to them, and each felt her heart swell and her spirit, along with those of the others, lift in absolute purity, abundance, and love. They all felt the oneness of their sacred circle and the happiness and light present within and all around them.

Knowing that the energy was now at its highest frequency, Flavia stepped out of the circle and stood near the fire ring. In a joyful voice, she said, "Ok, it's time to dance!"

She motioned for the music to begin again, and, as she did, powerful energetic sounds filled the space.

Flavia's hips swiveled and her feet beat out a joyous rhythm as she danced with her whole being and motioned for the other women to join in. They did, in a wild burst of jubilant emotion, dancing and singing to every beat.

Suddenly, bursts of light exploded in the sky from different locations all over The Orchid, illuminating the darkness with a brilliant array of colors and shapes. Red pinwheels, blue waterfalls, green stars, and purple flowers, each firework displayed its uniqueness, leaving its signature written across the night sky before disappearing from view.

Different songs and choruses continued with the sounds of fireworks accompanying them like the percussion section of an orchestra, creating a most magical experience. All were swept up in the excitement and euphoria of such a spectacle.

And then, just like that, the light show was over. The last firework faded in the dark night sky, leaving only the echoes of its sound and the memory of its stunning display. The dancing, however, continued for much longer, fed by different musical anthems from around the world, all invoking feminine power, strength, and freedom.

Eventually, the music wound down and the exhausted and exhilarated women found their places again on the earth, around the fire.

"How extraordinary it is to feel the power of our true existence, isn't it?" Mary asked of them. "Remember, that which you are experiencing—that strength, that power, that energy—is available to you anytime and anywhere because it is abundant *within* you."

Mary was looking at the faces of the amazing women with their souls shining brightly in their eyes as she said, "And now, taking advantage of this high vibratory state, I'd like to open our circle for sharing, inviting you all to go within, connect with yourself, and share that which is present for you in this moment. And if I may, I'd like to begin."

The women were excited. Until today, they had only heard Mary teach, giving insights as part of larger lessons, but had not heard her share personally.

She began, "I'm humbled by the opportunity that I am granted each week to contribute to the transformation of such beautiful beings. It is incredibly powerful to witness the change as it happens. We are all significant and we are all one." Mary placed both of her palms together over her heart. "My sincerest gratitude to you all for allowing me the privilege of being one with you during our time together."

When it was time to share, Nicole was the first to speak.

"I'm so thankful to you, Mary, and to the rest of the staff here, for all your patience, kindness, insights, and support. We are so lucky to have you to watch over us and encourage us as we go through our," she paused briefly, searching for the right words, "through our process. I certainly don't have all the answers yet. I'm not sure I'm supposed to, but I understand how the journey is mine, and mine alone, to decipher. I feel more powerful and capable than I've ever felt before. Thank you," she said and then sat down again.

She received a few pats on the arm and smiles in support from the others sitting around her.

Olivia stood next. "So much has happened this week. I don't know where to begin, but I think I'll focus on today. I consider myself a strong person, but today, today was special. The exercise of seeing ourselves in the mirror and declaring our love for ourselves was quite incredible. Then this evening, I saw my power multiplied, and then even that grew larger when we all danced together. I've never felt so powerful. I echo Nicole. Thank you all. Thank you, dear Lord, for bringing me here." She said these last words staring at the skies above. "And oh, yes, Mary, thank you for the wonderful fireworks. That was simply delightful."

"Yes, that was amazing and incredible, thank you," said a few of the women.

Jennifer stood up. "Before coming to The Orchid, apart from a rare mani-pedi, I couldn't remember the last time that I was kind or loving to myself. And I certainly wasn't prepared for how special and pretty I felt this afternoon when I said, 'I love you' to myself."

Jennifer paused and dabbed at tears rolling down her cheeks with the sleeves of her gown. "I was so lost before coming here. I didn't see myself. All I saw was a broken woman. A woman who was abandoned by her husband and was left with no future, no possibilities, and not a chance of ever loving or being loved again. Crazy, right? I don't even know who that person was. It feels like I've truly become someone else. I could go on, but that's what is present for me now. My gosh, even the way I speak is different. Who am I?" she said, laughing out loud. The others joined in.

Sofia was next.

"Ok, so let's just start with the fact that I'm not so angry anymore," Sofia said, grinning. There was some applause and laughter in the group.

"You go, Sofia," yelled someone.

Acquiescing to the smattering of applause, Sofia stood and spoke, "Only a day or so ago, I was still unsure if this was going to work for me or not. This stuff might have worked on you all, but not me. See, I was *different*. I was *special*," she said with sarcasm. "I could have easily walked out and that terminal uniqueness could have continued to ruin my life. Thank you, Mary, for believing in me, for not giving up on me even though I had given up on myself." She smiled as she walked over to Mary and gave her a warm hug.

"Today was so powerful," Sofia continued." I felt really exposed when I was speaking to my reflection in the mirror. I've never done that before. I don't think I had ever acknowledged me as, you know, me, much less told myself, 'I love you.' And the whole exercise of speaking to my brother and then my mom, it felt stupid at first, but after a while, the answers felt very real, profound, and sincere. As if they were the ones saying them back to me. Holy shit. Sorry." She said, slightly embarrassed. "Who knew? And tonight? What the heck? I kid you not, I felt superhuman. For a second, I felt this sensation that I understood *things*, even though I'm not fully sure what those things are. Anyhow…." She said with a huge breath, "Thank you. Thank you. Thank you all for, well, everything." And she returned to her place and sat down.

Stephanie stood up and simply held her hands together in front of her. She stood there and looked at all the others, turning her head slowly. The silence was the same as it had been earlier in the week, but what was different was her wide smile. She had stood before many groups in her previous life, but had been only a mannequin, showing nothing but her painted-on beauty. Now, though, she was modeling her soul; once hidden, it was now revealed to these women who had watched and helped Stephanie become a more authentic version of herself. "I don't know where to begin," she started. "How about, I love you all? I feel so connected to you, and there is no other place I'd rather be, and no other people I'd rather be with. It's like I'm on a natural high. I understand that I have a lot of work to do and a lot of issues to address." She took a ragged, deep breath before speaking again. "I was raped and I'm dealing with an eating disorder.... I have never said those things out loud to anybody. How's that for power?" She was nearly choked with emotion but pushed through and announced with confidence, "I AM powerful."

Unbidden the other women yelled in unison, "Yes, you are! Yes, you are."

"I AM complete," Stephanie added.

"Yes, you are! Yes, you are," the others repeated.

Stephanie's smile now grew bigger, adorning her stunningly beautiful face. She then sat down, enjoying the miracle of her life.

Through the remainder of the evening, the rest of the women stood and shared and celebrated. Many expressed how they felt weightless. Others spoke about being happy for the first in a long time. A few still had a lot of questions and even skepticism, but they admitted being encouraged by the changes they had observed in themselves and others since their arrival and were determined to continue embracing their process of transformation.

When all had spoken their piece, Mary said, "And now, please join me as we close this sacred circle and express our gratitude to the universe for all the blessings and miracles we witnessed today.

> Divine Presence, Spirit, Infinite Power, Higher Self, God,
>
> We offer our gratitude for revealing to us the greatness of our being and our interconnectedness with all that exists. We honor the forces that we have become aware of and commit to using them wisely and for the highest good.

Thank you for the privilege of being alive to experience this moment and for the opportunity to recognize the power and love that we carry within. As we embrace our new reality, we ask for clarity in resolving any remaining issues and for the continued expansion and understanding of our soul's journey.

We know this to be true. We feel it through all of our senses.

And so, it is.

Mary inhaled and then released a deep breath and turned to the women. "My dears, today has been a most incredible evening. Thank you all.

"Tomorrow we will learn the program's final lesson. We will discuss what to do with all the powers that we have at our fingertips. We will learn about manifesting our intention.

"Have a wonderful night and know you are loved."

Each woman felt the truth of that statement as they dispersed into the moonlit night to dream of the better tomorrow they now felt awaited them.

Chapter 47

Prayer

After the Evening Council ended, Nicole and Olivia found themselves walking together towards their respective rooms.

"How amazing was tonight? And the fireworks? They really do go all out to make us feel very special, don't they?" asked Olivia.

"For sure. It was so beautiful." Nicole answered.

"Nicole," continued Olivia "I can't thank you enough for yesterday. You were simply amazing. You knew exactly what to do during my panic attack. I don't know what I would have done without you."

"Oh, Olivia, please don't mention it. I'm glad I was there to help. It's what I'm trained for, but, honestly, anyone would have done the same."

"I know," said Olivia, "But it was you, and I appreciate you nevertheless. You were so calm and made me feel safe. Thank you, really."

"You're welcome, Olivia." Nicole replied. "That's what friends, I mean, sisters, are for. Just know that you're not alone, okay?"

"Thank you, Nicole, I really appreciate it," Olivia responded.

"I'm learning so much," Nicole continued. "I really do feel myself getting stronger. To be honest, it's made me realize that I need to muster the courage to tell a few people, especially my parents, how I really feel about a few things. But I need to find the right words. How do you do it, Olivia?"

"How I do what?" Olivia asked.

"Well, I assume you've had to argue and persuade people to change their minds many times. How do you decide what to say in those moments?" Nicole asked.

"Oh, I see, because I'm old you think I'm wise, is that it?" Olivia said with a laugh.

"No, not old, just older than me," Nicole said, worried that she had offended Olivia. "And yes, you certainly seem wiser to me."

"Well, Nicole, I read somewhere once that we only recognize wisdom that we possess ourselves, so right back at you, darling." Olivia said with a smile as the pair reached the path that led to Nicole's room. "But invite me in for a nice cup of tea and I'll share my secrets with you."

"Deal. Thank you, Olivia. I really appreciate you taking the time." Nicole said excitedly as she led the way to her room.

"My pleasure," said Olivia, "besides, I really wanted to see your fabulous room."

"Wow!" Olivia gasped upon proceeding past the waterfall and seeing the room's interior with its lush carpets and Moroccan lanterns. "This is some space. It's like out of a story book."

"I've never seen anything as exotic or as beautiful," Nicole said. "It is a dream."

"Hard to imagine someone created this so deep in the earth, right?" Olivia said as she admired the details.

Turning her attention back to Nicole, she said, "So what is it that you need to find the words to say, Nicole?" she asked.

"I need to tell my parents that…," Nicole hesitated, "that I'm … gay. And I think, I know, they are not ready to hear it," she spit out.

"Olivia raised an eyebrow and asked, "You mean they don't know yet? Are your parents very traditional?"

Nicole nodded, "No, they don't know. And yes, they are very traditional and deeply Catholic. No matter how many times I plan out what I'm going to say, when the moment comes, I can't find the words to go through with it."

"And what is it that you want them to do when you tell them? Still love you? Accept you? Change their dreams for you?" asked Olivia.

"Something like that," admitted Nicole.

"Ok. Let's see. Why don't you first pour me some tea, with two lumps of sugar, and we'll try to sort this out together," Olivia directed. "Life is always better over a cup of tea, darling."

Nicole went to gather the tea things and get the instant electric kettle boiling. As she gathered the cups, cardamom tea bags, and lump sugar, Olivia looked around the cave admiring the space.

When Nicole put down the cup in front of Olivia, she stirred it, took a sip of the fragrant tea, and sighed contentedly. Then Olivia turned to Nicole and asked, "So you want to hear my secret for choosing just the right words to say in any situation?"

"Please," said Nicole, sitting forward in her chair.

"Ok, honey, here it is. There are three things. The first is that I let go of all expectations and I surrender to the moment and simply do my best to deliver the most powerful message I can deliver. I remind myself that I'm not responsible for how people act or react, only that I've presented my most convincing argument, so I focus on that.

"The second thing I do is script every single word that I'm going to say. Scripting of the conversation, my parts anyway, helps me articulate my thoughts and piece the arguments together without missing anything.

"And the last, and this is the most important one. I use a ghostwriter."

"Huh?" Nicole said, looking confused.

Olivia continued, "Yes, I use a ghostwriter… the Holy Ghostwriter. I pray and invite God to step in. He sees the whole situation and farther down the road than I can, so I ask him to please give me the words to say. When I am standing in front of the person or people I have to address, I say, 'Ok, Jesus, please put in my mouth the exact words you need me to say,' and then I start speaking, and the right words come out. It never fails me, Nicole. Jesus never fails me."

Nicole blinked a minute and then said, "It had never occurred to me to ask God that directly for something so specific."

"Oh yes, honey, I have him on speed dial and I call him for everything. It never fails me. God always knows what to say and how to help us. We just need to ask. And when I don't get what I'm asking for, I assume that it is not his will. It's that simple," Olivia added.

"That makes sense," Nicole answered, somewhat relieved at the simplicity of Olivia's advice. "I guess I've got some praying to do," Nicole said quietly.

"You sure do, sugar, and you've got a great room to do it in—warm and dark and cozy, perfect for prayer and meditation. You do know the difference, don't you?"

"I don't," said Nicole.

"Prayer is where you talk to God and meditation is when he talks to you."

"I never thought of it that way," Nicole admitted.

"That's only because you aren't old and wise like me," Olivia teased, winking at Nicole.

"How I wish you could come with me to talk to my parents," Nicole said, her voice quavering a little. "I don't want to do it alone."

"Child, you won't be alone," Olivia stressed. "He is always with you."

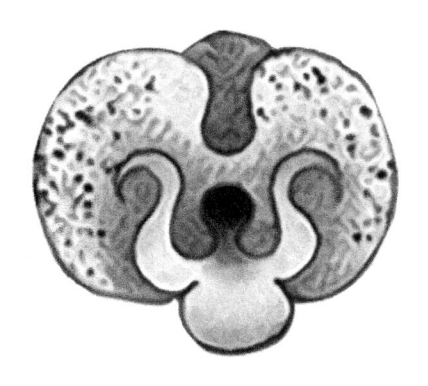

Part VII
Intention

The Orchid

Chapter 48

Morning Reflections

It was the early morning of the sixth day. Lights were on everywhere, and the combination of the Tibetan bell and an avian ensemble was announcing the commencement of the day's activities. It was always the case that, when the week was coming to an end, the women were more diligent about their schedules and being on time for their activities. Only a few days ago, getting out of bed so early was difficult. Today, many were up even before the sound of the first bell.

Olivia was in the middle of preparing a cup of hot hibiscus tea and was about to sit briefly to enjoy it. Just prior to this task, she had gotten on her knees to pray.

"Thank you, God Almighty, for this sacred place and for the individuals who pour their hearts out to enhance the lives of the women who visit here," Olivia began, her voice blending with the ethereal hum of the "om" sound resonating through the forest. "Thank you, Lord, for granting me the opportunity to gain such profound knowledge and insight and, through that journey, to learn about myself, my life, and my family. I hold a deep sense of gratitude, Lord, especially for the lessons on forgiveness. While I've been a person of gratitude, I've not always been forgiving. I ask for a special blessing for my father. May he find the answers he seeks. And may I garner the words, the courage, and the strength to one day sit beside him and exchange words of kindness."

**

Not far from Olivia, in her spectacular cave room, Nicole was journaling. She had been journaling a lot over the last twenty-four hours. Since her vision of Christ, Nicole had begun to see the pieces of her life fall into place. During the night, a desire had come to her to write a letter to her parents:

The Orchid

Dear Mom and Dad,

Yesterday, the theme of the day was acceptance, something I have not been particularly good at throughout my life. Let me begin by saying that I appreciate all the lessons, the teachings, and the values you both instilled in me. However, you should know that there has been a lot of pain in my life because of it. My truth and our family values have always been in direct conflict. As a result, I've lived with shame all my life. I've always known my truth, yet I felt I could never share it with you in fear of your judgment. The truth is I'm a lesbian. I battled my nature, believing I could change. I tried to suppress my feelings and even blamed myself for them, yet nothing alleviated my attraction to women or my burden of guilt and shame. You might wonder why I'm writing this letter. I believe you need to know the truth, my truth. I've felt unloved, uncared for, lost in the pursuit of a false image of the perfect, devout family. I felt constrained by the image of a punishing God that you instilled in me. But you know what? I experienced a new version of God. A God that is all-loving. Just yesterday, I spoke to Jesus and I was embraced by Him. You know what He said to me? He said what you should have said all these years. "Nicole my love, you are my child and you are perfect just the way you are."

When Nicole wrote these last words, she felt another surge of energy throughout her body, so much that she trembled and goosebumps rose on her skin. More stored energy was released and she fully integrated the prior day's encounter with Christ. She allowed the energy to travel through her body, and she felt the new sensation that was taking over, replacing the old fears and inhibitions. For the first time in her life, she accepted herself fully. She fell back in the chair, closed her eyes, and put down the pen. And, at that moment, she finally began to let go of her guilt and shame.

**

Up in her glass castle, Stephanie was in the lotus position listening to Tibetan "oms" playing quite loudly from her sound system. The vibrations reverberated through the forest far enough for a few other guests to hear them. It was as if the entire forest were singing as one. Stephanie was no stranger to yoga and meditation, but it had been a long, long, time since she had such a profound connection with herself. Though she had received a few insights, the most extraordinary thing for Stephanie was that she was at peace.

Still ensconced in her nest, Jennifer was lingering in bed, absorbing the final tranquil moments before the day called her into action. The ambient "om" sound pervading through the forest set a soothing background score to her morning reflections. The day before she had spoken to her children. She decided to call Brian's house where they were staying while she was away. He had fought the idea of them staying for the whole week, claiming he had no time, but, in the end, he agreed. Jennifer managed to speak with both kids for nearly a precious hour. They were missing her terribly, but she pushed down her remnants of guilt and said, "Thank you both for giving Mommy a chance to go away and get better. You'll see how much more awesome your mom is when I come home."

Brian was his usual obnoxious self, but what was different was that Jennifer wasn't bothered by his attitude. *Well, I am bothered a little*, she mentally corrected herself, *but at least I stopped my tongue before I took the bait and got into another screaming contest. Go awareness! Respond, don't react*, she thought. She made a mental note to work through that last little bit of reactionary behavior by putting more emphasis on gratitude and forgiveness.

As she lay in bed, she began to think about last night's ritual. How amazing to learn about those energies and later to put them all together in one singular force at her disposal. She felt powerful, like she felt years before when she was focused on her goals. What an incredible lesson Brian had been for her. *If you lose sight of your goals, life might just send you a few kicks in the butt so that you can get on course again*, she thought. Brian had been one big kick... and one big ass. Laughing out loud, she rolled out of bed and got ready for the day.

**

Sofia had gone outside to the wrap-around balcony to hear more clearly the sound of "oms" that were emanating from the trees. It was early and all the forest creatures weren't awake yet. She wore her bathrobe and wrapped a blanket around her as a hedge against the chilly morning breeze. On the horizon, she could see a sliver of coral spreading across the sky as the sun was inching its way up. Sipping hot coffee, she reviewed the week and enjoyed the thoughtfulness and kindness that had been awakened in her. An intense feeling of gratitude washed over her as her thoughts drifted to Monica, her childhood friend who insisted that she visit The Orchid. Monica and her family had always been the ones to show Sofia that there were different

The Orchid

ways of doing things and living life—better ways. Their approach was never forced, like a school lesson; instead they taught by example. Now she had learned some lessons on her own.

Sofia made a mental note to sit down with Monica and accept whatever decisions she made about their prospective business partnership without argument or trying to force her will. No matter if she chose to be her partner or not, Sofia would share with Monica how much she appreciated her and her family. That would be one good decision, she knew, because, if this week had taught her anything, it was to always lead with love.

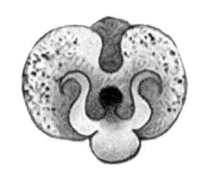

Chapter 49

Self-Empowerment

Their common experience and sharing of vulnerabilities had created an unshakeable bond among the guests at The Orchid. They were now often seen walking together, their heads bent in conversation, or gathered in small groups, continuing the sharing begun in the sessions. They spoke of love and pain, their conversations punctuated with both laughter and tears. Some walked alone, lost in spiritual introspection, and no one disturbed them. Everyone's needs were respected.

On the path to the Meditation Center, Olivia and Stephanie walked together and stopped to read the day's messages. They read a pair of messages focusing on the power of intention:

> Knowledge has no value unless you put it into practice. —Jane Goodall

> Use each interaction to be the best, most powerful version of yourself. —Marianne Williamson

> The secret of change is to focus all of your energy not on fighting the old, but on building the new. —Socrates

"These messages seem like someone has been reading my journal," said Olivia.

"Yes," agreed Stephanie, chuckling. "Who knew I'd be getting good advice from posted signs along a path? Oh well, I will take it where I can get it."

Sofia had taken the longer path in order to enjoy the peaceful surroundings. She came across a message that seemed placed there specifically for her.

> Be thankful for what you have; you'll end up having more. If you concentrate on what you don't have, you will never ever have enough. —Oprah Winfrey

The Orchid

She'd never stopped to think about things that way. *You may be getting smarter, girl*, she thought, as she smiled and continued up the path in silence.

When the women had reached the entrance of the Meditation Center, they noticed yoga mats had been placed outside in front of the building. "Today's meditation," a staff member said, "will be held under the vastness of the morning sky."

A few minutes later, Mary arrived. She was accompanied by Leyla. A very large, clear quartz crystal hung from her neck. She carried a wooden chest with both of her hands, as it was a bit heavy.

Olivia and a few women recognized her immediately. She was the physician Mary called on when Olivia experienced her panic attack and with whom Olivia met with in private later that morning for a quick medical checkup.

Mary welcomed them all with a joyous, "Good morning, everyone. Welcome to day six."

"Before we begin, for those of you who haven't yet met her, it is my absolute pleasure to introduce you to my dear friend and our center's resident physician, Dr. Leyla. She will be guiding us through this morning's meditation." Mary paused, inviting her to greet everyone.

"Thank you, Mary, and peace be upon you, beautiful souls," said Leyla. "In addition to being the physician here in this wonderful place, I am also a crystal energy healer and a seer. I'm originally from Turkey, and it's a great joy to be here with all of you today." Leyla's warm smile widened, her Mediterranean eyes sparkling with a blend of kindness and wisdom. She smiled broadly and looked towards Mary.

"And we are so happy to have you here with us," Mary said.

Nicole couldn't help but be captivated by the enchanting lilt in Leyla's voice, which carried the beautiful and specific melodies of her ancestry.

Having spent time with Leyla previously, Olivia was delighted to reunite with her once again. She deeply valued Leyla's comprehensive knowledge of both Eastern and Western medicine and had found solace in her unique perspective when they discussed her panic attacks.

Mary continued, "Today, we will connect with the power of intention. Therefore, let me please give you a quick overview of what we aim to accomplish."

"You have all been moving a lot of energy this week. By removing heavy energy and limiting beliefs from your life, you have created space for new energy to arrive and take its place. But if you are not vigilant, the energy that you have worked so hard to get rid of will return. In nature," Mary said, "vacuums do not remain empty for long periods of time.

"However, if you are intentional in what you ask for," Mary continued, "meaning, if you have a clear, mindful, healthy, and optimistic focus on what it is that you want to bring into your life, then you can send the universe that clear message and that is exactly what you'll get in return.

"Leyla, I, and all the healers here at The Orchid have witnessed, first-hand, this remarkable force. So as one of our concluding activities this week, we aim to introduce you to it. You, too, can use it to create the most exciting, prosperous, and successful life that you can imagine for yourself. You will do so by setting an intention.

"Intention is the process by which we plant a seed in our consciousness to grow what we want in our lives. The process of intention is essentially the process of you creating your future."

Seeing their excitement made Mary smile. She continued, "If intention is the seed of our future, then the water, the sunlight, and the nutrients that nurture that seed are our thoughts, our feelings, our words, and the actions that we take at every moment.

"It's powerful stuff. Essentially, you can create the type of life you've always wanted by ensuring that your thoughts, words, actions, and vibrations are clear and aligned, and then keeping them ever present at the front of your consciousness by giving them your constant focus and energy.

"And, since you are growing your future, it is important that the raw materials you use in your spiritual garden are of the highest quality. It shouldn't surprise you by now that you are at the best position to create such a future when you are vibrating at your highest energy level—that of love.

"That is the purpose of today's first meditation. Your goal is to elevate yourself to a high level of vibrational frequency so that you can then be in the best position to send your intention out to the universe.

"Are there any questions?"

"Yes," a woman named Susan said, raising her hand. "If intention is planting a seed in our consciousness, then what is manifestation?"

The Orchid

"Great question, Susan, thanks for asking it. Manifestation is like watching a plant grow from being that seed until it bears fruit. It's when a desire or idea you have turns into something real that you can touch or experience. For example, if you intend to be happier, you might start noticing more moments of joy in your life or find a hobby that makes you happy. If you're thinking about improving your health, you may start feeling more energetic or find that you get sick less often. And if you wish to have more meaningful relationships, you could end up meeting people who truly enrich your life.

"Does that make sense?" Mary asked.

"Yes, thank you." Susan replied.

"This—the idea of having a direct say in your own future—could be a difficult concept to accept, and that's okay. This is not something that has been broadly taught, not formally, anyway. But that's why The Orchid exists. We are here to help you see that you are more powerful than you think you are and to teach you how to use that power to create a better, more complete life for yourself."

Seeing that there were no more questions, Mary then turned to Leyla, who smiled and took over the session.

"Thank you, Mary. As you heard Mary explain, our goal this morning is to help you reach that higher vibration so that from that point you can send your intention into the cosmos.

"To get some extra help from nature, we have opted to do the meditation outside. Here, we can connect with Gaia, Mother Earth, and have her energy serve as our anchor. To begin, please stand next to one of the yoga mats and remove your shoes and socks."

The women did as they were asked. They were now all standing barefoot on the ground. Leyla herself was already barefoot, as she was most of the time, as part of her spiritual practice. Leyla then knelt and opened the chest she had placed at her feet. From it, she extracted three large translucent rocks. The clear quartz crystals reflected the light from the newly risen sun.

"Those are so beautiful," someone said out loud.

"Yes, they are. Our Mother conceals some of her most stunning items deep within the Earth," said Leyla. "She only reveals them to people ready to do more than admire their appearance; like those who are ready to receive their power."

Leyla placed the crystals in the center of the group on the bare ground. "The clear quartz acts as a transmitter, multiplying the intentions we will put forth during our session today and sending the energy we generate even more strongly out into the universe. Are you ready?"

Again, in a louder voice, full of vibrant energy, she asked, "Are you ready?"

"Yes, of course!" the women answered, eager to learn more about this powerful force.

"I'd like to begin with a few stretches and deep cleansing breaths," Leyla said. "This will allow us to make a deeper and stronger connection between ourselves and Mother Earth. So please place your feet hip distance apart. Inhale deeply as you bring both arms over your head. Lock your fingers and turn your palms upwards as you stretch. Release and bring your arms down. Now let's repeat that a few more times to open our channels."

After the stretches, Leyla said, "Now we will summon the energy of the Earth by connecting to the soil. Feel your feet as they make direct contact with Gaia. We ask that she sends her energy up through us like sap rises in a tree to fill our hearts with light so that we may have the clarity to see our true soul's mission during our meditation."

Leyla made fists with her own hands and said in a fierce whisper, "Allow the Mother's energy to flow up into you."

Many of the women *did* feel something. Their feet and soon their entire body sent down energetic shoots of themselves, like seeds germinating, and a buzz, a thrumming, ran through their blood upwards, toward their hearts. Those who managed to make the connection felt something greater than themselves, as if they were one with the Earth.

"Now, everyone, while staying connected to that energy, please lay down on your mats."

Once they were all comfortable, Leyla continued, "Now close your eyes and take a deep breath."

Leyla slowed down her speech and lowered her musical voice as it seeped into the consciousness of all present.

"Imagine yourself on a path embraced by majestic trees, vibrant and lush, with all of nature's grandeur cradling you. Whispers of the forest serenade your ears while the aroma of fresh rain and sweet florals permeate the warm air. Your footsteps are light. Your inner transformation has lifted burdens of loneliness, frustration, anger, sadness, and want. Distractions and disturbances no longer exist. Your face beams with smiles, happiness, and bliss.

"Following the path, you come upon an iron gate. Beyond it, a golden staircase rises through ancient trees, past the forest canopy, vanishing into the clouds.

"A sign greets you: 'Welcome, to the next stage of your journey. Come in. The life you yearn for is within your grasp.'

"You step through the gate, ascending the staircase at a tranquil pace. Calmness cascades through you, growing stronger with each step. Far off in the horizon, glowing purple letters form words which reveal themselves:

Joy. Peace. Gratitude. Freedom. Creativity. Connection. Abundance. Health. Purpose.

"When you begin your ascent, the first thing you encounter is Joy. This is a radiant space, where every particle of air seems to be filled with vitality and enthusiasm. It's as if every cell in your being starts to dance to a melody of eternal happiness. An aura of delight surrounds you, resonating with and amplifying your happiness.

"Advancing further, Peace greets you, represented by a wise, ancient tree that carries with it the wisdom of the ages and the serenity of time that heals all. You feel a harmony that transcends human understanding, as if you are merging with the very essence of the universe in eternal tranquility.

"Continuing the ascent, you encounter Gratitude. At this point, you sit in a sort of spiritual garden, where each flower represents an aspect for which to be grateful. You take a deep breath and feel overwhelmed by a gentle wave of appreciation that envelops every part of your being, recognizing the countless blessings that have been granted to you.

"With further elevation comes Freedom. You find yourself in an open space, a vast landscape that allows you to experience the feeling of being infinitely expansive. A gentle wind blows, reminding you that there are no chains holding you back, that you have the option to choose your own destiny and express your fullest potential.

"The journey up this stairway is a metamorphosis, a silent conversation between you and the universe. The emotions stirred are indescribable, the transformative power promising change and giving welcome to the new.

"After climbing more steps, you encounter Creativity. Imagine being in a celestial workshop where ideas flow like rivers of endless inspiration. This is a space where each idea becomes a star, illuminating new possibilities in your life. Your connection with the universe allows you to tap into knowledge in science, poetry, business, spirituality, and more and to use them widely and wisely.

"The ascent continues, and Connection beckons. Here, every stone, every leaf, and every drop of water seems to be in perfect harmony, like a natural symphony. You feel the interconnectedness with everything that exists, recognizing that you are an integral part of the fabric of the universe.

"As you move forward, you encounter the essence of Abundance. Imagine a treasure chest filled with everything you consider valuable: love, time, wealth, well-being. This is a place where you understand that everything you need is already within you or within your reach.

"Further ahead, Health awaits you in a space bathed in healing light. Here, you feel how every fiber of your being is revitalized, as if a current of well-being flows through you, purifying and strengthening you.

"Eagerly, you continue, knowing there's one more beacon to reach.

"Finally, you stand before Purpose. It is here where everything becomes clearer, and each of your movements is intentional and focused. Doubts and questions disappear, making way for a well-defined path where each step you take contributes to a greater good.

"Now your climb is done. At the top of the stairs, on the highest platform, set in the clouds, you turn and see all the steps you have climbed on this spiritual quest and all the phases of your growth awaiting their integration.

"Stand still, breathe deeply, and invite each of those powerful words that you met on your journey upward to integrate with you. Accept each with a warm embrace. Feel a new sensation start transforming every inch of your body.

"It begins from your feet and ascends, ever so gently, through to the top of your head. First your toes, then your heels, and onto the soles of your feet. It continues to make its way to your ankles and then your calves. Now it moves onto your knees and legs. The sensation feels soothing, natural, and even familiar. It continues coursing through you until it reaches your groin and buttocks. Then it arrives at your waist, your belly, and your lower back. You feel peaceful as it reaches your chest, your upper back, and your shoulders. Next, you feel it flow through your arms to your hands and each finger. Now you take a final deep breath and, in complete surrender, allow the sensation to go up your neck to your face, from your chin to your mouth, nose, eyes, ears, and forehead right through your scalp to the top of your skull.

"You are now completely transformed. All these new feelings of power are within you, filling you, becoming you. You feel happier, stronger, healthier, and clearer than ever before. You are enough and have plenty leftover to share. Every movement of your body is delicate and graceful. Your mind, your body, and your soul are all perfectly aligned, and you shine with pure love. You are complete.

Leyla paused and allowed them the opportunity to internalize and experience the essence of this new awareness.

"Take in and release a deep breath, and then another, experiencing these feelings and allowing them to mingle with your spirit.

"You are connected with all that surrounds you and all you do happens smoothly and effortlessly. Take in and release another deep breath. The feeling is becoming deeper and deeper. You are rejoicing in this version of you and life is good, perfect, and complete.

"You smile and suddenly there is a feeling that you need to descend back to where you came from, but you descend a different person than the one who climbed up. Your integration of all your spiritual phases is complete. Your new power comes with you. You accept that this is exactly what needs to be.

"You begin your descent, this time with a new awareness. You have been transformed and you are ready for the rest of your life."

Leyla stopped talking and stayed quiet for a while.

No one moved. No words were shared. Each in her own time, every woman walked back down the golden staircase. After she got a sense that all had re turned, Leyla looked around and softly announced the end of the meditation and invited everyone to open their eyes.

"Welcome back," she said, smiling. "What a truly special experience, right? Thank you for allowing me to guide you on this wonderful soul journey. You are all powerful, divine, and gracious beings, and it has been my honor to share this moment with you.

"I encourage you to remain in silence for as long as you can. Please drink some water, stay connected to nature and Gaia, and, if you feel called to it, this is a great opportunity for some journaling.

"Enjoy the depth of the experience and remember that your thoughts are capable of manifesting anything. Now you are vibrating at the highest levels—so go and intentionally create the life you have always desired. You are powerful, unlimited, and infinite beings, capable of manifesting anything you dare to dream.

"My love to each of you."

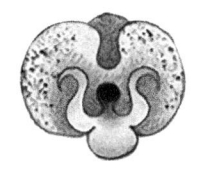

The Orchid

Chapter 50

LifeScript

Mary and several other familiar faces were awaiting the arrival of the women, who were making their way to the Activity Center for the last official lesson of the program. They had been through a profound transformation and were proud of their accomplishments. They were excited about what was still to come, but they also felt a bit sad that their experience at The Orchid was coming to an end.

Once the women entered, they were invited to take a seat at one of the tables. On top of each was a notebook and pen. When all were settled, Mary addressed them.

"Hello everyone, and welcome. Your embrace of all the information and teachings we have shared with you over this week has been truly exceptional." Nodding to her team standing beside her, Mary spoke for them all. "It is our privilege to observe such growth. We see it clearly and hope you see it in yourselves, too. Before we proceed, let's all come together to ground ourselves. Please close your eyes and take a deep breath." Mary waited until everyone had done so.

"Let's take another deep breath.

"And another.

"Allow yourself to feel the oneness that is present here within this amazing group of souls. Go beyond to connect with the energy of the room, the Earth, the air, the animals, the forest, and all that surrounds us.

"Take another deep breath."

Mary now placed both of her hands in front of her, palms towards the heavens, asking to access higher wisdom.

The Orchid

Divine Spirit, Higher Self, Universe, God,

> Thank you for your blessings, for your love, for your light and for all the gifts we are granted, both seen and unseen.
>
> Thank you for allowing us the understanding that we have the power to co-create our future and that our energetic vibration is the beacon that shapes and attracts that which we become.
>
> We ask that any fears, doubts, or limiting beliefs that may have held us back from embracing a life of abundance are fully released and transformed into loving energy that can propel us forward.
>
> We declare so with gratitude. We allow it to be. And so it is.

At Mary's words, the women felt how the energy in the room had become even lighter. Now the atmosphere was calm and peaceful, with a subtle electric current of anticipation. Mary channeled this as she spoke again.

"I trust you're as thrilled as we are to arrive at this significant and potent moment. Throughout the week, we've been unveiling the profound, life-altering forces available to you—awareness, gratitude, forgiveness, and acceptance. As my personal journey attests, and as you've begun discovering this week, these forces have the power to transform our lives."

Mary took a moment to make eye contact with all.

"Now," she spoke with even more intensity, "from that point of greater understanding and the higher energy in which you find yourselves, we will focus on the power of intention.

"As I shared this morning, intention is the process by which you plant a seed in your consciousness to grow and create what you want in your lives. When you live with intention, you fine-tune your thoughts, emotions, words, and actions so that they are aligned with the life you want to live. And that is what today's exercise is all about.

"You will imagine and write a message to the universe. We call this message your LifeScript. In it, you describe, in great detail, a day in your life three years from now. There are no restrictions or limitations on this exercise. Simply detail a script for your life exactly how you want it to unfold."

Mary paused, knowing that at this stage some women often felt a bit overwhelmed at the idea of having to write about their future lives.

"I know there may be some questions and perhaps even some hesitation about this task. Please keep in mind that this is meant to be fun and easy. Like everything else we have done here this week, I ask you to trust us and the process. I'll share with you a few general prompts that you can use in the process of deciding what to write about in your LifeScript."

Mary turned to a screen behind her where a list was being projected. On it were the words:

PERSONAL

- Health
- Intellectual
- Emotional
- Spiritual
- Values

RELATIONSHIPS

- Parents
- Romantic
- Children
- Pets
- Social
- Other

GOALS

- Ownership (i.e. property, home, other)
- Experiential (travel, other)
- Educational
- Professional
- Financial
- Life
- Other

"You can refer to these categories as you envision what to write.

"Another approach is to simply answer questions to jumpstart your imagination. Here are a few examples."

The Orchid

The projection changed and a series of directions and questions appeared on screen:

>How do you feel greeting the day? Describe your morning.
>
>Where do you live? (house, apartment, boat, other?) Describe it.
>
>What are the most important relationships in your life? (significant other, spouse, children, parents, friends, colleagues, pets, other?)
>
>What is your diet? (vegan, vegetarian, paleo, carnivore, other?)
>
>How is your health? What do you do to maintain it? (exercise, vitamins, regular checkups, other?)
>
>How do you maintain a spiritual balance? (meditation, prayer, religion, therapy, other?)
>
>How do you feel about your life in general?
>
>How do you relax and have fun?
>
>Are you happy? Describe how you experience happiness.
>
>Are you living in abundance? What does it look like and how does it feel?
>
>Are you active in your community? Describe how.
>
>Do you work? Describe your work. Do you enjoy it?
>
>Or are you retired? If so, how do you spend your time?
>
>What projects are you pursuing? How are you progressing with them?

Mary continued, "The next things I want to emphasize are five points we want you to keep in mind as you think about and write your LifeScript. They are integrity, achievability, sensory awareness, blessedness, and enjoyability.

"The first, integrity, is about ensuring that all the signals and instructions you send out for the universe to follow—thoughts, words, emotions, and actions—are aligned. This will require that you are disciplined, aware, mindful, intentional, and responsible.

"For example, if you want love and abundance, but your thoughts and actions are those of a person who lives in despair and lack, then love and abundance are not likely to manifest in your life. The same applies if you want peace, but your words and writings are about waging war with everyone around you."

Sofia was sure Mary was speaking directly to her and immediately felt a sting in her stomach. *Not long ago, those last words would have painted an accurate portrait of who I was,* she thought. *I'm so glad that's no longer true.*

"Next, we address achievability," Mary continued. "This part is all about properly framing your requests. While the universe possesses boundless power and can, technically, fulfill any wish, it's essential that your desires, however ambitious, remain within the realm of possibility. This is because you must genuinely believe that they are attainable.

"So, I don't recommend that you write about having twenty-million dollars a year of sales in a business that you haven't started or envision becoming a brain surgeon if you haven't gone to medical school. Whatever you write about, it should feel at least 50 percent achievable within the three-year time frame we are focusing on.

"The third point—sensory awareness—is equally important. As you write your LifeScript, make sure that you describe, in vivid detail, how all your senses—sight, hearing, touch, taste, smell, and even your intuition—are being engaged. By doing this, you ensure that the images you are creating in your mind are experienced vividly throughout your body. In this manner, the images and the feelings will have more energy propelling them, and their likelihood of manifestation will be greater.

"Blessedness is about ensuring that you end your LifeScript with 'This or something better, for the highest good of all concerned.' By now, you already know the importance of this statement. It is just in case the universe, my dears, has even better plans for you than you do for yourself.

"And lastly, because we should be aiming to have fun," Mary had a huge smile on her face, "just make sure that you are enjoying yourselves on this journey. You are creating your future, so give happiness the energy that it deserves."

Mary answered a few questions from the group and then, reminding them to ground themselves with a deep breath, directed them to begin.

"Take up your pens and tell the universe what you want it to deliver to you. This is more than daring to dream. It's about sculpting your own destiny. Let's turn dreams into realities, one stroke of the pen at a time."

The room was immediately silent as the women bent over their notebooks, their gazes turned inward.

**

The Orchid

Nicole had listened to all that Mary shared with the utmost attention. Half-hopeful, half-disbelieving, she sat there silently staring out the window and into the unknown. She was having difficulty reconciling Mary's directions for the exercise and all that had happened to her over the past few days with what she had been taught to believe since she was a child. The Bible sayings "Sin is crouching at your door; it desires to have you, but you must rule over it" and "Honor thy father and mother," kept running through her mind and seemed in conflict with the idea that she could have a more direct say in her future, let alone design it around her own desires. Was it in fact as simple as writing a very detailed and intentional letter about what she wanted? And if that was, in fact, true, then what about God's will?

She decided to raise her hand and share her conflict with Mary.

Mary walked over and asked, "What's on your mind, Nicole?"

Nicole explained, "I'm so conflicted, Mary. While I trust what I've been learning and experiencing in the program, I'm having difficulty reconciling that with what I've been taught all my life. If I have the ability to create my life, then where does Nicole end and God begin?"

Mary pulled over a nearby chair and sat facing her. Then, in a quiet but loving voice, she said, "What a wonderful question to ponder, Nicole. As with all such questions, the best way to answer is to go within, connect with yourself, and explore the potential answer with an open mind and heart. But please be patient and gentle with yourself as you navigate, for there is no one single answer. There is only the answer that is right for you, now.

"But I offer you the following: What if you simply look at the LifeScript as a kind of prayer to God? And perhaps view the instructions I've given you as a request for you to have faith and to be sure that your message to the future is sincere and heartfelt? For me, the words 'This or something better, for the highest good of all concerned,' are no different than 'Let Thy will be done.' When you look at them from this expanded perspective, the two approaches are not that different from one another, are they?"

Nicole thought for a moment. "No, not at all," she answered.

"My goal, Nicole," Mary said, "our goal here at The Orchid is to expand your thinking and, in the process, your understanding and appreciation for the power that lies within you to grow, change, choose, and create. Where that power comes from is not a question for me. It is the same power—all-knowing, infinite, omnipresent, and eternal—that has manifested itself in countless ways and been called by many names throughout time. What is different for me is that I now believe that this power is also inside of me and not somewhere else, out of my reach, guarded by others and waiting for me to be deserving of it. That power is my soul, right? And yours. And all of ours," Mary said these last words pointing to all the others in the room.

"The poet Rumi said, 'You are not a drop in the ocean. You are the entire ocean in a drop.'

"I'm not God, my dear, but God is within me ... and within you. I think one day soon, we will come to understand that there is no line dividing us."

Mary looked back at Nicole, waiting for a reaction. Nicole simply looked back at her, took a deep breath, and said, "Thank you, Mary."

With this newfound clarity of thought, Nicole went about writing her prayer to God—a day in her future three years from now:

> I'm waking from a restful sleep. As I open my eyes, I see Elena lying next to me and looking right back at me. We smile at each other, as lovers do. My heart skips a beat and I'm filled with joy and excitement. The room is quiet and peaceful. The white sheets and comforter are the softest I could find. All of a sudden, there is movement on the bed between us and a miniature head appears from under the sheets. It's Fifi, a tiny and fluffy toy poodle Elena and I rescued a year ago. Fifi's presence adds to the playful mood of the moment.
>
> We get up and go through our morning routines. It's Saturday, so we don't have to go to work, but we are up early just the same. Weekends are important to us and we tend to fill them with organic farmer's markets, local music festivals, museums, and all sorts of interesting and fun activities.
>
> I soon find myself pouring ground coffee into my French press, a housewarming gift we received from a friend when we moved into our house in the Montrose neighborhood of Houston. It is a funky neighborhood which has some modern townhouses, but also some ramshackle houses which are still somewhat affordable. Elena and I bought the house together and used our savings to turn it into our little love nest. We painted it bright yellow on the outside, added blue shutters, and put a vintage bird bath and a cactus in the front garden. Inside we restored the original wood floors, remodeled our bedroom, and are near the end of renovating the rest of the house now.
>
> After my transformative week at The Orchid, I realized that I needed to make some serious changes in my life. My most important goals were intertwined. I needed to stop hiding who I really was to the world, and I needed to salvage

my relationship with Elena. I knew that if I was going to have any chance of convincing her to come back into my life, I needed to remove the one thing that had been the thorn in our relationship. I needed to stop hiding and had to tell my parents that I was gay.

So, I picked up the phone and invited my mother and my father to coffee. I invited them together, because I assumed that I would only have enough energy and courage to have the necessary conversation once. We met in a local coffee shop because I hoped that the public venue might cut down on any shouting and hysterics. My plan was to get the words out before my parents stormed out. I rehearsed what I was going to say endlessly.

"Mom, Dad," I said when we were all seated. "I am a good woman and that is thanks to how you raised me, with rules to guide me, and the constant reminder to keep God at the center of my life. I appreciate that upbringing more than I can say, but I am grown now and it is time for me to live my own life." They both looked at each other as if they knew what I was about to say.

"I respect your beliefs, but they are not mine. I do have a relationship with Christ and would never consider leaving the faith, but I believe God is love and, as we are made in His image, love is what God wants for us all, even for me ... independently of who I love." My mother drew in her breath to speak, but I stopped her. "Please, Mom, hear me out."

My whole life, even as a teenager, I knew I was different. I never had a boyfriend and avoided those men you tried to set me up with because ... I like women. I was born this way and always have been this way. I have come to understand that my sexuality is as much a part of me as being tall, or the color of my eyes. It's how God made me.

I fought for years to reject this, to try to please you both, but I don't want to deny it any longer. To say I'm not gay is a lie and self-destructive. Instead, I want to turn towards love and acceptance of myself. I hope you can still love and accept me, too, now that you know the truth.

And oh, there is one more thing I have to tell you. Elena is not only my best friend, she is my lover, and has been for many years. Soon I hope to marry her. I love her. I love her with all my heart ... and I want to spend the rest of my life with her." I came to a shuddering stop then. It was hard to see my parent's faces through my tears.

They were silent. For the first time in my life, my father, but even more surprisingly, my mother, had nothing to say. They just sat there with their mouths open.

The conversation which followed was brief and cordial. To be honest, I wasn't *there to discuss anything. I was there to let them know what I was and how I was going to lead my life, regardless of whether they agreed with my choices or not. I was there to tell them that I was done with needing their approval. Afterwards, I got up from the table, gave them both a kiss on the cheek, told them I loved them, and walked away. I felt triumphant, empowered, and free. Since then, those feelings have never left me.*

Minutes later I was in my car heading to Elena's mother's house where Elena was staying. After telling her what had happened, Elena was beside herself with joy. A weight had been lifted from both our shoulders. At that moment, we simply picked up our life exactly from where we had left it, but now we were truly together. Now I was free and that made everything very different.

One day, some months later, my mom called. I let it go to voicemail as I now tended to do with all her calls. But this time her message was different. "Hi Nicky, this is mom. Your dad and I want to invite you and Elena to dinner here at home. I hope you can make it. What I mean is, I hope you give us the opportunity to say that we are sorry, honey."

Elena and I did go to that dinner. Since then, we've shared many somewhat awkward Sunday dinners until we all got comfortable with our new roles. Some months later, before it got to be 100 degrees in the shade, Elena and I married in my parent's backyard. It was a small and intimate ceremony. My father gave me away and looked very proud doing so. Things have been better ever since. There has been a lot of forgiveness. We are taking it a day at a time, but it is getting easier and easier.

After that, Elena and I bought our little funky house and now we are surrounded by a wonderful community, many of them gay or artists or musicians (or all three,) and we have made lots of close friends. I had to change schools as the one at which I taught didn't allow openly gay teachers. I now teach at an International School, where both the staff and the parents are more open-minded. It didn't hurt that the salaries were higher, too. Between Elena's cybersecurity business and my new salary, we make enough money to live comfortably.

One big thing is that Elena and I also decided to adopt a child and are in the final stages of that process now. We are just waiting for the call telling us it is time to come pick up our daughter. Elena will be the stay-at-home Mom since she can do her work remotely.

I have stayed in touch with the women I met that week at The Orchid. They continue to inspire me and when we catch up on the phone, they remind me that we have choices, and that we are powerful.

> *I've kept close to my continually-evolving faith with weekly Mass, daily rosaries, meditation, journaling, and lots and lots of intention. I've also continued my deep and enjoyable talks with my dear friend and mentor, Sister Consuelo. Her years are starting to show, but my goodness, that lady is unstoppable. She's even talking about running a half-marathon soon.*
>
> *It is hard to imagine I could be any happier and even harder to imagine what I was so afraid of three years ago. God is love and God loves me and mine. My time at The Orchid gave me the courage to step out in faith, not fear, and for that I am so very grateful.*
>
> *Oh yes, since I realized that God was with me always, I now have an ongoing dialogue with Jesus. He is my mentor, friend, and confidant.*
>
> *Thank you, God. Thank you, Universe. Thy will be done. This or something better, for the highest good of all concerned.*

**

Olivia, who had more experience than most putting her ideas on paper, began to write a monologue to her future self:

> *My week at The Orchid, three years ago, changed my life. It was there that I first realized, the world does not need me to save it, and that I needed to spend a bit more time loving me.*
>
> *With that new mentality, I spent the years which followed making important changes in my life. I began a new job, rekindled old relationships with friends, family, and even with my dad, (I'll get to that later). I have also begun new relationships, one in particular, (more on that later, too.) And I started exercising more, eating better, drinking more water, taking vitamins, and I even stopped drinking soda, a habit I never thought I would break. I'm also meditating on a regular basis.*
>
> *Since about a year ago, I've been working at the new job. I'm now the Senior Director at a private organization that funds NGO's, like the one I previously headed. It specifically funds those projects aimed at creating economic equity for women. So, my path is much the same, but I am approaching my work from a different and broader perspective. The work I do now is not only less taxing, but I actually feel like I accomplish more and, as a result, it is more rewarding. Because it is a private sector job, I am earning more money, which in turn has given me greater financial independence. I now can afford, financially and mentally, to take vacations. Relaxation and spiritual replenishment have become important factors in my overall well-being.*

With this new approach to life, I began to see old relationships differently. Gone is the pain from past incidents which had kept me from reaching out to old friends and relatives. I did allow many of them back in my life, reaching out where I needed to and accepting the overtures of those who reached out to me.

But the biggest shift came the day that I telephoned my dad and asked him to dinner. I flew down to Atlanta, where he now lives. I was pleased to see that he joined a 12-Step program, got sober, and that he began listening to the wise advice of his sponsor who encouraged him to get a job and even invest a small part of his earnings. He is now retired and lives off the yield from those investments, added to his small pension. He also found a very nice lady who is taking good care of him, and he of her. Theirs seems like a long-term and stable love. At first, he wasn't quite sure why I reached out to him and why, in his words, I "was acting so decent." We shared the meal alone and, by the time dessert was served, we were holding hands, apologizing to each other for past behaviors and reminiscing about times passed. We didn't dwell on missed opportunities, though he couldn't believe how I had been able to let go of all the pain and forgive him. Frankly, neither could I, but I did forgive him, and myself, for holding such anger and resentment all those years.

That dinner with my father was one of the most healing experiences I've ever had. It has made me very happy and brought me a lot of peace. We talked a lot about Mama, too. I think even Mama, rest her soul, was pleased that I was able to reconcile with my father. Dad and I still don't always see eye-to-eye, but we speak from time-to-time, which is quite nice and enriches my life. Ok, now for the juicy stuff. I met this kind, intelligent, and successful man with whom I share cozy evenings filled with fascinating conversations, fine wines, and the intimacy I never knew I longed for so deeply. I met "Mr. Wonderful" at an embassy cocktail party in DC. A mutual friend introduced us saying that we had lots in common and should get to know one another. Well, we did. We spoke the entire evening and then many evenings after that. Mr. Wonderful is a handsome, charming, athletic guy who is a few years younger than me (my friends tease me about my "boy toy"). He owns his own company, is cultured, well-traveled, and a great conversationalist. He shares my taste for opera, is educating me about fine wines, and has even gotten me dancing, something at which he excels. He is, above all things, a gentleman. He treats me with respect and affection, supporting me in my endeavors and never undermining me, but always building me up. He has grown children, all in college or recently graduated, who I have met and with whom I have formed good relationships. He and I have traveled together, most recently to Japan, where we had a wonderful time visiting Kyoto, Sapporo, and Tokyo, eating mountains of sushi, and laughing over delicious sake.

Though I never imagined this three years ago, I can see growing old with this man at my side.

My office is a short walk from a condo I just purchased. In a spur-of-the-moment decision, I decided to sell my old place and buy something more modern. This new apartment is truly a dream come true—it has a stunning kitchen, a lovely guest bedroom, that my friends and family use, and a balcony that offers breathtaking views of the Potomac River. It's also much more spacious than my previous place, with plenty of room for those occasions when Mr. Wonderful stays over.

My days are filled with lots of peace, excitement, and gratitude. When I wake, I still hit knees to thank the Lord for my blessings. After my prayers, I take a steamy shower and then sit with a fragrant cup of hot tea to read the news and review my schedule. Three times a week, I work out with a trainer at my building's gym. On alternate days, I do yoga and some Pilate stretches. Then I get on my "big girl clothes," beautiful-tailored suits, to be ready to meet with politicians, organizers, and other power players. I walk to work, wearing comfortable sneakers, and change into designer shoes (my weakness) when I get to my corner office.

As I look at where I am in my life, I am happy and content. I have no regrets and feel like I've accomplished a lot and have purpose. I'm not rich, not financially anyway, but there is more than enough money in my bank accounts for me to live a most comfortable life. Abundance surrounds me.

Between all my wonderful relationships, the many projects that keep me busy and give me purpose, and my love affair with Mr. Wonderful, my heart and my soul are full.

I still miss my Mama, but I do feel her near me, looking at me with a huge smile on her face. I can hear her say, "I'm so proud of you, Livy. You are still my precious baby and I couldn't love you more."

Thank you, Universe. Thank you, God. This or something better, for the highest good of all concerned.

Olivia

**

In another part of the room Jennifer was writing with a frown creasing her brow:

Three years from now, I still wake up early each morning. Now, however, I am careful to get a full night's rest and always wake up refreshed and energized. My bed is soft like a hotel's and I have a lot of pillows around me. After opening my eyes and indulging in a few yawns and stretches, the first thing I do is open the curtains and let the morning light in. Looking at the sun each morning brings me peace and reminds me of the sunrise at The Orchid. Depending on the day, I then either meditate or exercise. I still don't like going to the gym, so when I do exercise, I follow an online class that meets every other day.

After the class, I get dressed, and head to the kitchen for my first cup of coffee. There is something about the taste of the first cup of morning roast that feels homey, warm, and inviting. Tommy and Michelle, now 13 and 11, almost always wake up, shower, and dress without me having to nag them. I know! Can you believe I don't scream at them anymore? Since I returned from The Orchid, improving my relationship with them became my main focus. It was rocky in the beginning, but I figured it out, and now we are all working together to make our family a team. We now have meaningful conversations and the kids actually share what they are interested in (or even upset about) and I'm delighted that I have found a good balance between being their mom and their friend. Well ... almost.

I still love to "baby" them, sometimes by making their breakfast favorites (usually a stack of chocolate chip pancakes). I'm really grateful that my kids still love spending time with me, which is pretty cool (I used to think this was unachievable with tweens and teens). A few times a week I even manage to get the kids and I to sit down together for dinner. We talk about their day, friends, and school. As I listen to them, I am struck by how mature and thoughtful they have become. I take particular care making meals. I am now practicing intuitive eating, which really is listening more to my body and being more mindful about what I eat. Between that and the exercise, I have regained a pretty awesome shape and Jen Baby, you are looking pretty damn good, if I do say so myself.

Then I drive the kids to school in my new electric SUV. I love the smell of my new car and how the steering wheel is covered in ultra-smooth leather. It's silver with black interior and super-fast, though I promise I don't speed with the kids inside. It makes me feel safe, special, and the kids love it, too. Driving is a good test for me because it works like a barometer. Depending on how I react when someone cuts me off tells me quite clearly whether I am in a good place or not. Occasionally I do lose it, but I'm pretty proud of myself because it doesn't take me long to become aware of it and come back to a more centered place. It is getting easier and easier to do that. Fun fact: I keep a small printout of The Spectrum of Inner Growth on my car's visor.

Then, I drop the kids off at school (right out front because they are no longer embarrassed by me dropping them off) and then off to work I go. At least once a week, before arriving at the office, I make a quick stop to get bagels for my co-workers. We have a great team and I appreciate both their support and all they teach me. Thanks to them (and my own dedication) I am now doing really well at work. The people there have got my back and I've got theirs. When I arrive, I am greeted with smiles and warm hellos. I settle in at my desk and get to work, feeling very valued, focused and productive.

Another thing I did after returning from The Orchid was to go back to school for some accounting and management courses. I am now more confident and trust myself more in meetings and in general. My bosses, Rebecca and John, have been so good to me, and recently recognized all my hard work by promoting me to department head. I now oversee 5 people who are responsible for new business development. I feel excited and energized by the challenge, and I know that the team and I will do a fantastic job. With what I've learned at The Orchid, I also feel that I am better prepared to help my team members grow.

My days are still quite demanding, but now I feel excited for all the possibilities that each day holds. I know that there will be challenges along the way, but I feel confident that I am up to the task. It feels as if I have uncovered this superpower which lets nothing get under my skin and no one and nothing to bring me down.

Every two or three weeks, I meet with Brian over coffee to discuss things related to the kids. Brian also has changed. Somehow, after seeing that I responded differently, he also stopped reacting so hostilely to me. We became more open and less combative. We realized that fighting over the past was useless. I am struck by how easy it is to be around him now, how the pain I felt over our divorce has faded. We still have issues and disagreements, but it has gotten infinitely easier to work them out. This has made a huge difference, especially when making plans for the kid's future. Brian is doing well financially and he continues to send alimony and childcare monthly. Between his financial help and my new management salary, I have been able to save money and even move out of the old house.

Yes! I decided to sell it and did so "as is," so I didn't have to worry about getting anything fixed. A developer bought it for the land and I ended up with enough money to buy something in one of those new developments. It's smaller, but so much nicer, and requires almost no maintenance. The house has a ton of windows (to let in that sunlight that raises my spirit) and there's a patio perfect for BBQs with the kids. They each have their own room. Tommy's is covered with movie posters (he wants to be a Hollywood director) and Michelle has copies of fashion magazines everywhere. She spends all her allowance on fabric remnants and says that she wants to be a designer (look out fashion world).

> *After work, I usually head for one of Tommy's basketball games or one of Michelle's dance recitals. Brian also makes the time to be there as often as possible, as do both sets of grandparents. Everyone is involved in supporting the children and the kids appreciate that support, their eyes scanning the bleachers or the auditorium seats for us and waving when they spot us. My arrangement with Brian is that they'll spend every other weekend with him at his house. I make good use of that time alone. While they are away, I always manage to squeeze in dance classes and afterwards, I always feel stronger, centered, and more connected to my body.*
>
> *My relationship with my parents has also improved. Dad recovered significantly from his stroke and the paralysis has lessened with therapy, which means a lighter burden for Mom. They sold the dry cleaners and now they are fully retired. They spend their time between Lansing and Florida, where they have a condo not far from the beach. We've been there a few times and it is wonderful. The kids really love when we escape winter and spend a few days there on holidays. I feel my parent's love and support, and I am glad they are in our lives.*
>
> *I know you must be wondering, so I'll answer the unspoken question: No, I don't have a boyfriend. After all that happened, I wanted to take it slowly and simply date, which I have been doing. There are a lot of great and not-so-great men out there, so I'm taking my sweet time selecting a partner. I'm sure someone sexy, smart, well-grounded, and secure enough in his self to want to help me grow more as a person will come along when the time is right. In the meantime, I am enjoying dating, time with my kids, and being by my (very cool) self.*
>
> *That's my life now and it is pretty awesome. Sure, I am still figuring things out, but I have confidence I can handle whatever comes along. I'm really proud of myself for getting my shit together! You go, Jen!*
>
> *This or something better, for the highest good of all concerned. Thank you. Thank you. Thank you, Universe.*

**

Stephanie was pensive and was having a tougher time beginning her LifeScript, but, finally, she started to write, and her words began to flow:

> *I wake up in my house, to the sound of my alarm clock. I still live in New York, but we have moved to the suburbs, out in Westchester, to take the girls away from the intensity of the city. I sit on the side of the bed, and I stay there a few minutes, until I am fully awake. When I do I look around, I notice the photo of my family on the nightstand. My husband has left me a flower he picked from our garden*

with a little note on which he wrote, "I love you." I feel his love and support.

When I returned from The Orchid, the first thing I did was to come clean to James. I knew that if my marriage was going to last, I needed to speak openly and be vulnerable to him about my past and how it had affected me. What can I say? James was simply exceptional. After about an hour of me pouring my heart out, and sharing every single detail, I finally took a deep breath and waited silently for him to say something. He had been quiet all through my tearful recitation. When I was finally done, he grasped my shoulders, looked deeply into my eyes, and said, "Stephanie, darling, none of that matters. I love you and I'm just glad you finally are able to love yourself." You can't imagine the relief that washed over me with his words. An entire new world opened up in front of me and more healing happened then and has continued ever since. Every day I grow and learn more about myself and my journey.

So, continuing my day, I make my way to the bathroom and start my daily self-care routine. As I brush my teeth, I catch my reflection in the mirror and I no longer look for flaws. I'm healthier now, having worked hard to overcome my eating disorder with an experienced therapist, and I feel proud of the progress I've made. I remind myself that I'm strong and capable, and that I've come a long way.

After getting dressed, I head downstairs. I hear music coming out of the kitchen and find James already there making breakfast with the girls, who are enjoying every minute of it. We all greet each other with kisses and hugs. Our twin daughters are now eight, and they are becoming these wonderful little people. Their laughter fills the room. They fight a little with each other as they compete for one thing or another, but they listen to me when I ask them to stop. We sit down for a few minutes and we enjoy a wholesome breakfast. I feel grateful that we make this time to connect and spend this moment together as a family.

James has some meetings to attend, so he will be leaving early and, on his way, will drop the girls at school. Once they leave and the house is quiet, I sit down with a cup of tea in my home office. I have continued with many of the exercises I learned at The Orchid, and more I picked up afterwards. Self-forgiveness is one constant subject. I think I can never do enough of that work on myself. I also still journal, at least once a week, and burn it, just like they taught me. These practices continue to help me process my thoughts and heal from my past traumas.

On my computer screen at my desk, I review the beginning of the speech that I need to write for my next engagement. It reads: "My name is Stephanie and it is an honor to be here with you. I'm a survivor of sexual abuse and because of my inability to speak openly about it, or even properly address it to myself, I internalized a lot of pain. That led to many ailments, including depression, eating disorders, and other forms of self-harm. I am here to tell you that there is a way out, no matter how dark things appear to you now. You, too, like me, can heal."

That is how I always begin all my speeches. I share with other women across the country, my message of hope.

Aside from speaking engagements, I still run my design business and that is also doing well. I now have more clients and it allows me to express my creativity. I'm also in the process of forming a non-profit organization. I don't know exactly how the program will work, but it's meant to help young girls feel more confident and in control of their lives. The idea is to encourage them to speak up for themselves and not let anyone, including their parents, teachers, or partners, take away their power.

Talking about parents, at some point after my time at The Orchid, I realized that my relationship with my mom was not ideal, and I could not yet find a way to let go of all that I held against her. I'm working on that still and I am sure that I will find the answer soon, but in the meantime, I have created some space between us. She still lives in Singapore with my dad, and "sees" the girls regularly through video-chat. I only see my mother in person once or twice a year. I'm just more careful about our interactions. I'm still figuring that one out.

Additionally, I joined a group composed of former models, consultants, and other fashion professionals. Our goal is to disseminate information and education that helps identify illegal, unhealthy, or dangerous behaviors and practices before they happen. We are also initiating legal actions against individuals and organizations in the sectors that have allowed or tolerated it. One of those was Bellacroix and Elegant Models. It took a lot for me to step forward, but I'm glad I did. The case is still pending and I assume I will have to tell my story in court at some point. My heart is ok with the idea, but my stomach, not so much.

I still do a lot of meditation and yoga. Yoga continues to be an essential part of my healing, helping me build strength, flexibility, and grounding me. It just makes me happy to connect with myself and my body in that way. I've made many friends through a local yoga studio, and we get together once in a while at our respective houses. We have formed a pretty strong, if informal, support group.

Talking about support groups, I've remained in contact with Olivia, Jennifer, Sofia, and Nicole—Olivia especially. After we all left, she became somewhat of a mentor and advised me often on handling how to be a public persona and what to do to improve my speeches.

The Orchid

When the twins return home from school, I help them with their homework. We also spend quality time together, chatting about their day and sharing our experiences. That time together is very important to me. That is when I tell them that they can be anything they want to be and that the only person who will make those choices is themselves.

Today James came home late, but that's not always the case. In fact, since the pandemic, he has worked from home a few times a week, which has been wonderful. Those days that he is home, we prepare dinner together. Cooking has become another form of therapy for me, as I've learned to appreciate the nourishment and joy that food can bring when you have a healthy relationship with it. After dinner, we clean up together, and then we settle into the living room for some relaxation. We don't watch much television. Instead, we talk or play board games with the girls and enjoy the simple pleasure of being together.

We put the twins to bed early so that they can have a full night's rest. James or I, or sometimes both of us, read them a book or tell them a story. Even though they are eight, they still love to hear them, and then we give them each a hug and a kiss goodnight.

Not always, but I must say pretty often, James and I still find the time to have some intimate time together. That's another thing that has changed in my life.

Because I now love myself, I am able to enjoy lovemaking with my husband in ways that I never imagined. I feel a loving connection with him which grows stronger with every gentle touch and word of affection.

Just before ending the day, I take a moment to reflect on my journey. I acknowledge the progress I've made in my healing and the steps I've taken to create a brighter future for myself and my family. Through self-care, determination, and the support of James, the girls, my Orchid sisters, Mary, and many others who have given me love and lessons along the way, I have overcome the challenges of my past and built a future I can be proud of. I've learned the importance of self-compassion and forgiveness, allowing myself the space to grow and heal.

As I drift off to sleep, I feel a deep sense of gratitude for the love, support, and inner strength that have carried me through the darkest moments and into a life filled with hope, growth, and happiness.

(Thank you for listening to me, Universe. Please deliver this future or something even better, for the highest good of all concerned.)

**

Sofia was writing and writing as if she could set the paper on fire with the force of her pen:

> Hello beautiful Sofia,
>
> My week at The Orchid, three years ago, changed my life. All the things I learned there—awareness, gratitude, forgiveness, acceptance, intention, and love, helped me see life from an entirely new perspective. I am so lucky that I was able to attend.
>
> Thanks to that experience, my days are different now. I wake up early and the first thing I do is remind myself of all the things I'm grateful for. Each day I take the time to light a candle, burn some incense, and meditate. It all brings a sense of calm and self-love and it helps me start each day with a joyful attitude and to stay centered and focused.
>
> I still live in my wonderful apartment in Mexico City. I decided to embrace a minimalist lifestyle when decorating it, which has brought me a lot of peace. The apartment has a modern, simple design with open spaces that create a calm atmosphere. The wooden floors and white walls and furniture make it feel spacious, and the many windows offer breathtaking views of the city day or night. It's my favorite place to relax and unwind—it's like living on a cloud.
>
> I exercise frequently. I enjoy different classes according to the day, from yoga and Pilates, to dance and circuit training. Sometimes I even get pulled into doubles tennis. I feel my body becoming stronger and more agile.
>
> After exercising, I shower and do a simple makeup, hair, and fashion routine that leaves me looking quite beautiful. Plus, since I am free, calm, happy, and focused on the inside, I feel like I can take on anything. I really like the image I now project. I've learned that I need to do that for no one else except myself, so I do it to please me.
>
> My relationship with food is healthy, but I'm flexible, so it is not strange to find me enjoying some chicken street tacos from time-to-time. I feel satisfied with small portions and it's easy for me to maintain a consistent weight.
>
> I have to drive all over the city, and traffic in Mexico City can be challenging. Thankfully I no longer allow myself to get frustrated. Instead, when I drive, I do things that keep me vibrating on a high frequency. I listen to audio books to continue expanding my knowledge, laugh at the latest jokes on the radio, or simply seat-dance to loud music.
>
> Monica and I did reach an agreement to work together. We created a fabulous real estate company with a wonderful working environment. One of the biggest

lessons I learned was that when the team feels respected and empowered, the business grows even more. So, I made sure that everyone in our team was indeed respected and benefitted from the opportunities that emerged. I also made sure that we were always straightforward and honest with our clients. Thanks to these principles, we've enjoyed a lot of success.

I love sharing my knowledge and helping others achieve their goals, so I started mentoring other women in both business skills and personal growth. It's a way of giving back and contributing to the community. When they hear my story and see the change I've made, they feel more empowered and capable of doing the same. Who would have thought that I would become a mentor and symbol of personal achievement? I have The Orchid to thank for that. The experience there helped me see that I was more powerful than I realized.

Although it has been a long and sometimes difficult road, I made amends with all the people I had issues with in the past, including myself. All this forgiveness helped me a lot, and now it is clear to me that when I forgive, the person who gets the greatest benefit is always me. Since I no longer feel anger or resentment inside, it is easier to relate to others. Where there was anger, now there is only love, peace, and acceptance. Thanks to this, a lot of my earlier difficult relationships became easier and simpler. Today I have a more beautiful and respectful relationship with my parents and my brother. There's work to be done, but the relationships are getting stronger every day.

After going on many dates, I found a man who I liked a lot and wanted to get to know better. He is friendly, funny, intelligent, hardworking, confident, and communicates his ideas clearly. Additionally, he is comfortable being sensitive and believes that you can always improve yourself. Another thing I love about him is that he is successful and loves that I am successful, too. He isn't intimidated by me. We admire each other, and we have a relationship based on communication and respect. A few months ago, we decided to move-in together and that's going very well. I feel happy and grateful to have someone like him in my life and I'm enjoying the moment.

I still stay in touch with my sisters from The Orchid. Some have become like family. We are spread out over great distances, but we catch up from time-to-time. We are even talking about meeting up in some exotic place to see each other and continue talking about our spiritual growth. Maybe we can go back to The Orchid and visit that marvelous place again someday. Thanks to the tools, teachings, and everything we experienced there, we've transformed our lives.

I'm grateful for all the opportunities I've had and for the wonderful people who *have entered my life to teach me lessons. Although there are some moments of doubt, I'm committed to continuing to grow and learn.*

I have learned to let go of attachments and results, and am focusing on the present, knowing that everything is in its place, and everything happens for a reason.

Thanks to all of this, I feel that I'm on the right path to a life of continued happiness, peace, and fulfillment.

Thank you, The Orchid. Thank you, Mary. Thank you, Sisters. Thank you, Higher Self.

This or something better, for the highest good of all concerned.

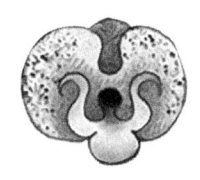

The Orchid

Chapter 51

Activities

As the rest of the afternoon unfolded, the women went about the last set of activities they had chosen.

Olivia surprised herself by picking a self-guided cycling tour in the heart of nature on the property's scenic trails. She relished the fresh air and the tranquility that the outdoors provided, pedaling away her insecurities and embracing a renewed sense of freedom. She realized that as the landscape around her shifted, so did her inner turmoil, giving way to a welcome sense of serenity.

Meanwhile, Sofia and Stephanie were guided to the Activity Center for a private yoga session. The movements and postures helped them release unexpressed stress and fears through the powerful flow of energy they were experiencing.

Jennifer, not always able to indulge and treat herself to special moments, enjoyed another spa treatment. This time, she surrendered to a skilled masseuse's gentle touch, rewarding her body with an aromatherapy massage. The intoxicating blend of essential oils invigorated her senses, allowing her to shed further layers of those stored emotions. As she lay there, she could feel the tension melt away, replaced by a blossoming sense of peace and contentment.

Nicole made a last-minute change to her schedule when she managed to find a spot in the improv comedy class. Along with a band of other nervous women, she found the stage and the improvised scenarios a platform for liberation and bold authenticity. Navigating the experience, Nicole realized it wasn't about the act but the freedom it offered. Improvisation had not just taught her to perform but to live authentically and embrace the idea that true confidence emerges from vulnerability and fearlessness.

The Orchid

As the afternoon ended, the women gathered and engaged in lively exchanges over dinner. The conversation flowed with a heightened sense of vigor and intimacy. Shared laughter rang out, punctuated by poignant moments of silence and profound realization, as each reflected on the journey they'd embarked upon. In the background of each lively exchange was the bittersweet realization that their transformative week was nearing its close, and this would be their last dinner together.

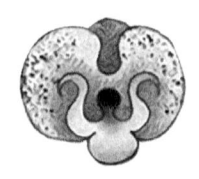

Chapter 52

Closing Ceremony

There was great anticipation as all the women headed towards the Sanctuary for their last Evening Council. Just like the first night, which now seemed an eternity ago, everyone arriving was greeted by familiar faces at the door. Mary, all the healers, and many of the staff were present, as the event would serve as both a graduation and a closing ceremony. The space was illuminated by hundreds of candles, the flames of which flickered and danced to the energy of the room.

At the front of the Sanctuary, two women were playing music. They tapped their bare hands on handpans, a round and convex metal instrument that resembles the shell of a turtle. The soft sounds generated by them were resonant, soothing, and uplifting and filled the room with a beautiful centering melody.

The music created a sense of connection and unity among all. They let go of their thoughts and allowed themselves to fully embrace that present moment, feeling grateful for the opportunity to be there, surrounded by such peace and serenity.

Everyone appreciated the attention to detail, knowing that every element, like all else this week, had been arranged with their spiritual well-being in mind. Despite having been in this space many times over the course of the week, the Sanctuary managed to look and feel even more grand and powerful than usual, echoing the emotional state of the women within.

Sofia, Olivia, Nicole, Stephanie, Jennifer, and the rest of the guests settled into their positions on the floor. Throughout the span of a week, these women, hailing from diverse corners, backgrounds, and life stories, had forged a profound connection. Drawing wisdom from various teachers and healers, they had championed one another on their individual journeys, creating a supportive network powered by shared learning and mutual encouragement. Still, despite all the love, beauty and energy that surrounded them, some felt a sense of sadness and hesitation as their departure neared. They wondered what it would be like once they returned to their normal lives and left behind the protective energy of their newfound community.

Regardless, they knew that they were capable of so much more than they had ever imagined, and for that they were eternally grateful. They were now different people than they were when they had arrived and had tools and knowledge that would ensure a different approach to life.

As Mary took center stage, the music gradually subsided. "Hello, my dear sisters." The softness of her voice was carried by the powerful vibrational energy that was present.

She stood there for a moment, basking in the energy of the room, her smile engaging everyone present. Then, placing her right hand over her heart, she met each gaze, offering a profound and heartfelt acknowledgement to every individual.

She continued speaking. "I am so excited about tonight's event. It marks the completion of this stage of your growth and transformation. But know this is not the end of your journey. This is just the beginning.

"Every single moment of every single day, you will learn new things about yourselves, about the universe, and about how you interact with both. Know that you are now more prepared than you have ever been for what lies ahead. Know that all you need is inside of you. The power, the knowledge, the insights, the inspiration—all is within, because God, the Divine Power, the Source of All, is within you.

"Please, everyone, let's stand, form a circle, and hold hands as we offer a centering prayer and invoke the presence of this force." Mary joined them and closed the circle.

"Take three deep breaths, releasing them slowly. Feel yourself become grounded and centered in the love that is within you and unites us all."

Everyone did as instructed. Afterwards, Mary raised her hands and began to speak:

> Beloved God, Universe, Creator, Source of All Power,
>
> We are grateful for the knowing that we are one with you, with each other, and with all that surrounds us. Thank you for giving us the

clarity that this oneness, and its infinite power and wisdom, gives us. It is all we require to live in love, abundance, and with purpose.

We ask for your guidance and support as we embark on this new path and for all heaviness to be lifted and transformed into that which can propel us forward.

We ask for awareness and mindfulness of thoughts and beliefs so that we can create our reality and our future.

We ask for gratitude, forgiveness, acceptance, kindness, and compassion, for ourselves and others, as we continue this journey of growth and self-discovery.

We are grateful for these blessings. We acknowledge them. We feel them. We know them to be true. Let it be so and so it is.

This or something better, for the highest good of all concerned.

Mary paused and then continued.

"Tonight, we shall have three activities. The first is to provide an opportunity for sharing, and the other two we will reveal as the evening progresses.

"So now, I'd like to invite everyone to take a seat and share what is present for you at this moment."

Nicole was the first to raise her hand.

"I'll start with gratitude. Thank you all. Thank you so very much. Like the saying goes, 'What a difference a day makes.' Yesterday, I was a mess...." Nicole stopped herself. "Let me be more careful with my words. Yesterday, I *felt* like I was a mess. Yet, being amongst you all, witnessing your fearless courage and vulnerability," her gaze shifted towards Mary, "our walk together, Mary, and then a very special conversation—so unique that I struggle to find words to describe it—changed that. Today, I see a change in myself as striking as the difference between day and night. It's hard to explain, but it feels like when you can't figure out a puzzle, but suddenly a piece falls in place and all the others follow swiftly. It is like that. Then, this afternoon when writing my LifeScript...."

Nicole stopped herself once again and looked at Mary. "Mary, is it ok if I share about our conversation this afternoon?"

To which Mary replied, "Yes, of course, Nicole. Please do."

"Well, this afternoon I was feeling uncomfortable with the idea that we can create our future, because it means that we see ourselves as God, which I don't think we are. And Mary's answer just clicked for me—God is inside of us, and *that* is what we are tapping into. This sealed it for me and then I went on to write the most beautiful story of love I could imagine for me and my partner. It is such a wonderful exercise to take a moment to visualize and write about my dream. It was really, really, powerful. Not only am I sending the message into the universe, I am also able to visualize what else I can do now to get closer to that vision. So, thank you."

Jennifer was next.

"This afternoon, when I wrote my letter to Santa … I mean, to Jen," she said, laughing a little, "I spared no detail. I pictured the perfect life. I wrote about a new house, a new car, a better relationship with my kids and with my work colleagues, more schooling, a promotion. Gosh, even a healthy relationship with my ex-husband. And you know what is interesting? I didn't think about this then, but it just came to mind now: when I was writing it, it didn't feel like I was wishing for something. It felt like something that I was living. It felt real, not any part in particular, but all of it. Feeling it, visualizing it, tasting it, sensing it made what I was writing feel incredibly real. For a second there, I think I was able to experience how this power of intention and sending the message into the universe allows me to create my future."

Olivia's sharing followed.

"I, too, saw my life completely changed. In my LifeScript, I wrote about having found peace and love three years from now. I saw myself changing jobs and enjoying myself a lot more. I also made some much-needed relationship reparations, the most important one with my dad. I saw us going to dinner together and showing him how I had forgiven the past. There was also romance. 'Mr. Wonderful,' I called him." She was slightly embarrassed revealing that piece, but a smile lit up her face as the other women made kissing noises and teasing remarks. "That was unexpected, but I ran with it and wrote about it in great detail to make sure he was exactly what I want in a companion.

"But, perhaps the most wonderful part of my day today was the golden staircase meditation. Oh my," she said placing her right hand on her chest. "That was so powerful. Taking each step and being so mindful about each of the powers being acquired was truly revelatory. Each one of those powers— joy, peace, gratitude, freedom, creativity.…" Olivia paused for a moment to recall what came next.

From around the room, different women yelled out, "connection," "abundance," "health," and "purpose."

"Yes, that's right. Thank you," Olivia said. "The attention and reverence given to each of those and the visualization of having them become part of myself, like an armor which gives me protection, was all very moving. It affected me so that afterwards, I went to my room and journaled for quite a long time."

Sofia stood up after Olivia and, with a beautiful smile, said, "Today was a very special day for me, too. The meditation, the LifeScript, everything took me a little further down this wonderful path of growth and discovery. I wrote about waking up, exercising, eating better, my home, a new boyfriend, my new business, and my new way of looking at and living life.

"The most powerful thing about my LifeScript was that I was able to write about it and envision it all with a calm that, until this week, had been absent in my life. The anger was all gone. And, because it was, the way I behaved towards everything and everyone was different. Where there was anger and pain, there is now a peace, calm, and a clarity of thought that I've never had before. Thank you, Universe. Thank you, Mary; thank you to all of you." She said these last thanks turning to look at all the team. She then bowed to them all, knowing that what they had given her was worthy of just such a respectful gesture.

Stephanie followed.

"Like everyone who spoke before me, and like my entire time here, today's experience was beautiful, special, touching, and beyond words. The meditation this morning left me feeling incredibly powerful. This was important for me because I now know that one of my challenges was that I had given my power away to different people. I now know that the power is mine, and the golden staircase helped me visualize that more clearly.

"And, the LifeScript, what can I say? I went ahead and wrote about all the changes that I needed to make in my life. I wrote about having a heart-to-heart conversation with my husband, something I intend to do as soon as I return home. I wrote about speaking publicly of my experiences so that others can benefit from it and about starting a foundation to help women. I also wrote about staying in touch with all of you. I want what we have here to continue."

The sharing went on, and many others followed Stephanie. They spoke about their different experiences, about feeling stronger, more daring, more capable

The Orchid

to pursue changes in their marriages, with their children, their parents, their bosses, their neighbors, and in every aspect of their lives.

After everyone who wanted to share had had the opportunity to do so, the first session came to an end. Mary gave a signal to the musicians, and the enchanting music began playing once again.

**

Following a break, the second part of the evening began.

This time, Mary was standing among the women and Wakinyan walked to the front of the room to address them all. "During this second part of the evening, you will each perform a powerful exercise we call the Tunnel of Love.

"It consists of every one of you individually walking between two rows of people lined up side-by-side and facing each other. As you pass through this human corridor, you will be surrounded by messages of love and words of encouragement and support. Walk at your own pace, carefully listening to and absorbing the heartfelt sentiments being offered to you.

"Those of you who stand side-by-side comprising the tunnel, the messages are of your choosing and we only ask that they be vibrationally centered on the power of love, gratitude, forgiveness, peace, and the like. Some examples are:

- You are remarkable.
- You embody beauty.
- You possess immeasurable power.
- Thank you for your benevolence.
- Love resides within you.
- Thank you for your friendship.
- I am here for you.
- You can accomplish anything you aspire to.
- You shine as brilliantly as the stars.

"Or anything special about the person you want to say. Perhaps you've noticed something wonderful or evolving in her during your stay here. Maybe it will be something helpful she has not even thought about herself. Ask the universe to provide you with the right words and for them to be for her highest good.

"And you, dear walkers, your job is simply to be present, to enjoy and open your heart, and to receive the love that will be shared with you. After you end your walk, simply take a spot at the end of the row and we will repeat this until each one of you has had the opportunity to walk through the Tunnel of Love."

Wakinyan asked everyone to stand, and the musicians began to play a spirit-lifting melody. The notes crafted an ethereal atmosphere, invoking ancient wisdom and the promise of a bright future. The music, with its heavenly harmonies, felt like a sacred hymn to love and unity, touching the heart of everyone present.

All was pushed aside, leaving the floor completely open. The staff helped the women form two rows about five feet apart from each other.

Stephanie was the first to walk through. She proceeded with purpose and intention, and, as she did, she made eye contact with the women standing on either side of her. Each offered her a phrase as she passed by. "You are radiant. You are kind. You are love. You are courageous. You are nurturing."

They had all become like family over the course of the week, and their words of love, gratitude, and encouragement filled her soul like a symphony of beautiful melodies. Along the way, Sofia extended her arms, offering Stephanie an embrace, which Stephanie accepted, surrendering to the warmth and tenderness of the act.

At that moment, Sofia whispered in her ear, "You are powerful beyond belief." Stephanie pulled back, tears filling her eyes, as those words opened a floodgate of emotion within her. On she walked, deeply touched, holding hands, giving and receiving hugs, and expressing deep gratitude to all of her new sisters.

Olivia, who had been standing opposite Stephanie, was next. As she entered the tunnel, she placed both of her hands across her chest as a symbol of the incredible gratitude she felt for all. Her movements were as graceful and fluid as ever as she took each step. "You are such an inspiration. You are beautiful. Thank you for your kindness and dedication, Olivia. You are impactful and effective with your words. You are a gentle soul. You are a true expression of love." Her eyes met each woman's, lingering for a moment on their faces and offering her lovely smile in return. She, too, had grown attached to these beautiful souls over the past week.

As she moved, she received, and offered in return, deep appreciation and thankfulness for the present moment. When she reached the end of the walk, she extended her arms to the heavens in a gesture of proclamation and

The Orchid

liberation, grateful for the loving bond she felt and that they all shared.

Jennifer followed. As she did, the messages, "You are complete. You are not alone. You are love. Thank you for your kindness. You are a powerful woman capable of anything you set your mind to. You are a wonderful mother. You are worthy of love, especially self-love," flowed from the mouths of those who cheered her on as she paraded through the tunnel.

Each step taken brought her closer to a place of peace, solace, and strength. The walk heightened her energy and the energy of all present in that room. She held hands, received kisses and embraces, and her heart swelled with emotion. She was thankful for Mary, for The Orchid, and for all these other smart, kind, gentle, and fearless women with whom she had forged such a powerful connection. The thought crossed her mind of how much knowledge she had acquired in just a few days and how her self-love and inner power had replaced the thoughts of pain and lack she held when she had arrived. Today, those dark thoughts and fears could not be further from her mind. She recognized that she owed that all to this place, these women, but, above all, to herself.

By the time Sofia entered the center of the tunnel, the celebratory mood of the exercise was at its height. Hers was the largest smile, and the self-love that she had just discovered bubbled over. The walk was a bit overwhelming, and she wasn't sure she could contain all the love she felt.

"Your strength inspires me and your love fills me with joy," Nicole said to her. Other similarly loving words followed. Then she heard, "The power of your kindness is beyond measure," and when she looked at who had said it, she realized it had been Stephanie, who was returning the same kindness Sofia had given to her. Olivia held both of Sofia's hands and looked her in the eyes as she told her, "You are an incredibly strong and capable woman, raise your head and embrace your power." The touching comments continued, all based on the strength of the collective love that enveloped Sofia and all others.

It only took a few steps for the words "You don't have to hide, for you are perfect just as you are" and "You are a child of God" to make Nicole weak in the knees. She paced herself along the path, absorbing all the lovely invocations and affirmations being offered to her. "You are a divine being having a human experience." "It's loving, not who you love, that defines you." "You are a powerful beacon of light." Nicole absorbed it all and used the moment to acknowledge herself for having done such hard work during her time at The Orchid.

She thought of Elena and how she, too, would benefit from this marvelous place. Then she mentally corrected herself. *Every woman I know would benefit from more self-love, more self-forgiveness, more self-acceptance, and the camaraderie of other women. We don't have to be enemies or even competitors. There is enough love for everyone. We just have to replace all the limiting beliefs that we have been fed and embrace love.*

One by one, all the other women had their moment, all experiencing the same flow of emotions and sensations. All around, affectionate, endearing, and gracious messages of love, kindness and support were offered and received as each walker marched down the glorious path. The words and messages themselves became more heartfelt and beautiful with each step taken. "You are smart and a joy to be with." "The divine in me salutes the divine in you." "You are brave." "Rejoice in knowing that you are perfect." You are the love you seek." "The love within you is infinite." "Love, your love, is the answer."

As the last one finished her walk, bringing the exercise to a close, the doors to the Sanctuary were thrown open, revealing a roaring bonfire spreading warmth and light into the surrounding clearing.

The women were radiant with the power and the transformative energy of the exercise in which they had just participated. The experience had stirred something profound within them, sparking a surge of empowerment that infused their beings and emanated from their every pore. It was as though they had each been touched by the divine, their souls ignited with a newfound sense of purpose and strength.

**

Following the celebration around the fire, Mary addressed them again.

"And now it is time for the third and final act of the evening. If you will, please follow the instructions of our wonderful staff as they direct you to where we will conclude our evening, just a short walk from here."

The women were guided into the lushness of the forest. The path contained a few twists and turns that had been illuminated by candles, giving the walk a sense of mystery.

Some minutes into their walk, they arrived at a clearing surrounded by tall trees, illuminated by many tea candles. At its center, there was an old stone arch entwined with sapling branches and ivy.

The Orchid

The women fell quiet, understanding this was a place of reverence.

The structure itself did look like a door to another world, an entrance to a sacred place. It was a mystical place that resided deep in the heart of everyone who had previously crossed it. A few of the healers and teachers waited near the arch for the group to arrive.

As the women trickled in, they could read the words carved across the top of the arch:

> When you walk through this doorway, we shall be sisters, and awareness, gratitude, forgiveness, acceptance, intention, and above all, love, shall be our bond.

Once all were gathered at the front of the doorway, Mary began to speak.

"This portal is a most special place here at The Orchid. It's a high frequency and powerful gate, capable of transporting those who cross it with enlightened intention to any realm of their choosing. Today it will be your turn to cross under it, as thousands of women have before you. And as you do, we will deliver a special prayer and blessing so that you are able to embrace the full greatness of your existence. May it serve as a confirmation of the incredible transformation that you have undergone since your arrival."

The women were all experiencing a sense of exhilaration, wonder, and humility and were ready to take the leap into the next stage of their lives. It was faint, but as they waited, some of them thought they noticed a sound and vibration coming out of the portal, as if the power stirring beyond it wanted to make itself felt.

They gathered closer together, many holding hands, waiting for the ceremony to begin.

"Ok," Mary said, "who wants to go first?"

There was a brief silence, and then Sofia stepped forward and claimed the spot. "I will, Mary." And taking advantage of the moment, she turned to Mary, to the staff and healers, and to all of the women who stood behind her. She paused to allow her words, which had fled from her mind momentarily as emotion flooded it, to return. "Thank you, my dear sisters. Thank you for supporting me and for helping me see how powerful and perfect I really am"

"You are so very welcome, my dear," Mary replied on behalf of all. "Are you ready for your blessing?"

"Yes!" Sofia answered excitedly.

"Very well, Sofia. Step forward and stand in the center of the portal. When ready, place both hands in front of you, palms facing upward, to symbolize your openness to receive this blessing. Repeat after me:

> I, Sofia, stand here tonight at this powerful portal, surrounded by the mighty forces of awareness, gratitude, forgiveness, acceptance, and intention.
>
> I recognize my divine right to be happy and of my power to manifest such happiness. I acknowledge that such power exists within me, because I am one with love—the infinite source of all.
>
> I shall act lovingly and responsibly with myself and all that surrounds me. I shall be mindful of my sisters, knowing that that which happens to one, happens to us all.
>
> I ask all my family line—past, present, and future—for their blessing so that I may fully become the highest and most complete version of my unique self. From this moment forward, I stand in the greatness of my perfect soul, which is but a reflection of the perfection that is the source of all.

One by one, Sofia repeated each of the lines, and, when finished, she took a step, crossing the threshold of the portal into the sacred space beyond.

The rest of the women cheered and all waited for the blessing to be bestowed upon them, too. They knew that crossing under the arch marked the beginning of a new chapter in their lives.

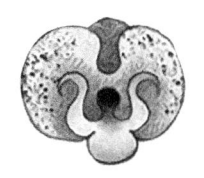

The Orchid

Part VIII
Farewell

The Orchid

Chapter 53

Connect with Mother Earth

It had been a long and celebratory night, and a few of the women had not slept at all. Most had slept very little. The expectations and high energy of the prior night's ceremonies seemed responsible, but it was more than that. There was a desire and a need to not let go of each other.

They wanted to continue conversing, to get to know one another just a bit more, and to speak of anything they had not had the opportunity to discuss before. At first, when no one knew what to expect, a week had seemed like an eternity; now, no one could believe how rapidly time had come and gone and how wonderful it had all been.

The activities within the rooms were a familiar scene, reminiscent of any hotel on departure day. Tidying up and packing clothes, gathering personal items, and ensuring nothing was forgotten all was part of the routine leading up to the mid-day checkout and subsequent journey home.

With none of the women scheduled to leave until mid-afternoon, there would be ample time for heartfelt farewells—to bid adieu to Mary, the team, and the rest of their new sisters.

All were still enjoying the last few moments of tranquility and reflection in this wonderful space that had served as a reset button for their lives. The views, the silence, the sounds of the morning, the canopy of the lush forest, the beauty of the risen sun, all of this pristine and wonderful environment had contributed profoundly to their experience. They continued to make mental notes of the changes they would make in their homes and lives to create a personal space that was reflective of the peace and joy they found in this one.

The Orchid

After enjoying a cup of coffee or tea, praying, meditating, and packing, the women began their last walk to the Central Plaza, where they would gather for the final group event of their shared time at The Orchid.

It was another beautiful morning, filled with expectation, and, though many of the guests were tired, none showed it. As they walked, the women read the quotes and messages that had been posted along the path.

> Owning our story and loving ourselves through that process is the bravest thing that we will ever do. —Brené Brown
>
> It's not your job to like me, it's mine. —Byron Katie
>
> The biggest adventure you can ever take is to live the life of your dreams. —Oprah Winfrey
>
> I did then what I knew how to do. Now that I know better, I do better. —Maya Angelou

Good morning, dear ones. It's a pleasure to see you here. I hope you managed to get some sleep," Mary said, knowing full well that they hadn't.

"At the end of each program, we aim to merge the magic and learning of the week with the promising path that awaits you. And what better way to do so than by planting a seed in Mother Earth, the very essence of this sanctuary that has sheltered us."

Mary pointed to a path winding between the trees. "Let's follow this path to the heart of the plantations. There, the soil awaits to receive our gift."

Lucía and her team awaited them, and upon arrival, they offered gloves, shovels, and tender avocado plants. "Before our hands touch the soil," Lucía said, "let's connect with it and ask for its blessing.

> "Oh, Great Mother, source of all life, today, as we plant these seeds, we honor our connection with you and symbolize our rebirth. Just as these plants seek to grow and flourish, so do we aspire to do the same. We celebrate the interconnectedness of all and give thanks for every moment we are connected to you. So be it."

With full hearts and ready hands, the women inserted the plants into the earth, leaving their fingers for a moment to whisper intentions and express wishes, many of which had emerged during the past week. Upon completion, a feeling of gratitude and connection enveloped them. They knew that, just like these plants, their growth and transformation, nurtured at The Orchid, would continue to blossom in the outside world.

Mary, radiating the calm and wisdom that had been the beacon for all during the week, offered them some words. "My dear ones," she began, "this activity is not merely the end of our week together, but the beginning of your new journey. The plants you've sown today are a reflection of what you've cultivated within: strength, self-love, and a deeper connection to the essence of life. As these plants grow and strengthen, may your spirits and hearts do so as well."

The Orchid

Chapter 54

Because I Am You, and You are Me

The women walked back to the central court and, as they reached a shaded area not far from the Sanctuary, Mary spoke again. "Let's sit here a while and share some freshly-squeezed fruit juices, and, as we enjoy our beverage, I'll be delighted to address any final questions you may have."

All were excited by the idea of sitting with Mary and the others just a while longer.

"I know," said Mary, "that the last day of the program is often filled with doubt, apprehension, and perhaps even anxiety. Often the main question in everyone's mind is, 'Now what? What happens after I leave this wonderful place, and I return to my daily life? How can I remain connected? How can I ensure I remain anchored to this new version of myself, my real self that I've now uncovered? How do I nurture the light I've found and not allow it to be extinguished?'"

Many of the women looked at each other. A few lowered their heads, ashamed that they had been doubting themselves already, and they had not yet even left The Orchid.

Mary asked, "Are any of those questions running through your minds?"

"Yes, ma'am," admitted Olivia.

"You got me," yelled Sofia, half-smiling.

"Definitely," said Jennifer.

"Know this," Mary continued, looking straight at every one of them. "You *will* lose your connection. You *will* find yourselves reacting from time-to-time like the earlier version of yourself. You *will* fall from the heights you have achieved here. But know this, too. When you do—without shame, without judgement, and without giving into discouragement—you will get up, gather yourself, take a deep breath, and simply say, 'It's ok, I am a spiritual being having a human experience.'"

The women laughed with relief at that simple reminder that they needed only to remember that most basic of lessons.

"Our human experience is filled with imperfection, and noticing that is a lesson in itself. But you will always have the opportunity to correct yourself and start again. As you do, remember what you learned here this week. I promise you the time it will take for you to realize the disconnection has happened will get shorter. Eventually, you will become better at both avoiding and correcting such imperfections, and, one day, you will realize that you have mastered the art of conscious and deliberate living."

Mary stopped speaking to allow for questions.

Jennifer was the first to speak. "Mary, what should I do tomorrow, a month, or a year from now, on that one day when I'm likely to look at myself in the mirror, and, no matter how hard I try, all I see is a fat slob, full of doubt and despair?"

"Jennifer, if you don't mind, I'm going to rephrase your question some," said Mary. "You want to know what techniques you can use to manage limiting beliefs and overwhelming feelings of self-doubt when they present themselves?"

"Yes. Thank you for wording it that way," said Jennifer.

"No worries. But, please, don't forget," Mary looked at all of them when she said this, "try your best to be impeccable with your thoughts, your words, your emotions, and your actions."

"Now, about your question," Mary continued. "When that day comes, and, make no mistake, it will come, simply go back to the basics you learned here. Go back and access the power of awareness, gratitude, forgiveness, acceptance, and intention. Accessing the power of those concepts will trigger a response within you, and it will jolt you. And, when it does, you will remember who you really are. You will remember that the true you *is* perfect and complete.

"Whenever you have a strong surge of unhelpful energy, dig deep within yourself, perhaps pick up a pen, a piece of paper, a candle, and journal. Write in that journal like your life depended on it. Free yourself of the energy behind those thoughts and the discomfort you are feeling. You now know, and have experienced first-hand, that such thoughts are not real. As you have now learned, your thoughts do not define you, for you are the master of your thoughts."

Stephanie raised her hand. "Mary, how can I help others in my life, particularly other women, to embrace their own self-worth and to practice self-love?"

"Thank you for that question, Stephanie. As you probably can tell by now, nothing is dearer to my heart than what you have just asked. I would say, speak to them about your experience at The Orchid. If you are willing, speak to them also about your breakthroughs. By you being so open and vulnerable, they can see that they are not alone.

"I believe one of our most pervasive misconceptions, and potentially the one that most hinders women from seeking answers to their questions, is the mistaken notion that we're alone in our experiences. We tend to feel embarrassed, mistakenly believing that our feelings are singular and unique to us. So, please, share your knowledge. Share what you have learned. Share the tools and solutions that helped you. Let them know that they are not alone and that they don't have to carry the pain of their traumas, their fears, or their limitations for the rest of their lives. There is hope and freedom from such unbearable weight, and it is as available to them as it was to you.

One important thing to remember is that when you do share your stories, do so without insisting that the listener adopts your views. You don't need to convince anyone. All you need to do is speak about what the experience has meant for *you*."

Mary paused as she thought of what else she wanted to share.

"I find that another of our biggest challenges is that, too often, we spend an enormous amount of time and energy fighting each other, being jealous of and criticizing one another. That, my dears, is one big limiting belief we need to resolve. The idea that we are supposed to be in competition with one another is outdated and false. Look at how you have refuted it just this week by becoming soul sisters with women you hadn't even met a week before. You and many other women out there are realizing that there is no greater power than working together, collaborating, and co-creating. Spread that belief by your actions when you leave here. If I may add, it's important to be aware that the philosophy of mutual support transcends gender barriers. There are people of all genders who embrace these same ideals and join us as genuine allies, actively propelling this wave of change and optimism. I invite you to seek out these allies, regardless of how they identify, and collaborate with them to spread a message of love and inclusion. Collectively, we have the energy and power to reshape the world in which we live."

Olivia asked, "What characteristics should I look for in a potential partner that indicates they will support my journey towards self-love and personal growth?"

"Ah, you are asking about 'Mr. Wonderful' I see," Mary joked. The other women joined in laughter and teasing sounds. "Well, there is no secret answer," Mary continued. "The most important thing is to trust yourself. Trust your intuition. Your conscious self may not know, but your higher self knows everything. Sometimes things happen because there are lessons you need to learn, and sometimes those lessons are painful. My suggestion? Go within. Ask for guidance. Journal. Meditate. Pray.

"But remember, real love is not blind nor does it leave you powerless. On the contrary, I find that when I love myself fully, I am empowered, liberated, and full of clarity. All I want in a partner is someone who subscribes to that idea, someone who is not afraid to let me be the greatest and best version of myself that I can be."

Nicole raised her hand next. "How can I ensure that I'm making time for self-reflection and personal growth when I have such a busy schedule?"

"Good question, Nicole, and a very important one," Mary commented. "It helps to start with small steps and to be consistent. It is better to do something for a few minutes consistently every day than to do something big, inconsistently, throughout the week. Aim to integrate short and daily practices of self-reflection that may work for you. Ten to fifteen minutes each morning meditating, journaling, gardening or dancing will go a long way in helping you process your emotions.

"Things you do each day become second nature. Brushing your teeth, drinking coffee, driving to work are examples of things you do almost without thinking, as you've done them so often. A good approach is to attach new habits to those regular ones, so the rote actions become triggers to remind you to practice your helpful new habits. For example, you can silently repeat an affirmation while brushing your teeth or write a page or two in your journal as you drink your coffee. Listen to a spiritual podcast or audio book as you drive to work. Be creative, but whatever you do, be consistent. Studies suggest that when an action is practiced daily, it can become a habit in as little as three weeks."

Mary paused and looked to see if there were other questions.

"I'm a little concerned about being able to set healthy boundaries and then not keeping them in place with other people," said Nicole. "I've been kind of a pushover in the past, and I'd like to change that. How can I maintain the healthy boundaries I want to create?"

"Another wonderful question, Nicole. Thank you.

"The most important way to maintain healthy boundaries is to know yourself well and to know what those boundaries are or should be for you in the first place.

"Prioritize yourself. Know and accept that at any time you, *you*, are the most important thing in your universe. If you are well, then all that surrounds you will be well, because you will be able to manage it. Learn to discern when a 'yes' or a 'no' is the answer you truly want to give and then give it. Often, many of us do not know how to say 'no' or that 'no' is a complete sentence. Nothing more need be said. But, this way of answering, of really speaking your mind and holding your boundaries, will seem foreign to you, so practice it. Use it. Learn to know when you need some time alone to yourself, and don't be afraid to let others know. You will get more comfortable with saying what you mean when you have done so many times."

Mary continued, "Also, communicate clearly. It is important that you eliminate any ambiguity when you are dealing with boundaries. Be clear and communicate what you want and don't want, first with yourself and then with others.

"That clarity comes from being aware. That is why awareness is our first lesson of the program. Be aware because all is dependent on you knowing yourself. Look at yourself from a distance, and observe what is working and what is not. Then make changes to your life as appropriate."

Mary looked around the group, awaiting the next question.

"How can I remain optimistic and grounded in situations that are testing my patience? You all might have noticed I have, in the past, been a little lacking in that quality," Sofia asked with a chuckle.

"We are all still growing and perfecting ourselves," Mary reminded Sofia with a smile. "Nobody's perfect ... yet. The first thing is to remember that your thoughts, your actions, and all your reactions are choices you make, Sofia. It is you who do the choosing and therefore it is you who are in control. That awareness is critical to remain grounded in the face of any situation, even those that try your patience.

The Orchid

"When you are aware, you are in a better position to choose and prioritize between something that is elevating your vibration and something that is lowering it. Take your time to allow yourself to respond to a situation as opposed to reacting to it. You can use specific techniques such as meditating, taking a hot bath, reading uplifting books, or talking things out with a trusted friend. You can ground yourself in Mother Nature by walking barefoot outside, having a stress-relieving massage, drinking a soothing cup of herbal tea, or spending time regulating your breathing. And, never forget, you can always pray to whatever force you conceive your higher power to be. You have choices."

"Mary," another woman asked, "our LifeScript, what should we do with it?"

"Your LifeScript is your intention for the type of life you want to live. Read it regularly, every day if you can. When you do, don't forget to feel it, live it in your mind as if it was happening already. The more you visualize it, the more you can bring it into sharp focus; and, the more concrete you can make it to reality, the sooner the universe will deliver it to you.

"As time goes by, add to your LifeScript. Modify it. Update it. However, let me say this. Like with all habits, be consistent. If you are constantly changing the instructions that you are sending to the universe, then all you will get is chaos and confusion in return. Be clear and consistent in what you are asking."

The exchange continued for some time.

When there seemed to be no more questions, Mary asked the women if they had any last words they wanted to share before their time at The Orchid was over.

There was silence as they all contemplated the inevitable end to this magical experience.

Finally, Olivia stood up. "Mary, and all of you," she looked at all the teachers, healers and staff present. "Thank you. Thank you. Thank you. I am a different woman. I have discovered so many things about myself this week. I have forgiven. I have let go of much pain and hurt that was swirling inside of me for so long. I've let go of limiting beliefs that were controlling me. And I've come to understand that I am free, that I am enough, and that I do not need to carry the weight of the world. I just need what is mine to carry, and even that can be lighter when I let go of all that holds me down. Lastly, I have learned to be kinder to myself. I am leaving with a renewed sense of self-worth and a commitment to practicing a greater level of self-care. Thank you so very much for this most incredible experience."

Jennifer spoke next. "For five years, I struggled to find closure and heal from my 'failed' marriage. I needed to break free from allowing it to determine who I was and how I acted. I was so lost that I was willing to let it all go to waste—my life, my children's life, our happiness. My gosh. I'll be honest, not for a moment did I believe that change would happen, let alone believe in the huge transformation that has taken place. This place is unique, and I am thankful that I was given the ultimatum to come here." There was laughter around the group. "Thank you for giving me the opportunity to prove not only to the world, but, more importantly, to myself, that I am powerful, complete, enough, and that I love and need to continue dancing. Thank you for giving me the greatest gift of all, the ability to love myself."

Stephanie boldly spoke up next. "I was so lost before I came here. I'm not sure how long I would have been able to carry the load I was carrying. You," Stephanie looked at Mary directly, "quite literally, saved my life and I will forever be grateful. Thanks to you Mary, The Orchid staff, and to all of you."

Stephanie looked around at the other women, her eyes eventually coming to rest at the tight-knit group sitting together: Olivia, Sofia, Nicole, and Jennifer. "You are so very precious to me. I thank you for your love, for sharing your stories, for your laughter and your tears, and for accepting me. You are the most powerful women I have ever met, and I am so happy that I can count you as my friends and as my sisters. This week has shown me the power of sisterhood and the strength that exists in togetherness. I love you."

Nicole continued. "I learned that God loves me just as I am. I thought I knew that already, but it wasn't until this week—surrounded by your support, your love, and your wisdom—that it finally sank in and I truly understood it. I spent so much of my life doubting myself and feeling unworthy. The support and love I've experienced here have shown me that I am enough and that I have unique gifts to offer the world. I am perfect just as I am. We are all perfect just as we are. Thank you all."

Sofia couldn't stop smiling. Joy suffused her face as she said, "I came to The Orchid weighed down by anger and abusive, destructive behaviors that hurt many people around me and, above all, also hurt myself. I'm so glad you lived this week with me because I don't have the words yet to properly explain the profound shift that has taken place within me." She raised her hands to the skies as if she were speaking to the universe and all the people in it, "To everyone I hurt, abused, or exploited, please know that I am sorry. I didn't know better, and, now that I know better, I will do better." The other women applauded and whistled in support and admiration.

Sofia continued, "Mary, you all, and this amazing place have given me the opportunity to think back on my actions, and I am deeply grateful for the support, understanding, and guidance I've gotten from all of you. I leave ready to change my life. I'm going to do my best to be more self-aware and grateful, to forgive who I have got to forgive and ask forgiveness from those I've mistreated. I am going to aim for acceptance and include intention in everything I do. *Las quiero con todo mi corazón.* I love you with all my heart," she said as she blew a kiss to them all.

There were many embraces, kind words, tears, kisses, and heartfelt farewells shared as their last session at The Orchid came to a close. Mary watched as they hugged and listened and acknowledged the challenges, hard work, and eventual triumphs they shared with each other. They were all remarkable women and the growth they had experienced in a few short days never failed to amaze Mary, though she had seen the miracle thousands of times.

As the partings wound down, Mary spoke one last time to them all, these shining lights.

"Many years ago, in my own despair, I found strength, love, and wisdom in the teachings of some wonderful people all over the globe. Once I realized that all the answers were inside of me, and that I had all the power to craft any life I wanted to live, I knew I wanted to share that power with others, especially with other women.

"Each week, when we close another program and I hear profound messages of love, gratitude, growth, and empowerment like those I've heard from you today, I am reminded of my purpose on this Earth and of my desire to live the rest of my days in service to others.

"On behalf of myself and all of us at The Orchid, as well as the graduates that have come before you, I thank you for the privilege of your presence and I welcome you to our sisterhood.

"Know that each of you will be forever in my heart.

Because I am you, and you are me.

Namaste."

The Orchid

Part IX
Acknowledgements

Acknowledgements

To you, dear reader: With hearts overflowing with gratitude, we thank you. We hope that by immersing yourself in this narrative, through the stories and transformations of its characters, you've found inspiration to rediscover your light and the powerful potential within you.

To us, life and writing partners: Our journey together has been nothing short of magical. Every day by your side is an invaluable gift. I love you.

To our daughters: Every laugh, every challenge, every moment with you reaffirms that it's all worth it. Thank you for teaching us so much.

To our family, friends, and all who have crossed our path: You are the embodiment of unconditional love and the true essence of unity. Each of you has been a fundamental piece in this mosaic of life.

Special thanks to all who co-created with us, illuminating each page of this book. What a fantastic team!

To the teachers and guides who have accompanied us: Your teachings have been beacons on our path. Every word, every gesture has enriched our journey of love and understanding.

To all the authors whose words have nourished our souls: You've planted wisdom in our inner garden.

To every experience, high or low, laughter or tear: Each and every one of these moments has shaped who we are today. And finally, our deepest gratitude to that wonderful energy that has been called by many names throughout time. To that Divine Light, thank you for choosing us to convey this message.

With all our love and gratitude.

**

We invite you to visit theorchidbook.com. There, you'll discover more about this journey, the authors, exercises, audiobook and book club support materials, other information and resources aimed at helping us all grow together.

Also, if you were moved by the message within these pages, we humbly request that you take a moment to leave a review where ever you purchased your book, or in our website theorchidbook.com. Sharing your experience can pave the way for other readers to discover and connect with The Orchid.

Lastly, we remind you that the exercises in this book are tools and guides, but they do not replace professional help when needed. If you feel it's necessary, always seek expert support.

The Orchid

This, or something better, for the highest good of all concerned.

-The End-

ABOUT THE AUTHORS

Rocio Aquino and **Angel Orengo**, a wife-husband team of twenty-three years, and devoted parents of two teen daughters, merge their rich imaginations and global experiences in "The Orchid." Stemming from Rocio's 30-year quest for self-love and self-forgiveness, and Angel's search for meaning and purpose in his life, the book is a culmination of their shared ambition to lead an authentic and empowered life. Their transformative journey includes living experiences around the world, holistic retreats, indulging on hundreds of enlightening books, numerous interactions with healers, sacred trips and a two-year certification on spiritual psychology. These profound experiences paved the way for revelations about personal freedom and age-old forces such as awareness, gratitude, forgiveness, acceptance and intention. Desiring to share these insights, they first turned to writing. "The Orchid" stands as a universal reflection on their hurdles and victories, and their desire to urge readers, especially women, to embrace their unique paths towards a more powerful existence.

Printed in Great Britain
by Amazon